PRAISE FOR CHRISTOPHE

D1111360

"Christopher Golden is o   ,
smartest, and talented writ~~ ~~ ~~ his~~ generation, and his
books are so good and so involving that they really ought to
sell in huge numbers. Everything he writes glows with
imagination." —Peter Straub, author of *In the Night Room*

"A new book by Golden means only one thing: the reader is
in for a treat. His books are rich with texture and character,
always inventive, and totally addictive."
—Charles de Lint, author of *Promises to Keep*

"A master of his craft." —SciFi.com

"Harkens back to classic Stephen King." —*Dark Realms*

"A major player in horror fiction."
—*San Francisco Chronicle*

"Christopher Golden's storytelling is spellbinding."
—*Boston* magazine

"Christopher Golden collides the ordinary and the super-
natural with wonderfully unsettling results."
—Max Allan Collins, author of *Road to Perdition*

"Golden [has a] blistering ability to enchant and entertain
[and] conjures up new ideas and characters into moments of
high drama with a flawless sleight of hand."
—SFCrowsnest.com

"Christopher Golden brings intrigue to old-fashioned horror
by complementing the unknown with the eerily familiar."
—*Alternate Reality* webzine

"Golden's work is fast and furious, funny and original, and I can't wait until his next book."
—Joe R. Lansdale, author of *Lost Echoes*

PRAISE FOR TIM LEBBON

"Tim Lebbon displays the sort of cool irony and uncanny mood-making that drive the best 'Twilight Zone' stories."
—*New York Times Book Review*

"Tim Lebbon is a master of fantasy and horror, and his visions make for disturbing and compelling reading."
—Douglas Clegg, author of *The Queen of Wolves*

"Tim Lebbon is an immense talent and he's become a new favorite. He has a style and approach unique to the genre."
—Joe R. Lansdale, author of *Lost Echoes*

"A firm and confident style, with elements of early Clive Barker." —Phil Rickman, author of *The Fabric of Sin*

"Tim Lebbon is an apocalyptic visionary—a prophet of blood and fear."
—Mark Chadbourn, author of *Hounds of Avalon*

"One of the most powerful new voices to come along in the genre...Lebbon's work is infused with the contemporary realism of Stephen King and the lyricism of Ray Bradbury."
—*Fangoria*

"Beautifully written and mysterious...a real winner!"
—Richard Laymon, author of *The Beast House*

Christopher Golden and Tim Lebbon

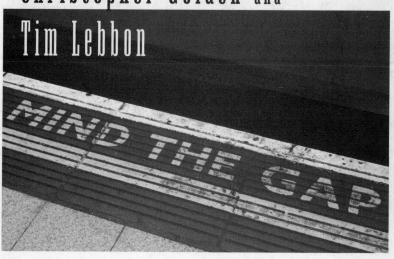

a novel of the hidden cities

bantam books

MIND THE GAP
A Bantam Book / June 2008

Published by Bantam Dell
A Division of Random House, Inc.
New York, New York

Book design by Carol Malcolm Russo

Bantam Books and the rooster colophon are registered
trademarks of Random House, Inc.

Library of Congress Cataloging-in-Publication Data
Golden, Christopher.
  Mind the gap : a novel of the hidden cities / Christopher
Golden & Tim Lebbon.
    p. cm.
  ISBN 978-0-553-38469-7 (trade pbk.)
  I. Lebbon, Tim. II. Title.

PS3557.O35927M56 2008
813'.54—dc22

                                        2007047391

Printed in the United States of America
Published simultaneously in Canada

www.bantamdell.com

10 9 8 7 6 5 4 3 2
BVG

For our dear friends, convention buddies, and fellow writers, Mark Morris and Sarah Pinborough

acknowledgments

A big thanks to our editor, Anne Groell, who had a clear vision of the Hidden Cities, and to Josh and everyone at Bantam. Also a massive thank-you to Howard Morhaim and Katie Menick, and to the supremely talented Graham Joyce.

mind the gap

Chapter One

little birds

Even before she saw the house, Jazz knew that something was wrong. She could smell it in the air, see it in the shifting shadows of the trees lining the street, hear it in the expectant silence. She could feel it in her bones.

Dread gave her pause, and for a moment she stood and listened to the stillness. She wanted to run, but she told herself not to be hasty, that her mother had long since hardwired her for paranoia and so her instincts should be trusted.

She hurried along a narrow, overgrown alleyway that emerged into a lane behind the row of terraced town houses. Not many people came this way, out beyond the gardens, and she was confident that she could move closer to home without being seen.

But seen by whom?

Her mother's voice rang through her head: *Always*

assume there's someone after you until you prove there isn't. Maybe everyone had that cautionary voice in the back of their mind; their conscience, their Jiminy Cricket. For Jazz, it always sounded like her mother.

She walked along the path, carefully and slowly, avoiding piles of dog shit and the glistening shards of used needles. Every thirty seconds she paused and listened. The dreadful silence had passed and the sounds of normalcy seemed to fill the air again. Mothers shouted at misbehaving children, babies hollered, doors slammed, dogs barked, and TVs blared inanely into the spaces between. She let out a breath she hadn't been aware of holding. Maybe the heat and grime of the city had gotten to her more than usual today.

Trust your instincts, her mother would say.

"Yeah, right." Jazz crept along until she reached her home's back gate, then paused to take stock once more. The normal sounds and smells were still there, but, beyond the gate, the weighted silence remained. The windows were dark and the air felt thick, the way it did before a storm. It was as if her house was surrounded by a bubble of stillness, and that in itself was disquieting. *Perhaps she's just asleep*, Jazz thought. But, more unnerved than ever, she knew she should take no chances.

She backed along the alley for a dozen steps and waited outside her neighbor's gate. She peered through a knothole in the wood, scoping the garden. The house seemed to be silent and abandoned, but not in the same ominous fashion as her own. Birds still sang in this garden. She knew that Mr. Barker lived alone, that he went to work early and returned late every day. So unless his cleaners were in, his house would be deserted.

"Good," Jazz whispered. "It'll turn out to be nothing, but..." *But at least it'll relieve the boredom.* To and from school, day in, day out, few real friends, and her mother constantly on edge even though the Uncles made sure they never had any financial worries. *No worries at all*, the Uncles always said....

Yeah, it'd turn out to be nothing, but better to be careful. If she ever told her mother she'd had some kind of dreadful intuition, even in the slightest, and had ignored it, the woman would be furious. Her mother trusted no one, and even though Jazz couldn't help but follow her in those beliefs, still she sometimes hated it. She wanted a life. She wanted friends.

She opened Mr. Barker's gate. The wall between their gardens was too high to see over, and from the back of his garden she could see only two upstairs windows in her house—her own bedroom window and the bathroom next to it. She looked up for a few seconds, then brashly walked the length of the garden to Barker's back door.

Nobody shouted, nobody came after her. The neighborhood noise continued. But to her left, over the wall, that deathly silence persisted.

Something is *wrong*, she thought.

Mr. Barker's back door was sensibly locked. Jazz closed her eyes and turned the handle a couple of times, gauging the pressure and resistance. She nodded in satisfaction; she should be able to pick it.

Taking a small pocketknife from her jeans, she opened the finest blade, slipped it into the lock, and felt around.

A bird called close by, startling her. She glanced up at the wall and saw a robin sitting on its top, barely ten feet away. Its head jerked this way and that, and it sang again.

Above the robin, past the wall, a shape was leaning from Jazz's bedroom window.

She froze. It was difficult to make out any details, silhouetted as the shape was against the sky, but when it turned, she saw the outline of a ponytail, the sharp corner of a shirt collar.

It was the Uncle who told her to call him Mort.

She never bothered with their names. To her they were just *the Uncles*, the name her mother had been using ever since Jazz could remember. They came to visit regularly, sometimes in pairs or threes, sometimes on their own. They would ask her mother how things were, whether she needed anything or if she'd "had any thoughts." They never accepted a drink or the offer of food, but they always left behind an envelope containing a sheaf of used ten- and twenty-pound notes.

They told Jazz that she never had to worry about anything, which only worried her more. When they left, her mother would slide the envelope into a drawer as though it was dirty.

But what was this one doing in her bedroom? Whatever his purpose, Jazz didn't like it. They had never, ever come into her room when she was at home, and her mother assured her that they did not snoop around when she was out. They were perfect gentlemen. *Like gangsters,* Jazz had said once, *and we're their molls.* Her mother had smiled but did not respond.

The Uncle turned his head, scanning the gardens and alleyway.

He'll see me. If the robin calls again and he looks down to locate it, he'll see me pressed here against Mr. Barker's back door.

The bird hopped along the head of the wall, pausing to peck at an insect or two. Jazz worked at the lock without looking, waiting for the feel of the tumblers snicking into place. One...two...three...two to go, and the last two were always the hardest.

The Uncle moved to withdraw back into the room, and Jazz let go of her breath in a sigh of relief.

The robin chirped, singing along with the chaotic London buzz of traffic and shouts.

The Uncle leaned from the window again just as Jazz felt the lock disengage. She turned the handle and pushed her way in behind the opening door, never looking away from the shadow of the man at her bedroom window.

He didn't see me, she thought. She left the door open; he'd be more likely to see the movement of it closing than to notice it was open.

The robin fluttered away.

Jazz did not wait to question what was happening, or why. She hurried through Mr. Barker's house, careful not to knock into any furniture, cautious as she opened or closed doors. She didn't want to make the slightest sound.

In his living room, she moved to the front window. The wooden Venetian blinds were closed, but, pressing her face to the wall, she could see past their edge. Out in the street, she saw just what she had feared.

Two large black cars were parked outside her house. *Beamers.*

Jazz's heart was thumping, her skin tingling. *Something's happened.* Rarely had more than three Uncles visited at once, and now there were two cars here, parked prominently in the street with windows still open and engines running, as if daring anyone to approach. *They're a law unto themselves*, her mother sometimes said.

Her mum had rarely said anything outright against the Uncles, but she never needed to. Her unease was there on her face for her daughter to see. But Jazz could not just sit here and spy on her own house, wondering what had gone wrong.

She and her mum had talked many times about fleeing the house if trouble ever came to the door. They'd made plans, created a virtual map in their minds, and once or twice they'd pursued the escape route, just to make sure it could really work.

All Jazz had to do now was reverse it.

She found Mr. Barker's attic hatch in one of his back bedrooms. This was a cold, sterile room with white walls, bare timber floors, and only an old rattan chair as furniture. She lifted the chair instead of dragging it, positioning it beneath the hatch, then stood carefully on its arms and pushed the hatch open. It tipped to the side and thumped onto the timber joists.

Jazz cringed and held her breath. It had been a soft impact, muffled in the attic. Unlikely it would travel through to her house; these places were solid.

Got to be more careful than that.

Fingers gripping the edge of the square hole in the ceiling, she pushed off the chair, trying to get her elbows over the lip of the hatch. The chair rocked, tipping onto two legs and then back again with another soft thud. She let her torso and legs dangle there for a while, preparing to haul herself up and in. Jazz was fitter than most girls her age—others were more interested in boys, drinking, and sex than in keeping themselves fit and healthy—but she also knew that she could easily hurt herself. One torn muscle and . . .

And what? I won't be able to run? She couldn't shake the sense of foreboding. The sun shone outside, a beautiful summer afternoon. But gray winter seemed to be closing in.

She lifted herself up into the darkness, sitting on the hatch's edge and resting for a moment. Listening. Looking for light from elsewhere. She still had no idea what had happened. If the Uncles were waiting for her to come home, perhaps they'd also be checking her house. And that could mean the attic too.

When her eyes had become accustomed to the darkness, she set off on hands and knees. Mr. Barker's attic had floorboards, so the going was relatively easy. The old bachelor didn't have much stuff to store, it seemed; there were a couple of taped-up boxes tucked into one corner and an open box of books slowly swelling with damp. Mustiness permeated the attic, and she wondered why he'd shoved the box up here. She hadn't seen a bookcase anywhere downstairs. There were rumors that Mr. Barker's wife had left him ten years ago, so perhaps these books held too many ghosts for him to live with.

At the wall dividing Barker's property from hers, Jazz crawled into the narrowing gap between floor and sloping roof. Right at the eaves, just where her mother said it would be, was a gap where a dozen blocks had been removed. *Lazy builders*, she'd said when Jazz had asked. But Jazz found it easy to imagine her mother up here with a chisel and hammer, while she was in school and Mr. Barker was at work.

She wriggled through the hole into her own attic. There

were no floorboards here, and she had to move carefully from joist to joist. One slip and her foot or knee would break through the plasterboard ceiling into the house below. She guessed she was right above her bedroom.

A wooden beam creaked beneath her and she froze, cursing her clumsiness. She should have listened first, tried to figure out whether the Uncle was still in there. Too late now. She lowered her head, turned so that her ear pressed against the itching fiber-wool insulation, and held her breath.

Voices. Two men were talking, but she could barely hear their mumbled tones. She was pretty sure their voices did not come from directly below. Her room, she thought, was empty—for now.

There were two hatches that led down from the attic into the town house. One was above the landing, visible to anyone in the upstairs corridor or anyone looking up the stairs from below. And then there was the second, just to her right, which her mother had installed in Jazz's bedroom. *Emergency escape*, she'd said, smiling, when Jazz had asked what she was doing.

Everything you told me was right, Jazz thought. She felt tears threatening but couldn't go to that place yet. Not here, and not now.

She crawled to the hatch, feeling her way through the darkness. When she touched its bare wood and felt the handle, she paused for a minute, listening. She could still hear muffled voices, but they seemed to come from farther away than her bedroom.

Jazz closed her eyes and concentrated. Sometimes she could sense whether someone else was close. Most people called it a sixth sense, though usually it was a combination of the other five. With her, sometimes, it was different.

She frowned, opened her eyes, and grasped the handle.

Maybe there was an Uncle standing directly below her. Maybe not. There was only one way to find out.

Jazz lifted the hatch quickly and squinted against the sudden light. She leaned over the hole and found her room empty.

Good start, she thought. Everything her mother had said to her, everything she had been taught, shouted at her to flee. But there was something going on here that she had to understand before she could bring herself to run.

Jazz lowered herself from the hatch into her room, landing lightly on the tips of her toes, knees bending to absorb the impact. She remained in that pose, looking around her room and listening for movement from outside.

Her drawers had been opened, her bookcase upset, and clothes were strewn across the floor. The cover of her journal lay loose and torn on her bed like a gutted bird.

Mum! she thought. And for the first time, the fear came in hard. The Uncles had always protected and helped them, even if her mother had little respect for them. But now they seemed dangerous. It was as if their surface veneer had been stripped away and her perception of them was becoming clear at last.

She glanced back up at the ceiling hatch, close enough to her desk that it would be easy to jump up and disappear again.

The voices startled her. There were two of them, seeming to come from directly outside her door. She slid beside her bed and lay there listening, expecting Mort to enter her room at any second. He would not see her straightaway, but he *would* see the open hatch. And then they'd have her.

"We could be waiting here forever," one voice said. Mort.

"We won't. She'll be home soon." This other voice was female.

The only time a woman had ever accompanied the Uncles was the day after their house had been broken into years before. Jazz had been young, but she could still remember some details about that day. The woman had tried to soothe and comfort her mother, while all around them the Uncles had been busy packing their belongings. By early evening they were in a brand-new house: this one. And the woman—whose voice was cold and uncaring, even then—had called herself Josephine Blackwood.

"What if she isn't? What do we do then?"

"We stay calm and proceed," the woman said. The same voice; the same coldness. "She's just one girl."

"She's more than that," Mort said.

"Shush! *Never* in public! Never outside!"

The Uncle sighed. "So, is she definitely . . . ?" He trailed off, as though there was something he did not want to say.

"Of course," the woman said. "I saw to it myself."

The two fell silent again, their presence suddenly filling the house. Jazz lay there, turning over what they had said. *I saw to it myself*, the woman had said. Saw to what?

"I'm going downstairs," the man said at last. "No need to guard this door anymore, at least."

"All right. Let's go down."

Jazz listened to the man and woman slowly descending the stairs.

No need to guard this door anymore...

There were more voices from down there, subdued and indistinguishable.

Is she definitely...?

"Mum," Jazz whispered, and the world seemed to sway.

She closed her eyes and breathed deeply several times, then stood and crept from her room. She moved fluidly, drifting rather than walking, feeling the air part around her and guide her along. She knew where every creaking floorboard was, and she didn't make a sound.

Her mother's bedroom door was closed, and there was a smear of blood on the handle.

It was small—half the size of the nail on her little finger—but she saw it instantly. Her heart thumped harder as she turned and glanced downstairs. There was no one at the bottom of the staircase looking up, but she could still hear their voices elsewhere in the house.

What have you done to my mother? she thought, touching the handle, opening the door, stepping inside, and *seeing* what they had done. And also smelling and tasting it, because so much blood could not be avoided.

Her legs began to give way. She grasped the handle and locked her elbow so she did not fall. Then she closed her eyes.

But some things can never be unseen.

Her mother lay half on the bed, her upper body hanging down so that her head rested on the floor. A line had been slit across her throat, a dark grin gaping.

I saw to it myself, the woman had said.

Jazz felt strangely numb. Her heart hammered in her chest, but her mind was quiet, logical, already plotting out the next few minutes. Back to her room, the phone, the police, up into the attic to await their arrival, listen to the Uncles and that Blackwood woman panicking as the sirens approached...

And then she saw the writing on the floor. At first she thought it was a spray of blood, but now she could see the words there, and she imagined the determination her mother must have had to write them while blood spewed from her throat.

Jazz hide forever.

She bit back a cry, steeled herself against the tears.

Her mother stared at her with glazed eyes.

Jazz looked at the words again, then glanced at the staircase to her left and started backing away.

As she reached her own door, she realized that she'd left her mother's bedroom door open. They'd notice, know she'd been here.

She darted back across the landing and closed the door. Her last sight of her mother was bloodied and smudged with tears.

The words on the floor shouted at her even when the door was closed.

Jazz hide forever.

She had always listened to her mother.

Lifting herself back through the ceiling hatch in her bedroom, Jazz wondered what kind of life those words had doomed her to.

They were sitting together in the park, watching as ducks drifted back and forth on the pond, squabbling over thrown bread and scolding the moorhens.

"Pity there aren't any swans," her mother said.

"I love swans," Jazz said. "So graceful and beautiful."

"They may look gentle, but they're hard as nails." Her mother shuffled closer to her on their picnic blanket. The remains of their lunch lay beside them on paper plates, already attracting unwanted attention from wasps and flies. "If there were swans here, we'd have a full hierarchy. Swans would be the rulers of the pond, ducks below them, moorhens below them. Then there'd be the scroungers, the little birds, like that wren over there." She pointed to a tiny bird hopping from branch to branch in a bush that grew out over the water.

"So what are we?" Jazz asked. Even then she was a perceptive girl, and she knew that this conversation was edging toward something.

"We're the little birds," her mother said. She smiled, but it was sad.

"I think you're a swan," Jazz said, flooded by a sudden feeling of complete love.

Her mother shrugged. "Maybe you," she said. "One day, maybe you."

The wren dropped to the grass and hopped across to the edge of the pond. It started worrying at a lump of bread that the other birds seemed to have missed, but the movement brought it to the attention of the mallards. A duck splashed from the water and came at the wren, wings raised and head down, bill snapping. The wren turned and hopped away slowly, almost as though it was trying to maintain its dignity. The duck took the bread.

"Wise thing," her mother said. "If you're on the run, you *never* run unless you know they're right behind you."

"Why?"

"You never call attention to yourself." Her mother lay back on the blanket, looking around the park as though waiting for someone.

Never run unless you know they're right behind you.

Jazz was afraid that if she did start running, she'd brain herself on a lamppost. She was doing her best not to cry—that would draw attention—but the pressure and heat behind her face was immense.

For a minute or two, she had considered calling the police from Mr. Barker's house and waiting until they arrived. But she had known that if she paused any longer, she would never move again. So she had left the way she arrived, walking the length of Barker's garden, hurrying along the alleyway, emerging out onto the street, and putting more distance between her and her mother with every step she took.

She hated blinking, because whenever her eyes closed she saw the blood and that twisted, splayed body that had once been her mother.

That woman slit her throat. Cut her and left her to bleed to death! And they had been waiting for Jazz to come home.

To do the same to her?

She walked past a coffee shop and glanced in the window. A man and woman sat turned to face the street. The woman was sipping from a cup, but the man stared straight out at Jazz. He wore a smart dark suit and sunglasses, and his lips twitched into what might have been a smile.

Jazz hurried on, turning into the next side road she came to, rushing through a lane between gardens and emerging onto another street. She passed an old woman walking her dog. The dog watched her go by.

It took Jazz ten minutes to realize she had no idea where she was going. Where could she hide? And how could she just leave her mother?

She emerged onto a busy shopping street. It was noisy and bustling and smelled of exhaust fumes and fast food. A cab pulled up just along the street and a tall, elegant woman stepped out. She brushed an errant strand of hair from her eyes, paid the cabbie, and walked away with her mobile phone glued to her ear.

And Jazz's mother was dead.

She was dead, murdered, and now Jazz was more alone than she had ever been before.

They'll be on the streets, she thought, and the idea bore her mother's voice. *Once they know you're not coming home, they'll be on the streets looking for you.*

She stepped into the doorway of a music shop and scanned the sidewalk and the road. No big black Beamers, but that meant nothing. Maybe they'd be on foot. Maybe, like her mother had been telling her for the last couple of years, they had so many fingers in so many pies that none of them knew the true extent of their reach.

She wiped her eyes and looked both ways. A dozen people turned their heads away just as she looked at them. A dozen more looked up. In a crowd such as this, there was always someone watching her.

"Oh shit, oh fuck. What the hell am I going to do?" she whispered.

A black BMW cruised around the corner. Jazz pressed back into the door but it was locked, the damn shop was shut, and then the BMW passed and continued along the street.

She hurried back out onto the pavement, resisting the temptation to keep her head down. She had to watch, had to know what was going on.

A tall man emerged from a fast-food joint, carrying something that looked like steaming road kill in a napkin. He was dressed in a sharp black suit, and as she paused six steps from him, he adjusted a lump beneath his jacket.

Gun, Jazz thought.

He looked up, glanced around at her, and smiled. "Too hot to eat," he said, raising the food toward her.

She ran. The man called after her, and even though he sounded friendly and alarmed, she could not afford to stop, not now that she'd started running, because she was drawing attention to herself. And if and when she did stop, she'd collapse into a heap, and the white-hot grief would start tearing her up.

The grief, and the loneliness.

She ducked into a Tube station, grateful for the shadows closing around her. The smell of the Underground seemed to welcome her in.

Chapter Two

behind the beneath

Jazz flew down the stairs two at a time, sure that she would trip and break an ankle but unable to stop herself. Images of her mother's brutalized corpse—and the warning she'd painted on the floor in her own blood—flashed across her mind. But there was no going back. Over the years her mum had said a lot about running, but one refrain echoed in Jazz's mind.

Once you start running, don't stop 'til you're well hidden.

A glance over her shoulder revealed several men descending after her, but they seemed in no hurry. Still, best to be sure. To be safe. The blood on the bed and floor could so easily have been her own, and if she slowed down it still might be, though now it would spill on the concrete stairs or tiled floor of the Tube station.

She hit the bottom of the stairs and sidestepped a bickering middle-aged couple with three tagalong children who huddled close to their parents, afraid of the world. *Wise little ones*, Jazz thought.

In her pocket she had a crumpled wad of notes—little more than forty pounds, she guessed—and her rail pass. Hurrying toward the turnstiles, she thought of simply vaulting them, both for speed and because her pursuers could not be so bold. But in the fugue of grief and fear that warped her thoughts, she knew that would attract attention she did not want. She pulled out the rail pass, stuffed her money back into her pocket, and fed the card through the slot on the turnstile.

Get lost in a crowd, her mother's voice whispered in her head.

All of the things she had told Jazz over the years, while tucking her into bed at night or sending her off to school in the morning, were the words of a ghost. Jazz had a ghost in her head now.

People milled about the platform, waiting for the train to arrive. The electronic sign above their heads declared the next was three minutes away. *Three minutes.* Jazz glanced over her shoulder at the men who had come onto the platform behind her, and she knew she did not have three minutes. These weren't the Uncles, but she had seen the black BMW slide by on the street above. Dressed in dark suits, they seemed cut from the same cloth as the ugly-eyed men who had kept Jazz and her mother like pets and whose leader had put Mum down like a sick dog.

Bile rose into the back of her throat, and she had to breathe through her mouth to keep from throwing up. She tasted salty tears on her lips and wiped them away, plunging into the crowd of suited commuters, snaking through them, hiding among them on the platform.

Trembling, she stopped. Eyes on the advertisements across the tracks, she tried to blend as best she could, steadying her breathing. *Do You Know Who You Are?* one advert asked. She had no idea what it was trying to sell, and for a second she felt the whole world bearing down on her, pressing in from above and all around.

She closed her eyes and breathed deeply. How many times had she taken the Tube in her life? Hundreds, surely. If she could be normal for two more minutes, pretend that all was well, perhaps she could truly become invisible in the crowd.

She squeezed her eyes tighter, trying to hold back the tears. A dreadful mistake, for on the backs of her eyelids she found the grotesque tableau of her mother's bedroom. She opened them wide, staring across the tracks at the grubby tiles, the colorful advertisements, breathing too fast. The questions had begun—who were the Uncles, really, and why had they done it? But they were not new questions to Jazz. She had been asking versions of them for most of her life.

Someone shouted. She glanced along the platform. A mother held the hands of her two girls, twins about six years old. An old man with long silver hair and an enormous nose leaned with great dignity upon a cane. Beyond them, among a sea of tourists and business suits, she saw a flash of dark jacket, moving quickly.

"Here, love." A hand landed on her shoulder. "Everything all right?"

Jazz opened her mouth to scream but no sound emerged. She stood paralyzed for a few frantic seconds, and then she bolted to the right, toward the end of the platform. Colliding with an old biddy in a frumpy dress, she didn't wait to apologize. A teenage boy got in her way, one hand out as though he might try to stop her. She shot him an elbow to the chest and kept going.

"Mad fucking cow!" he called after her.

Her face flushed with heat as her heart thundered in her chest. She darted in and out of the crowd, knocking over shopping bags and bumping briefcases.

"What's happening?" someone shouted.

"Who is that?"

"Don't *push*, don't *shove*!"

Jazz felt the ripples of unease spread across the platform, all originating from her. *A fine way to stay hidden*, she thought, but she could not help running. She thought of shouting *Bomb!* but people would panic and some would get hurt, and she could not bear that on her conscience.

She burst from the crowd to find herself alone at the end of the platform, tile walls to her right and straight ahead and the train tracks to her left. If the Uncles really had come down here after her, they would be on her in seconds. Her skin prickled with the attention of strangers' eyes, as though the tiles themselves observed her.

A ledge jutted twelve inches from the wall, a lip of concrete that continued past the end of the platform as though the wall had not always been there. Desperation drove her forward. The cry of metal upon metal and the screech of brakes approached from behind, and a great gust of wind blew along the tracks. The train's arrival imminent, she put one hand on the wall and hung her head out over the tracks. In the gloom of the tunnel, she saw that the wall went on perhaps six feet and then there was an opening where the platform seemed to continue. In the darkness, she thought she could make out some kind of metal grate—the sort of thing they used to partition off unused areas of the Underground.

"Here, girl, what do you think you're up to?" a voice called.

Jazz pressed herself against the wall and moved around onto the ledge. The shriek of the slowing train grated along her spine. The light of its headlamps picked her out on the ledge as it bulleted into the station from behind her, slowing, slowing...

Face sliding against filthy tiles, Jazz shuffled swiftly along the ledge, forcing herself not to imagine falling backward or being blown off by the wind of the passing train. If she fell beneath it, her mother would never forgive her.

The train hissed as it slowed, the front car coming toward the end of the platform, nearly adjacent to her now. The conductor would see her. Someone would be called. More people would chase her into the darkness, and then where would she hide?

Her left hand suddenly pressed against nothing. She slipped around the end of the wall onto a stretch of forgotten platform. On the track, the train hissed a final puff as though frustrated by her survival, and then she heard the sounds of disgorging passengers and others climbing aboard. A recorded voice announced the time of the next expected train and advised those getting on and off to mind the gap.

It seemed she had already been forgotten.

Jazz laughed softly and without humor. Mind the gap,

indeed. Never knew when you'd find yourself falling into one of the cracks in the world. Here she was, living proof. Alice down the rabbit hole.

The train hissed again, doors closing, and started forward. In the light from its headlamp eyes, she stared at the iron grating before her. Beyond it lay another stretch of platform, eight feet deep and perhaps twenty long. A rusted, padlocked chain locked the gate. Some cinema action hero might have been able to snap the rust-eaten chain, but not Jasmine Towne. The train rattled past, gaining speed, and with it her pulse began to race again.

She saw the shapes of people at first, and the occasional blur of a face, but the faster it went the more those people seemed to blur into one.

The illumination from the train's interior flickered off the black iron grate, but at the upper edge of her vision was a rectangle of darkness that seemed to swallow the light. Jazz studied it, blinking at the realization that either a section of the grate had been broken away or whoever had installed it had left a transom window above.

She gripped the iron bars, propped the rubber sole of one trainer against the metal, then hauled herself up. If Jazz could be said to be gifted at anything, it was climbing. Her mother had often called her a monkey for her love of scampering up trees and rocks and the way she could always manage to break into their town house if her mum had lost her keys. She'd thought, once upon a time, of becoming a dancer. But little girls always wanted to be ballerinas or princesses, and people like her weren't allowed dreams for very long.

Her foot slipped, but her hands found a grip on the

transom. One knee banged painfully against the gate, rat-
tling the chain and sending a shower of rust flaking to the
platform. But she pulled herself up across the bottom bar of
the transom and through to the other side like a gymnast.

She landed in a crouch and paused for a moment, listening to the roar of the train fading into the distance. Light
from the station reflected off the tiles on the other side
of the tunnel, giving her just enough illumination to see.
Voices came from beyond the wall: bored commuters talking into phones and excited tourists nattering in a mixture of
languages.

She stood frozen, like a rabbit caught in oncoming head-
lights. And when someone shouted, Jazz bolted. As the train
passed, its light had shown her the outline of a tall door,
and she guessed it to be an old exit up to street level. The
Underground was rife with such things, she'd read, coming
up into the storage rooms and basements of chemists, mar-
kets, and pubs that had once been Tube stations or buildings
associated with them.

Dark shapes scurried and squealed around her feet: rats.
As long as they ran away from her, not toward her, she could
put up with that.

The door stood open a few inches, the frame corroded.
Whatever lock had once sealed it had been broken, leaving a
hole where the knob ought to be. Jazz had a strange feeling
that the door had been forced closed, not open.

She reached out. The metal felt warm to the touch and
pulsed with the thrum of the Underground, like a beating
heart. Jazz leaned her weight against it, and it scraped open
across the concrete floor.

Blinking, she waited for her eyes to adjust. The stairwell

ought to have been pitch black, but a dim blue glow provided light enough to see that she had been wrong. The spiral metal staircase did not lead toward the surface. Rather, it led deeper into the ethereal gloom.

She could go back. For a moment she considered it. But to what? The Uncles and her mother's corpse, and the murderous woman with Jazz on her mind? No. There would be no going back now. If she returned to the surface, it had to be far from here. If she got onto a train, it could not be at this station. Somewhere in the underground labyrinth, there would be another way up.

The spiral staircase created an echo chamber, and the sound of her breathing surrounded her as Jazz started down. Such evidence of her panic forced her to calm down, to slow her breath, and soon her pulse slowed as well. Still, she heard her heartbeat much too loudly in her head.

It was at least thirty feet until the staircase ended. The blue glow brightened into silvery splashes of light from several caged bulbs, metal-wrapped cables bolted to the curved stone walls. She wondered who would come down here to replace these bulbs when they blew.

More hesitant now, Jazz stepped away from the bottom of the stairs and along a short tunnel. It emerged into a vast space that made her catch her breath. Above her was a ventilation shaft that led up to a louvered grille. Daylight filtered down, a splash of light in the false underground night. Like distant streetlamps, other vents served the same purpose in the otherwise enduring darkness of that long-abandoned station. The platform had been removed, and beneath her feet there was only dirt and broken concrete. In a far-off puddle of light, a short set of steps led up to where the platform had once been, but now they were stairs to nowhere. Without the platform, she noticed for the first time how round the tunnels were—long cylinders bored through the city's innards.

Peering along the throat of the tunnel, past the farthest splash of light, she saw only darkness. But somewhere down there, where the platform had once ended, there must be another door.

Jazz started in that direction, but as she moved beyond the first pool of light, the dirt and broken ground underfoot disappeared in the dark. She moved to the tracks and crouched to place a hand on the cold metal. Once it had been a working artery, pumping blood to the city's heart. Now it was dead. She stepped over the rail and between the tracks. Simple enough to match her stride to the carefully placed sleepers.

The sound of her movement echoed around her: scraping stones, sharp breath, footsteps.

Walking into the darkness did not make her feel lost. A pool of light waited ahead and another remained behind her. She could see those areas of the tunnel well enough. Yet when she looked down at her feet she saw nothing, and even her arms seemed spectral things.

Water dripped nearby, but she could not locate its source. She studied the walls, searching for any sign of an exit. Without a way out she wouldn't get far, at least not without a torch.

Something rustled off to her left. Jazz froze, listening

for it to come again. Seconds passed before she took another step, then she heard the sound again. Not a rustle, but a whisper. A voice in the darkness, speaking gibberish.

"Who is it? Who's there?" she said, flinching at the sound of her own voice.

The whispering went on and, from behind her, back toward that spiral staircase, came another voice, secretive, furtive. The Uncles or their lackeys—those dark-suited BMW men—had followed her.

"Shit," she whispered, and started moving more swiftly.

The whispers followed, but though they certainly must have seen her, no one shouted after her.

"Bloody Churchill," one of them said, but this was no whisper. She heard it clear as a bell. "Thinks he's a general but hasn't the first idea how to fight a war. Get us all killed, he will."

A child laughed.

A burst of static filled the tunnel, followed by music—a tune she knew, something her mother had hummed while making dinner.

Are the stars out tonight?
I don't know if it's cloudy or bright.
I only have eyes for you, dear.

Sometimes Mum sang little snippets of it, and Jazz had always cherished those rare moments when her mother seemed to steal a moment's peace, from the fear that ran through her every day, like deep water under a frozen river. Jazz had asked her several times about the song. All but once, Mum had seemed not to know what she was talking about. That once, she'd relented.

"Was a time your father sang it to me, and meant every word," she said. She never spoke of it again.

Churchill? What was that about? The music crackled, a tinny echo, as though it came from some old-time radio. Someone *was* down here in the tunnel with her, but it wasn't the Uncles or their other BMW men.

The song continued to play, but the child's laugh did not come again.

Hope and dread warred within her. Whoever lurked in the tunnel could point her way out, if they weren't mad as a hatter. But that business about Churchill pricked at her mind, and the memory of that voice seeped down her spine.

Retreat not an option, she went on, peering into the darkness for a face. The radio crackled again and other whispers joined in. Jazz's breath caught. How many people were down here? She caught a few snatches of words, but nothing that made any sense. What had she discovered, some sort of subterranean enclave?

"Sir?" a voice called. "Paper, sir?"

Before she turned, in that singular moment, she understood something that had been niggling at the back of her mind. The laughter, the voices, even the music . . . they made no echo. The tiles did not throw the sounds back at her.

Her skin prickled as she turned and saw the boy in his cap and jacket, the shape of him more a suggestion in the dark, a fold in the air. He held something out, a newspaper, as if to some passerby. But no one else was there. He did not seem to have noticed Jazz at all.

She backed up, caught her foot on the rail, and sprawled on her ass.

When she sat up, breath hitching, shaking in confusion, the ghost had gone. For what else could it have been? Hallucination or phantom: those were really the only choices, and she feared madness more than haunting.

The music and whispering had stopped.

Jazz stood and stepped carefully back between the tracks. With a quick glance at the spot where she'd seen the darkness form its lines and shadows into a shape, she hurried on, wondering if the whole day might be some kind of breakdown, a series of waking nightmares. What if she was sitting in her bedroom right now, or in a hospital, and none of what she had seen was real?

The thought brought the threat of tears, and she bit her lower lip. The rail glistened with weak light that filtered down the vent shaft ahead. The dripping noise remained, and from far above she could hear car horns and the roar of engines. She moved into the pool of daylight, and it made her wonder just how dark it would become down here when night fell.

She glanced around, searching for an exit. Again, as she had back on the station platform, she felt the burden of strangers' eyes upon her. Twisting, she peered back the way she'd come, but there were no signs of anyone there.

Taking a breath, she started into the darkness again, hurrying toward the next shaft of light. Focusing only on her footing, she stepped from sleeper to sleeper, catching the glint of the rails just enough to avoid stumbling over them.

The key's in adapting, her mother's voice muttered in her head. *Remember, they can't find you if you can't find yourself.*

That particular comment had been made while out shopping for a winter coat, the day Mum had bought her the red one with the fur-fringed hood. It hung in her closet now, and would forever, until someone packed it up with the rest of her things and it vanished into another closet or some charity shop.

Jazz swallowed but found that her throat had gone dry. Mum spoke to her from the surface world, from the life that had ended just an hour ago. How much might be memory and how much her own imagination, she did not want to know.

Perhaps she'd become just another ghost in the Underground.

"How'm I doing, Mum? Lost enough?" Jazz said aloud, her voice quavering, the echo soft.

Halfway to the next splash of light, the whispers began again. The Churchill hater spoke up, so close. *Too* close. Jazz spun around, crouched down, and now the walls she had built to keep out the fear gave way and it crashed in around her, drowning her. Her eyes searched the tunnel for ghosts.

"Where are you? What the hell are you doing here?" she cried into the darkness.

A horn beeped loudly behind her.

Jazz spun and saw the car coming at her along the tracks. On instinct, she threw herself to one side. But the car existed only as a shade—a pale, translucent image. As it passed, she heard the engine buzz in her ears, but the tunnel did not echo the sound.

A cacophony of sound erupted around her. Voices. Cars. The music started up again, crackling radio static. "Pennies from Heaven" this time. The newsboy hawked papers. And as she spun, eyes wide, body shaking with the influx of the impossible, the tunnel came alive with faded images. Gas lamps burned on street corners, and she saw the city unfold around her. London—but not the London she knew. The clothes were of another era. The Churchill hater stood outside a pub, blustering drunkenly at another man; couples walked arm in arm, the men in suits and the ladies in dresses.

The ghosts of London.

All she could do to escape was close her eyes, but when she squeezed them shut, an all too earthly image slashed across her mind instead.

No escape.

Jazz screamed, and when she ran out of breath, she inhaled and screamed again. And when she finally opened her eyes, the ghosts were still there. On one corner stood a man in an elegant tuxedo, top hat, and white gloves. He fanned a deck of cards to an unseen audience the way the newsboy had offered his papers to invisible passersby. With his right hand he drew out a single card, and her eyes followed that card for only an instant but long enough for the rest of the deck to vanish. He opened his arms as if to welcome applause, and doves appeared in his hands, spectral wings taking flight. The birds vanished when they reached the roof of the tunnel, passing through as if by some other illusion.

She kept screaming, turning. Nowhere to run from this. Nowhere to hide, if not here.

Another scream joined hers. Higher. A keening, grinding wail that did not issue from a human throat. A siren. But its significance was lost on her until she saw the specters begin to scatter. The newsboy raced toward a regal-looking structure and vanished inside.

An air-raid siren, then, and this was a shelter in those hellish days when the Luftwaffe crossed the Channel and the bombs rained down and the fires burned out of control.

The first explosion knocked her off her feet.

Jazz stopped screaming. She lay on her side on the tracks as dust sifted down from the ceiling, and she told herself the impossible could not touch her. There came another thunderous roar and she felt the ground shudder, and that drove her back to her feet. She staggered toward the next splash of light. In the distance, she saw the ghost of a building reduced almost to rubble, valiant walls standing like jagged, ancient ruins.

Not real, she told herself. *It's not real.*

But her mother's voice came back, stronger than her own. *Trust your instincts, Jazz. Always. Down deep, we've all got a little of the beast in us.*

This time the voice didn't sound as though it came from inside her head but from the darkness, clear and strong as the Churchill hater's.

Jazz raced, panicked, for an exit, but nearly halfway to the other end of the abandoned station, she had nowhere to run. The siren rose and fell. Voices shouted from the darkness, but the sepia mirage that had appeared around her had thinned, fading.

To her right, Jazz noticed an anomaly on the wall—a round metal pipe that followed the curve of the roof and then went up through the ceiling of the tunnel. Some other sort of vent, going to the surface. But it came from the floor beneath the abandoned station, and that didn't make any sense at all. What could be deeper than this?

The air-raid siren became a whisper and then a strange

electrical buzz. No, the buzz had been there all along. It came from the pipe bolted to the wall. Jazz put one hand against it and thought she could feel the slightest vibration. She glanced back the way she'd come and found herself truly alone again. With a shuddering breath, she nearly went to her knees with relief. Her ears still rang with the effects of the siren.

With no sign as to where this vent might lead, she continued on her original course but against the wall now, letting her fingers drag along the tiles.

She saw the hole before she reached it. Tiles littered the ground where someone had shattered the wall, tearing down bricks to make a passage. Practically adjacent to one of the ventilation ducts above, the hole in the wall was bathed in light. Beyond the hole was a short passageway, at the end of which another metal door—this one painted a deep red—stood open, and Jazz could see the top of another spiral staircase leading down. This one was cast in concrete. Words had been painted on the passage's wall, faded now but readable even after so many decades had passed.

DEEP LEVEL SHELTER 7-K

On the door were two posters. Jazz stepped through to peer at them. The top one featured a beautiful illustration of St. George slaying the dragon and, in large type, the declaration *Britain Needs You at Once*.

Jazz put a hand over her mouth to keep from crying out again, remembering the phantoms fleeing the air-raid siren. *Britain needs me*, she thought, her mind feeling frayed. She uttered a short bark that might have been a laugh.

The other poster had been torn at the top as if someone had tried to strip it from the door. The letters she could make out made it clear it had been issued by the Metropolitan something or other.

A man and four women were charged and convicted at Great Marlborough Police Court on the 8th March, 1944, with disorderly conduct in a public Air Raid Shelter. Further, on the 13th March, 1944, at Clerkenwell Police Court, a man was sentenced to one month's imprisonment for remaining in a public Air Raid Shelter while drunk.

It is in the best interests of all that shelters should be kept respectable. Will you please assist in an endeavor to meet this end?

—C.F.S. Chapple

Afraid to go on, afraid to go back, mind numb and body exhausted, Jazz stood and stared down that spiral staircase. The descent appealed to her. Down and down and farther down, as deep as she could burrow into the ground, where no one would ever find her. Down into the darkness to hide forever, just like Mum had told her. But without light...

Yet there *was* light.

"Can't be," she whispered. The bulbs in that stairwell off the main station had been a surprise enough. But who in their right mind would keep a light burning down here?

Hands on the walls of the narrow stairwell, she started down, counting steps. Only the dimmest glow came up from below, and she felt blind. She probed with her foot before each step. The twenty-first step was broken. A piece of stone crumbled away under her heel and she slipped, one leg shooting out in front of her, hands flailing for purchase. Her head struck the steps and pain exploded in the back of her skull. Hissing, she squeezed her eyes closed and saw a cascade of stars.

"Fucking hell," she muttered through clenched teeth, reaching around to gingerly touch the back of her head. She winced at the pain, and her fingers came away sticky. In the dark, her blood was black, but she knew the feel of it. She knew the rusted-metal smell of it. Jazz had become intimate with that odor today and would never forget it.

By the twenty-seventh step, the light had brightened considerably.

The thirty-third was the last.

At the foot of the steps, an orange power cable ran along the ground. To her right she could see several more dangling from the open circular vent—an answer to the mystery up above. But this was nothing official. Someone had jerryrigged the cables, used that old vent to steal power from the surface.

Deep Level Shelter 7-K was operational, but Jazz had no idea what it was being used as shelter from. This place had never been a Tube station. It was round, just as the train tunnels were, but the way the ceiling arched in a half circle, she wondered if there was more shelter space under the floor, making up the bottom half of the circle. The tunnel might have been two hundred feet long. Work lights hung from hooks all along its length, connected by black or orange cables. At least half of them were out and had not been

Wayne Public Library
461 Valley Rd.
Wayne, NJ 07470
(973) 694-4272
www.WaynePublicLibrary.org

Item ID: 32352054685554
Author: Golden, Christopher.
Title: Mind the gap : a novel of the hidde
n cities
Date due: 8/29/2017,23:59

Item ID: 32352054597903
Author: Katz Cooper, Sharon.
Title: Aristotle : philosopher, teacher, a
nd scientist
Date due: 8/29/2017,23:59

Item ID: 32352054951121
Author: McManus, Lori.
Title: Meet our new student from Japan
Date due: 8/29/2017,23:59

Item ID: 32352056633685
Author: Heinrichs, Ann
Title: Japan
Date due: 8/29/2017,23:59

Thank you.

replaced. There were crates and boxes all along the walls, as well as mattresses stacked with blankets. Metal shelves and cabinets that appeared to have been part of the original design lined one wall, and she could see bottles and cans of stored foods. As she moved closer, she confirmed her suspicions that these were not ancient supplies but far more recent ones. A bit dusty, but they had been put up within the last year or so.

Her gaze froze on one shelf. A trio of black heavy-duty torches were neatly lined up. She grabbed one and turned it on. Nothing. That didn't make sense. Organized people— whoever had made use of the shelter—wouldn't have the torches as backup lights without keeping batteries. She searched the rest of the shelves, then opened the nearest cabinet and found what she was looking for. An entire box of batteries.

Jazz loaded up one of the heavy torches and flicked it on. Despite the lights that already burned in the place, the bright beam thrown by the torch thrilled her. The hidden people who had used this shelter could not have rigged the entire tunnel system with lights. There would be many dark passages underground. If she meant to find her way out, far from home and the Uncles, the torch would guide her.

"Hello?" she called, suddenly nervous that the hidden people, likely thieves themselves, would attack her for thievery. She feared them, but they needed blankets and torches and canned beans; therefore, they were flesh and blood. Not phantoms.

"Anyone here? Hello?"

Her only answer was the echo of her own voice.

Jazz glanced around again and wondered what these people had run from, why they were hiding, and if they meant to hide forever.

"Mum," she whispered, hidden away far beneath the city. Her tears began to flow and she put a hand over her eyes. At last the fear that had driven her gave way to grief.

"Oh, Christ. Mum."

Shaking with exhaustion now that adrenaline had left her, mind awhirl with mourning and ghosts and hopelessness, she made it to the nearest mattress and collapsed there. Jazz held the torch like a teddy, drew a blanket over herself, and pulled her knees up tight, as she did on the coldest winter nights.

In silence, buried in the grave of another era, she cried for her mother and herself.

Chapter Three

flesh and blood

Her dead mother's whispering woke her up.

Jazz jerked upright, and for a few seconds she thought she was still dreaming. She was surrounded by a pressing darkness, lessened here and there by dusty bulbs hanging suspended from a high ceiling, and if she'd been in her bedroom, she'd be looking at a movie poster of Johnny Depp. Instead, the poster that hung on the rough brick wall above her was of a man lighting a cigarette, and the words said,

"Let 'em all come"
Men 41–55
Home Defense Battalions

Jazz felt a weight on her chest. She reached out and touched cool plastic; the comfort she had gained from the torch had all but vanished.

She sat up, taking in a few rapid breaths to dispel the dreams she could no longer remember. They had been bad, that's all she knew. Her mother had been there—alive or dead, she could not recall. But the echoes of her dead mother's words still reverberated in her mind. She knew that they always would.

She was cold and uncomfortable, and it felt as though she'd been asleep for a long time. Her muscles were stiff, her neck ached from where she had been resting her head at an awkward angle, and her right hand tingled with pins and needles.

Jazz clicked on the heavy torch and shone it around the shelter. She was alone. The Uncles had not come down here and found her, and although she knew the likelihood of that was remote, she still felt incredibly vulnerable, as though the trail of tears she had left behind was something they could follow.

Who's to say? she thought. *Until today I had no idea of what the Uncles were really capable of.* She aimed the strong beam all around the shelter, then clicked it off, satisfied that she was really alone.

They were waiting to kill me. The facts were punching back into her life like knives reinserted into old wounds. *They killed Mum, and they were waiting there to kill me as well!* The *why* still did not matter, though she thought it would soon. The simple fact of that terrible truth was enough for now.

She stood and stretched, letting out an involuntary groan that echoed around the shelter. She crouched down, startled. No reaction from anywhere; no sudden burst of activity from the shady corners or behind the shelving units fixed along the walls.

There was food here. She could smell it beneath the odor of old dampness and forgotten corners, and she went searching. Starting at the end of the tunnel farthest from where she had entered, Jazz began looking through the stacked shelves. She was immediately struck by the huge variety of goods down here. This was more than just a hideaway, it was a store, and many of the items she found were distinctly out of place. One shelf was piled with hundreds of CDs, ranging from Mozart to Metallica. The next shelf down held boxes of plant seeds still in their packets, and below that were piles of random-sized picture frames, all of them lacking pictures. *A family that never existed*, Jazz thought, and the idea chilled her more than it should.

Between the shelving stacks, on the floor, were small cardboard boxes. Rat traps. She had no wish to look inside to see what had been caught.

On the next stack were models of fantasy figures still in their boxes, empty sweets tins filled with one-penny pieces, a shelf of sex toys of varying shapes and sizes, tourist guides to London and beyond, stacks of watches still in their boxes, a variety of cacti, flat-packed furniture, jewelry, books, bedding, bumper stickers, children's cuddly toys, dining sets, garden gnomes, empty wallets and purses, empty rucksacks...

Peeking out from behind the units were old wartime posters, some of them unreadable but a few still quite clear. It felt peculiar, reading these exhortations to a lost generation that had feared losing itself. One in particular struck her:

Keep Mum,
She's not so Dumb!

Across the print a newer message was scrawled in marker pen:

Make them go away!

The tone behind that desperate plea was more disturbing than the age of the poster it was written on. It chilled her but at the same time made her realize how much her life had changed. Up until recently, things had been controlled and overseen. But now she was...

Free? she thought. *No. No fucking way. I'm more trapped by Mum's murder than I ever was before.*

Fighting back tears—Mum would want her to look after herself, not stand here crying—Jazz moved on, and on, and eventually she found a series of shelving units with lockable doors. No doors were locked, but they were all closed, and when she opened the first one her stomach gave an audible rumble of pleasure.

She plucked out a pack of bourbon cream biscuits and ripped it open. They were soft and probably well past their use-by date, but the first one tasted exquisite. She had no way of telling the time, but she felt that she had been down here for a long time. Even if she'd had a watch, it wouldn't have done her any good; she could never wear one, because they always broke when she put them on. Her mother suspected the radiation from dental X-rays, though whether this was paranoia or a joke, Jazz had never been sure. Either way, she ignored it as absurd.

Whatever the hour might be, Jazz decided it was lunchtime.

Several biscuits eaten, she moved on to the next cupboard. There was plenty of tinned food in here but no tin opener, and she did not feel inclined to go searching for one. A box of crackers looked more inviting, and when she opened the last unit she found four fridges, stacked two high and all working. Inside—butter, cream cheese, salads, and milk.

She closed her eyes and breathed in the scent of fresh food, and something moved behind her.

Jazz fell to her knees and clicked off her torch. She was still bathed in stark light, and for a moment she thought she was pinned within the beam of someone else's torch. Then she remembered the fridge lights, and she slammed the doors closed.

That had definitely been a movement. An echo, perhaps, of something farther away, but definitely not dripping water. More ghosts? She imagined an endless procession of people fleeing endless bombing, but the things she had found down here were at odds with that image. Ghosts did not eat biscuits, drink milk, or listen to Metallica.

Jazz scanned the shelter by the poor light of the hanging bulbs.

Keep your wits about you, her mother had once said. *That's the best weapon you can have.*

"See?" she said. "Richard Kimble's got his wits. Evades capture. Runs. And he's saving himself too."

"*The Fugitive* is just a film, Mum," Jazz said. She was sitting on the sofa with her legs tucked up beneath her, eating strawberry ice cream straight from the tub. Her mum's whiskey tumbler was almost empty again, but although her eyes glittered and her face was flushed, her words were as clear and concise as ever.

"But you can learn a *lot* from a film. Why shouldn't you learn from fiction? It's a vast array of ideas, and you can take what you need from that. Look at him. You can see the planning in every movement of his eyes, everything he does. He knows not to stop running. He knows to lose himself and how to find himself again after that."

"But he's just an actor, Mum. Not flesh and blood."

"Flesh and blood?" her mother said, and she froze for a few seconds, her eyes seeing something much farther away.

"Mum?"

"Flesh and blood," she repeated, words quieter than ever. "Not everything real is flesh and blood, Jazz. Not everything at all."

Those ghosts were not real, Jazz thought, running low and fast toward the other end of the shelter. She wanted to get as far from the spiral staircase as possible, and she remembered seeing some cupboards and storage units piled haphazardly against the end wall. Perhaps there she would find cover from whatever was coming.

She could hear the footsteps now, a single set descending with confidence.

Whoever it is, they're not expecting anyone to be down here. It gave her a moment's hope, but still she was terrified.

She almost fumbled the torch and held her breath, looping her index finger through the handle. If she lost that, she really would be in trouble.

If whoever came down was threatening, she could blind

them with light, then run for the stairs. It wasn't so far to the surface. A hundred feet, maybe? A bit less, a bit more?

She reached the end of the shelter, paused, and heard those footsteps still descending. She should have been counting steps, she knew. Should have been trying to work out how long she had, how close they were, how fast they were descending.

There were a dozen cabinets here, stacked against the crumbling brickwork, and most of them were full with all manner of goods. She started panicking again. She could lie down on one of the mattresses and pull a blanket across her, but how effective would that be? She had to hide, and now she was starting to wish she'd just gone to wait at the entrance tunnel, ready to clout the visitor over the head with the torch and run for her life.

She found a cupboard that was only half full, coats and jackets piled flat on its floor. She could fit in there.

The footsteps echoed so loudly that she was sure they were right behind her.

She glanced back, stepped into the cupboard, pulled the metal doors shut behind her, left an inch gap through which to see, and the person stepped into view.

He paused for a while at the end of the entrance tunnel, looking around the shelter, nose raised.

He knows I'm here. Oh fuck, he knows I'm here. He can smell me, see me, sense me!

The man was tall, easily six feet, and stood proud and straight. She thought he was older than his appearance suggested. He had long black hair that was tied in a loose ponytail and wore a trench coat that had seen better days. Its material was ripped in several places, and there seemed to be stains beneath both large pockets, as though he kept something in there that leaked. From this distance, Jazz could not make out his features, but his face looked pale and long, only the chin and cheeks darkened by stubble.

He held one hand out before him, fingers moving gently as though he was playing the air.

Jazz knew for sure that he was no ghost.

She tried to breathe slow and deep, but she was out of breath from her mad dash along the shelter. The torch was held between her knees; if it slipped and banged the cabinet, she would be found out.

The man looked around, moving his fingers before him again. *What can he see?* she thought. She shifted slightly and looked at the array of cupboards and shelving, trying to picture what it had been like when she arrived and make out how it had changed. Some doors were open, but they had not all been closed to begin with. The fridges were closed, the cabinets housing them shut. Some of the blankets on the mattresses were messed up—had she done that as she ran?—and...

She could just make out the biscuit packet, still half full but discarded carelessly on the floor.

Jazz shifted again until she could see the man. He did not seem to be looking in the direction of the biscuit cupboard. Indeed, he now seemed to have his eyes closed and his face raised, as though smelling the air of the place.

"You can come on down now, my pets," he said. "We're very much alone."

The man walked gracefully into the shelter, and then Jazz heard the whisper of many more feet descending the spiral staircase. From where she was hiding, the footfalls sounded like fingers drumming on a tabletop, distant and ambiguous.

The man took something from the pocket of his trench coat, stuck out his tongue, and placed the something on it. He chewed thoughtfully, only turning around when the first shape appeared behind him.

It was barely a shadow, slipping into the shelter and dashing across the concrete floor. Jazz tried to keep track, but the poor lighting defeated her. It was as though this shape—whoever or whatever it was—knew just where the lighting levels were lowest and took advantage of that.

Another shape came from the entrance tunnel, then another, all of them much smaller and slighter than the tall man. They came low and fast, parting around the man like a stream flowing around a rock. Jazz counted four, six, perhaps nine shapes flowing from the tunnel. When she did catch sight of their faces, she saw only pale skin and dark eyes; the light was too poor, and they were moving too fast to truly make out any features.

They were all carrying something on their backs.

What am I going to see? she thought. *I've moved on from one danger to . . . what? Something worse?*

The man raised his arms and turned slowly around, and then all the shapes stopped and turned to look at him.

They were kids. Teenagers and younger. Pale, scruffy, yet most of them with a smile on their face, and a couple with expressions of outright joy.

"Ahh, my pets, there's nothing like coming home," the tall man said.

Home, Jazz thought, with a sudden longing.

"Now, then," the man continued. He groaned slightly as

he sat on a large blanket in the center of the floor. "Cadge, if you'd be kind enough to illuminate our day's haul, I'd be most grateful."

"No problem, Mr. F." A boy to Jazz's left disappeared out of her line of sight, coming close to the cabinets and apparently slipping between two of them to whatever lay behind. She had thought they were lined against a solid wall, but maybe not. Seconds later, the rest of the strung lights lit up, and Jazz had to squint against the glare.

There was a brief cheer from the kids and a satisfied smile from the tall man—or Mr. F., as the boy Cadge had called him.

Cadge came into view again and performed an elaborate, slow bow. He was a short, skinny kid, maybe fourteen, with an unruly mop of bright ginger hair, baggy jeans, and a denim jacket studded with button badges. He wore a pair of wire-rimmed glasses, which seemed too delicate for his face. He glanced back once—Jazz held her breath—then he slipped the rucksack from his shoulders and went to sit close to Mr. F. From the brief glimpse of his face lit up by the lights, Jazz was sure she had seen no lenses in his glasses.

The children gathered around Mr. F., sitting on blankets, mattresses, or bare concrete. They all took off rucksacks or duffels and placed them beside them on the floor, and the tall man looked around with a warm smile. "Good day, my pets?"

"Best I've 'ad in a while," one boy said.

"Ah!" Mr. F. clapped his hands. "If Stevie Sharpe tells me he's had a good day, I know we'll be eating well tonight."

Stevie Sharpe smiled tightly, the expression hardly changing his face. He tipped up his rucksack, and Jazz gasped. Dozens of wallets and purses fell from it, pattering to the floor like dead birds. "American bus trip broke down," the boy said. "They had to catch the Tube to meet up with a new bus." He picked up one wallet and flipped it through the air.

Mr. F. caught it and put it to his nose. "Real leather, of course," he said. Then he opened the wallet and flipped through the contents. He smiled. "Yes, eating *very* well tonight. That's if you all don't mind fillet steak bought with honestly earned money?"

The children laughed and started offering their own hauls to the man sitting in their midst.

What the hell is this? Jazz thought. And as she watched the strange display before her—more loot, more celebrating, more banter, and plenty of laughter—another realization struck her: she needed to pee.

Wallets and purses were the main hauls, handed to Mr. F. as though he were some ancient god to which the kids had to pay tribute. Jazz guessed that the youngest was maybe twelve, the oldest eighteen. A couple of them were about her age—seventeen—and old enough to pass as adults.

She closed her eyes and tried not to concentrate on her bladder. However desperate her situation, she was too proud to piss herself while shut away in some cupboard. Some *smelly* cupboard, she realized. The coats and jackets compressed beneath her seemed to be exuding an old, musty odor, a mixture of damp and sweat and something more spicy and exotic.

When she looked again, several of the children were gathering their haul and starting to store it away. They shoved it seemingly at random into cupboards and cabinets, but they worked in a way that convinced Jazz there was some sort of system here.

No coats today, she thought. *No jackets, no coats or jackets, please, not today.*

But remaining undiscovered was simply delaying the inevitable. Unless she could stay here until these people went out again, what hope did she have?

Mr. F. stood and strolled to the other end of the shelter, opening the fridge cabinets and taking out a bottle of beer. He popped the top and drank deep, turning around to watch his kids hide away their stolen goods.

Bunch of thieves. Nothing more, nothing less. Jazz actually felt disappointed. Discovering this subterranean place had instilled a sense of mystery in her, distracting to some small degree from the seriousness of her situation. The *hopelessness.* She had been thinking only minutes, maybe hours ahead—avoid capture by the Uncles, maybe plan forward to where and when she could go back up to the surface. And then the ghosts—

(though she had not really seen them, had she? Not really. The stress, the strain, the trauma had thrust visions at her from the darkness, that was all)

—and the discovery of this strange place had combined to help remove her even more from the world. She had not only come deeper, she had come *farther away.* That had felt good.

"Just bloody thieves," she whispered.

"Mr. F.?" One of the girls walked to the tall man, holding something in her hand.

Jazz held her breath. What had she left? What had she forgotten?

"So who's the litterbug?" Mr. F. asked. "Cadge?"

"Not me, Mr. F. I'm clean an' tidy."

Mr. F. smiled and held up the half-empty biscuit wrapper. "Someone craving bourbons? It's hardly surprising. They are, after all, members of the biscuit royalty, though I'd only bestow a princehood on them. The king being...?"

"Chocolate Hobnobs," a tall boy said, rubbing his stomach and sighing.

"Right. So...?"

A chorus of no's and shaken heads, and then the strange group went back to tidying their haul.

"As ever, I believe you all," the man said. His voice was lower than before, and Jazz could see the confusion on his face.

Damn, she really needed to pee.

Jazz sobbed. She couldn't help it. She quickly pressed her hand to her mouth, squeezed her eyes shut, and the torch slipped between her knees. The handle touched the metal wall of the cabinet, making a sound as loud and striking as a school dinner bell.

Oh fuck!

"Guests?" she heard Mr. F. say.

She tried to open her eyes, but fear kept them glued shut. Tears squeezed out and tickled her cheeks, and when she finally found the strength to look, the shelter was frantic with activity, children darting here and there as they searched for the intruder. The only person not moving was Mr. F. He was once again standing on the blanket in the center, turning slowly around until his gaze settled in her direction.

"Cadge?" he said.

"Mr. F.?" The voice came from very close by, and Jazz's breath caught in her throat. She leaned forward slightly and saw the ginger boy, Cadge, standing six feet away.

"The coat cupboard," Mr. F. said.

Jazz kicked open the doors and went to leap out and brandish the torch as a weapon. But her left leg had gone to sleep, and instead of leaping she stumbled, falling to the ground and sending the torch spinning away.

Cadge was on her quickly, knocking her left hand away and sending her falling painfully onto her side. He sat astride her and pinned her right arm beneath his legs.

Jazz struggled for a moment, then realized it was far too late.

"Mr. F.!" Cadge called. "'Fink we caught us a proper lady!"

"Is she wearing a hat?" one of the girls asked, and everyone laughed.

"Trust Hattie to think of the most important things," Mr. F. said. He came into Jazz's field of vision, sideways because she still had her face pressed to the cool concrete, and he looked even stranger close up. His skin was so pale as to be almost white, and even beneath the stubbled chin and cheeks it looked like flesh that had been underwater for too long. He had a large Roman nose, a wide mouth, and deeply piercing eyes. She thought they were green, but it was difficult to tell in this light.

There were very fine, very intricate tattoo swirls beneath both ears and disappearing down under the collar of his coat.

"Who are you?" Jazz asked.

"We ask the questions down 'ere," Stevie Sharpe said. "In fact, you don't even talk. Not a word. This is our place, and the walls hear only our words."

Mr. F. pursed his lips and raised an eyebrow. "Don't you think, my pets, that we should hear this girl's story before we start imposing such rules?"

"She could be trouble," a tall girl said.

"She could be, Faith. But weren't you trouble as well when I found you?"

Faith shrugged, still staring at Jazz. "Suppose."

"First thing I wanna know is how she found us," Stevie said.

Cadge remained silent, still pressing her down. Jazz could sense that he was tensed and ready to move should she try anything foolish.

"I really need to piss," Jazz said.

Mr. F. frowned. "We don't swear and curse down here, young lady. Avoid vulgarity, please."

"Right. Pee."

Mr. F. regarded her for a while, expression unchanging.

"She does look a bit desperate," a short, chubby boy said.

"Hmm." The tall man squatted and turned his head so that Jazz could see him straight on. "Well then, Hattie, would you be good enough to take her to the loo?"

"No problem. Cadge?"

Cadge stood from Jazz, gently, so that he didn't hurt her.

Jazz sat up slowly, shifting her foot to test whether she had feeling back in her leg. It seemed better, but she didn't want to collapse again in front of these people. So she waited awhile, looking around, trying not to appear as confused and frightened as she felt.

"My name's Harry," Mr. F. said. "And nobody here will hurt you." Jazz believed him. There was something about his voice that made her suspect that she would believe it if he told her black was white. It was smooth, intelligent, and assured. *Mum would like him*, she thought, and the thought surprised her. She looked down at the ground and stood, rubbing away a tear as she did so.

Facing them, feeling their attention bore into her, sensing the suspicion coming off them in waves, she realized that there was no reason at all to lie.

"My mum's dead," she said. "She was murdered today. And the people who did it are looking for me."

Harry's expression did not change, but the kids around him all reacted in some way.

"Then you're lost too, just like us," Harry said.

Lost, Jazz thought. *Can it really be this easy?*

Hattie led her to the loos. There was a narrow opening in the end wall of the tunnel, the same place Cadge had gone to switch on the rest of the lights. The walls were bare brick festooned with cables and spiderwebs, the concrete floor damp from several leaks that looked decades old. As they walked past a room off to the right, Jazz felt a draft that could only have come from a vent to the world above. Light from the corridor shone into the room just enough for her to see several clotheslines hung with drying laundry and an ironing board.

Hattie noticed her looking and laughed softly. "What, didn't think a bunch of tunnel rats would want clean clothes?"

"No," Jazz said, not wanting to offend. Then she shrugged. "The iron surprises me, though."

"Mr. F. likes things neat and tidy," Hattie said. "A bit of cleanup makes it easier to go unnoticed up above."

The passageway went on another dozen feet before opening into a large round room. Jazz knew this place had been built as a bomb shelter but still found the chamber remarkable this far underground. At its center stood three roughly plumbed basins. On one end were two curtained shower stalls, and on the other there were four toilet cubicles. The room smelled faintly of piss and shit and, underlying that, the stench of old bleach.

"Best we can offer," Hattie said. "'Spect you're used to bidets and people handing you the toilet roll."

"No," Jazz said. "Not at all." She went into one of the cubicles and peed, not minding for a second that the girl was still standing outside.

"Sorry about your..." Hattie said, unable to continue the sentence.

Jazz could not reply. She looked at the floor between her feet, reaching for small talk. "Is Hattie your real name?" she asked at last.

"No. But I like hats, so Hattie it is. What's your name?"

"Jazz." She realized that none of them had asked her this until now, and that was strange. Surely a name was the first thing anyone asked?

"Ha! You like music?"

"I do, but it *is* my real name."

"Right," Hattie said, and Jazz could hear the smile in her voice. "Well, it's strange enough to keep, I guess."

Jazz finished and flushed the loo. A trap vented into a flowing sewer, then slammed shut again.

"You'll want to use the spray," Hattie said, and Jazz

noticed the cans on a shelf above her. She sprayed the air around her, trying to screw her nose up against the stench.

"That is fucking foul," she said.

"Hey," Hattie said, "Harry meant it. We don't swear down here." The admonishment seemed strange coming from a girl her own age.

"So who are you all?" Jazz asked, stepping from the cubicle and going to wash her hands. The water wouldn't get hot, and she shivered as she thought how cold the showers must be in the winter.

"We're the United Kingdom."

Jazz stared at the girl, waiting for the teasing smile. But none came.

"Come on," Hattie said. "I'll let Harry tell you himself."

Chapter Four

all the world

"Gather round, my pets. Time to have a chat with our little wandering note, our Jazz girl. Leave off the dinner prep just now, Stevie, and come to circle."

The boy looked up from perusing the contents of the tribe's many refrigerators. He must have been eighteen or so, tall but slender with muscles like whipcords. He wouldn't be very strong, but he'd be quick as the devil. His black hair hung straight to his shoulders, and his eyes were a coppery brown. Jazz couldn't help taking a second glance at him, and a third, and when he noticed, she turned her eyes away.

Now that she'd calmed down a bit and the panic of her urgent bladder had passed, Jazz took a closer look at the nine runaway urchins who made up Harry's United Kingdom. Hattie and Faith seemed like opposites: Hattie a bit odd and wild but happy enough, and Faith with grim blue-steel eyes and suspicion deep as a knife wound.

The boys seemed to lack any real leader aside from Harry, unless the silent Stevie filled that role. The youngest among them was twelve-year-old Gob, but Jazz couldn't be sure if the nickname came from his lurking in the tunnels like some hobgoblin or from the fact that he never seemed to stop nattering, even to breathe, unless Harry hushed him.

Cadge had a bit of the peacock in him. The prize pupil, he obviously fancied himself a miniature Harry, even mimicking the man's body language, that particular quality that bespoke an earlier life as a gentleman. Just a few minutes watching him scramble about revealed that Cadge must be the procurer among them, the most adept with his fingers. He seemed also to know where every item in the old shelter had been stored.

"Come, come," Harry urged, gesturing for them to move in closer.

The United Kingdom formed a circle, seated on the cold ground. Somewhere a train rumbled past, and Jazz remembered where they were, how deep, with the whole of modern London looming over their heads and only the echoes of the past around them. She studied Harry's face, searching for guile or cruelty, but saw only a gleaming pride in his tribe, a love for them that seemed simultaneously out of place and all too natural there in the forgotten cellar of the city.

Harry settled down, leaving Jazz the only one standing. He gestured for her to take a place beside him in the circle.

"Small comforts in our kingdom, love, and chairs not among them. Do join us, please."

For a moment, Jazz was struck by the upturned faces of Harry's followers. The word *urchins* would not leave her head, though surely many of those nine children were far too old to bear the word comfortably. Still, urchins they were. Lost and dirty children, far from whatever homes they might once have had. They looked to her like schoolchildren waiting for the teacher to begin reading, eyes alight with the eager anticipation of story time.

I'm Wendy Darling, she thought. But Jazz understood her foolishness instantly, and a tremor passed through her. Neverland did not exist in the rotting belly of London, under the feet of the world, and these were not the Lost Boys. Wendy Darling had run off on a girlish whim, heart aflutter with the allure of Peter Pan, and when she'd gotten over her crush, her parents were waiting for her with open arms, ready to whisper happily-ever-afters as they tucked her into bed.

There'd be no fairy-tale ending for her. Not with those words her mother had written in blood.

"Thank you," Jazz said, her voice quavering only a little.

She sat down beside Harry, and a collective sigh of relief seemed to sweep over the tribe of urchins—the United Kingdom. Did that make Harry the king? she wondered.

"The circle is for sharing stories," Harry began a bit ceremoniously, though his eyes were gentle. "Whether it be the day's adventures, or the nightmares that wake us in the night, or the longings for times gone by, what's spoken here is never judged, never questioned. We bring only truth to the circle."

The nine apostles nodded their assent and Jazz followed suit.

"A time for proper introductions, then," Harry said, turning to Jazz. "Harold Pilkington Fowler, at your service."

He made a bow of his head and spoke the words with a courtly flourish of his hand. Jazz gnawed her lower lip for a moment, glancing nervously about. Shouldn't she still be running? Or was there simply nowhere left to run? She had no reason to trust this odd band, save that they seemed the utter opposite of the Uncles and their BMW men. Harry Fowler's tribe was the opposite of everything, really. Opposite of the world as she'd always known it.

A twitch of a smile touched her lips. Their oppositeness suddenly seemed more than enough reason to trust them. Thieves, ruffians, and scoundrels they might be, but she sensed the nobility in them and a sense of honor she'd rarely encountered among the tidier folk aboveground.

Jazz returned Harry's bow and offered her hand. "Jasmine Ellen Towne, Mr. Fowler. And she's grateful for your hospitality."

Harry beamed. He shook her hand and then adjusted the lapels of his coat as though chairing a meeting of the board of a brokerage or similarly snooty enterprise.

"Now then, my compatriots, my fine filchers, do likewise please and make yourselves known to our Jasmine—"

"Jazz," she interrupted. "Just Jazz, please."

Hattie sighed, rolling her eyes. "'Course it's just Jazz. I said as much, didn't I? We don't care much for proper names down in the kingdom. No use for 'em."

She wore a pale peach bonnet with faux flowers on the brim and a smear of black grease along one ragged side. Jazz wondered how many hats she had hidden about the shelter.

"Jazz it is, then, and a fitting name. Improvisation is vital to our little enterprise, so I hope you shall earn the appellation," Harry said. "But back to our introductions. Round the circle, if you please."

And they began. The boy to Jazz's left had small dark eyes set back in his face above a long thin nose that had been broken more than once. She'd thought his name would be Rat, or some synonym, but he went by Bill, an ordinary enough name. Bill did not introduce himself, however. That task fell to Leela, an Indian girl who sat beside him. Leela's eyes seemed to have their own luminescence, but they dimmed a little when she explained that Bill had no voice of his own. Whether the boy was actually mute or simply chose never to speak, Leela did not reveal, and Jazz hadn't the heart to ask.

Cadge was next, and for a moment the confidence he had when imitating Harry faltered and he gave Jazz a shy smile. The names came too quickly. She'd already marked Hattie, Faith, Gob, and Stevie. Another of the boys was called Switch, and still another Marco—after the explorer Marco Polo, according to Harry—but by the time they'd gone round the circle entirely, Jazz couldn't recall which was which.

"Good to meet you all," she told them, "and thanks for not running me off."

Some of them smiled in return, but others sniffed at her words and one or two eyed her with open suspicion.

"Nonsense," Harry said with a flutter of his hand. "It's not our way, love. You're a stray. We've all gone astray ourselves, but now we're lost together. Far better than being lost on your own. Now, then, let's have your story. I see it's all still fresh, a bit of glaze in your eyes, but pain needs telling, Jazz girl. Pain always needs telling. The only way to stanch the wound."

Jazz squeezed her eyes shut and a moment of vertigo washed over her. If she hadn't already been seated, she'd have fallen. Was she really supposed to share her story with them all, like some tale told round a campfire?

Nothing's for nothing, her mother had once said. *Those that help mostly help themselves.* Jazz could hear the echoes of that voice whispering in her head, and she wanted to claw into her brain to stop it. It felt now as though her mum had been preparing her for this all her life. But Jazz wasn't ready to be alone. How could she survive down here in the dark by herself?

She opened her eyes again and saw those faces, all watching her curiously. Her mother's whispers became more insistent, but Jazz shut them out. After all, her warnings had been about people up in the world, people like the Uncles, not about the discarded, like Fowler and his United Kingdom. Even if she told them, how could they hurt her with the truth? They lived down here. Who would they tell?

"My mum's dead," she said. "Murdered, just today." Jazz frowned and looked upward, as though she could see through hundreds of feet of earth and stone and pavement. "Or yesterday. I'm not sure what time it is. I was walking home from school and a queer feeling came over me, and then I saw the cars."

"Cars?" Harry asked.

Jazz nodded. "The Uncles were there, but there'd never been so many visiting at once and I knew something was wrong. Mum brought me up paranoid, made sure if things took a turn I'd suspect it right off, and I did. I went up the alley that runs behind the house..."

She left out any mention of ghosts or whispers, fearful that they'd think her mad or doubt every word if she started up talking about phantoms. By the time she finished recounting the hours leading up to their discovery of her, like Goldilocks in Baby Bear's bed, Jazz felt exhaustion beginning to claim her again. Her tears flowed freely while she spoke, and several times she had to pause simply to catch her breath. The sympathy on Harry Fowler's face and the empathy shining in the eyes of the urchins were the greatest gifts she had ever received.

Jazz never would have imagined herself crying so openly in front of anyone, let alone a roomful of strangers. But she could still smell her mother's blood. Her life had new rules, now and forevermore.

When she fell silent, no one spoke for a moment. Harry reached out as though to lay a comforting hand on her shoulder but hesitated. Then he cupped the back of her head and looked into her eyes. Had anyone else done such a thing, Jazz would have slapped the hand away.

"You're well hid, Jazz girl. Well hid. So you've done as your dear mother asked," he said, his gaze intense. After a moment, he withdrew his hand but continued to stare at her.

"You can keep running if you like," Harry went on. "No one will try to stop you. We'll give you a bit of food, let you keep a torch, even an extra set of batteries. But know that you're not alone down here, and I'm not talking about us. There are old empty stations all through the Underground, and shelters like this one as well, and other places besides.

The whole city's got a warren under it, and a wonder it doesn't collapse right down into the earth. Sometimes I think the old tunnels are growing, spreading like the roots of some invisible tree.

"Point is, others have retreated down here over the years. Some come and go. Mostly they're hiding, like you, or don't trust anyone up above, like me. They aren't all as hospitable as the United Kingdom, I'm sorry to say. There are lots that are homeless as well, not hiding so much as fallen through the cracks. You'll see them in your rambles underground. And there may be other things down here, wild dogs and the like. Pets lost to the tunnels.

"So I say this: go if you like, and Godspeed. Stay if you like, and welcome. But if you stay, you've got to contribute, just like the rest."

Jazz glanced at the hard ground at the center of the circle. "By contribute, you mean steal."

Harry laughed at that, the sound a harsh, barking cough. "Steal from them topside? Surviving isn't thieving, Jazz girl. We're scavengers, so we are, living off the corpse of a decaying society. If we pick a pocket or snatch a purse, or forage for food or supplies, they don't miss it. Not really. We're invisible down here, girl, just as we like it. It's a world of monsters up there.

"There are the rich and the poor, and the poor must stick together. If we don't, the rich will pick our bones."

Even without the encouragement on the faces around the circle, Jazz felt the truth of Harry's words. The world above had taken her mother, or at least turned a blind eye while killers spilled her blood. Rich men who followed the rules. The world had shaken her off like a dog shakes off fleas.

Her mother had told her to hide, but Jazz understood the deeper meaning of the word, communicated over the course of years. Mum had wanted her to survive, above all else.

"I might not stay forever, or even for very long," she warned.

Harry only smiled. He clapped his hands and stood up.

"I'm famished. Let's have a nibble, eh? Then we'll see if Jazz girl's got the knack."

Half the cast was crowded into the green room while a quartet of volunteer mothers applied the final touches of the stage makeup. Mrs. Snelling darted her head back and studied Jazz, then put down the brush—done with blush, apparently. Unsatisfied, she picked up the coal pencil and darkened the lines around her eyes. At last she smiled, sat back, and nodded.

"Gorgeous, love. You're ready for your close-up."

Jazz thanked her and hurried out of the room. In full costume, she had to reach down and gather up the bustle of her dress to squeeze through the crowded space. Making a point, Tom Rolston gestured broadly and clipped the edge of her bonnet. Had Jazz not flinched away from him, he might have dislodged the hat, pins and all.

"Oi! Watch it, y'lummox!" she said.

Rolston laughed and rolled his eyes. "Sounds more like Eliza than Mrs. Higgins."

Jazz explored her hair and bonnet to make sure all was

still in place, then shot him a dark look. "Lucky boy. I won't have to kill you today, apparently."

"What a glorious death it would be, though," he said, waggling his eyebrows suggestively.

Smiling, Jazz exited the green room. Though her role in *My Fair Lady* was that of a lady, the entire cast had taken to imitating the rough, cockney speech of Eliza Doolittle backstage. Sometimes a well-placed *guv'nor* could reduce the whole stage to fits and giggles.

She rushed down the half dozen stairs to the door leading out into the auditorium. The hinges squeaked when she opened it, and she made a mental note to remind the director—the English teacher, Mr. Morris—to have someone take care of it before the first performance tomorrow night.

Today was the dress rehearsal. They were all in full costume and makeup for the first time. Though Jazz was a slender girl, her costume cinched her waist so tightly that she felt it might rip at any moment. The girl who'd been handling costumes promised to let it out tonight, and Jazz hoped she remembered, or there was the real possibility she'd pass out onstage.

The door squeaked shut behind her and Jazz glanced up onto the stage, where the hands were moving sets around with only a modicum of thunder. Then she glanced out over the auditorium. Most of the five hundred or so seats were empty. The director and the school's principal sat with half a dozen teachers, patiently waiting for the dress rehearsal to begin. Twenty or thirty parents had come as well, along with a handful of kids who were the younger siblings of members of the cast.

Jazz felt a moment of crashing disappointment when she

did not see her mum. Then her gaze flickered to the back of the auditorium and the figure standing just inside the doors, and her smile returned.

She hurried up the central aisle and presented herself to her mother, spinning once to show off her dress and then curtsying like a lady.

"What do you think?"

Her mother smiled nervously. "You look lovely, Jazz. I could do without all that makeup—"

"It's stage makeup, Mum. You've got to wear it or the audience won't be able to see the expression on your face."

"Well, you do look lovely. Hardly a girl at all anymore. A young lady."

Jazz basked a moment in the compliment, but then she saw that her mother's attention had wandered, gaze darting around to take in the auditorium, the doors at either side of the stage, and the nearer corners of the room.

"What is it?" Jazz asked, seeing her mother's brows knit.

Her mum nodded toward the stage. "And you'll be up there, will you? The entire time?"

"Hardly," Jazz replied. "My part's not very big. It's not as if I'm playing Eliza."

"Yes, but when you are on, you won't be out in the audience at all?"

"Of course not."

"That'll have to do, I suppose. Can't be too careful, sweetheart."

Jazz stared. Her mother had always been paranoid, and she suspected it had to do with the suddenness of her father's death. Jazz tried to assuage her fears whenever possible, but sometimes she couldn't bite her tongue.

"Honestly, Mum. What's going to happen? It isn't as if someone in the audience is going to try to hurt or rob me in the middle of the show."

Her mother's thin smile seemed to pain her. She gave a shake of her head. "No, of course not, love. Still, you can never be too careful. Never know what's out there looking to do us harm, do we? Just look after yourself."

But the following evening, and at all three performances that weekend, whenever Jazz spotted her in the audience, her mum was standing at the rear of the auditorium, not watching the show but instead studying the audience and the shadowy corners of the room, always on guard.

But that was her mother. Always on guard. She never seemed to know precisely what or who might pose a threat, so she mistrusted everything and everyone.

Jazz never participated in another play after that. She could find no joy in it.

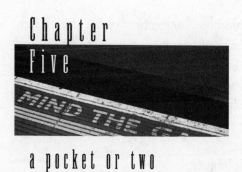

Chapter Five

a pocket or two

Holborn station stood at the juncture of High Holborn Street and Kingsway, the foot traffic a mixture of hurried Londoners, business travelers, and enough casual tourists to warrant a map vendor on the curb outside the station's entrance. The facade of the building looked more like an old theater marquee than a Tube station, but the red circle and blue band that marked the Underground gave it away.

On a pleasantly warm day—a workday, though she'd lost track of which one—Jazz stood near the magazine stand across the street from the station and pretended to talk into a disposable mobile. The phone had been fetched from the garbage in Tottenham Court Road station after having been discarded there and made a useful prop. Jazz had never seriously entertained thoughts of becoming an actress, but her few excursions onto the stage had come effortlessly. She'd been born to pretend.

"Can you believe it, Sally?" she asked into the inert mobile. "And he sent flowers the next day. He's got no shame. I've half a mind to—"

She felt a tug behind her, on the hem of her skirt. Then Cadge whipped the back of her skirt up high, revealing her lavender thong and far more of her than she would have liked. A breeze fluttered the skirt, and then she forced it down, covering herself again and dropping the phone in the process. The mobile cracked when it struck the pavement. She spun on him.

"You cheeky little bugger!"

Cadge laughed merrily, his cheeks flushed with excitement and embarrassment. Though older, he looked no more than twelve.

"Nice arse, love. Let's have a look at the rest!" he cried.

A man at the newsstand shot him an angry glare. He'd just bought a magazine and now stuffed his wallet back into the inside pocket of his suit coat.

"Here, now!" the man said. "There's no call for that."

"Bloody right," Jazz snarled, and she started toward Cadge.

"Oh, tough bird, are we?" Cadge said. "Come on, give us a show."

"Right!" the man in the gray business suit said, catching hold of Cadge's arm. "That's enough. Leave off now. Get out of here."

Jazz didn't hesitate. The man had gotten an eyeful of her backside, and she knew she looked good. The skirt and blouse had come from the dress-up closet Harry Fowler's

United Kingdom had filched over time. Hattie had helped her choose the clothes and Faith had done her hair. Harry'd even managed enough hot water so that she could shave her legs. No one looking at her would have guessed that she'd been living in the Underground for an entire month.

Yes, she'd gotten the bloke's attention. Now the business suit had to be her knight in shining armor. Couldn't resist a pretty girl.

"I'll have you, you little shit!" Jazz said, and she lunged for Cadge.

Businessman put himself between them—or at least later on he'd think he'd done that out of chivalry. Really, Jazz made sure to catch the man between herself and Cadge. She cursed and damned him and his relations and ancestors going back several generations. Cadge kept laughing, egging her on.

"Jesus, girl!" the man said, now alarmed to be stuck between them. "Get off."

As the businessman struggled to keep hold of Cadge and to prevent her from clawing the boy's eyes out, Jazz put to use everything Harry and the United Kingdom had taught her over the past few weeks. The fabric of his coat whispered as her fingers slid against it.

Finally she darted around him, spit at Cadge, shouted a final curse at him, and walked away. "Someone's got to pay for that phone," she told Cadge. "You'd better hope you don't see me again!"

Jazz marched across the street and into Holborn station. She didn't bother thanking the man. Time was of the essence now. She descended the stairs and felt the comfort of being enclosed again. It had been good to go aboveground again, but she'd felt eyes on her everywhere, the breeze whispered about her, and buildings stared down like sentinels.

Jazz went through the turnstile and took the escalator down. Leela waited for her on the platform. The sign above them declared the next train to be two minutes away. Jazz and Leela stood near each other for a moment, neither acknowledging the other. The Indian girl had downplayed her looks to be less conspicuous, which had to be difficult for someone with such natural beauty. But Leela managed it. Her right arm was looped through the handles of a big bag that seemed half purse and half briefcase, something she'd snatched earlier in the day.

Stevie and Bill emerged onto the platform. From their smiles, Jazz presumed they'd also had a successful day aboveground. The train arrived and all four of them stepped on through different doors.

At Tottenham Court Road station, Jazz got off. The other three would travel up to the next station.

"Mind the gap," a voice warned.

Jazz let out a long breath of relief as the doors closed and the train pulled away. She went to a bench and picked up a discarded copy of that morning's *Times*. A few minutes later, Cadge darted onto the platform.

Grinning, she got up.

"Right, give me the news. How'd I do?" she asked as Cadge approached.

"Perfect," he said, clapping softly. "Like you were born to it."

She felt herself swelling with pride, and it took her by surprise. Jazz had been reluctant at first. Of all the things she had one day imagined she might become, *thief* had never been on the list. But Harry and his tribe—*your tribe too now*—had persuaded her otherwise. Topsiders were all about money and merchandise. They lived for the illusion of success. And the rich bastards, the ones with more than they needed—if their wallets were a bit lighter at the end of the day, most of them would barely feel it. That's why it was so damn easy to steal from them, to pick their pockets or con them on the street. They were hardly aware of what they carried, because they could afford to lose it.

And how else were they to survive down there in the Underground? The rich, Harry insisted, would happily pick their bones. He did not pretend to be some modern-day Robin Hood, robbing from the rich to give to the poor, but Jazz figured the same rules applied. If she was to hide down beneath, she had to survive. A little petty thievery from the arrogant and rich did not trouble her overmuch.

And the way she'd been raised—weaned on paranoia, caution, and suspicion—had laid the groundwork for a life of thievery. She'd learned to be stealthy and to blend in a crowd, and with her natural agility it almost seemed as though her past had been the perfect preparation. Jazz knew she shouldn't take pleasure in discovering a talent for stealing, but the thrill was undeniable.

"Well, what's your haul, then?" Cadge asked.

Jazz glanced around. By now the mark would have noted the theft, but unless he'd done so quickly enough to follow Cadge, there would be no way they would be caught. She plunged her hands into her pockets and drew out their contents. In her left hand she held the man's wallet. She hadn't checked to see how much money he'd been carrying and it wasn't safe to do that here, but it felt thick with cash.

In her right hand she held his mobile phone. Down there in Harry's United Kingdom, they hadn't any need for phones. No one to call. And it would be turned off by morning. But there was no telling when they'd find a use for it, so when her fingers had brushed against it in the right-hand pocket of the man's jacket, she had liberated it.

"Well done, you," Cadge said.

His own hands were empty. Today had been her first time hitting the street with them, and Cadge had been assigned to work the mark, not to do the actual nicking.

Jazz glanced nervously at the entrance to the platform. "We should go."

Cadge nodded. "Wait for the train."

Two minutes ticked past with excruciating slowness until the train pulled into the station. People were disgorged and others got aboard, and then it rumbled away again. In moments, they were alone.

Cadge led the way to the edge of the platform. He glanced both ways along the tunnel. According to Stevie Sharpe, there were other ways to get to the unused platforms at Tottenham Court Road, but the tracks were fastest. With great care, they picked their way along the side of the tracks, retrieved their torches from a nook where they'd stashed them, and fifty yards along they split off along a section of unused track. The abandoned tunnel ran past the old platform, but they didn't slow. It wasn't the moldering platform they wanted but this lonely, abandoned track. Following it would take them back to Holborn station, and from there they could descend to one of the older, deeper stations that had sheltered air-raid refugees during the Blitz. They would meet up with the others and make their way back to Deep Level Shelter 7-K, their sub-subterranean home.

Home.

A chill went through her. It was the first time she'd thought of the underground refuge as home, and something about it felt very wrong to her. She knew she had to hide, knew that if she ever tried to return to her real home, ugliness and murder awaited her there, perhaps along with truths and revelations she had no interest in ever learning. But to think of the shelter as home was to submit to the idea of living there forever, and that she could not do. Silently, she promised herself she'd never think of it that way again.

Ever since the moment Cadge had yanked up her skirt, Jazz's heart had been racing, adrenaline pumping through her. Now, at last, far away from any chance of discovery, her pulse slowed and the thrill began to lessen.

And then she heard the music, distant and tinny at first, then growing in volume. A plinking piano, a jaunty violin, a tooting horn...and then a sudden chorus of wolf whistles and lecherous howls so loud that Jazz felt surrounded.

"Oh, Jesus," she whispered, and clapped her hands to her ears.

Frantic, she whipped around, shining her torch into the shadows on both sides of the old track. With the light shining, she saw nothing at all, but when she swung the torch away, she saw spectral images in the darkness left behind. The piano player, the violinist, and the trumpeter, who swayed his hips to get a laugh. And the audience roared.

Jazz spun and saw them there, rows and rows of them, applauding. They were dressed not in the thirties' garb of the spirits she'd encountered before but the clothing of an earlier era. Still wartime, though. Always wartime. The music hall had phantom walls and curtains, a stage, and above her hung a ghostly chandelier.

For a moment the whole room flickered and became a tavern full of men locked in serious debate, and on the plate-glass window at the front she could read the reversed lettering of the name of the place—the Seven Tankards and Punch Bowl. Then the moment passed, the tavern blurred, and the music hall returned, accompanied by laughter and those wolf whistles.

Voices called out a name. "Marie!"

"Marry me, Marie!"

"Get yer knickers off, Marie!"

But the voices weren't addressing Jazz. She could see in the faces of that spectral audience—many of them in uniform—that their focus was on the stage. Jazz turned just in time to see the tall blond woman sashay suggestively onto the stage. A microphone awaited her. She ran her fingers down the smooth contours of her body, over the sparkling material of her dress.

And she sang.

"I didn't like you much before you joined the army, John," Marie cooed, "but I do like yer cockie now you've got your khaki on."

The audience erupted with hoots and applause.

Jazz fell to her knees and slapped her hands over her ears. She squeezed her eyes closed tightly. The sound of her own breathing filled her head, and her heart thundered in her chest.

When she felt fingers on her shoulder, she screamed.

Scrambling away, she rose to a crouch, ready to flee. Blinking, she saw that the apparitions had gone. She had left her torch on the tracks a dozen feet away, and the light shone off into the darkness.

Cadge stood staring at her, torch trained on her, his eyes wide with concern.

"Get that light out of my face," she said, but couldn't manage the scolding tone she'd attempted.

He lowered the torch, and they stood staring at each other in its diffused glow.

"You hear them too," he said.

Jazz cocked her head, staring at him doubtfully. "What are you saying? You heard that?"

Cadge moistened his lips. He hesitated a moment as though afraid to confess, but at last he nodded. "A song, this time. And cheering. It's always different. Almost always."

Torn between relief that she wasn't mad and astonishment at this confirmation, she stared at him. "Are we the only ones?"

The boy glanced away, shifting nervously. "Harry hears 'em, I think. Just echoes, he says. Echoes of old times. But he told me never to mention it to the others. They'll think I'm a nutter."

"Echoes," Jazz whispered. Then she narrowed her eyes and studied him. "You see them too?"

Cadge gave a small shrug. "Sometimes. Like bits of fog. Used to think my eyes were going, the way things would blur. Once . . . once I thought I saw a face."

Jazz swallowed and found her throat dry. He might have heard the phantoms lost down there in the tunnels, the ghosts of old London that had manifested to her twice since her descent, but it was obvious Cadge could not see them the way she did.

She didn't tell him that. Not yet. But she wondered about Harry. If he heard them, maybe he saw them too.

"So, echoes?" she said.

"Like memories," Cadge said. "The city's memories; something like that."

They fell into step together, more cautiously this time, making their way deeper beneath London.

"Not ghosts?"

His eyes widened a little. "No, not ghosts."

"Why not?"

Cadge glanced away. "'Cause I'm afraid of ghosts."

"Just echoes, Cadge," she said, and she sensed Cadge more at ease beside her. It felt strange, her trying to calm him, but though she seemed to hear and see much more, she could not find it in herself to be frightened. There was something about the visions she'd just seen, a sort of sad innocence, that perhaps had a little to do with the old times they were from.

"Hear 'em now and then," he said. "That's all. Now and then."

"So let's keep them between us for now, yes?"

Cadge turned to her and smiled, and she saw his pleasure at their complicity.

"All right by me," he said. "Besides, there's plenty else to be scared of down here. Ask Harry to tell you about the Hour of Screams sometime."

Jazz frowned. "What's that?"

"Told ya, ask Harry. Don't even like to talk about it

myself." He shivered theatrically, to make sure she got the point. But then he smiled. "We'd best get moving."

Jazz shook her head in amusement. "You are so odd."

Cadge offered a courtly bow, grinning, and then they walked on. Rats scurried out of their way, avoiding the torchlight. Now and then they heard the rumble and rattle of a train in the distance, like the Underground grumbling in eternal hunger. A wind pushed through the tunnel from ahead of them, carrying stale scents of dust and despair. Jazz had always sensed that down here, every time she'd traveled somewhere with her mother. *London has more than its share of sadness*, her mother had said once. *Like an old person, an old city can sometimes get wistful and melancholy.*

Old city, Jazz thought. *That's for sure.* She sniffed the breeze and thought of so many people dead and gone, and the sadness of growing toward death.

Her mother had been forty-four years old when she died.

Chapter Six

old news

Jazz had been down beneath for over a month, but still she searched for news of her mother's death. Harry made it his duty to keep tabs on what was going on aboveground, and every day one of the lost kids would return from an excursion with a newspaper, bought or nicked. Harry read them, then left them stacked beside one of the storage cupboards, ready to be used to light the occasional fire they had when the tunnels grew cold. Jazz had been looking through these papers, and nobody had interrupted her. They all knew what she was searching for.

So far, nothing.

No mention of the Uncles in their black BMWs. No reports of the bloody death scene in their house, no stories about the dead mother and the missing daughter who was yet to be found. Nothing. A blank, as though what had hap-

pened was so far below the normal surface of things that nobody knew.

"*Someone* has to know," Jazz said. Cadge was sitting beside her, as usual, watching as she scanned the discarded
copy of the *Times* she'd picked up from the station platform.
"Someone has to know *something*."

"From what you said, lots of people know stuff," he said.
"Just that the ones that know don't wanna tell the papers."

She turned another page and read some more old news.
Everything here described events happening in another
world, and she could not find it in herself to care about another rise in inflation, a minor royal's indiscretion with a
pop star, or the latest record-breaking celebrity divorce set-
tlement. None of that mattered. None of it ever had. Her
mother had told her that, and it was her *mother* who mattered, and between these pages of cold dark print there was
nothing concerning her mother.

Up there, her mother's murderers still walked free.

She had burned with the injustice of things since spying
that initial smear of blood on her mother's bedroom door
handle. But now, for the first time, Jazz's thoughts were
clouded with revenge.

They celebrated that evening with hot dogs cooked over
an open fire, while Harry Fowler relayed a tale of his time as
a gentleman. Exaggerated and ridiculous—travels in Africa,
hunting tigers in India, and carrying out expeditions to find
the Yeti in the Himalayas—but the kids were all entertained,
and Jazz found herself caught up in the banter and enjoy-
ment.

But that night she dreamed of her mother, as an idea
rather than a real person. In her dream, Harry sat her down

one day and broke a terrible truth. *Jazz girl, pet, you've been down here with us forever,* he said. *You were born down here and you'll die down here. The upside is just where we go to hunt tigers.*

She woke up with a start and cried in the dark, vowing to never let the memory of her mother fade away.

Three days after her first nick, Jazz went back up with Cadge, Stevie, and Hattie.

"Money's all good and nice, pets," Harry said, "but our United Kingdom needs plenty more besides. There's stuff money can't buy, but luckily it's not just pockets our hands can worm their way into." Everyone listened, but he was speaking to only Jazz.

They caught the Tube to Covent Garden and parted company before the station exit. Stevie and Hattie went their separate ways, and Jazz watched Stevie disappear quickly into the crowds. For someone so striking, he hid well. She wanted to say good-bye, wish him luck, touch his hand, and try to catch a smile from him. But during the entire Tube journey, he had sat opposite her and stared over her head through the dark window. Never once had his eyes flickered down to meet her own. And in his feigned disinterest, she wondered whether there was something to find.

Time will tell. Her mother had said that, using it as a full stop after telling her stories about the Uncles, and other people, and what the future might hold for her. *Time will tell.* And it certainly had.

Cadge went with Jazz, and the two of them browsed shop windows, chatted, and laughed, keeping one eye on the time. There was a place to be and a time to be there, and everything was leading up to that.

Cadge seemed even more ebullient than ever. Once or twice he touched Jazz's hand, blushing and looking away as he laughed at something she said. He carried an outwardly cheeky confidence, all bluster and defiance, but it was obvious that there was a deeper side to him that was both vulnerable and delicate. In the beginning, his attentions had made her feel awkward, but now she was flattered. Still, she did her best to temper her response. She liked Cadge—he had a good heart, and she believed he could be a very good friend—but there was an age difference that she could not shake from her mind. She was still all but innocent of the opposite sex, but she knew enough to realize that Cadge was just a boy. So while he touched her hand and exuded an image of togetherness, she thought of them more as brother and sister.

Jazz did not like facing out into the street. She felt exposed. There were eyes upon her, and she expected an Uncle to emerge from the crowd at any moment and bury a knife in her gut. They'd go for Cadge too, of course, and drag him into some shop doorway, and the last thing she'd see would be the Uncle's face pressed up close to hers, the last thing she'd smell would be his garlic breath, and he'd pant in excitement as her blood pulsed over his hand.

Her murder would be quick and quiet, a brief disturbance in a street filled with everyone minding their own business. London was like that. So many people pressed so closely together, and the more people there were, the more alone she felt. Nobody seemed to pay attention to anyone out here. If the street was virtually deserted, passersby would nod a brief hello, maybe give a smile, and if there was only her and someone else, they'd pause for a chat. But in crowds like this, everyone kept to themselves. The more people there were, the less human they seemed to be.

So she looked in shop windows and studied the reflections of the street behind her. Cadge nattered on, pointing out things in the window displays—CDs here, clothes there, books and shoes and sexy lingerie—but Jazz's eyes were always searching beyond these things. Was that a man in a black suit staring at her back from across the road? She shifted sideways, and no, it was just the shadow thrown by a slowly closing coffee-shop door. They walked to another shop, and Jazz looked past the display of hats and handbags at the reflection of a man standing motionless behind her. Cadge made some quip about Hattie not being here, and Jazz lowered her head and looked at the reflection. Still not moving, still staring across the road, his immobility in such a bustling street marked him.

Like picking a scab, the urge to turn was impossible to resist. But the man was only a mannequin placed on the pavement outside a clothes shop. Its arm was raised, finger pointing at her accusingly. In its blank pink face she saw a hundred expressions she did not like.

Someone nudged into her and passed by without apologizing.

Windows lined the buildings above her, any one of them home to an enemy.

"Cadge, let's get a drink," she said. "Got half an hour yet."

"Sure!" He grabbed her hand and headed for a newsagent's stall, but she held back and nodded across the street.

"Coffee," she said. "Somewhere inside."

"Oh." He looked grave for a second, then smiled and nodded. As they dodged traffic across the street, he held her around the waist and leaned in close. "It was like this for me the first few times back up," he said.

"Like what?" Jazz asked. They reached the pavement and negotiated the equally busy streams of human traffic.

Cadge looked up at the ribbon of gray sky between rooftops. "Too exposed."

She felt a rush of affection for Cadge then, and she opened the coffee-shop door and motioned him in first.

Harry always sent them up with some money. Jazz had a cappuccino and Cadge a milk shake, and they drank them quickly.

"So what's your story, Cadge?" she asked. "I feel so self-ish. Things are bad for me, but I've never asked about you or any of the others, and that's bad too."

"Don't feel guilty," he said over the top of his glass, and she sensed a maturity in him then, something that belied his outward image. He suddenly reminded her of herself at that age. "My story ain't too much fun to tell either."

Jazz sipped her coffee and glanced around the busy coffee shop. Everyone in their own world, nobody looking at them, and she no longer felt so out of place. She glanced at her watch. "We've got time."

"Well..." He sucked up more milk shake through his straw, then licked his lips. "To be honest, it sounds like a really bad soap. 'Cept it ain't. It was real lives ruined, and no one to watch but me. See...I came home from school one day and found my dad and auntie...you know. Doing it. Thought they hadn't heard me, but as I was creeping out, Dad ran downstairs an' caught me. Gave me the beatin' of

84 Christopher Golden and Tim Lebbon

me life. Never was one to hold back with his fists, my dad. So he beat me, and my auntie came downstairs without clothes on, tried to stop 'im, and he hit her too. Just smacked her one in the eye and she fell down, all naked and that. Mum came home later—she'd already heard what had 'appened from her sister—and she and Dad had a row. Real screaming, shouting match right in front of me, while I held a cold flannel against my mouth and cheek where he'd hit me. I thought he'd hit her too, but he didn't, and then she ran away. Just...left." He shook his head, looking down at the scarred timber table, as though searching for clues to his mother's whereabouts in the scratched names.

"What about your dad?"

"Kicked me out. Said he'd never wanted me, I'd ruined his life, and told me to piss off an' ruin someone else's."

"Fucking hell, Cadge."

He grinned. "Told you. Not much fun." He noisily sucked up the dregs of his drink, and a few eyes turned their way.

"Just fucked-up adults, Cadge, that's all. They didn't mean it, I'm sure."

"Maybe not Mum," he said. "Maybe not her." He seemed to drift away for a time. Jazz let him. She finished her drink and scanned the street outside. Tourists, office workers—she could tell them apart with ease—and she spent a couple of minutes picking out people who'd have fat wallets. She seemed to be a natural at this thieving lark. Her mum had always told her to be observant, cautious, secretive.

She gasped and closed her eyes, catching a whiff of perfume that reminded her of so much. *Waking from nightmares and she's there for me, ready to calm and soothe . . . Arriving home from school and she gives me a kiss, and I can always sense her relief that I'm okay . . . Passing her bedroom in the morning, seeing her staring into the mirror, smelling that perfume she always used and feeling both contented and sad . . .*

"What is it?" Cadge asked. His hand closed around her upper arm, warm and protective.

Jazz opened her eyes. "Beautiful," she said. "Perfume my mum always wore." She glanced around and saw a tall, smart woman just sitting down at a table. Perhaps she had a daughter too, and perhaps her daughter would not appreciate her fully until she was gone.

"Beautiful," Cadge said. "That's something to hold on to, Jazz."

She nodded. "It is. Come on, let's go."

"Yeah." He slipped from the stool and grabbed her hand, and Jazz gave him a brief squeeze. He beamed. "Yeah! This'll be fun."

They exited the shop and turned left, and the crush of pedestrians forced Cadge to let go of her hand. Jazz weaved through the people, head down but eyes always looking forward.

The chemist was on a corner at the T-junction of two streets. A pub took up the opposite corner, one of those old London boozers with leaded stained-glass windows and history oozing from every glazed brick. There was not quite so much bustle here, and a woman smiled thinly at Jazz as she walked by. *What does she see?* Jazz thought. She'd come topside that morning wearing nondescript jeans, a baggy T-shirt, and a denim jacket, the clothes worn but not tatty. *Why did she smile?* Jazz turned and watched the woman walking away, and Cadge frowned a question.

"Nothing," Jazz said.

"Calm down," Cadge said. "You know how it'll go. Take it easy. This is what I'm good at. Just follow my lead." With those few words, Cadge took charge. He glanced at his watch, listened for the sound he was waiting for—raised voices—and then walked past Jazz and approached the shop.

Timing was crucial, and Jazz marveled at how perfectly it flowed.

Hattie ran from the shop, screeching and scattering packets and bags behind her: toothpaste, throat lozenges, corn plasters, and sun cream. She darted straight across the road and pelted down the street, waving a bag over her head.

A man shouted in the shop, a deep, angry roar, and then Stevie Sharpe leaped from the door. He stood there looking around for a few seconds, eyes skimming past Cadge, pausing briefly on Jazz, and passing on. His long hair swung as he spun around and saw Hattie disappearing along the street.

A man appeared beside Stevie wearing the white coat of a pharmacist, and Jazz froze. *He's caught!* she thought. *He should have run faster, shouldn't have looked around for us, shouldn't have looked at* me!

But then she saw what was happening.

"I'll get her, mister!" Stevie said. And he took off after Hattie.

Cadge did not break pace at all. He slipped into the shop behind the man, casual but quiet, and Jazz followed him in a few seconds later. The man's attention was focused wholly on the fleeing girl and the boy who had given chase, and he was thumbing a number into his mobile phone as he watched.

The law, Jazz thought. *And they'll not take long to get here.*

Cadge was moving smoothly and confidently, and Jazz took a second to scope out the shop. Gob had already been here three days before and so they knew the layout: two island units, three aisles, one main counter. Jazz was pleased to see just one woman behind the counter and no other customers. The man remained outside.

Cadge walked right up to the counter and looked the flustered woman in the eye. "I'd like some condoms, please," he said. "Ribbed."

"Oh, well...er..." The woman lowered her eyes and moved along to the other end of the counter, pointing along the side aisle to Jazz's right.

Jazz grabbed a handful of small boxes containing painkillers, two boxes of plasters, and some cough medicine, slipping them into her pockets as she browsed slowly along the shelves.

"Where?" Cadge asked from out of sight.

"Just there...er...past the aftershave."

"Can't see 'em."

Jazz rounded the island unit, smiling in mock sympathy at the obviously embarrassed woman, and entered the central aisle. Cadge was beyond the second island unit, rustling boxes and dropping several of them to the floor.

"Hold on," the woman said, and Jazz heard the sound she had been waiting for: the creak and bump of the counter hatch being opened and the woman coming to help. She heard her footsteps and Cadge mumbling something. The woman sighed.

Jazz took three paces to the counter, sat on it and rolled over, falling behind and remaining on the floor for a couple of terrifying seconds.

"Nah, I don't like that make," Cadge said, and Jazz grinned at the cheek in his voice. "Itchy."

"Well, please make up your . . . we've just had a girl take some . . . Oh dear."

Jazz crouched down and ducked behind the obscured glass screen that separated the pharmacy storage area from the rest of the shop. Harry had told her what to look for: amoxicillin. She scanned the drawer tags, looked at the bottles already full and half full on the stainless-steel counter, then saw the name just as she heard the man's voice again.

"Little bitch took off like a bat out of hell," he said. "Boy went after her; wouldn't be surprised if he was part of it. Law are on their way. Jean?"

"Over here, Terry, just trying to help this young man."

He's back inside! Jazz had hoped for at least another thirty seconds before the owner came back in. Maybe they were used to thefts. Just another part of life as a pharmacist.

She was suddenly terrified. *If I get caught and the police get me . . .*

They're all in it together, her mother had said. *All tied up, dropping money in one another's pockets, and information, and . . . other stuff. Promises. So promise me, Jazz, that you'll never trust anyone.*

If the police got her, the Uncles wouldn't be too far behind.

"Johnnies!" Cadge suddenly shouted, wielding a packet of condoms, and Jazz heard rapid footsteps as he, too, ran from the shop.

"Wait!" the woman, Jean, shouted.

"Little bastard!" The man's voice faded again as he went back outside, obviously chasing after Cadge.

Jazz snatched up the bottle marked *amoxicillin* and walked to the counter again, sliding across and heading straight down the central aisle. She pocketed the bottle just as she bumped into Jean emerging from the side aisle with a box of condoms still clasped in each hand.

"Busy day today!" Jazz said.

The woman rolled her eyes skyward. "I sometimes wonder why I stay working here," she said. "Last year it was a man with a knife."

"It's only stuff," Jazz said. "And I'm sure he's insured. Bye!" She exited the shop and turned right, not walking too fast or slow, not looking around, trying to appear for all the world as though she belonged.

Jazz was amazed at how smoothly things had gone. Harry had told her that people were easily fooled because they were never prepared for things to go wrong and that confusion was the United Kingdom's best tool when working on a nick. And now Jazz had seen how right he was. A bit of chaos, a bit of misdirection, and the man and woman in the chemist had been thrown off-kilter long enough for her to lift what needed lifting. It was a delightful ruse: get them concerned with Hattie taking a few minor items so that she, Jazz, could slip across the counter and take what they really wanted.

Infections were common down in the beneath, and

amoxicillin was essential to ward off illness caused by all the bacteria crawling around down there.

She walked confidently through the streets, aiming for the rendezvous she had arranged with Cadge. Stevie and Hattie would be long gone now, heading back belowground and through the Tube and tunnels to their home shelter. Though Jazz still felt exposed out here on the streets, she was enjoying the feeling of sunshine on her skin.

"Jazz." The voice was low, called from the shadows of an alley, and Jazz froze in her tracks. Someone walked into her and uttered a curse under his breath, but then the crowd parted around her. She was as invisible to the crowds as she ever had been, but . . .

"Jazz, in here."

An Uncle? She should run. She looked to her left and right without turning her head, spotting at least three escape routes, marking the side road thirty yards along the street as the most likely to lead her somewhere safe. The road was busy here, and she would dart across without checking for traffic. It moved slow; if something hit her, she'd just roll and keep running.

And then she realized how much she was fooling herself. This Uncle hidden down an alley wouldn't be on his own, and soon they'd close in and—

"Fuck's sake, girl, in here!"

Jazz looked into the shadows and saw the unmistakable outline of Stevie Sharpe. As she saw him, he stepped forward and grabbed her arm, guiding her into the alley and walking quickly away without saying anything. She assumed she had to follow.

They passed a pile of refuse with split bags spewing rotting food and alive with flies. Jazz held her breath and waved the flies away, but Stevie seemed unperturbed.

"What's this about?" she asked.

Stevie stopped and turned, looked over Jazz's shoulder, and then stared at her. His expression barely changed as he gave her a frank, shameless appraisal. He examined her face, her shoulders, arms, chest, down her body and legs, then back up again very, very slowly. It felt as though it went on forever. Her tingle of anticipation changed to one of discomfort, but then he spoke at last. She even thought she saw the ghost of a smile.

"Did good today," he said. He looked down at her pockets and she tapped them, assuring him she had what they had come for. "Did good." Then he gave her a casual wave, turned, and ran along the alley.

"Wait!" Jazz called.

"See you back home!" he shouted over his shoulder, and she was sure she heard a laugh as he disappeared around a corner.

Jazz hurried back onto the street, more ruffled than she had been since first emerging into the sunlight a couple of hours before. She was sure her expression would give her away—Hi, *I'm a thief and I'm on the run, but not just from people I've thieved from*—and she walked faster, head down as though to deflect attention.

What had that been about? There'd been no reason for Stevie to hold back and see her. Even the muttered *Did good today* was something that could have come much later, deep beneath the city. There had only been that look, examining her, *perusing* her, and, much as she liked Stevie, she still felt unsettled.

She turned a corner and a police siren suddenly blasted through the air. She gasped and almost stumbled back as the white car sped by, curious tourists staring after it, seasoned Londoners using the brief distraction to move that much faster toward their destination.

I'm getting way too damn twitchy now, she thought. The boxes and bottle in her pockets felt heavier than ever, begging to attract attention even though they could not be seen. She was at least a mile from the chemist and there was no chance she'd be caught, but the sky was suddenly way too wide, the buildings too tall, and the people too likely to stop, turn to her, and say, *It's her, there she is, take her!*

She did not want to think about who would respond to such a call.

"Jazz?" Cadge said.

She jumped a little, then sighed. Jazz grabbed his shoulder and pulled him close, enjoying the contact as they hugged.

"Hey," he said, and she could hear the smile in his voice.

"Bit spooked," she said.

"You were late, so I started walking down this way." He pulled away and looked into her eyes, but he did not spook her like Stevie. She could only find benevolence in Cadge. "I was getting worried."

I should mention Stevie, Jazz thought. *There's no reason not to, is there?* But she simply shrugged and looked around, glancing up at the clear blue sky.

"Got you this." He handed her a small box, blushing, turning away as she held out her hand and accepted whatever the gift might be.

It was a pink box with gold lettering: *Beautiful.*

"Said you liked it," he said.

Jazz felt tears threatening, but she held them back. She nodded, unable to speak for a few seconds, and the sharp reality of the box's weight and corners pinned her to the world. "Thanks," she said at last, and it came out husky and gruff.

Cadge nodded, but he could not keep the smile from his face.

"Really," Jazz said. She looked at the box again and remembered what these boxes had looked like on her mum's dressing table, the way she'd always kept the perfume inside instead of disposing with the box and just keeping the bottle, the way she had liked the fact that however empty the bottle might be, the box always looked new. "Really, Cadge, thanks."

He nodded, face flushed. "Pleasure," he said. "Now it's time to go. We're not far from Oxford Circus here. And Harry'll be waiting for us when we go down."

"Harry?"

"Told me he'd meet us. He does that sometimes, especially with someone new."

"Why?"

Cadge shrugged but looked away. "Sometimes Harry likes to talk in private."

He would not be drawn out any more, so Jazz followed Cadge along the bustling streets and into Oxford Circus Tube station. As the shadows cooled around her, she felt a calm sense of relief closing in with them.

Chapter Seven

the silent tree

"Do you trust me?"

"Of course I do."

"Good. That's good. But why?"

"Because you're my mother, of course." Jazz didn't like the way her mum's conversation was going this morning. They'd started out commenting on the architecture of Oxford Street, but now they sat in the back corner of a coffee shop and her mother had embarked on one of her lectures. At least Jazz thought it was likely to turn into a lecture. It had that feel: a difficult question, followed by a few moments of silence, and soon would come her mother's sad expression and alert eyes as she started to speak of hidden dangers, covert groups, and the risks of trying to live a normal life. *Life for us can never be normal*, she'd said during one of these discussions a couple of years ago, and Jazz had never forgotten that. Out of all the advice her mother had given her, it was this statement that stuck most in her mind. Sometimes she hated her mum for telling her that. Surely such harsh truths were something a girl should find out on her own?

"That's not good enough reason to trust me," her mother said. "Lots of kids trust their parents and are inevitably betrayed by them. It's a word bandied around too readily nowadays, like *love*, and *fate*, and *hate*. But it's a precious thing. Analyze your trust, Jazz. Study it. Does it have rough edges, or is it thoughtless and complete? Because nature abhors sharp edges, so something with them can't be natural."

"You'd never betray me," Jazz said firmly. She was starting to feel upset and anxious at the way this was going. *Mum was her bedrock! Her solid pedestal from which she was starting to live life as an adult!*

Her mum smiled. "No, I wouldn't. But if I was someone else, just because I never have betrayed you doesn't mean I never would."

"You're scaring me, Mum."

One of the coffee-shop staff paused by the next table, cleared away mugs and sandwich wrappers, and started polishing its surface. The silence was uncomfortable, and the young girl threw them a nervous glance and hurried away, the table still smeared and dirty.

"Don't be scared," she said. "Be warned. You're the only person you can really, truly trust. *You.* The *only* one. You'll need to be careful, Jazz, as you get older. Make sure you're certain of people's intentions toward you."

"You mean boys?"

"I mean everyone." Her mother looked suddenly sad then, and Jazz was mortified when she saw tears in the woman's eyes. "You can never really know someone."

"Mum?"

She shook her head and waved Jazz away, dabbing at her eyes. "I'm fine. I'm fine." But she didn't look fine. And that brief, intense conversation about trust stayed with Jazz for a long, long time.

Harry was waiting for them below the surface, behind the grubby wall and bulky grate at the end of the station platform. He was alone. He carried two heavy torches, and he gave them to Cadge and Jazz. He trusted them to light his way.

"A good nick today, Jazz girl?"

Jazz produced the boxes of painkillers, plasters, cough mixture, and antibiotics. She kept the Beautiful to herself.

"Nice!" Harry said. "Nice, my pets. I don't like the thought of my kids being ill, not when they're such an *honest* bunch."

The word *honest* was a strange one, Jazz thought, as applied to a bunch of thieves. But it also made her proud. They might nick things, but they were all honest to one another. At least, *almost* all of them. The image of Stevie Sharpe hidden in the alley shadows had failed to leave her, and being down here in the dark only seemed to make it more solid.

"It went okay," Jazz said. "Cadge had to do a runner too, but I had the stuff by then. And I left without them even suspecting me."

"And what did *you* fetch, Cadge lad?"

"Nuthin'."

Jazz frowned—she remembered him running with a box

of condoms in his hand. But she kept walking and did not look at the boy.

"Nothing at all?" Harry asked.

"Dropped it," Cadge said. *And I wonder how scarlet he is right now?* Jazz thought. *These shadows are good for hiding a lot.*

They veered left into a disused tunnel, walked for a hundred yards, and came to an abandoned station platform. From there they made their way down an old maintenance staircase, hearing the rustle of rats retreating before the wash of their flashlights. Cockroaches scurried out of sight. In the drier tunnels, they were rarer, but in the damp, rotting places, cockroaches and other bugs were plentiful. Jazz forced herself not to take much notice of them.

The stairs were slippery here, layered with a thin green slime, and at the bottom of the staircase a curtain of water fell in a continuous waterfall. Harry produced a small retracting umbrella from his pocket, opened it up, and diverted the water far enough for Jazz and Cadge to step through. "One of the oldest water-distribution systems in the world, down here," he said as he stepped through. "More water leaks into the ground than reaches Londoners' taps." He brushed a few droplets of water from his coat shoulders. "Lucky for us, eh? Free water whenever we want it. I only wish they could heat some of it for us. Then life would be grander than grand, eh, Cadge?"

"Life's grand as it is, Mr. F."

"It has its moments, for sure."

Something rattled in the distance and Cadge spun around. They were at one end of a short brick-lined tunnel, and the steel door at the other end was twisted open. The noise came from beyond.

Rats? Jazz wondered. *A train in the distance?* She was already becoming familiar with how strange the noises were down here.

"It's nothing," Harry said.

Cadge glanced at Jazz and smiled. "Really was a good nick," he said. "You're becoming an expert."

"I think she has the light hands and gentle touch of a thief, for sure," Harry said. He squeezed Jazz's shoulder. "I think you'll go far."

"I'm still not sure . . ." she said, but she trailed off.

"Still not sure you want to stay," Harry finished for her. "That's to be expected, and I honor that, Jazz girl. Honor it completely. If ever it's time for you to go, you'll go with our blessing. I tell that to all my kids, and I mean it."

Cadge walked ahead of them, pretending to check out the open doorway.

"I'm certainly not going yet," she said. Cadge turned around and smiled.

Something screeched in the distance. It seemed to come in from a long way off. Jazz was already learning to judge sound down here, and this one had lost many of its lower frequencies, swallowed by concrete, brickwork, and the solid rock of London's legs.

The smile froze on Cadge's face. Harry cocked his head and frowned. "Mr. F.?"

The screech came again and Harry shook his head. "No, Cadge. I think it's just metal on metal. Something collapsing somewhere far off, maybe. Or perhaps someone else taking a secret tunnel to somewhere we don't know."

"Collapsing?" Jazz asked.

Harry nodded. "Old places down here, Jazz. And some

bits are older than you believe. Sometimes it's just time to fade away."

"Sounded like a scream to me," Cadge said. "And comin' closer."

Harry shook his head again. "I've heard it often enough," he said.

"Heard what?" Jazz felt scared and excluded, and she looked back and forth from Harry to Cadge.

"Hour of Screams," Cadge said.

The phrase chilled her, the echo of Cadge's voice fading away to nothing in her ears.

"You mentioned that the other day," she said, then turned to Harry. "Cadge told me I should ask you about it, but I'd forgotten. Is that what we just heard?"

Harry frowned at Cadge. "Not at all." Then he turned to Jazz again. "Walk with us. Let's get back to the kingdom. I wanted to tell you about this in my own time, in my own way. But it seems young Cadge has preempted me."

"Sorry, Harry," Cadge said.

"Don't apologize, lad. It's good to be worried about the Hour of Screams. Good to be scared. It's something not to be trusted."

Jazz thought of her mother's advice on trust, and how precious it was, and how easily it was given out nowadays. *I trust Cadge*, she thought. And the idea gave her great comfort.

As they shone their torches ahead and Harry began to talk, Jazz reached out and held the boy's hand.

"It's something we've learned to live with," Harry said, "though no one was meant to live with it. I would've told you about it earlier but, truth be told, it's been months since we've had the Hour of Screams come through. I should've warned you sooner, Jazz. I've been meaning to. Just didn't want to scare you off."

"But what is it?"

"It's a dead thing, the Hour. An old, dead thing."

"I don't understand," Jazz said. "Is this about the... echoes?"

Harry frowned, shot a glance at Cadge, and then refocused on Jazz. "You hear them too, do you, or has Cadge just been speaking out of school?"

"I hear them," she said, thinking how strange it was to be speaking so normally about something she would have thought impossible not long ago. But her perception of the possible and the impossible had changed radically of late. "Sometimes I *see* things too."

He studied her. "What things?"

"Like silhouettes. Just flickers, really," she lied, though she wasn't sure why she withheld the truth. It felt personal to her. Intimate. "I thought they were ghosts."

"Perhaps they are. But either way, they're old things, whispering down here the way the beams and boards in an old house will creak when the wind blows. Nothing to concern yourself with."

Jazz hesitated a moment, then forged ahead. "You've seen them too?"

"A glimpse now and again," Harry admitted, still watching her curiously. Then the moment passed and he waved a hand as though to erase the conversation. "Nothing to worry about, though. I don't talk about the echoes with the others. They've enough superstition among them already. But everyone knows what I'll be telling you now, Jazz girl.

It's the Hour you've got to be careful of. Just because things have been quiet down here doesn't mean they'll *stay* quiet."

Cadge led the way through the twisted steel door and into a huge circular tunnel, which had been ground into the rock and unlined. There were not even any supports built here for line and platform. It was unfinished rather than abandoned; this place had never formed a true part of the Tube. Perhaps a plan had been drawn wrong, or money had run out, but this was a route that led nowhere. There was graffitti on one wall, but it had faded with time, washed away by a continuous trickle of water penetrating the tunnel at its highest point and following the curve.

"We call it the Hour of Screams," Harry said. "Though it doesn't last an hour, and sometimes it's more a long sigh than a scream. It echoes through the Underground—at least, through all those places hidden away, where people aren't supposed to be or even know about. Or where there are people like us. Because in a way, I suppose some of us are as lost as the spirits that make the scream."

"Spirits?" Jazz asked. "But you said you didn't think—"

"It's old London that cries out, young Jazz. You know the saying, *If a tree falls in a forest and there's nobody there to hear it, does it make any noise at all?* The Hour of Screams is a bit like that falling tree. It happens whether there's anyone to hear it or not, because it's just a part of how things must be. Trees grow, age, and die, and then they fall. So it is with history. History's all about rise and fall, you know that, girl?"

Jazz did not respond, because she thought it was a question that did not call for an answer.

"Everyone knows about the Hour of Screams," Cadge said from ahead, as if anticipating her thoughts.

"True," Harry said. "But not everyone knows not to listen. To hear it is...painful. Perhaps damaging. I've seen people driven mad, and some of them never get better, Jazz. It touches them and leaves something of itself in them; living people shouldn't bear the burdens of the dead. When I first came down here—before the United Kingdom came together, when I was on my own—the Hour screamed through one day. The lady I'd hooked up with for a while, Kathryn, she refused to cover her ears, refused to sing her song. Said she was proud. Well, proud she may have been, but after the screams she was mad as well. She ran. Tried to catch her, but she ran faster than I. She went deeper than I ever had or have since, and for all I know she's still running and still going deeper."

"You said she'd be dead by now," Cadge said.

Harry nodded and sighed again. "And I'm sure she is. But still I wonder, and hope."

"But what *is* the Hour of Screams?" Jazz asked. "You say spirits, but what spirits?"

"Old London," Harry said. "The restless spirit of the old city, wailing in grief. In pain too. No one knows for sure, not even I. But perhaps it's the remnants of London's past not yet at rest: people, places, events, dark deeds, and there are plenty of those. The tiring soul of one of the world's oldest cities."

"What does it have to do with the...the echoes we've heard?" Jazz asked.

Harry studied her. "Perhaps nothing. And perhaps the Hour's what happens when the whispers wake up for a bit."

"Maybe it's just the sound of trains in the distance," Jazz said.

Cadge laughed. "If you'd 'eard it, you'd never say that."

"It's not just a sound," Harry said. "You mustn't listen, that's true enough—choose a song now, Jazz, and cover your ears and sing it when you know the Hour's coming. But it's everything else besides: the smell of age, the sight of weary shadows, the taste of rot, the feel of the scream rushing past your skin, the wind as though it wants to carry you away."

"But it doesn't last an hour?"

Harry shook his head. "Sometimes only seconds."

"Just feels like an hour," Cadge said. "Here we are. The way down."

They had reached the end of the desolate tunnel, and Cadge aimed his torch at a rough hole in the wall to their left. It had been hacked into the concrete rather than formed, and there was a metal frame that held a heavy grille gate bolted in. The gate seemed to be closed, but Harry stepped forward and shoved it open. It creaked.

"Another way back to the United Kingdom?" Jazz asked.

Harry smiled. "There are several," he said. "It wouldn't do to live somewhere down here with only one way in or out."

Why not? she wanted to ask. But maybe she'd had enough information for now.

The Hour of Screams...

She'd seen things down here, heard them, and out of everyone she seemed to see and hear the most. What that meant for her when the Hour of Screams came, she really didn't wish to know.

Maybe it would be best if she did not hang around long enough to find out.

The remainder of their descent passed in silence. Cadge went first, moving smoothly and easily along the flashlit tunnels, ducking under pipes and sidestepping pools of stagnant water that reflected rainbows of grease. Jazz followed, marveling at Cadge's dexterity and grace. He was a natural down here.

Harry Fowler followed them both, trusting them to guide his way with their flashlights, and Jazz wondered how long he had been down here. He must have a history, a profession, perhaps a wife and children somewhere above, tales to tell, people to avoid, crimes to forget, or destinies yet to fulfill. He was much older than all of them, and older people had more to tell, and perhaps more to fear.

Like Mum, she thought. *She always feared more than me. Tried to make me as scared as her, but it took this to make that so.*

They heard sounds in the distance, and Jazz froze at every one. But Cadge did not, and Harry always calmed her with a smile or a shake of his head. They knew the sounds of the Underground, which belonged and which did not.

Jazz knew that she had a decision to make. The time would come for the Hour of Screams to storm through her new home. She had to decide whether to wait for that to happen. And if she did wait, she had to decide whether she would choose a song to sing or open up her senses and listen.

In the final short tunnel that led to the shelter, Jazz paused. Cadge went on before her and Harry stood beside her, looking down.

I'm being watched, she thought, but she could not say that. "Need a minute."

"Of course," Harry said. "Cadge and I will ensure

there's food being prepared. Time alone to think is good, Jazz girl. Time alone is fine. Part of the reason I came down here in the first place was for time alone."

"Don't get much of that now," she said, smiling.

Harry smiled back and shook his head, and she saw something then that didn't surprise her as much as it should: he was content. Perhaps more content than any adult she had ever known. Then he walked on, whispering something to Cadge. The boy turned and looked back at Jazz, and though she tried she could not give him a comforting smile.

Because I'm being watched!

As soon as Harry and Cadge disappeared through a blank doorway, Jazz scanned the tunnel around her, probing every nook and cranny with the powerful beam of her torch, chasing shadows away to reveal the truth of what hid beneath.

She turned the torch off to see how much more she could see.

The tall, elegant man she had seen during her first hallucination stood at the end of the short tunnel. He was looking just to her left, an enigmatic smile on his lips, tuxedo well fitted, and tall hat touching the ceiling without effect. His white-gloved hands rose before him, fingers flexing as if preparing for some infinitely intricate trick.

No voices, no crowds, no rowdy catcalls from a ghostly audience... This man was alone. He made no sound. She could smell a vague hint of lotion, something sweeter and more pleasant than the usual underground smell of dust and age. His expression was the fixed, tired smile of a performing magician, but as his hands closed together, his eyes shifted slightly until they were staring directly into her own.

Jazz shivered, nerve endings jangling as though a breath of freezing air had wafted through the tunnel.

The ghostly man pressed his hands together, and when he pulled them apart a chain of sparks hung between them. It swung low and heavy, ghost fire given weight, and he seemed to be trying to communicate something to her with his eyes.

And then he spoke.

All in the touch, the ghost said.

He brought his hands close together again, and just before they met, Jazz saw the sparkles darken, and within them a dozen small forms danced and squirmed. *All in the touch.*

Jazz ran. She reached the shelter quickly, went to Harry, and hugged him, comforted only a little when he hugged her back. And an idea pounded at her, one that she could never, ever say.

How do I hide from ghosts?

Chapter Eight

the appointed hour

"Why don't we ever nick anything from the Tube? Seems like easy pickings down here, with people waiting for the train, minding their business."

Cadge's face grew serious, his wide eyes narrowed with an expression that seemed almost an imitation of wisdom, like a small boy mimicking his father.

"Harry hasn't given you that speech yet? Surprised at that," he said. "Can't ever nick from the station platforms. They're our doors and windows, like. Hard enough for us to come and go without drawin' too much attention. We start snatching bags and wallets down here and too many people will remember our faces, be on the lookout. An easy place for the law to keep watch for us too. That's why we gotta go topside."

"Right. Of course," Jazz said. "I should've realized. Sort of a stupid question."

Cadge shook his head sagely. "Nah. Not stupid. You've only been at this a couple of months. You've got good 'ands and all. Scary good. Stevie said Harry's got big plans for you—"

"What plans?"

Her face flushed, and she couldn't decide if the reaction came from knowing Harry was impressed with her or that Stevie had been talking about her. He kept to himself so often, but sometimes she caught him watching her with a kind of veiled curiosity that made her breath catch in her throat. He almost never came over to talk to her but seemed always to be hovering nearby, as though he couldn't decide if he was protector or predator.

"Plans," Cadge repeated, as though that was an answer. "Mr. F.'s got grand ambitions for you. For all of us, I guess. You've inspired him, like. Says we ought to move up in the world, now we've some of us got good enough to do more than nick a purse here and there."

Jazz wasn't sure how she felt about that. It sounded like Harry's grand ambitions—as Cadge called them—would mean engaging more with the upside world, and that didn't sit well.

"Anyway, what I was saying is, there ain't any stupid questions, yeah? Down here's got a whole different set of rules from up above. And nobody trained you to think like a thief, so you got to learn."

Jazz uttered a soft laugh as they reached the bottom of the steps and strolled into the Tube station. Over her shoulder she carried a heavy bag she'd nicked from a tourist foolish enough to put it down while paying for a newspaper. Inside it were two wallets she'd also filched, as well as a nice linen jacket, a small sack of groceries, and a plastic bag from Waterstone's with a few suspense novels inside. All stolen. Cadge carried a small duffel bag he'd brought upside with him that was now stuffed with fruit, drinks, and a heavy industrial torch he'd grabbed when some workmen had wandered off for lunch and left their tools unattended.

They'd had a very successful day.

"I think I'm doing all right," she said.

"More than all right," Cadge said, with such warmth in his voice that Jazz looked at him. Face a bit flushed, he glanced away.

On the train platform, Jazz scanned the waiting commuters. Her constant lookout for the Uncles and their BMW men had become almost unconscious by now. Half the time she caught herself looking around warily and only then realized what precisely she'd been looking for. Yet she felt more at ease in the Tube station than she did aboveground, and the deeper she went, the more comfortable she became.

She worried that she was becoming too comfortable, down there in the dark. But the upside world held only danger for her, and up there she would be on her own. Better by far to be safe and in the company of friends. And if she had ever had any real friends, certainly Cadge fit the bill.

The train slid into the station. The exhilaration of thieving and the threat of capture still prickled her skin as she stepped on and took a seat, setting the bag on the floor between her feet. Cadge sat beside her, and they kept silent for the brief ride to Holborn.

They stepped out onto the platform. Before the rush of disgorged passengers could subside, they slipped over the rail at the end of the platform and down to the shadows beside the tracks. When the train left the station, they ventured into the dark.

"What about that torch?" Jazz asked.

Cadge grinned like it was Christmas morning. She knew he'd been itching to try it out, but he waited until they'd left the main track, following an abandoned branch out of sight of anyone who might be in Holborn station, and then unzipped the duffel. When he clicked the torch on, the light sent rats scurrying and picked out some of the rust and scabrous growth that covered old piping along the walls and ceiling.

"Maybe less light is better," Jazz said.

Cadge laughed. "Be it ever so humble..."

Jazz flinched. The down-below had become her sanctuary, a hiding place, and the United Kingdom behaved like a family, but no matter how long she remained there she refused to think of it as home. Once, on the day of her first topside nick, the word had come unbidden into her mind, and she'd vowed to herself that it wouldn't happen again.

Cadge paused and glanced at her. "Hear that?"

She realized she did hear something—had been hearing it for a couple of minutes already. A susurrus of low voices like the hush of a flowing river ran nearby. Now that she paid attention to it, the noise grew louder.

"A crowd, sounds like," Cadge said.

Jazz nodded. They both knew it couldn't really be a crowd—not down here. Which meant it had to be phantoms.

The ghosts seemed to blossom to life around her. In the

darkness they were shadows with a hint of ethereal illumination, but in the glow of Cadge's torch they were revealed as true specters.

A Victorian carriage rattled by, drawn by a single horse, a lantern swinging from a hook beside the driver's high seat. Cadge stepped quickly away from the startling sound of horses' hooves but glanced around as though blinded. He heard the phantom near him but could not see it.

A couple of weeks ago such a vision would have terrified Jazz, but now she caught her breath in wonder. There was something almost comforting about them. The Underground was a forgotten home to lost people, and it seemed only right that it would echo with forgotten moments, the dreaming memories of London itself.

A sweet aroma reached her, a mélange of different scents that made her inhale deeply. She shuddered with the delicious odors, closed her eyes tightly to shut off all but her sense of smell. When she opened them again, she stood in a marketplace sprawled across cobblestones. There were carts full of vegetables and stacks of wooden crates overflowing with fruit. A little girl sold fresh flowers from a basket to specters who strolled about investigating the wares of the vendors. The smells were invigorating and such a wonderful change in the damp tunnels whose ordinary odors were rust and sewage.

A man rode by on a creaky antique bicycle with wheels so large and unwieldy it seemed mad to think anyone could keep such a contraption from crashing.

"You see something," Cadge said.

Jazz had almost forgotten him. She blinked and turned to focus on his face. "What?"

"I saw your eyes. You see them, don't you? The things I'm hearing. You see somethin'. More than just glimpses, like you said before."

For a moment she did not breathe. *Never trust anyone*, that had been her mother's advice. Her rule. But her mother had never had to create a brand-new life in a brand-new world, and her mother had never met Cadge.

"Sometimes," she said.

Cadge gazed at her with open admiration. "Wish I could see them. Did you smell it too? The fruit?"

Jazz nodded. "Made me hungry."

"I've only got apples and some pears in the bag. We'll go to the market later this week, get ourselves something juicy—oranges or kiwis."

"A pineapple," Jazz said.

Cadge laughed. "You nick a pineapple, where d'you suppose you'll hide it while you're slipping off, eh? Bit prickly, I'd think."

Jazz gave him an arch look but said nothing. They shared a quiet laugh and then started along the tunnel again. Around them, the ghosts of London were fading, and Jazz was saddened by their departure.

She shifted the big bag from one shoulder to the other.

"Let's have that, then," Cadge said, gesturing toward the bag. "I'll carry it for a bit."

"I've got it, thanks."

He blinked and looked away, and she realized she'd been too sharp with him. Jazz had bristled at the suggestion that she might not be strong enough to do her part, but Cadge had just been making a clumsy attempt at chivalry.

"You've got enough to carry," she added.

Cadge brightened a little. "Yeah. We'll both be glad to set these down. Mr. F.'s gonna love this torch too."

"We should've nicked some batteries for it," Jazz said.

"Nah. We've got loads, all sizes."

They fell silent then, trudging onward. Cadge led her up onto a platform that had been abandoned for decades, its walls covered in a thick layer of dust and grime, floor scuffed with years of boot and shoe marks left behind by the United Kingdom and perhaps other subterranean travelers. They eschewed the chained gate blocking the way up and instead followed a corridor that led to yet another train track.

Jazz had been astonished when, after just a couple of weeks, she had come to know her way around the labyrinth of abandoned stations, tunnels, and bomb shelters beneath the city.

Across the tracks was a smaller platform, part of the same long-closed station. A rusted metal door set into the far wall of the platform drew her attention. It had a heavy handle that had been left in a raised position, the door open just a few inches for forgotten ages.

As Jazz and Cadge dropped down to the tracks, she could not stop staring at that door.

Cadge stopped to glance back at her. "Jazz?"

It felt as though someone had set a hook in her chest and was drawing her in. She took a step and then paused, fighting the urge. Whatever called to her from behind that rusted metal door, it frightened her in a way the ghosts of old London no longer could.

"What's through there?" she asked without looking at Cadge.

"Through where?"

She pointed to the door.

"Dunno. Stairs, I guess. Some kind of emergency exit. Could just be storage. Or toilets. Never know what you're gonna find behind a door down here."

Cadge walked back to Jazz and took her hand. That intimate contact allowed her to drag her gaze from the rusty door. She smiled at him halfheartedly, gave his fingers a squeeze, and then pulled her hand away. The boy was sweet, but he was just a boy. If she'd let her hand linger in his, he might get ideas.

"Want to go over there? Have a look?" he asked.

Jazz blinked. The temptation to say yes nearly overwhelmed her.

"No. No, let's go," she said.

Cadge waited for her this time. When she started walking again, he turned off his torch and stored it in his duffel bag. Drains and grates high above them let daylight filter down, along with the sounds of the cars, trucks, and buses growling by above. Somewhere close, a train roared through the Underground. Dust sifted down from the ceiling and a breeze blew along the tunnel. This track might be closed, but others nearby remained in regular use.

A hundred yards farther on, they arrived at the door that led into a staircase down to the sublevel. The circular stairs were quiet as a tomb, the rock closing in on all sides. Jazz shuddered, feeling a claustrophobia unusual for her.

"What's that?" Cadge said.

Jazz listened, thinking at first that perhaps more phantom echoes of London were about to appear. But then she heard a girl crying out for Harry and recognized the voice.

"Hattie," she said.

They rushed down the last half dozen steps and pulled open the door. The tunnel curved off to the right. The entrance to Deep Level Shelter 7-K was just around the bend. Above, dim light filtered down from screened vents that went all the way to the surface.

There came another scream, followed by the shouts of angry men and the sound of scuffling. Cadge and Jazz exchanged a glance, and she saw her fear reflected in his eyes. Turning away, she started along the tunnel. All that remained of the former rail line here were occasional railroad ties on top of dirt and stone, and she kept close to the wall to avoid tripping over anything in the gloom.

"Vermin!" a man shouted. "Filthy little vermin."

Jazz dropped her stolen bag and all of its contents and started running. The others needed help. From behind her, she heard Cadge utter her name like a curse and give chase.

She came around the bend in the tunnel and staggered to a halt. Cadge bumped into her and nearly sent the two of them sprawling. Tendrils of gas roiled along the floor of the abandoned tunnel, crawling as though with hideous purpose. At first glance, Jazz thought the yellow mist another phantom, a glimpse of some moment out of London's past. But then Hattie came racing toward them, hacking and choking, the gas parting around her legs.

The girl collided with Cadge. He managed to hold her up, but only barely. She began to retch and pushed away from him, dropping to her knees and vomiting.

"The others..." Hattie choked out.

"Go on to the door up to the old Holborn tunnel. Hide in there until I come to fetch you," Cadge told her.

Hattie managed to stagger away.

Jazz pulled her shirt up to cover her nose and mouth and ventured farther into the tunnel, through the slowly rising fog of yellow gas. Cadge came after her and they picked up their pace.

"Nothing but bloody sewer rats, what you are!" they heard a man shout.

The gas thinned, almost a gauzy film over the shadows. The entrance to the United Kingdom's lair stood open, the metal door hanging wide, and that ugly gas roiled up from the throat of the stairwell beyond.

Not far from the door, four men stood around Harry, who lay on the ground. They spat on him, shouted obscenities, and kicked his back and legs and ribs, even as he tried to protect his face and head with his arms, pulling himself into a fetal ball.

"Don't belong down here, rats. Gotta flush you out," one of the men said.

The four of them wore white filter masks over the lower parts of their faces. They'd thrown something down into Deep Level Shelter 7-K—tear gas or worse—to drive Harry and the kids out of there. Jazz didn't know what had happened to the others, but she could only hope they'd gone out the emergency exit while Harry'd gone up the hatch to buy them time.

Harry let out a shout of agony as a heavy boot caught him in the back. He arched his body, letting a fusillade of profanity loose upon his attackers. But words would not drive them off. They only kicked him again, harder. They hadn't yet noticed the two witnesses in the deeper shadows of the tunnel.

"What do we do?" Cadge whispered.

Images of her mother's corpse flashed through Jazz's mind. She saw the blood again, and the message scrawled on the bedroom floor. Her mother's last thoughts had been of her survival. But if she'd reached home while the killers were in the midst of murder, she would never have chosen to run. Nor could she now.

She bolted toward them. One of the men heard her approach and looked up. Jazz stopped short, just near enough to taunt them with her presence.

"Oi! Leave off, fuckers!"

All four of them looked up, and for the first time she got a decent look at them. Three were dressed in boots and work clothes, sleeves rolled up as though they'd just come from the docks. The other wore black trousers and a thin black tie that hung over a white shirt. With the right cap and jacket, he'd have looked like a rich man's chauffeur.

In the eyes of all four of those men, Jazz saw sudden recognition. One by one, they focused not on her and Cadge but on her alone, and they *knew* her.

The phantoms of the London Underground might not frighten her anymore, but the look in the eyes of those men sent ice shooting through her and dread skittering down the back of her neck. She caught her breath and stood staring back at them.

They stepped away from Harry. On the ground, the old thief coughed and spat up blood and bile. The men watched her with a terrible malice.

"Well, now," said the man with the black tie. He reached up and pulled down his mask—most of the gas had dispersed—and Jazz uttered the smallest sound, a kind of whimper that she despised.

She recognized him. He had been one of the men the Uncles sometimes sent to watch over her and her mother, to pick up groceries or do a bit of repair on the pipes or the electric. And he had been standing outside her house, on guard, while her mother's killers had been inside. Jazz didn't know his name. In her mind, he was simply one of the BMW men.

He took a step toward her.

"Cadge, run!" she cried.

Jazz turned, caught her foot on a railroad tie, and stumbled. She risked one glance over her shoulder and saw the men running. One of them tripped and fell, but the others did not hesitate.

She ran. Her breath sounded too loud in her ears, and the walls of the tunnel seemed to be closing in. They gave chase, shouting to one another as though on a foxhunt. And Jazz knew what happened at the end of the hunt. The copper stink of her mother's blood rushed back to her as though she had returned to that death room. Her breath came faster.

Cadge ran just ahead. The only noise he made was his footfalls. As they rounded the bend, legs pumping, dancing amid the remnants of train track, Cadge snatched up his duffel bag.

"Nowhere to run down here, kids!" one of the men called.

Jazz had been thinking almost exactly that a moment before, but now she realized how wrong he was. There were an infinite number of places to hide in the down-below. The men had beaten Harry and scared off the others, but the United Kingdom had scattered. They'd be hiding now, like the rats these men thought they were. Like Hattie. The girl had passed them only moments ago, but Jazz ran by the stairs she and Cadge had come down and the door was now closed firmly. In the shadows, it looked unused.

"You're slow and old, you ugly shits!" Cadge called to their pursuers. "I hope you all have heart attacks and die down here."

"Christ, Cadge," Jazz rasped, running, chest burning with the effort. She'd already been exhausted when they'd walked into this chaos. What was Cadge doing?

When he glanced at her and she saw his expression in the gloom, she understood. He wasn't taunting the men out of amusement, but to make sure they knew he and Jazz hadn't gone through that door. If one of them opened it and found Hattie there, she was dead.

Well done, Cadge.

He started to slow, the extra burden of the duffel weighing on him. Jazz glanced back and saw they'd lengthened the distance between themselves and the thugs. She couldn't even see them now around the bend in the tunnel—could only hear the clomping of their boots. But if Cadge slowed...

"Drop the bag," she whispered.

He shot her a look of terror. "But the torch—"

Jazz tore the duffel from his hands and let it fall to the floor of the tunnel, hoping one of the bastards would trip on it. Cadge wanted the torch in case they had to hide somewhere that the light from above didn't filter in and where there were no electrical lights still siphoning power from the upside world. But they couldn't afford to lose a step.

Better to live in the dark than die in the light.

Her face burned with exertion and hatred, not only for these men but for herself. The BMW man proved it, and she'd seen that recognition in all of their eyes. They were here for her. Jazz had brought blood and perhaps even death to Harry and his United Kingdom. Her heart tightened into a fist in her chest. She couldn't let them catch her. The pain they would inflict on her would be terrible, but far worse would be the knowledge that her mother had spent so many years preparing her to survive and that she had failed at the task.

She had to live for Mum.

"Here," Cadge said.

The only light came from vent shafts twenty yards in either direction, but her eyes had become used to the dark in the past couple of months and she saw immediately what Cadge pointed to. A small narrow platform was set into the left side of the tunnel. Against the far wall were thick pipes that thrust deeper into the Underground and ran up to the ceiling of the tunnel. They branched off there, some following the tunnel both ways and some going straight up through the ceiling toward the surface. Others, however, turned and vanished into a crawl space atop the platform wall, no doubt once having carried water or power into other tunnels and stations from here. Many of the pipes had large wheel valves, but it was the ladder that mattered.

She gave Cadge a push and they ran for it together.

As they climbed onto the platform, the men rounded the bend in the tunnel.

"Where d'you think you're going?" one of them called, and then laughed.

As the laugh died out, Jazz heard another sound. Cadge

had reached the ladder ahead of her, but he turned and stared back down the tunnel—not at the men but beyond them, as though he could see the source of the distant shriek that came whistling up the tunnel, building in volume.

"Fuck me blind," Cadge whispered.

The BMW man reached the platform first and leaped up onto it. He lunged at Jazz. She turned and squared off, letting him come, and then swung her leg to kick him in the balls. He was ready for the attack, as she'd figured he would be. It had been a feint.

She drove her fingers into his eyes.

He screamed, reached for his face, and Cadge slammed a shoulder into him, knocking him off the platform. The others tried to catch him, but the BMW man slipped through their hands and hit the ground.

"Jesus, my eye!" he cried. "It's bleeding. Bitch popped my eye!"

The words were a shout of fury and pain; otherwise, Jazz would never have been able to hear them—not over the shrieking wind that came hurtling along the tunnel. The howling noise grew louder. To her ears it sounded like a train derailing and the terrified screams of the passengers, all merged into an infernal chorus.

The Hour of Screams.

A hundred rats ran along the tunnel, all in the same directions, ignoring the humans and seeking darkness once again.

"Jazz, a song!" Cadge shouted, his lips right beside her ear.

Her hair whipped past her face. The wind buffeted her, and now she saw that it had spectral texture. She nodded and huddled with him at the base of the ladder. Jazz clapped her hands against her ears to block out as much of the noise as she could. The banshee wail of the Hour of Screams grew louder, grating on her mind, stripping away her thoughts.

Harry had said to pick a song but hadn't elaborated much. Jazz knew it had to be something that she felt in her heart, that meant something to her, or she wouldn't be able to concentrate on it. But as she tried to focus, tried to choose, the Hour of Screams grew so loud she could barely think, and nothing came to mind. Snatches of lyrics, but she couldn't think how any of those songs went.

The stars, she thought. *Something about the stars.*

And then she had it, a song she could never forget, a melody that would never leave her.

Are the stars out tonight?
I don't know if it's cloudy or bright.
I only have eyes for you, dear.

Jazz sang the words softly at first and then louder, defiantly. Her eyes were squeezed tightly shut, but she felt Cadge at her side, huddled against her. Fear cradled her and she surrendered to it. Her sanctuary had been shattered. Her blood would soon stain the Underground, and the vanishing that had begun the day of her mother's murder would be complete.

The Hour of Screams bore down upon them. Jazz shook, breath hitching in her chest. Things slipped past her that might have been gusts of wind but were not. They caressed her, and she knew these were not ghosts like the phantoms she had encountered before.

"I only have eyes for you," she sang.

Beside her, Cadge shouted as though to drive the screams away and then began singing louder. She forced herself to open her eyes against the buffeting winds to make certain he was all right. Cadge had his own eyes screwed shut and hands clamped over his ears. His lips moved along with a song, but over her own singing and the howling of the Hour of Screams, Jazz couldn't make out the words or the tune.

Motion on the tracks caught her eye. She looked and saw the men crumbling to their knees. Ethereal shapes whipped around them, darting in close and then drawing back, pulsing in the air. The men beat their arms uselessly against the wind. Their eyes were wide with terror, and their shrieks joined the symphony.

And then it passed. The wind began to diminish and so did the volume of the screams, until moments later it lingered as nothing more than a distant whistle, just as it had been the first time she'd heard it from so far away with Harry and Cadge.

The men did not rise immediately, nor did they curse or shout. One by one, they looked up, eyes still wide. One of them wore a grin that seemed slashed into his face. He started to laugh and the BMW man slapped him, which only made the thug laugh harder.

The BMW man's gouged eye bled down his cheek. He glanced around with his one good eye and spotted her, then he bared his teeth and growled like an animal. His upper lip curled back to reveal crooked teeth.

One by one they rose, driven mad by the Hour of Screams.

"Rats," one of the men muttered, staring at Cadge and licking his lips. "Drive 'em out."

"Jazz," Cadge whispered.

The men were moving slowly. The first one reached the platform and began to haul himself up.

"Jazz!" Cadge shouted. He grabbed her arm and whipped her around, shoved her toward the ladder. "Climb!"

Heart thundering in her ears, she grabbed hold of the rungs and scrambled upward. Cadge shouted after her, urging her faster. Jazz caught his face with the heel of her shoe, so quickly was he following.

"Go! Go!" he yelled.

At the top, hands sliding over dust and grime, she pulled herself into the crawl space between the thick pipes. It couldn't have been more than two feet high but wide enough that she twisted sideways and rolled into the darkness. Turning around to face the way she'd come, she reached out to grab hold of Cadge's hand as he topped the ladder.

He froze, clung tightly to the top rung, and she saw a terrible understanding in his eyes: *they had him.*

Cadge knew he wouldn't be getting away.

The BMW man roared in triumph as Cadge's fingers were torn away from the rungs.

Jazz screamed for him. And for herself.

At the edge of the crawl space, she could see down onto the platform. The BMW man dropped onto his knees on Cadge's chest and began to beat him. There was a cracking of bone and the wet slap of skin on skin, growing slippery with blood. The others pulled him off, desperate to have their turn. They had been sent down into the underneath to hurt or even to kill, but they were madmen now. They kicked Cadge in the side and the head.

In the dim gloom of the tunnel, she thought she could see the life go out of his eyes. But Jazz knew it before the men did, and so her own screams turned to numb horror and she edged backward through the crawl space, deeper and deeper. Eventually, it would lead to some other tunnel or passage, but she would be the only one to emerge.

The BMW man still growled like an animal, but soon the wet noises and the thumps of their blows ceased. One last smack echoed through the tunnel and into the crawl space, and then she heard them.

"What was that? That wind. What just happened?"

"Fuck's sake, look at him. What'd we...?"

The sound of vomiting followed.

"Couldn't stop myself," one of them whispered.

The ladder grated, metal upon stone, as one of them climbed up to the crawl space. Jazz held her breath. She saw the silhouette of a head blocking out most of the ambient light from the tunnel. The BMW man. She could smell the blood on him, could hear the low snarl that came up from deep inside him. The madness of the others might be passing, but not this one. He was broken forever.

"Come on, Philip," one of the others said. "Girl's long gone. Work's done for the day."

The BMW man hesitated. He reached up to touch his ruined face, but she was far enough back in the darkness that he could not see her with his remaining eye. After a few moments, he descended the ladder.

Jazz could hear them moving off but worried that it was a trap. So she lay there quietly, waiting for some sign that they were really gone, waiting for Cadge to tell her it was time to come out. Dear, sweet Cadge, who'd fancied her so much. She wished now that she'd given him a kiss. Just one. He was so young, but what harm could one kiss do?

Perhaps she could still give it to him.

Maybe he'll know, she thought. *Maybe he'll see. All the ghosts of old London are down here. Now they've one more to join them.*

Chapter Nine

the river flows

Time blurred, and Jazz did not know whether she stayed in the crawl space for long minutes or hours. When at last she overcame her fear and tamped down her grief enough to act, her left arm had gone numb and prickled with pins and needles as she moved. Her neck and hips were stiff and ached to the bone.

A foot from the ledge, she hesitated. The top of the ladder was visible, and if she closed her eyes she knew she would see Cadge's fingers being pulled away from the rungs. She kept them open.

Something shifted in the tunnel. She heard breathing, which stilled her own. For long moments she considered her best course. The thugs who'd been driven mad by the Hour of Screams knew she had come into the crawl space. They might not have been able to squeeze in there to come after her, but they knew she was there. If they'd stuck around, surely she'd have heard them?

So whoever or whatever was out there was on their own and didn't know Jazz hid so near. She could try to back up, but that might make enough noise to draw attention. Or she could inch forward just a bit, enough to see who it was.

A low sigh came to her then, and a new thought rose in her mind. *Cadge?*

Jazz slid to the edge and looked down onto the platform. Her heart sank when she saw the bloody figure lying there, limbs akimbo like some cast-off marionette. She drew in a shuddering breath.

Someone moved in the shadows on the other side of the tunnel. At first glance she thought it was a ghost. An image crossed her mind of the magician's specter performing sleight of hand in the midst of old London's echoes. She half-expected him to emerge, drawing colorful kerchiefs from the sleeves of his jacket.

But the silhouette resolved itself, and she recognized him.

Stevie Sharpe.

He moved away from the wall, stepped over the old railroad ties, and climbed up onto the platform. Stevie pulled out a white rag and knelt to wipe some of the blood from Cadge's swollen face. One side of the boy's skull had been caved in. Jazz put a hand to her mouth to hold in a scream.

There had been enough screaming today.

"Are you coming down?" Stevie asked, still gently wiping at Cadge's face.

He glanced up at her. She was surprised to see tears on

his face. Stevie would not cry aloud; Jazz knew that much about him already. His expression seemed carved in granite. But his tears gave him away.

"Jazz, come down," he said.

It took her a moment to realize that she was supposed to reply. But she couldn't open her mouth. She crawled to the ladder and stared at the rungs where Cadge had tried so hard to hang on. Cadge, who had a touch of whatever awareness Jazz had found here in the underneath. Cadge, who'd only ever been sweet, who'd tried to make her feel at home.

"Jazz—"

Stevie stuffed the rag in his pocket and went to the ladder. He climbed up, boots clanging on the metal rungs, and gently reached for her, putting a hand on her wrist.

"Come down," he said.

His eyes always seemed shielded. They were supposed to be the windows to the soul, and while Jazz couldn't be sure she believed in souls, she did have faith in her ability to read someone's heart in their eyes. But not Stevie. He hid himself down deep. She supposed they had that in common.

"I'm afraid," she whispered.

Stevie nodded. "Good. We should be afraid. But you can't stay here. The others will be gathering at the rendezvous point soon, and we've got to check on Harry before we meet up with them."

Jazz wrapped her fingers around his wrist and they gripped each other's arms for a moment. From the first, she'd seen that Stevie differed from the others in some intangible way. She still didn't know what it was, beyond the age difference, but Jazz felt certain she had not imagined it.

The contact went on a beat longer than was comfortable. Stevie pulled his hand back and averted his eyes, then started down the ladder.

"Let's go."

Jazz took a breath and spun around. She scooted over the edge and began to climb down after him.

"Did you see them?" she asked as she came off the ladder onto the decrepit old train platform, purposefully avoiding looking at Cadge's body.

Stevie nodded. "I sent the others away, but I doubled back to see if I could help. After the Hour of Screams went by, I heard them shouting and I knew what had happened. I hid when they ran past, then came as fast as I could. Did you see anyone else?"

"Hattie. If she's still where we left her. And Harry. They did a job on him. We should check on him."

They knew me, she wanted to say. *They recognized me, and one of them I've seen before. They were here for me. What they did to Cadge . . . it's my fault.*

But she couldn't say any of that, no matter how true it felt. She'd sometimes gotten the feeling that he didn't trust her, didn't want her there. If she told him the truth, he'd never let her stay with them.

"Let's have a look," Stevie said. "But quietly. No telling if they're really gone or if there might be others. Nowhere's safe down here now, until we've had a proper look around to make sure it's clear."

Jazz had been avoiding looking at Cadge too closely, but when Stevie turned to jump down from the platform, she did not follow. Almost robotic, she forced herself to look.

This time her anguish did not rip into her as it had

before. Her eyes did not burn with tears. Instead, a cold fury spread through her. Slowly, she went and knelt by the ruined boy. He looked so small, and his wrecked face was gruesome to behold. But she did not allow herself to look away. Cadge deserved that much, at least.

"Let's go," Stevie said, though there was kindness in his urging.

She kissed the first two fingertips of her right hand, then pressed the kiss to Cadge's bloodstained cheek. Something had shifted in her, just in those few moments. Jazz had had enough of grief and enough of fear. Enough of running.

"Enough of hiding," she whispered to the dead boy.

She stood and turned to Stevie, holding out her hand. "Give me your jacket."

He frowned but slipped it off and handed it to her without question. Jazz placed Cadge's arms over his chest, then covered his corpse with the jacket. The others might need her, and Cadge was beyond anyone's help now. Beyond fear. Beyond the painful memories of his father's disdain.

Of them all, he was the only one who was safe.

"What are we going to do with him?" she asked, looking down from the platform at Stevie. "I won't just leave him here."

The older boy—almost a man, really, though his dark, narrow features still had a child's aspect—cocked his head, studying her. "You've been down here for a few months, but you haven't learned much. We take care of our own, Jazz. You should know that."

For a moment they indulged their anger by glaring at each other. Then Jazz dropped down to the remnants of the train tracks. So close to Stevie, she had to look up at him and felt his nearness keenly. An awkward tension rippled between them. She thought he might take her into his arms to comfort her, and as much as her mother had taught her never to rely on anyone—especially a bloke—the thought gave her a feeling of warmth inside.

But Stevie did not embrace her.

Wrapping her arms around herself, shivering now with the cold and damp of the tunnel, Jazz turned and started retracing her steps. When she reached the metal door to the stairs that she and Cadge had descended earlier, it hung partway open.

"Hattie was supposed to wait in there," she said.

Stevie pulled the door wide, revealing nothing but darkness within. He swore, but Jazz didn't waste time staring at the emptiness of the stairwell. She picked up her pace, jogging around the bend toward the entrance to Deep Level Shelter 7-K. The chemical smell of the gas the bastards used still lingered in the air. From behind her, she heard the sound of the metal door closing tight—they'd been taught to leave as little trace of their presence as possible—and then Stevie's footfalls as he pursued her.

When she came in sight of the door to the United Kingdom's lair, she staggered to a halt. Hattie knelt on the ground where the thugs had beaten Harry. For the first time since Jazz had met her, the girl was without a hat. The cute little cap she'd been wearing fashionably askew had been left behind, and Hattie hadn't noticed.

Harry lay beside her on the ground. Jazz couldn't see his face—Hattie blocked her view—but the man wasn't moving. Not at all.

Stevie caught up to Jazz but didn't slow. "Harry, no!" he shouted as he rushed toward the old thief.

Hattie spun around, eyes wide with fear. When she saw them, the girl shook with relief.

Then Harry moved. He reached up one hand to pat Hattie's arm, a gesture of fatherly comfort. His legs shifted and he tried to sit up but couldn't. Stevie reached them and dropped down next to Hattie. Jazz had been frozen with indecision, not knowing where her life would go from here. But for the moment, at least, such thoughts would have to wait. Harry had been kind to her. Cadge might be dead, but Harry was alive.

Jazz ran to them. She stood behind Stevie, looking down at the bruised, bloody face of Harry Fowler.

"I thought..." she said.

"The worst," Harry said. "I thought the same, love. But I'll be all right. Need some rest. Cracked some bones, I think. But a few weeks and I'll be right as rain."

"Think they'll be back?" Stevie asked.

Harry nodded. "Might be."

"So what do we do?" Hattie asked, her voice a desperate whine.

At that, Harry beamed, though he winced with the pain the smile caused him. "Why, Hattie, dear, what do you suppose we do? When the big bad wolf blows down the house, the smart little pig moves somewhere safer."

Hattie and Stevie nodded, but Jazz felt a darkness enveloping her, a grim hopelessness that she feared she could never escape.

"They caught Cadge," she said.

Harry frowned deeply. "Is he bad off?"

"He's dead."

At those words Harry—who'd made himself both monarch and jester of the Underground—began to cry.

And Jazz thought she loved the old man, just a little.

"What is this rendezvous point, anyway?" Jazz asked. "Nobody ever mentioned it to me."

Hattie led the way. Jazz and Stevie helped Harry as best they could, the old thief's arms around them for support. At first he'd had to lean on them quite a bit, but as the minutes passed and some of his stiffness retreated, he seemed to need them more for balance than anything else. Jazz stretched her own neck and arms, glad to have his weight off her.

"Couldn't be sure about you at first, Jazz girl." Harry coughed, spat a wad of bloody spittle, and kept walking. "If you were just passing through, it wouldn't do to give up all our secrets."

"And now? You're sure I'm not just passing through?"

"I'm not sure of anything except that those bastards attacked my family in my home, killed one of my children, and are going to pay for it."

Harry stepped on a loose stone that shifted beneath him, and he stumbled a bit. Jazz and Stevie caught him, but she saw the pain in his face and wondered how many bones were cracked or broken and whether he had damage inside him that none of them could see. Losing Cadge had gutted her. She wondered what would happen to the United Kingdom if Harry died as well and decided not to think about it.

"As to the rendezvous, here we are. You'll see for yourself."

Jazz narrowed her eyes. Hattie had gone down into the bomb shelter and fetched one of the heavy-duty torches. Its illumination shone into the tunnel ahead, but the darkness seemed to swallow it up. There were no shafts here to bring light down from the surface. Jazz couldn't have said how long they'd been wandering through the various tunnels and corridors that made up the labyrinth of London's true Underground, but she thought nearly an hour had passed.

The torchlight glinted on the tracks—there were still rails here—and on the walls and roof of the tunnel. But after a few more steps, the darkness seemed to yawn before them and they stepped into what had to be a vast subterranean cavern.

"What the hell?" Jazz whispered.

"Stevie, get the lights," Harry said.

The old thief released both of them, moving gingerly ahead. Stevie slipped off to the left, and Hattie aimed the torch just ahead of him. Jazz saw a platform. She and Hattie kept up with Harry as they came to a set of steps that led upward. At the top of those stairs, they stopped and waited.

"Stevie!" Harry called, one hand pressed against his side. "Let's have those lights."

"Give us a minute," Stevie replied, his voice floating to them from the darkness.

As promised, a moment later there came a loud clank and the hum of electricity, and lights began to flicker on high above their heads. Jazz turned slowly, mouth open in amazement. She had never seen a Tube station so beautiful. The pillars were marble and chandeliers hung from the ceiling high above. Frescoes had been painted on that vaulted surface. It seemed to her more like a cathedral than a train stop on the Underground.

"You've got to be joking," she said. "Who builds something like this and then abandons it?"

Hattie laughed and pirouetted in the middle of the station. "Isn't it lovely, though? Wish we could live here instead of just using it for emergencies."

"Why wouldn't you?" Jazz asked, turning to Harry.

He shook his head. "Too open. Can't heat it with a fire or a space heater. Never any direct light. Hard enough to keep the electric working. And once every few years they let a bunch of professors come down here and take pictures for their studies on the lost Underground."

Stevie appeared.

"They'd just finished building it when the war started," he said, strolling over to stand by Jazz. He gazed up at the ceiling. "The track was meant to connect two other lines, with this as the axis. Crown jewel, all of that. Then the bombing started. Used to be a ministry building up above. The whole thing came down, collapsed onto the station, and the walls on the stairs caved in. The Germans buried the place and nobody ever bothered to excavate."

"Why not?" Jazz asked.

Harry laughed. "Did a bit of research on it myself, once upon a time. See, on paper they said it was too dangerous. The ground above's unstable, they said. Have a look at the crack up there."

He pointed to the ceiling, and for the first time Jazz noticed the jagged line that cut across the ceiling on the far side, beyond the last chandelier.

"But it's stable enough they built a hotel on it," Harry continued. "Ask me, I'd say they just wanted to forget the place existed. After the First World War, the ministry never spent a penny rebuilding the military. When Hitler came to power, they hadn't the money or the army to fight him properly, had to beg and borrow to make a go of it. The last thing they wanted the people to see was how much money they spent on vanity and opulence. Bombs burying this place was their good luck. They weren't in any rush to dig it up again."

As Jazz listened to the tale and gazed around, studying the station, others moved out of the darkness down on the tracks and emerged from behind marble pillars and counters. The grand staircase had collapsed long ago, and the steps were strewn with rubble. From the shadows there, Gob and Leela appeared.

"Mr. F., you all right?" Marco asked, as he and Faith approached.

Bill and Switch stood by Stevie, all of them studying Harry.

"Gather round, pets. We've a lot of work to do and ought to do it quick."

Jazz noticed Stevie staring at her, but when she caught him, he looked away.

"Now, then," Harry went on. "Things have taken a turn, haven't they? Enemies have found us out, and they may be back. We're going to have to move, of course. Don't like it one bit, and I'm sure you don't either. But so it goes. I'm a bit bunged up, but I'll be all right. Stevie and I picked out a new place more than a year ago, just in case. We'll show you the way, and then you'll have to go back to the shelter and start moving our goods. Watch for trouble. Careful not to be seen. Anyone comes, anything starts, you run, and whatever you do, don't lead them back to our new home, right?"

They all nodded and grunted their agreement.

"First, we've got another task," Harry said. "A terrible task, indeed."

"Hang on," Leela said. "Who were the bastards? Got to tell us that much. They weren't police and they weren't building no new tracks or anything. So why'd they bother with us?"

Harry had wiped most of the blood from his face, but now his expression darkened. He lowered his head, face in shadow.

"The mayor's men, pet. Bone-breakers and life-takers," he said. "Running for reelection, isn't he? The nasty bastards didn't say as much, but I'm no fool. I've been reading the papers, seeing the signs. Mayor Bromwell said as he was gonna clean up the city, stop the thieving, protect British subjects and tourists alike. I knew we'd have to be careful, but I never thought they'd come down the hole after us."

As much as Harry seemed to believe it, Jazz could not. They had come down here searching for *her*. Someone must have seen her on the upside and followed her down, told the Uncles where she was. Jazz still did not know why her mother had been murdered, but obviously they still wanted her dead as well.

She would have to tell Harry, but now wasn't the time. Not with all of the others there.

"Bromwell's corrupt as they come," Harry added, but he didn't say it the way a man in a pub might complain about city government. It seemed more personal than that. "He sent these men down to clean us up. But we'll get him, pets. I promise you that. We'll get him."

Harry shook with fury and a grief that Jazz knew the others didn't yet understand.

"Hey," Gob piped up. "Where's Cadge?"

Jazz turned away from them. She hugged herself. Hattie came over and slid her arms around Jazz.

"Harry?" one of the boys prodded.

"They caught him. The Hour of Screams caught up to them. They might've done it anyway, madness or not, but they beat him. I'm sorry, pets. I loved him so. Sweet boy, swift of mind and hand. But he's dead. That was the other task I mentioned—saying good-bye to Cadge."

Jazz heard the water before she saw it. The soft hiss and gentle burble echoed off the stone walls of the old tunnel. Where they walked now, no train had ever run. This corridor seemed part of an ancient structure, the cellar of an old London building that had been destroyed. No doubt some other edifice had been erected in its place, but its roots remained.

Stevie led the way with the industrial torch Cadge had nicked that morning. Leela and Bill took up the rear, also carrying lights. Jazz and Hattie stayed on either side of Harry, just in case he stumbled. More than anything, he needed to rest and recuperate, but he refused to do so—refused even to let them begin the process of moving to their new sanctuary—until Cadge had been seen to.

Marco and Switch had gone with Stevie to get the body. *Yeah, the body. Not Cadge. It's not Cadge anymore. Just the shell he left behind.* Jazz figured if she kept telling herself that, she might stop wanting to scream every time she had to be near his corpse. In the shelter, their old home, they'd managed to find a suit bag—the kind business travelers carried—and zipped him into it. The sight troubled Jazz. It might not have felt so wrong if it had been black, but the bag was a bright cobalt blue. Marco and Switch carried it between them and, though the others offered to take a turn, they refused to share the burden.

They passed through a stone archway at the end of the corridor and emerged on a stone-and-earth embankment. Stevie clicked off his torch, for enough light filtered down through grates above them to see perfectly well.

A river flowed beneath the streets of London, thirty feet wide and deep enough that the water churned as it sped by. Jazz stared at it in amazement, then looked around at the crumbling foundations of the walls on either side, at the newer stone supports, and above at the concrete and steel in the roof that hung above the river.

"Where the hell did this come from?" she asked.

"Didn't come from nowhere," Stevie said, staring at the water. "River came first. Y'know Fleet Street? Named it after the Fleet River. Once upon a time it was aboveground, but they buried it. Must run for four or five miles under the city."

Harry stepped between them, reaching out to put one hand on Jazz's shoulder and one on Stevie's. "True, Mr. Sharpe. The River Fleet's got a great many stories, some of them full of mystery and some of sorrow. This part of the river here used to be called the Holbourne, which meant *hollow stream* or some such in the old Anglo–Saxon. That's where modern Holborn originated, with the river. But like so many other pieces of London's history, the river has been buried and forgotten."

Silence descended. The kids all gathered on the river-bank. Marco and Switch set down the suit bag with Cadge's body in it.

"Take a moment, my friends," Harry said at length, his voice a rasp of emotion. "Cadge was a good lad. One of the sweetest boys, one of the kindest hearts we'll ever know. The world above might have forgotten him, but we never will."

"Never," Hattie agreed.

"Never," the others all echoed, Jazz included.

Her chest tightened and she wiped moisture from the corners of her eyes.

"We won't forget what Cadge did for us nor what was done to him."

Jazz glanced at Harry, wondering if he would cry. But instead his face was grim and cold. He did not look like the kindly old thief she had always seen him as. Just then, Harry Fowler looked dangerous.

"All right, lads," he said, and nodded.

Marco and Switch picked up the suit bag, swung it once, and launched it as far out into the river as they could. It struck the water and went under, dragged by the weight of the dead boy inside, but then bobbed up again, moving swiftly in the current.

"Where—" Jazz began, but her voice broke. She cleared her throat and looked at Harry. "Where does the river come out?"

The old thief reached into his pocket and came out with a handful of coins. He shook them in his fist and they clinked together.

"Depends what you believe. The River Fleet goes along under the city, all the way to the Thames, and spills out there. But I figure there's another river here, and that's the Styx, Jazz girl. Runs beneath the surface of everything, all the way to the underworld."

Harry hurled the handful of coins into the river. They plinked into the water and were gone.

"What was that for, Mr. F.?" Gob asked, wiping at his eyes.

"To pay the ferryman, lad. Always got to pay the ferryman."

Several minutes passed in relative silence, each of them saying good-bye to Cadge in their own way. Jazz found it hard to accept that he was gone—that she would never see him again. Only hours ago he'd been smiling shyly at her, stealing a momentary touch of her hand. But she'd seen him brutalized, seen the broken, hollow thing that they'd made of him.

Death came swiftly. She'd seen it with her mother and now with Cadge. Before that, when she'd been just an infant, her father had been taken from her just as abruptly. It was a lesson she wished she had never had to learn.

Stevie began herding the others back into the corridor. Time for them all to see their new home, and then the process of moving would begin. But as they moved back into the ancient cellar, heading for the labyrinth of the forgotten Underground, Harry touched her shoulder.

"A moment, love."

Jazz watched Stevie disappear through the archway, then studied Harry's face. "What is it?"

"Curiosity, really. You've been quiet. I wondered if that

meant you'll be moving on now? Many do, you know. Some let the Crown care for them, others live on the streets. No way to live, really. I won't stop you, of course. Godspeed and all that. But I hope you'll stay with us."

Jazz turned from him and stared at the river, watching it churn away and disappear into darkness and stone.

"Cadge said he heard you talking, that you had big plans for me. Grand ambitions."

"You've quite a talent, there's no denying it. You're a natural. I think we could accomplish great things together."

"Would any of those things involve hurting the men who killed Cadge?"

Harry narrowed his eyes. His face betrayed no trace of his usual smile. What she saw now was a different man, perhaps a man he had been in his mysterious past.

"Thieving is what we do, Jazz. We steal to survive. To live. We make a life for ourselves that others would deny us, and we do no real harm. But you have such a gift that it makes a man ambitious. It may be possible to do better than merely survive, and I'd like to provide those opportunities for all of you. But there's a way to do that and to hurt Mayor Bromwell and his lackeys along the way. I swore I would make the bastards pay, and I will. To our benefit, and their detriment. And so yes, there is a role for you to play in all of this."

The river seemed too loud in her ears. Jazz nodded.

"Then I'm not going anywhere."

Chapter Ten

finding cruel patterns

Jazz and Stevie Sharpe were sitting on an old bench beneath an oak tree in Willow Square. They listened to the bustling sounds of rush hour around them, watched people in suits march briskly through the small park, and purposely did not stare too long at number 23. They pretended to be young lovers, yet though they sat close, Stevie's shoulder *just* avoided touching Jazz's, and his thigh was a whisker away from coming into contact with hers. He sat with his arm splayed casually along the back of the bench, but his hand did not rest on her shoulder. She wished he would touch her, but it was the last thing she was going to ask.

She turned to him and he smiled, but she knew that he was merely keeping up appearances.

The previous morning, Hattie had sat on the other side of the small park reading a trashy paperback novel. The morning before that, Gob and Switch had been here, playing Frisbee with a stray dog they had befriended. They'd fed it well before bringing it here, bought it a collar, brushed its matted fur, and made up a name that it seemed to like. They said they'd had a lot of fun, and the target had even lobbed the Frisbee back at them when it sailed out of the park and across the residential street. Harry had been concerned about that, but Gob had assured him that the target had not made them. *Too busy talking into thin air,* he'd said. *Thing plugged in 'is ear. Looked like someone out of* Star Trek.

"So what now?" Jazz said. She'd been plucking up the courage to ask for several minutes, but Stevie shot her down.

"He comes out and goes to work the same time as before, and the nick's on."

Jazz sighed. "Don't mean here, this. I mean..." *Us,* she wanted to say. But that sounded so intimate, and she was not sure there was any intimacy present in Stevie Sharpe. There really was no reason for her to think of her and Stevie as an *us.* But sometimes she got the feeling that he wouldn't have minded so much, and she couldn't deny that he intrigued her.

Stevie shifted on the bench. His hand dropped on her shoulder, light as a bird's touch, and she felt the warmth of his leg against hers. *Was that an answer?* she wondered. She shook her head slightly and smiled ruefully. She didn't want to play games like this.

Jazz stood and stretched, walking a few paces before squatting down and picking some daisies. It was hot already, even though it was barely nine in the morning. For the first time since going underground, it felt truly good to be out again. This was a wealthy street, the houses far apart and sep-arated by this small park, and the windows she could see were too far away to bother her. She did not feel spied upon, did not feel watched, and the sky above her was almost light enough to lift her away.

She picked another flower and remembered the daisy chains her mother used to make. When she was a little girl, she'd thought they were magical, and when her mother showed her how they were done, she remembered being disappointed.

Maybe she'd make one for Stevie.

"Jazz," Stevie said.

She glanced back at him. He was looking at her with lazy, lidded eyes, trying to affect a casualness that neither of them felt. "Is he out?" Jazz asked.

"Front door's open; he's gone back in to set the alarm."

"Same again," she said. The target had done the same yesterday and the same the day before. Three days in a row meant routine. And routine meant an easy score.

Jazz looked back at the ground before her, picked another daisy, and stood. As she turned around, keeping her head down, she lifted her eyes to glance across the street. The house's facade was tall and imposing, three stories high with four windows on each floor, an attic window in the steeply sloping roof, and plant pots on balconies outside the first- and second-floor windows. The pots held the dried remains of last summer's flowers. There was a large gate in the cast-iron fence around the small garden and a set of steps up to the front door. Beside these steps, in the shadows, hid a smaller gate that must lead down to a basement access. The light stonework was darkened from years of exhaust fumes and London smog, and Jazz wondered at someone who could live somewhere so opulent without caring about its appearance.

The front door stood open, and she saw the shadow of the owner approaching from inside. He'd set the alarm, and now he had however long the delay lasted to close and lock the front door.

Jazz heard Stevie counting very quietly beside her.

Something about the man caught Jazz's attention. She should be turning away from him, she knew that—they'd seen enough to know he had his set routines—but as he emerged backward from the house and slammed the front door closed, she realized what had grabbed her.

He had a ponytail.

Plenty of people have ponytails, she thought. Her heart stuttered. The first time she'd met the ponytailed Uncle, he'd said to her, *Hello, little Jazz, you can call me Mort*. She never had. When they visited her mother, she always avoided speaking to them, if at all possible. But over the past few weeks, when she thought back to that fateful day, she'd often wondered whether he had been joking with her even then. Playing with her. Giving her a clue as to how their relationship would inevitably end.

You can call me Mort.

"What is it?" Stevie whispered.

She'd dropped the daisies and grabbed Stevie's upper arms, fingers digging in. She heard his sharp intake of breath, but she could not loosen her fists.

Turn away, she thought. *If it's him, and he glances across here and sees us, it's all over. Cadge died because those people knew me. I can't have Stevie on my conscience as well.*

"Jazz?" Stevie said. "You're hurting, and you're going to draw attention."

The man dug his car keys from his pocket.

Black suit, black sunglasses, like a reject from Reservoir Dogs, *and it should look ridiculous, but it doesn't, because I know how dangerous these people are.*

"Jazz, for fuck's sake."

The man began to turn around, and when Jazz saw his profile she dipped her head, turned, and buried her face against Stevie's neck. She gasped, breathed in his scent, and managed to ease her hold on his biceps.

Uncle Mort, she thought, and any thoughts of revenge or retribution were swallowed by a moment of outright terror.

"Stevie," she whispered. She put her arms around his waist and held him tight, and Stevie lowered his own face against her neck and hugged her as well.

"Hey," he said. She felt his warm breath against her ear, and it gave her some comfort. He was no longer acting the part but playing it for real, and she hoped that later he did not suspect she had put this on. She wasn't yet sure what she was going to tell him—her mind was a muddle—but she grabbed this moment as hard as she was grabbing Stevie Sharpe. She felt his dark hair mingling with hers. She let out a sob, one shuddering exhalation that shook her body.

Jazz raised her head, careful not to turn around. Stevie looked up as well. They were so close that she could not focus on his eyes.

"Has he gone?" she asked.

"Just getting into his Porsche."

"Porsche," she said. "Tacky. Yeah, tacky suits him, I guess."

"You know this guy?"

Jazz shook her head. "Not yet. Tell me when he's gone. And I mean away, completely out of the square."

She heard the motor start behind her. A horn beeped and another beeped back, and she sensed Stevie's expressions change as he smiled.

"He can't drive for shit," he said.

Jazz giggled, and it felt good. There was suddenly something uniquely thrilling about being here, thirty yards away from a man who had probably spent weeks looking for her and who would likely kill her if they ever crossed paths. If she'd been on her own it would have been different, but although she knew Stevie would be in danger as well, they were accomplices in this deceit. Tires screeched, and Mort drove away from the girl the Uncles wanted most.

"He's gone," Stevie said. "We should go too. But we're not going straight back down."

"We're not?" Jazz asked. But she already knew that. Stevie still had not let go of her waist.

Stevie shook his head. "I know a place where we can talk."

They left the square as they had entered an hour before, holding hands and smiling. The smile still felt false, but now Jazz was sure the holding of hands had meaning. It was hot, her palm was sweaty, but she did not want to let go.

Music blasted from the speakers at about a million decibels, so loud that Jazz felt her stomach and chest rippling in time with the beat. It produced a wall of noise she thought she could probably climb. She didn't know who the band was, but the song screamed about rock and roll, drinking, and doing the horizontal dance. At least two of the three were actively being pursued in here.

Though it was still early morning, the café was packed. The front portion of the shop consisted of a secondhand record-and-CD dealership, but at the back there was a surprisingly well-appointed coffee counter selling coffee, tea, hot chocolate, and a selection of cakes and snacks. A few people had brought their potential purchases here to mull them over while having a drink, but most of the dozen tables were taken by obvious regulars. They sprawled casually across the chairs, drinking something from large mugs that most definitely did not resemble coffee. It did not steam, for a start.

But though the music was loud and the clientele all seemed to know one another, Jazz felt completely comfortable. Part of it was the anonymity, she guessed, but she also felt as though this was somewhere people came to get lost. Everyone here was doing their own thing, laughing and talking with friends of a similar bent, and there was no hint of tension or exclusivity in the air. It certainly was not the sort of place where shoppers popped in for a quiet coffee before their cab home.

"I thought you said we'd come here to talk!" Jazz said into Stevie's ear.

He smiled and shrugged, and leaned close to her. "At least we won't be overheard."

They were both drinking coffee, and Stevie had bought a selection of small cakes, which sat on a plate before them. Jazz didn't feel at all hungry, but she felt obliged to take a nibble. She chose a caramel shortbread and it was gorgeous, obviously homemade, rich, and sweet. She smiled in appreciation.

"So he was one of the guys who murdered your mum?" Stevie asked.

Jazz stopped chewing and felt instantly queasy. She lowered the cake and closed her eyes, nodding slowly. "How did you know?"

"Pretty obvious," Stevie said. "Your reaction. You were terrified."

"He was there," she said. "The day I went home and found Mum...He was there. In my room, watching for me."

Stevie frowned and drank more coffee. He looked around the café, up at the concert posters on the walls, down at the scratched table—anywhere but at her.

"And now we're going to do his house," she said.

"We are?" He looked at her, the expression of surprise honest and open.

"Bloody right we are!"

"But...you said they were still looking for you. You were scared to come up here for the first few weeks."

Jazz nodded. *Yes, he's right. I was scared and I still am. But there's something more here, something far beyond what I know.*

"And now you want to go and do his house?"

"Harry chose the place," Jazz said. "It's got something to do with Mayor Bromwell, and he's the one responsible for Cadge, so there's no way I'll pull out. Not now. And as Harry keeps telling me, without me it can't be done."

Stevie smiled at that, nodded. "He's not far wrong. You're fucking good."

At Stevie's words, Jazz felt a flush of pride—and the heat of something else entirely. Without making it too obvious, she picked up another cake and slid sideways as she started eating, leaning against Stevie. He did not move away. She took that as a good sign.

"Are we going to tell Harry?" Stevie asked.

"No. No need for him to know." *And I want to get inside,*

she thought. She was confused, she couldn't find the big picture, but there was something behind and beyond all this that connected things. *Don't believe in chance*, her mum had always told her. *Don't trust in coincidences. They do exist, but they're best held in suspicion. Things happen for a reason, life has a pattern, and sometimes that pattern is cruel. So watch out, and see meaning in everything.*

"What if you're caught?" Stevie asked. His concern was very real, even though he managed to maintain his cool expression, and Jazz felt so grateful for that. Cadge's death had done something to all of them; it wasn't weakness but a closer tie among the kingdom members that put more emphasis on danger. With one of their number killed, everyone else had realized how fraught their existence really was.

"I won't be," Jazz said. "I can do this."

Stevie nodded, frowning.

"Don't tell Harry," she said. "Please. Afterward I'll tell him, talk to him. Ask him what's going on. But if you tell him now, he'll stop what's happening, and..."

"And there's stuff you need to know," Stevie said.

Jazz nodded. *Yeah*, she thought. *And you understand that, don't you?*

"You ever think about later?" she asked.

"Later?"

"The future, I mean. I suppose it's all right for Harry. He's on in years, isn't he? But d'you really think you'll spend your whole life underground?"

Stevie frowned at that, but then his expression softened. "We're not all hiding from killers, Jazz, but we're all hiding from something. Not sayin' I haven't thought about it, though.

I owe Harry a lot. For now that's enough. But I don't think I'll be down there forever, no. Got to make a life, haven't I?"

As though realizing he'd said too much, his gaze sharpened and he studied her. "You won't say nothing, will you?"

Jazz shook her head. "Course not."

He hesitated a moment, and she had the feeling he was weighing whether or not he could really trust her. Then he nodded, smiling at her in a way that gave her a pleasant squirm.

They finished their coffee and cakes without saying anything more, and when they left, nobody turned to watch them go. Outside, they split up, both of them heading back belowground. Stevie left Jazz and headed for an alternate station. He seemed reticent about letting her travel on her own, but she nodded and smiled and said that she'd be fine. In truth she'd have preferred if he *had* traveled with her, but Harry would have questions about that, because he drummed caution into them all the time. And right now she didn't want Harry suspicious.

Besides, he was still on the mend. She didn't want him to worry. The mayor's men had done a good job on him, broken several ribs and cracked his wrist. For a day or two after the attack, he'd been coughing up blood, though only Hattie, Stevie, and Jazz had known about it. A rib had scraped his lung, he said, and however much they begged, he refused to go aboveground to find a doctor. It was almost as if, once he depended on someone other than himself again, his time down here would be finished.

Jazz descended out of the sunlight and into the station. She moved far along the platform and waited beside one of the chocolate vending machines that no one ever seemed to use, and when the train arrived she dashed on first. She was lucky to find a seat, and she stared down at her shoes as they rattled away into the tunnels.

As she traveled, she thought about what she had seen. Had that really been Mort? She had already decided it was, but there was always the possibility that she'd been mistaken. Her mother's words about coincidence and chance came back to her, but her mother was dead, and it was up to Jazz now to translate events. If it was Mort, then he was connected to Mayor Bromwell somehow, and that meant the Uncles were as well. What *that* meant... she was not sure. But Harry had chosen this house—the third posh place they'd have hit in as many weeks—for a reason: revenge.

Maybe the time had come to double up on vengeance.

When she got off the train, she stood on the platform for a minute, fumbling in her pockets for change and pretending to use the chocolate machine. When the platform was empty, she dashed to the end, slipped over its edge, and headed into the tunnel.

The first time she'd come this way after the United Kingdom had moved, the first thirty yards had scared the crap out of her. She was very conscious of the train tracks close to her left foot, and she knew that if a train came along she'd be done for. Even if there was just room for her to press against the wall, the suction of the train's passing would pull her into it, and she'd be battered between train and wall before being deposited on the tracks. Maybe people would see her, maybe they wouldn't, but either way they'd never reach her before the next train came along to finish her off.

Timing, Switch had said. He never spoke much, and after

almost three months this was the first thing he'd said directly to Jazz. *Off the train, down, thirty yards to the door. Find it, get in, you're okay. Miss it, you're fucked.* He'd stared at her, grubby face revealed by ghostly torchlight. *Don't miss it.*

She walked quickly, running her right hand along the wall and counting her steps. She heard a sound in the distance, a screech and squeal, and for a second she feared it was the Hour of Screams coming in again. But then she remembered how close she was to the surface. The Hour only swept through the lower, more remote levels. Places, Marco had told her, where living people shouldn't be.

She found the steel hatch, grabbed its edge, and pulled. Once through the gap in the wall, she closed the hatch and breathed out.

Away from the station, away from the line, she still had a long way to go. Their new home was deeper than before. She only hoped it would be safer.

The clank of metal doors, the dust of abandoned tunnels, the flicker of uncertain lights, scampering rats and the tickle of spiders, damp walls and leaking domed brick ceilings—all were becoming familiar to Jazz. Worst were the cockroaches, which always seemed to scuttle just at the edges of any light. Once she'd stepped into a nest of them; she'd become more careful since. The United Kingdom kept several torches hidden in an alcove close to the surface, and she took one now and made her way back down to their new shelter. It had been built for royalty, and so they'd started calling it the Palace.

As long as Jazz didn't have to call it home, any name was fine with her.

The Palace was more comfortable than Deep Level Shelter 7-K, and sometimes when the air was right they could hear faint, unidentifiable music coming in from somewhere high above, down pipes perhaps, or through a fault in the ground.

But she was distracting herself. She was almost there, and she knew that soon she would have to pass the wall.

It wasn't that it spooked her. Not really. But she was still getting used to the Underground, the nooks and crannies, and the idea of miles of abandoned tunnels and places never seen by anyone alive. The United Kingdom had made some of these places their homes and haunting grounds, and there were plenty of other people living under London, the homeless and disenfranchised and mad. They kept away from others as much as possible, keeping their own location secret to avoid the theft of food or supplies. When Jazz passed others in the Underground, she usually ignored them the way Harry had taught her, but sometimes she couldn't help giving a smile or a wave or a quick hello, just to let those lost people know there were those who hadn't forgotten them, who still saw them and acknowledged their existence.

They were harmless, mostly. But Harry often alluded to other, less normal inhabitants beneath the city. One night around a fire he'd told them all the story about a tribe of people who had lived down here since the 1800s, and how their descendants were born down here and had never seen daylight. *Hear a scratch*, he'd said, *see a face at the bottom of some unplumbed pit, and it's likely one of them.* She'd asked him afterward whether he'd said it to scare them, and he'd paused for a while, looking at her. Then he'd smiled and nodded. *Of course, Jazz girl*, he'd said.

She'd believed him then because she needed to, but now she was not so sure.

She walked on, along a narrow access tunnel between a subterranean room and a shaft that housed an old metal ladder. She checked the shaft before descending—

(no pale face down there staring up with milky, sightless eyes)

—and then carefully lowered herself down.

And here it was. The bottom of the shaft widened in a bell shape, and its base was a dozen steps across. One quarter of it opened onto an old brick-lined cavern, its use long since lost to time. But opposite this opening was the bricked-in doorway.

Something back there, Jazz thought. *Something not dead.* It was the same notion she'd had the very first time they'd come this way, all of them following Harry in those painful, confused hours after giving Cadge to the river. Then she'd not had time to pause but had turned away from the old opening and walked on. Now, as every time since, she stopped to look.

She remembered what Cadge had said about that other metal door that had held her fascination. *Never know what you're gonna find behind a door down here.* Well, once there had been a doorway here, and somebody had seen fit to brick it up. They had brought all those materials down here—bricks, sand, cement—and worked in these cramped, uncomfortable conditions to fill the opening perfectly.

Jazz felt as if she could walk straight through the bricks. She tried, but they were solid and damp. Something scurried away up the wall, its many-limbed escape scratching at her hearing.

She turned her back on the wall and walked away. It wasn't easy. Maybe it was just because it was a mystery, and sometimes mysteries can exert a powerful influence.

Jazz went on, leaving that strange place behind.

Ten minutes later she found the room of alcoves. It was a long, thin room, the ceiling blank concrete instead of the usual vaulted brick, and along the wall to her left were five alcoves. The door she wanted—the one that led to the back entrance of the Palace—was in the middle one.

It was open, of course. Harry and the others were expecting her and Stevie, eager to hear their report. If all was good—and she would make sure it was—there was a job for them to pull in less than twenty-four hours.

Harry said the Palace was an old nuclear shelter from the 1960s. There was a big steel door at the entrance that was wedged open, completely immovable. Inside were a series of rooms, a dozen in total, set in two levels around a round central space, which served as their main gathering area. The largest of these rooms was filled with a hundred shelves of inedible tinned and dried food. They'd opened a few of the tins out of curiosity and found a powdery substance inside, which perhaps had once been soup or beef stew or Spam. They hadn't tried any more.

Jazz wasn't convinced. Search though they had, they had not found any sign of a plant room to draw in or process fresh air. The atmosphere down here was heavy and damp at best, but surely in a nuclear war they'd rely on more than the depth of this place to ensure the air was uncontaminated? Neither was there a control or communications center, which she'd seen in documentaries about the shelters built by the government through the late fifties and sixties. She'd asked her mum about who would go down there if there was a war.

The government, she'd said. *Politicians, their assistants, soldiers to guard them, doctors to look after them. And the royals.*

Lucky them, Jazz had said.

Her mother, in one of her darker but more humorous moments, had laughed out loud and changed channels to *The Simpsons. Yes, lucky them! Survive Armageddon, and when they come out there's no one to rule over, no one to canvass for votes, and no one to print stories about your latest indiscretion with your secretary!*

Maybe it *was* a shelter of some sort, but Jazz believed it more of a retreat than anything else. It could have been government, could have been private, but whatever the case one thing was sure: it was long forgotten now.

When she stepped through the rear entrance of the Palace and walked along the corridor into the central area, Stevie was already there. Damn, he was fast! They locked eyes, she frowned, he shook his head slightly. Good. He hadn't said a word.

"Jazz girl!" Harry gushed. He stood and came to her, wrapping his wounded arm around her shoulder. "It's good to see you safe and sound," he said, quieter. "So come and sit with us, have a drink and a bite, because now that you're back we're all together again. And I've got something to read to you all."

Jazz nodded greetings and took a cup of tea offered by Marco. Hattie brought a plate of sandwiches and a huge bag of potato chips, and Jazz helped herself to a generous portion. The shock of that morning and the effort of her descent had made her hungry, and they'd not had time for breakfast.

"So Gob was up early this morning, lifting wallets on Oxford Street, and, bless him, he knows how much I like to read a paper. He brought down the *Times*—the only true paper for a gentleman, as I'm sure you all know. And lo and behold, at the bottom of page eleven, we get a mention!"

Cadge! Jazz thought. But no, that was more than two weeks ago. His memory was precious, and she would not want it sullied by some impersonal newspaper report.

Bill tapped his plate with his mug and held his hands out, shoulder up. *What is it?* Nobody had ever heard him talk when he was awake. Sleeping, he sometimes cried out words that none of them could quite make out, as though he spoke in a long-forgotten language. And then only when he had nightmares. Jazz felt sorry for him, but she also couldn't help finding him a little spooky.

"Patience, Bill!" Harry said. He rustled the paper, trying to pretend it wasn't already open and folded at the correct page. He coughed several times, made himself comfortable on his chair, and began.

"*Bromwell Crisis of Control* is the headline. *Piers Taylor, a longtime friend and supporter of London's Mayor Leslie Bromwell, has spoken out against the mayor at a vital point in his campaign for reelection. Taylor's London home was broken into ten days ago by a gang of professional thieves, who made away with family jewelry and an undisclosed sum of cash.*"

"They called us professional!" Hattie said.

"Of course, my girl!" Harry said. "We've got the talented Jazz on our team. There are cat burglars aplenty, but in just a couple of months she's become a shadow burglar, for sure. Got an aptitude for stealing and a heart for hiding. Now, listen: *In a statement read by his public assistant, Taylor, an industrialist who made his fortune in oil and diamond mining in South Africa, said, 'Mayor Bromwell's avowed aim is to clean up London's streets, ridding us of the plague of violent crime and robbery that blights this nation's proud capital. He has been less than efficient in succeeding in this task, which is self-evident from the number of burglaries and street crimes still reported every day. Even if I had not been a victim of such a crime, I would be speaking out now, because I believe the mayor is a man who has been distracted from his path.' Asked by this reporter what the distraction entailed, Mr. Taylor's assistant refused to comment. Efforts to contact Mr. Taylor for an interview have met with silence, but it is telling that someone once so close to Mayor Bromwell is now speaking out against him.*" Harry sat back in his chair, rested his head, and looked at the ceiling. "Ah, my pets, what a fine vintage is revenge."

"Ten days ago," Jazz said. "That was the first house we did."

"The first," Harry said. "The one with the fancy topiary and swimming pool in the garden."

"What about the second?" she asked. "The one we did five days ago?"

"No mention yet." Harry stood and dropped the paper. "But it was well chosen, Jazz. Well chosen by me."

"And what about the third?" Stevie Sharpe asked. Jazz could have hugged him. One day soon, she promised herself there and then, she would.

All eyes turned to her.

"Yes, Jazz girl," Harry said. "What about the third?"

"Tomorrow morning," she said. "Easy. But we need to plan."

Harry grinned, bowing to Jazz like a performer at the end of a play. "Then plan we shall."

Chapter Eleven

thieving the thief

Jazz chose her moment well. Between traffic passing along the street, front doors closing, curtains being drawn open, the postman passing by, and pedestrians clicking their expensive shoes and high heels as they hurried to work, she walked across the street from the park, through the front gate, and down the several steps to the house's basement entrance.

She looked back across the street at Switch. He was reading on a bench in the park, and though he had his back to her and the house, she knew he'd been watching her. If there was any sign that she'd been seen, he'd let her know.

He turned a page, rubbed a hand through his hair, and carried on reading.

Jazz checked her watch. Five minutes. She was hidden from the road by the bulk of the steps leading up to the main door, and the basement door was set into the steps' side wall.

The only way she would be seen was if Mort decided to visit his basement in the few minutes before leaving.

They'd decided that Jazz would be the only one to go inside. *Too many cooks*, Harry had said, and he was right. The more who went in, the greater the chance of being caught. But the others were here, providing what Harry had called protection and distraction. Switch sat reading in the park, Gob and Hattie walked up and down a neighboring street, Marco did as his namesake and explored alleys, back streets, and service roads in the area. Stevie had taken one of the most dangerous jobs—scruffing himself up and sitting at the corner of Mort's street, begging. They all knew that he'd be moved on by the police soon, but that was one more distraction for the local beat bobbies while Jazz did her thing.

Switch looked at his watch and closed his book. That was the signal that the time had come. Jazz had already inserted the skeleton key into the door's lock, and now she started turning and probing, feeling the tumblers click back as the key found its way in. Still listening for the sound of the front door opening above her, she concentrated hard.

If Mort opened the door, set the alarm, and came out before she had this one open, it was all over. Even if he didn't see her—and the chance of him missing her was close to zero, by her estimation—they would have missed their best opportunity to get inside. There were other ways, of course, but with an alarm system like this, it was best to fool it right at the start.

There! The lock snicked open and she grabbed the handle, ready to go inside.

The front door opened above her. She turned the handle, pushed the basement door open, and started counting.

One, two...

She slipped through, turned, and pushed the door shut behind her. She eased the handle closed with her hand, not wanting to risk its springs snapping it back into place. She had no idea of the layout of the house, no inkling of how sound could carry.

Three, four...

Jazz paused for a heartbeat to get her bearings. The basement had once been a well-appointed room, perhaps a separate dwelling in its own right, but now it was crammed full of old furniture, boxes sealed with packing tape, and a huge bookcase packed solid with old hardback books. Her route across this space would be slow, and the far door was closed, perhaps locked.

Five, six...

There was a motion detector in one corner of the room, flashing red where it was fixed just below the ceiling. Once the alarm was set and the flashing stopped, it would be active.

Jazz moved. Over an old sofa, clouds of dust puffing up around her and tickling her nose. Through a forest of dining chairs, upright and upside down, and her rucksack caught on one of the legs. She paused and spun around, catching the chair just before it hit the ground.

Seven, eight...

She stepped around a pile of small sealed boxes, wondering what they contained.

Footsteps came from above as Mort hurried along his hallway, needing to set the alarm and close the front door by the count of thirty. After that, he'd set it off himself and have to explain to the police what had happened.

Nine, ten...

From her rucksack, she pulled a canvas cozy Hattie had made, elastic band sewn into the edges. Stretching it with her fingers, she slipped it over the motion detector, let it snap into place, and then ran on.

Thirteen, fourteen...

She made the far door and tried the handle. She sighed when it opened, then stepped out into a dimly lit corridor, the only light bleeding through a glass-block wall at one end. There were two doors on each side, and any one of them could be the one leading upstairs.

A motion detector watched the corridor as well. This house was well protected.

Seventeen, eighteen...

She snapped another cozy over the detector in the hall. When the alarm activated, the motion detector would be effectively blind. She tried the door five steps along from the basement door. It opened onto a blank space, a basement that had never been completed. Bare concrete walls and exposed ceiling joists were swathed in spiderwebs and dust. She closed it and crossed the corridor to the door immediately opposite.

Twenty-two, twenty-three...

Last chance. She'd have to stop soon, because she couldn't trust counting in her head. Three seconds off and everything would be ruined.

I'm in his house! I'm in Mort's house, and if the alarm goes and he comes in, catches me, he could kill me here and now. Or knock me out, tell the police it was a false alarm because he didn't set it in time, see them on their way with a cup of tea and a friendly wave, come back down to where he left me, slit my throat. Kill me when I'm unconscious.

Twenty-five, twenty-six . . .

Jazz opened the door and saw the short staircase leading up. Here, too, a motion detector flashed its readiness. She closed the door gently behind her, hurried to the top step, and pressed her ear against the door. A third canvas cozy was clutched in her right hand.

Twenty-eight . . .

She heard hurried footsteps, the front door slamming shut, and then a few seconds later the alarm let out one long beep. That was it. Set.

Jazz froze. She turned her eyes up and to the side and saw the steady LED of the motion detector.

Now was when the long, slow, fun part began. She'd hoped to avoid it, but no such luck.

Harry had told her that motion detectors used in domestic house alarms were only so sensitive. They could be fooled, but it took someone with a steady nerve and grace of movement to do so. He'd said that if Jazz moved as slowly as she could, she would be able to cross a room covered by a detector. It would take a while. And any slight jerk, sneeze, or slip could set it off. But it was possible.

Jazz reached up slowly and closed her hand around the door handle. She shut her eyes—slowly—and willed it to be unlocked.

It was an old-fashioned round brass handle, similar to those on the basement doors, and she had to grip it tight to provide enough friction to turn it. She moved her hand clockwise, hearing the lock squeal slightly, amazed at how tensed her muscles had become in her efforts not to move.

She was crouched on the top step and her right leg was below her, already aching and burning where it took her weight.

She could not ease up, stretch her leg, or shift position. Every movement now had to be relevant and necessary. Surely only the main corridors would have motion sensors, and even then perhaps only on the lower floors.

It was going to be a long, slow journey through the house, but she had all day.

The handle slipped in her palm, all the way back to the closed position.

"Shit!" Tempted though she was to slap the door, she could not.

She turned her eyes again, looking up at the red eye of the motion detector and silently cursing its electrical patience.

It turned off.

Jazz gasped. It was no trick of the light or a fault of her eyes. Did this happen once the alarm system was set? It had been maybe five minutes. Did all the detectors suddenly switch off the LEDs even though they were still active? She thought it unlikely—they were there for a reason, after all, and it seemed strange that they would no longer display their alertness.

She heard a sound beyond the door. It was a light metallic click, like a tool snapping shut or a door latch finding its home.

Mort! He hadn't gone to work after all. He must have forgotten something, returned home, and . . .

But she had not heard the front door open, nor the beeping of the alarm that would count down the period he had to get inside, enter the code, and disable it. She'd have heard all that. She had been concentrating on the handle, true, and the beaded sweat on her forehead attested to that. But she would have heard Mort coming home.

Footsteps passed by outside, very soft, as though barefoot. Mort always wore expensive shoes. She remembered that of him; he'd prided himself on his appearance, and there was no way he'd have left the house in anything other than exquisite dress.

Jazz had still not moved, for fear that the detector was active—but if it was, then whoever was out there would have set it off. If Mort had returned, then he must have deactivated the alarm system without her hearing. Remote control, perhaps?

If it wasn't Mort, then she had to see who *was* out there.

Wincing, preparing herself for the shriek of the alarm, Jazz stood and backed down a couple of steps.

Nothing happened. She let out a sigh of relief, then a groan as pins and needles rushed into her leg. Kneeling, she looked under the door, able to see right across the hallway. The dark-oak floor was highly polished, broken up here and there with rugs, and across the hall stood at least two closed doors. She turned and looked to the left, just in time to see a foot lift out of view onto the staircase. It had been wearing soft-looking shoes, like a dancer's. And now it was gone.

Jazz's heart thumped. Who could it be? Maid? Cleaner? But no, not if Mort had set the alarm on his way out.

She kept looking for a while, waiting for the foot's owner to come back down. But there was no more movement.

Another thief? What were the chances of that? But right then it was all she could think of. There would have been no reason for Mort to set the alarm if he knew there was going to be someone in the house; therefore, he did not know. So whoever owned that soft-shoed foot was not supposed to be here.

Jazz took a deep breath and considered her options. She could turn around and leave, pick up the others and go back down below, tell Harry that someone had beaten them to it. But that felt like failure, and it also meant that she would have no more opportunity to find out about Mort, his relationship with the mayor, and what it had to do with her and...

Mum. She shouldn't forget her mum. The owner of this house had been there when she was murdered—not in the same room perhaps, but certainly in the same house. Maybe he'd heard her fighting, heard her gurgling as her throat was slit and the air rushed from her lungs, blood spewed from her arteries...

No, if Jazz left now, it was not only knowledge that would elude her. It was some measure of revenge.

She held the door handle and gently turned it. When she felt the latch disengage, she opened the door an inch and peered through the crack. The hallway was large, hung with several expensive-looking paintings and adorned with four huge porcelain vases on their own metal stands. The porcelain was cracked and chipped in a couple of places, which meant that they were old and probably worth a lot.

She'd save them for on the way out.

The staircase was wide and it curved up and to the left. Banister and newel posts were ornately carved from oak and polished to match the hall floor. The stairs ended with a wide landing that overlooked the hall, and there was no one in sight. Whoever had climbed the stairs was busy exploring the second floor.

He or she doesn't know I'm here, Jazz thought. *Need to keep it that way.* She slipped off her trainers, tied the laces, and slung them around her neck. Her socks left sweaty imprints on the floor as she walked across the hallway, but by the time she reached the stairs and looked back, they were already fading away. *Like a ghost's*, she thought, and smiled.

She stood on the lower stair. The whole first floor was available to her to explore. There could be a study down here, a drawing room, library, other places where she could find stuff worth taking and perhaps something that would tell her more about Mort. She fingered the short folding knife in her pocket and looked at the paintings, and the urge to destroy was great. She hoped that Mort loved this place, hoped that his parents had handed all these nice things down to him, because she was going to ruin them. Petty and basic, maybe, but it would make her feel a little bit better.

But upstairs called to her. Whoever the other person in the house was, they seemed to have forsaken the first floor to go up. Which led Jazz to believe that they knew something she did not.

She climbed the stairs quickly and quietly. The open landing at the top had one door at the end, which was closed, and beside this another, smaller staircase led up to the third floor. To her right, a corridor branched away, lit by open doors.

She peered around the corner, counting two doors on each side and another corridor at right angles at the end. Many places to hide, and many places from which the other intruder could emerge and surprise her.

She fingered the knife again. Considered opening it. Decided against it. If it was a man and he turned aggressive, her mum had told her often enough what to do. *A swift kick to the balls, love, and then a knee in the face when they double up in pain. A bloke's life is led by what's between his legs, so it follows that it'll hurt the most.*

And if it was a woman...? Then perhaps they could share notes.

Jazz glanced once more at the closed door at the end of the landing. She went to it, put her ear against the wood, then pressed the handle. The door clicked open and she peered through. A clean, spartan bedroom: one bed and a chair, a small window, and little else. She left the door open slightly and turned back to the corridor leading deeper into the house.

She feared creaking floorboards, yet found none. Though the outside presented a different picture, the inside of this house was well kept. It was old, yes, but it reeked of care and of money well spent. The wallpaper in this corridor probably cost more per roll than some people earned in a month. She could almost smell the money seeping from walls and rising from expensive carpets. And that made her think: *What can you steal from someone who has so much, to make it really hurt?*

Jazz would return to the United Kingdom with a backpack filled with stuff to sell. But she would also find something special. A trophy, something priceless beyond money. She knew that it would be here, and she was confident it could be found.

There were picture frames lining the walls, photographs of people and places that must be personal to the owner. She paused to look at a couple that showed Mort smiling on some exotic seafront. She wondered who had taken the picture, and the thought of someone intimate in his life came as a shock. Whoever it might be, would they know what he was? Would they understand?

She moved on and paused beside the first two open doors, directly opposite each other. The one on the left smelled like a bathroom, damp from a recent shower and loaded with aftershave aromas. The door on the right led into another bedroom, and as she edged a few more inches forward, she saw the messed-up bed, open wardrobe, and clothes strewn across a chaise longue. There was a magazine open on the bed, and even from here she could see the pale spread of naked flesh.

Charming.

The next two doors, standing half open, led into further bedrooms, both of them smart and well presented but lacking any touches that indicated they were used. There was no sign of the intruder.

At the junction with the next corridor, Jazz paused and listened hard. She must be nearing the rear of the house now, and every room she looked in, every corner she turned, took her closer to the other intruder.

Unless they're upstairs! It was possible. But she could hear nothing—no footsteps, no flexing floors, no doors creaking open or closed. Maybe whoever it was knew she was here and they were waiting for her to pass by—or until she was close enough for them to attack.

For a crazy moment she considered calling out, asking who and where they were and telling them she wasn't here to hurt them. But no thief was likely to share their loot with her, and giving away her position would be madness.

Jazz glanced around the corner into the new corridor. It ran in both directions, finishing at both ends with a large stained-glass window. Four doors were spaced evenly along the far wall, two in either leg of the corridor. They were all closed.

More bedrooms? she wondered. *That'll make eight, for a house occupied by one man and his porno mags.*

There were also more photographs on the walls here, a lot more, and as she turned the corner she peered closely at them. Most of them were of Mort, usually on his own or with a tall, beautiful woman with dark hair and a melancholy expression. Her smile was never quite a smile, reminding Jazz of the *Mona Lisa*. Some of the settings she recognized because they were famous—Pompeii, Paris, New York, other places in America, Edinburgh. Still listening for any sign of the other person, she walked along the corridor, mindful of the closed doors. *If one starts to open, I'll be back around to the landing,* she thought. *And if they see me and call out, I'm out the front door, and fuck the alarm.*

Then she saw a picture of a group of people lined up in front of a building she did not recognize. It was London, she was sure of that, but there was no way to say where. Still, she recognized them. The Uncles. Mort was standing on the left, the others strung out to his right, with Josephine Blackwood among them, her face stern yet powerful, and if Jazz had ever had any doubt about who was in control, it now vanished.

Next to her, at the center of the group, stood...

Stood...

Jazz looked closer. For a mad moment she couldn't quite place the face, not because she didn't know it—she knew it well, so well, not from life but from a hundred other photographs—but because there was no way he could be there. No way!

"Fuck," she whispered. "Fuck, fuck, fuck…"

Her father. He looked sad and vulnerable, as though he knew he should not be there, but other than the Uncles and the Blackwood woman, he was the only other person in the photo.

"Dad," Jazz whispered. "Fuck," she said again. She shouldn't be talking, should be moving, but she didn't understand any of this.

Carefully, she lifted the picture from the wall, slipped the rucksack from her shoulder, and dropped it inside. On impulse she walked down the corridor and took another framed photograph of the Uncles. This one did not contain her father.

She began to doubt, thinking maybe she'd been mistaken. She was tense and wired, and perhaps she'd seen something dredged from her subconscious. But no. She did not have to look again, because she knew what she had seen. Her mother had made Jazz a strong girl, certain of herself, and she had never been one to check the keys in her pocket a dozen times or wonder whether she'd actually locked a door. Jazz was in control.

"I know what I saw," she whispered, and the door at the far end of the corridor opened.

Jazz didn't think. The instinct for survival was programmed into her. She turned across the corridor, grabbed the handle of the door next to the stained-glass window, turned it quietly, and pushed the door open with her body. There was no time for caution or stealth, she simply had to hide. Once inside, she swung around and pushed the door until it was almost closed. She squatted down and pressed her face to the crack, waiting to see who would emerge from the far room.

The pictures! Their absence on the opposite wall was obvious to her, but then, she had taken them. Thankfully, there were no lighter patches of wallpaper where they had been, but the hooks were prominent and cast shadows both ways from the two windows. If the intruder was observant enough—had looked around the corridor before entering the far door—he or she would notice.

Jazz breathed lightly through her mouth, trying not to pant.

She heard the door along the corridor close, but she could not yet see whoever had emerged.

She watched. A shadow shifted toward her along the carpet, and then a man stepped into view, silently, gracefully, almost floating. He stood at the junction of the two corridors for a second, head tilted to one side as if listening. She could see him only in profile: tall, thin, long-limbed. He wore a suit and tie, and over his right shoulder he carried a small bag.

Don't look this way, Jazz thought. *Don't see me.*

Even when he was standing still, she could sense the strength in him, and when he moved away he was nimble and elegant.

He walked along the corridor and back toward the landing. Jazz opened the door another inch and listened for other doors opening, but there was nothing. She guessed he was heading for the next floor. His bag had looked empty, so whatever he'd come here for, perhaps he had yet to find it.

She cast a quick glance at the room behind her. Not a bedroom, as she had suspected. The large room contained a long, expensive-looking table surrounded by a dozen chairs. The walls were unadorned, and there were no other furnishings apart from heavy curtains hanging on either side of the two floor-to-ceiling windows. A meeting room. And only twelve chairs, so when the Uncles met here, they met alone.

Spooked, Jazz left the room to follow the man. The pursuit excited her. She had to be completely silent, watching every shadow, every breath, ensuring that he could not hear her, see her, smell her. She felt like a great cat stalking its prey, but if he was a cat burglar, then what did that make her? *A hunter*, she thought. And that felt good. Too many times since her mother's murder, she had felt like the hunted.

Back at the landing, she looked down into the hallway first, just to make sure he had not gone downstairs. Then she heard a sound above, a footfall perhaps, or something being lowered to the floor. There were more sounds: the snick of wires being cut, low metallic noises, then a single soft electronic beep.

She took the opportunity to dash quickly into two of the rooms on that floor—one a sort of office or library and the other Mort's bedroom—nicking small items and dropping them quickly into her rucksack. In the bedroom, a hurried glance through Mort's sock drawer turned up a wedge of cash, which went into the bag as well. More footfalls above, and she knew she was risking too much. She went back into the hall.

At the foot of the second staircase Jazz looked up, listened, watched for movement. This was not quite so grand as the stairs from the first to the second floor, and she guessed perhaps the floor above had once been servants' quarters. But what was up there now? Surely not more bedrooms?

She started to ascend. Her heart was beating so rapidly that she feared he would hear, but even in such a silent house there was traffic noise from outside.

The stairs ended with a small landing, only one door leading off to the left. It was wide open. Crouching down at landing level, she peered around the doorjamb. She was expecting to see another corridor, narrower perhaps, with further doors heading off left and right. What she was not expecting was one large room.

It must have been forty feet square. It had an open ceiling and a front wall lined with windows. Close to the doorway, a small electronic device hung on three wires from a fitting in the wall, and spaced around the room just above floor level she saw dozens of sensors. Lasers, perhaps? That certainly was heavy-duty protection, but this man had disabled it with barely a pause.

In the sloping ceiling was a skylight—the one she had seen from the street, assuming an attic room—and it made this the brightest room in the house.

It was also the strangest.

The floor was carpeted, and spaced irregularly around the room were timber pedestals, all of them bearing display cases or racks of some kind. Every case and rack carried an item, and many of them were unknown to Jazz. In one case sat what looked like a human skull, but there were curious protrusions at either temple that could have been the roots of horns.

Another pedestal held a water-filled tank, murky with algae, and there was a bare suggestion of movement inside. She saw a stuffed duck-billed platypus with a head and beak at both ends, and an old Hessian sack, tied closed at the mouth, stained with what could have been dried blood. One stand held a simple top hat, and she had a sudden flashback to the ghostly conjurer she had seen twice now down in the Underground. The hat had a small hole in it halfway down. Nothing jumped out.

Jazz was so amazed that she almost forgot caution, and it was only when the intruder darted out from behind a high, wide display of dried rushes that she ducked back from the door. For a second she thought she'd been seen, but he was dashing about the room, going from one arcane exhibit to the next as if searching for something very particular.

He tipped a suitcase from a timber stand, fiddled with the locks, and broke it open. Something inside hissed and he slammed the lid again, but not in panic, not in fear. It simply was not what he was looking for.

Jazz was petrified and fascinated. Part of her almost wanted to rush into the room herself, because there was a globe she could see that glowed from inside and a huge closed book with a very tempting bookmark. But she could not be seen. She did not know who this man was, why he was here, or what he was after. And if his burglary of Mort's house was intentional, it could mean that he was just as dangerous as the Uncles, if not more so.

The man grunted, then gasped. He stood still, suddenly as motionless as the exhibits he had been examining. He was partly blocking what he was looking at from view, and Jazz resisted the temptation to lean farther into the doorway to see what it was.

"And here it is," he whispered. "At last, here it is." He leaned forward, reaching with both hands, then hesitated. He wiped his hands on his trousers—his first sign of nerves, the first indication that he was anything other than completely composed—and reached forward again. Once more he paused. "Blast." He shook his head, looked around, and headed for the rear of the room.

Jazz stretched around and saw that there were three doors there, all closed. The man opened the middle one and disappeared inside.

And at last she could see what had enraptured the man so. It looked like a short wide sword, one curved edge serrated, and close to its tip was a hole through the blade the width of her wrist. Its handle was metal as well, rounded and textured for grip.

The man was still gone. *Looking for something to wrap it in,* Jazz thought. *Something to pick it up.*

Jazz didn't think about what she did next. It was almost as if someone was guiding her, and as she stood and walked into the room, she had a momentary whiff of her mother's perfume. It was from her own slightly perspiring skin, of course. She'd worn Beautiful every day since Cadge had presented her with a bottle. But still...

She moved quickly, dodging around display pedestals, careful not to nudge them as she passed but unable to tear her eyes away from the sword. There was something about it...something almost familiar, yet alien and unsettling. As she reached out and grabbed it with both hands, she knew what that feeling was.

Here was something powerful, something calling to her like whatever lay behind that metal door and the blocked-in doorway belowground. There was intense mystery here and the threat of more things she could not possibly hope to understand. And there was also the promise of many revelations.

It was as if there were a hundred ghosts crowding her, unseen and unheard yet struggling to communicate, and it was all she could to do to prevent herself from talking to them there and then. *Yes*, she thought, *I want to hear you, but not here and not now.*

She lifted the sword from its rack. It came easily, almost gratefully, and she turned and hurried back across the room to the staircase.

Jazz didn't stop to think about what she had done. She had come into this house to thieve, and she was now leaving with two great mysteries; the photos in her backpack, and this thing nestled in her arms.

She reached the staircase, glanced back at the door the man had disappeared through, and headed down.

He's still in there, she thought. *I might really get away with this.*

Down the stairs, onto the landing, and then she heard a sound from above her. A gasp perhaps, closely followed by one muttered word: "No."

She did not wait to see if he had anything else to say. She ran, all pretense of secrecy thrown to the wind, holding the sword in both hands as she trotted down the curving staircase. Soon he would be there at the corner of her eye, emerging onto the landing and shouting at her to stop, to give him what he had come for.

When she reached the hallway, she saw the paintings and vases, but any idea she'd had to smash and slash them now seemed puerile and ineffective. She had the definite feeling that the loss of what she carried from this house would hurt Mort much more than a shattered pot and a ripped painting.

"Stop," a voice said. She froze in her tracks halfway

across the hall to the basement door. The voice was so refined, calm, and commanding that she could do nothing else.

Her heart thumped, pulsing in her ears.

She turned around.

"That's mine," the man said. He was standing up on the landing, leaning on the handrail and looking down at her with soft, mournful eyes.

Basement? Jazz thought. Then she had a better idea. Risky, but it would give her more of a chance to get away. There'd be lots of running, lots of trouble, but she thought if she went out the front door, things might still go her way.

"It's mine now," she said. Then she ran for the door.

She searched for the alarm box and found it next to a row of coat hooks, one of them bearing a smart jacket. A small gadget hung below it, suspended by stripped wires protruding from a break in the bottom of the unit. She reached out with the sword and pulled the wires free, and as the deafening shriek of the alarm cut in, she heard the man shouting one more time.

"*No!*"

His voice was suddenly filled with agony, as though he'd just seen his nearest and dearest killed.

Jazz glanced back one more time to see him running for the stairs. Then she unlocked the front door, flung it wide, and ran out into the blazing sunlight.

Chapter Twelve

intersection

The burglar alarm wailed like an air-raid signal. Jazz flew down the front steps, desperation mixing with a strange euphoria as she tucked the blade into her rucksack. She heard the thief shouting after her, but if he thought a harsh word would stop her, he was a fool. A black taxi cruised by and a courier scooter whipped past, but the streets around Willow Park had little traffic this time of day. That didn't mean there were no witnesses, though. An old woman out walking her dog stopped to stare. Two mothers picnicked in the park, one with a little girl playing on the grass beside her and the other with a baby sleeping in a pram.

The alarm woke the baby, who started to cry.

A well-dressed man stood on the far corner, a mobile phone clapped to his ear. He turned his back and covered his other ear, far too intent upon his conversation to be distracted by something as mundane as daylight robbery.

Jazz glanced back as she crossed the street. The thief shrugged on his jacket and stuffed something—gloves, perhaps—into his shoulder bag as he trotted along the sidewalk, appearing for all the world like a businessman in a hurry, no less ordinary than the self-important fool on his mobile half a block away. He'd shut the door behind him. The alarm still blared and he cast a casual, almost annoyed look back at the house he'd just tried to rob. Other than the handful of people who must have seen him emerge, no one would have thought him responsible.

"Fuck," Jazz whispered. One glance around revealed that everyone in the park and on the street had their eyes on her. Even the old woman's yappy dog focused on her, barking madly.

She ought to have played it cool until she was out of sight, like the suave bastard stepping briskly along the sidewalk parallel to her as she reached the other side of the street. But it was too late for subtlety. She leaped onto the sidewalk and kept running past a posh restaurant. Most of Mayfair consisted of luxury hotels, office space, and residences that had once housed nobility or ministry officials. Some still did. But London was a rat's warren of alleys, even in Mayfair. She had to vanish as quickly as possible, before the police arrived.

A familiar whistle drew her attention. Jazz looked up and saw Hattie coming toward her, head adorned with a pink felt hat with fake flowers pinned to the brim. She ducked into a dress shop and Jazz followed.

"Annie, there you are, love!" Hattie said excitedly, embracing her for the benefit of the shopgirls. Her hand clutched the strap of Jazz's bag, which was heavy with the strange blade and the other shiny bits she'd taken from Uncle Mort's house. "Give us the bag," she whispered.

"Lovely hat," Jazz said in reply. She snatched it off Hattie's head and plopped it on her own, then slipped out of her sweatshirt and handed it over. "Leave me the bag, go."

Hattie might have suffered a certain amount of brain slippage, but she wasn't daft. The girl nodded, pulled on the sweatshirt and zipped it, then hurried out of the shop. She turned back the way Jazz had come.

From inside, Jazz peered out of the shop windows. The thief had been marching toward the door, but now he altered course toward Hattie. Even as he reached her, another figure hurried along the sidewalk—Mr. Stevie Sharpe. As the thief reached for Hattie, Stevie purposely collided with him. The man ought to have fallen, but he spun away from the impact, reached out and grabbed Stevie by the wrist, and then cuffed him in the temple.

Stevie staggered backward. The thief—looking like a stockbroker or barrister—tried again to get hold of Hattie. This time Stevie didn't bother trying to make it look like an accident. He tackled the man, and the two of them spilled into the street. A screech of tires followed as a taxi skidded to a halt, slewing sideways.

"Can I help you, miss?" one of the shopgirls asked.

Jazz did not even glance at them, hoping they wouldn't be able to recognize her face if she managed to get nicked for this.

She went out the door, turned right, and hurried along

past a jeweler's and a men's clothing store. When she reached the corner, she turned right again and broke into a run, darted diagonally across the street, and slipped into the service alley behind the Grand Jubilee Hotel. Her trainers were nearly silent on the pavement. An enormous black Dumpster sat by the hotel's loading dock, and she had to fight the temptation to toss away Hattie's pink bonnet. The girl would never forgive her.

After the hotel, the alley went behind a pair of older buildings, lovely Georgian structures transformed into offices. The alley narrowed here, but she hurried on. Her temples throbbed and her heart pounded, but a grin began to spread across her face as she switched her bag from one shoulder to the other. Things had not gone as planned. Things had, in fact, been completely bollixed by the arrival of that handsome thief. Now that she was away and the terror of capture had passed, she almost felt giddy. The bloke had been startlingly good-looking. Some of the girls she knew had been attracted to their teachers, but older men had never done a thing for her, save the occasional actor. This one, though... She'd liked the way his eyes flashed with anger.

Not that she wanted him to catch her. That was the very last thing she wanted. From the way he'd sought the sword that she now carried, and the fury in his voice when she'd stolen it right from under his nose, she thought he might do anything to get it back. That made him a very dangerous man, indeed.

She'd been damn lucky. Setting off the alarm hadn't bought her the head start she'd hoped. Stevie, Hattie, Gob, and Switch had been meant to take turns looking out for her with some of the others, but Jazz wasn't supposed to leave the house until the mark returned home in the early evening. If Hattie and Stevie hadn't been alert when the whole thing went tits up, she never would've gotten away from the guy.

Hope they're all right, she thought. Particularly, she hoped Stevie was all right. By now the police would have responded to the alarm. The thief wouldn't have stayed behind to turn in her friends for fear of witnesses reporting him fleeing from the house. One way or another, they'd all be away by now.

The question was, how much damage had the thief done Stevie before taking off?

The alley ended ahead. Jazz clutched the strap of the bag tightly and stepped onto the street, turned right, and dropped into a brisk walk. Now would be a terrible time to draw attention to herself—though the pink flowered hat would be conspicuous enough.

No shouts greeted her emergence and no sirens blared.

At the next corner she crossed the street into a narrow arcade of trendy boutiques and gift shops. A small Italian restaurant and an antiquarian bookstore stood at the end of the arcade, where a fruit-seller had set up a cart on one side and another bloke sold flowers on the other. The arcade let out on a main road where traffic roared past in both directions, belching exhaust fumes and snatches of music.

Jazz joined the bustle on the sidewalk and made her way to the light at the corner. Across the street was Green Park. Jazz caught a glimpse of a man in the crowd waiting to cross. Thin and dapperly dressed, he carried a shoulder bag much like the thief's. She hesitated, but then the light changed and the throng began to move, and she saw that this was a much older man with pug Irish features and glasses.

"Silly girl," she whispered, and swept across the street.

The trees of Green Park cast long fingers of shade across the lawns. She spied an empty bench and recalled sitting with Stevie yesterday, pretending to be more than just his mate. Pretending to be a normal seventeen-year-old girl who fancied an entirely ordinary boy. Much as the upside world had its terrors for her, the memory of those hours made her strangely sad.

Without another glance at the trees, she grabbed the railing and hurried down the stairs into Green Park Tube station. The bag over her shoulder felt heavier with every step and she shifted to accommodate it. Jazz moved past a cluster of tourists trying to figure out the map of the Underground and reached into her pocket for her Travelcard. Her flight from Willow Square to Green Park had taken less than four minutes; her heart still raced. She cast a quick look around but saw no familiar faces—neither friend nor foe. Then she slipped through the turnstile and hurried down a tiled corridor toward the platform.

From the tunnels came the rumble of an approaching train and the squeal as it began to brake. Jazz held the bag against her, still feeling the weight of that strange blade, and picked up her pace. The train arrived as she joined the crowd on the platform. Out of habit and the instinct Harry had worked to instill in her, she plunged into the thickest part of the crowd as though heading for a door in the center, then cut across toward the next car. She stepped onto the train and immediately began walking. Jazz unzipped the bag, stuffed the pink hat into it, then zipped it closed again, moving as unobtrusively as possible.

People jostled one another, a few taking the open seats but most standing, holding on wherever they could. Jazz stood beside the doors between cars and put her back to the wall. She kept her head forward so her hair veiled her face. The train pulled away and she exhaled, willing herself to calm down.

Like some amusement-park ride, the cars rattled over the tracks, twisted through the Underground, and soon began to slow for the next stop. Just before they pulled into the illuminated area of the station, she glanced out the window and saw the flicker of motion, the luminescent outline of one of the ghosts of old London. Jazz blinked, startled to see a specter beyond the limits of the abandoned parts of the Underground. But then she saw the top hat and the way the magician shot his cuffs just before a trick. She bent to peer out the window, and just before she lost sight of him, he produced a phantom dove from thin air. It flapped white silk wings and flew up into the darkness of the tunnel.

The train hissed as it slowed, crawling into the station.

"Piccadilly Circus," a recorded voice said. "Next stop, Leicester Square."

The doors slid open.

"Mind the gap," said the voice.

People flooded off the train. Piccadilly was a major stop. Jazz took an empty seat in the corner and kept her head down. Someone settled into the next seat, bumping her, and another crowd began to fill the car.

The man beside her set down his shoulder bag.

"You're very good, you know," he said. "Stealthy and quick, with a deft touch. I'd no idea anyone else was in the house."

Jazz froze. The doors closed and the train began to pull out of the station. Leicester Square seemed a thousand miles away. The other people in the car loomed up around her. To them, she might as well have been invisible. She'd done that much correctly. No one had noticed her—or the well-dressed man seated beside her. But with the people packed in, she had nowhere to run.

"On the street, though, you could use some work," he went on. "You were watching for pursuit by foot, never considering an alternative. The taxi that nearly struck your little friend and me? I hired it. Once you came out of the alley and crossed to that arcade, it was obvious you were headed for Green Park. Had you hired a taxi of your own, it would have made things difficult. And I suppose if I'd been unfamiliar with this part of the city, you might have lost me when you first entered the alley. That much was intuition on my part, I confess. Where else could you have gone so quickly? A shop or restaurant wouldn't guarantee you a rear exit unless you'd planned that in advance, and your friends' clumsiness made clear that you had not considered your retreat carefully enough. So, the alley.

"From there, it was easier than you'd imagine to avoid detection while following you down into the Tube station. And so, here we are."

Jazz gripped the strap of her bag so tightly that she felt her fingernails cutting crescents into the flesh of her palm. She forced herself to lift her head and look at the man. Only inches separated his face from hers. She inhaled slowly, steadying her nerves, and when she did she breathed in the warmth of his own exhaled breath. The intimacy of the moment startled her.

She closed her eyes and cleared her head. When she opened them, she thought she would find anger on his face. She'd thought his words were mockery. But he studied her with open fascination, his eyes an intense icy blue that she could not turn away from. He carried himself like an older man, but could not have been more than thirty-five. The game of cat and mouse that had begun back in that house in Willow Square had just come to a conclusion. For a moment, she nearly apologized for stealing the treasure he had gone there seeking. To her it was nothing more than an artifact, something to sell, or for Harry Fowler to put on a shelf or in a box with his collection of trinkets and oddities the others had brought home for him over the years. Jazz had stolen it on a whim, but it had been this man's only goal.

But she would not apologize. She would simply deny it, play the encounter as coyly as possible, and look for an opportunity to flee. With Stevie, she'd rehearsed a number of things a young woman might scream to make onlookers think she was being accosted.

But she said none of those things.

"You're not angry anymore," Jazz said. "Why?"

"The day has taken a curious and unexpected turn," said the thief, "but an interesting one."

The train began to slow. Jazz glanced at the doors, tried to determine if she would be able to push through the crowd and get out before him, and if there was anything she could do to slow him down. No way would she lead him back to Harry and the others, not when they'd just had to relocate. Well dressed he might be, but she had a feeling this man would follow her—and the contents of her bag—anywhere.

So how could she escape him?

The answer troubled her. She would have to hurt him, because otherwise there was every chance that he would hurt her. No way in hell was this bloke going to let her walk away with what she'd stolen.

When she glanced at him again, he must have seen dark thoughts in her eyes.

"Ah, that's a shame, then. I'd hoped to avoid ugliness."

"How?"

The speakers on the train crackled. "Leicester Square," said the electronic voice. "Next stop, Covent Garden."

The thief gave her a charming, beguiling smile. "Continue on with me one stop. There's a lovely café that reminds me a great deal of Paris. Let me buy you a coffee and we'll have a chat. We experienced a remarkable coincidence today, and I can't imagine you aren't at least a tiny bit curious about how we happened to come together. For my part, I'm certainly curious about you."

The doors hissed open.

Jazz tensed, ready to plunge through the people jammed onto the train to get off. The thief only watched her, making no move to keep her there.

The moment went on for several beats and then the doors closed again.

They sat side by side in silence. When the train pulled into Covent Garden station the thief rose, threaded through commuters, and stepped off onto the platform. He started walking away, then paused and looked back.

Jazz got off the train and followed.

When he'd said the café was in Covent Garden, Jazz had assumed he meant on the piazza. She'd only been there a few times and, to her, the restaurants and shops and the street performers entertaining the crowds on a summer day on the piazza *was* Covent Garden. But the Augusta Café was nestled away amid the trees and flowers of Embankment Gardens, away from the crowds.

"Would you like the patio or the terrace?" asked the hostess, a girl not much older than Jazz. Her accent revealed her as a northerner, likely in London for university. "The patio's lovely today, but you can see the river from the terrace."

The thief looked quite at home in the midst of the fancy café, and he charmed the hostess with his roguish smile. "Not sure I want to look at the Thames. Never quite makes me want to go for a swim."

The dark-haired girl wrinkled her nose, grinning. "Can you imagine? It's pretty to look at, but you'd catch something dreadful. So it's the patio, then?"

Jazz had felt invisible to them, but then the thief looked at her as though they shared some grand jest. "What do you think, love?"

"It sounds perfect," Jazz found herself saying, as though they'd rehearsed these lines. That was what it felt like—a performance.

The hostess led them on a winding path among the tables on the patio. Several were occupied by men and women who were obviously there on business, with clients or associates. At one sat a burly bearded man in a T-shirt and jeans with an attractive dark-complexioned woman who held his hand across the tabletop. From their clothes and the relaxed air about them, she marked them as Americans. From another table came a steady stream of French spoken by a pair of fiftyish women holidaying together.

Jazz observed them all, careful not to let them notice her attention. When the thief pulled out a chair for her, she sat down. The hostess left them with menus and then hurried back to her post, where a white-haired gentleman with a newspaper under one arm awaited her.

In a tank top and cotton trousers, Jazz soaked up the warmth of the sun. She had deprived herself of it for so much of the time since she had gone on the run that she could not help relishing it now. The tables all had umbrellas that provided shade, but she wanted to feel the heat on her skin. The breeze that blew across the patio and rustled in the leaves of the trees was redolent with the scents of a dozen different flowers.

"You approve," the thief said.

Jazz had been avoiding his blue eyes. Now she forced herself to look at him. The man sat in the shade of the umbrella. At any other time, he would have blended perfectly into the scene on the patio. Jazz would have blended as well—just an ordinary London girl, out and about on a summer day. But together, they were an odd enough pairing to draw attention. It worried her.

"It's beautiful here," she admitted, reaching up to tuck a lock of hair behind her ear. "I'm just not sure what I'm supposed to say to you. Given how we met, I mean."

He cocked his head, studying her, and tried to hide the

smile that touched his lips. "Well, I certainly think we both worked hard today. I'd say we've earned a peaceful moment or two, not to mention coffee. They do the most remarkable Italian coffees here. The cappuccino is lovely. There are iced coffees as well. Or if you prefer tea—"

"I'm fine with coffee."

"Good." He leaned forward and tapped the menu. "The last page. They've got quite the variety."

With that, he began perusing the menu as if they had nothing more important to discuss than coffee. Jazz stared at him for several moments, but then she glanced nervously around. What the hell had she been thinking, coming here with him?

Certainly he had made her curious, but Jazz wasn't shallow enough to become a fool just because some handsome man intrigued her. He'd given her no choice, really. If she'd fought him, even if she'd managed to get the better of him on the train or in the station, they'd have drawn enough attention that the police would be summoned. She might get nicked, which terrified her. Her mother had taught her that the police could not be trusted, and given what the mayor had been up to, that seemed truer than ever. But if she'd simply run, she would have led him back to the United Kingdom, putting her friends in danger.

No choice.

She glanced around again. Sitting on the patio of the café, perusing a menu of exotic coffees, felt like a masquerade. Out there in the open, anyone might see her. The Uncles and their BMW men couldn't be everywhere, but this was simply throwing caution to the wind. Jazz did not enjoy the damp and the darkness of the Underground, but it represented safety.

Laughter rippled in the air. She glanced across the gardens and saw a little girl, no more than three, chasing a boy of around the same age while their parents strolled along a path behind them. The father held a red balloon.

Jazz felt the muscles in her neck and shoulders begin to loosen.

An hour in the sun. A cup of coffee. It wouldn't kill her. She thought of Cadge as she watched those children play and how he would have smiled to see them. He would have hated this handsome gentleman thief on principle, but the café . . . Cadge would have loved the café.

The waiter—a tall, athletic bloke with a shaved head and artfully groomed chin stubble—approached.

"Hello, I'm Rob. Have you decided what you'd like, or shall I give you more time?"

Jazz and the thief regarded each other over the tops of their menus. He arched an eyebrow, lips pressed into a thin smile.

"Look at you," she said. "So bloody pleased with yourself."

He blinked in surprise and then grinned.

Jazz looked at the waiter. "Iced coffee with a double shot of espresso and just a dash of cream."

Handsome Rob nodded, smiling bemusedly. "Excellent." He turned to the thief. "And you, sir?"

"Cappuccino, frosted with cinnamon. And a glass of ice water, if you would."

"Straightaway."

He gathered their menus and headed back into the café. When he'd gone, and without the menus to focus on, Jazz and the thief had nothing else to distract them from each other.

"I suppose the first order of business ought to be names," he said. "I'm Terence." He offered her his hand, leaning out of the umbrella's shade.

"Jazz," she said, reaching out to shake.

His grip was firm but brief. Meant only as a greeting, not to intimidate.

"An interesting name."

"Short for Jasmine."

"Beautiful. Seems sort of a shame to have a name like that and not use it."

"So nobody's ever called you Terry?"

Terence smiled. "Not my friends."

"Have a lot of those, do you, *Terry*?"

He laughed, then nodded in appreciation. "A precious few, Jasmine. Do you fence?"

"What, you mean like with swords? Do I look like some posh tart, then? Next you'll ask me if I sail."

"I don't see you as a sailor, actually. But fencing…you'd have a talent for it, I think."

Jazz sat back and crossed her legs, enjoying the sun, wishing she wore a skirt or shorts instead of long trousers. "And why is that?"

"You clearly relish the sparring and the quick riposte. You're quick on your feet, light and agile. As I mentioned on the Tube, you managed to slink around the house while I was there, with me none the wiser. And believe me, I was alert for the presence of others. It's a rare creature who can trump me the way you did today."

A waiter brought a tray of sandwiches to a table of well-coiffed professionals at the far side of the patio. As he walked past her, Jazz inhaled the aroma of the food and her stomach rumbled. She ignored it but thought back to the moment on the train when Terence had sat so close to her, had spoken to her, and she had inhaled his warm, sweet breath.

"Do your friends share your view of yourself, or are you really as much an egotist as you sound?"

"Both, I suspect."

Jazz smiled. "Of course."

"I don't suppose you're going to tell me where you learned your craft?" Terence asked. Thus far he had carefully avoided mentioning whose house they had been at or anything even remotely resembling a discussion of theft. There was something thrilling about having this conversation where others could hear yet making it oblique enough that no one would understand what they were talking about.

"I can't do that."

He sat forward and slipped out of his jacket. "Of course not." Neatly, he arranged the jacket on the back of one of the two empty chairs at their table. His clothes were stylish and impeccable.

"Do you always dress so well for work?"

"I dress to fit the job. Shall I tell you where you learned your craft?"

"You're a psychic now as well? You have so many marketable skills."

Terence sat back, perhaps unconsciously mimicking her pose. "You're a tunnel rat."

Jazz flinched inwardly but tried to keep her expression neutral. How the hell did he know that?

"Oh, you could have somewhere aboveground, but I don't think so," the thief went on. "The pallor of your skin gives you away, and your clothes have a bit of a moldy smell that might've come from your auntie's damp basement or something, but taken together with your complexion, tunnel rat's the safest guess. I suspect you've learned sleight of hand that would make the finest prestidigitator proud, relieving passersby of the burden of having to carry their wallets, purses, mobiles, and whatever else your fingers might reach.

"You haven't been away from home very long. Your education makes that clear. And the way you're constantly on guard, even this far from the scene of our encounter, makes it clear you're running from something other than your bravura performance earlier."

The waiter interrupted with their coffees. He set down napkins, then Terence's cup and Jazz's glass. "Can I get you anything else?"

"We're perfect, thanks, Rob," Jazz told him.

He liked her using his name. Pleased, he put his tray under his arm and threaded back through the patio to the café.

"All right, you've read your share of Doyle," Jazz said, turning to Terence. She picked up her iced coffee and took a sip, wrinkling her nose. It needed sugar. "I won't argue. Rather, let's just cut to the 'so what?' I had the good fortune to get to something you wanted before you did and you're upset."

"You have skill, not good fortune."

Jazz shrugged. "Whatever. And what of it? You think I'm a tunnel rat. Pretty sure you live a bit higher than I do, breathe a rarer air. How does any of that lead to fancy coffee in the garden?"

The bag with the money and knickknacks she'd stolen from Mort's house—along with the strange holed blade—sat on the fourth chair, within reach of either of them. She was pretty sure that Terence hadn't even looked at it.

"What you did today was far beyond the scope of what you and your accomplices would normally attempt. That's simple deduction."

"We aspire to greater things."

Terence stirred his cappuccino and set the spoon aside. "Admirable, wanting to improve your lot." He took a sip. Jazz could smell the cinnamon wafting off the top. "But you'll forgive me, I hope, if I say I have difficulty believing in today's coincidence. I suspect, whether you're aware of it or not, there is another reason you were in that house today."

Her thoughts immediately flashed to the framed photographs in her bag. The shock of seeing her father in that old picture, standing with the Uncles, remained fresh.

"What do you know of the apparatus?"

Jazz frowned. "The what?"

Terence cocked his head, obviously surprised by her reply.

"The object you stole today," he whispered, glancing around, no longer as confident as he'd been. "What made you take it?"

Jazz smiled. She also whispered. It wouldn't do for them to be overheard, now that they were no longer skirting their subject. "I nicked plenty of things today. I only took the sodding blade because I saw it was what you were looking for and figured it was valuable."

He studied her, and Jazz saw the moment where he decided he believed her. Terence sighed and gave a small, self-deprecating laugh. "It's worth more to me than you can imagine, but to you it's worthless. You really only took it because you saw I wanted it?"

She nodded.

"And that house?" He lowered his voice further. "Mortimer Keating's house? Who chose that house in particular? You're new to this line of work. Your friends have been in the game longer, but neither of them seemed bright enough to organize a tea party, much less a high-society burglary."

"You underestimate them."

Terence raised his cappuccino in a mock toast, then sipped it. "Maybe so. Regardless, someone sent you to that house. But I see you won't tell me who it was. Fair enough. Can't say I blame you."

He set the cup down. "Have you ever heard of the Blackwood Club?"

Jazz started to shake her head but faltered. She'd never heard of any Blackwood Club, but the name Blackwood was familiar enough to stir up nausea in her gut. Josephine Blackwood had been present at her mother's murder—indeed, she "saw to it herself."

"No?" Terence asked.

"No," she replied, barely able to get the word out.

Now, at last, he looked at her bag. Since she'd set it on the chair, he had behaved as though it wasn't there at all, as though it did not contain the very thing for which he went to such great lengths at the house of the Uncle who'd once told her to call him Mort. *Mortimer Keating*. She let the name settle in her mind and found she liked having his identity. It made him less terrifying to her—made her feel like she could hurt him, if she could get close enough.

"If I ask you for it, would you give it to me?" Terence said, voice low.

"If I say no, will you try to take it?"

He chuckled softly, but then his expression grew serious again. "All that time, down there in the tunnels. I'm sorry, Jasmine, but I can't believe it's all coincidence."

"I couldn't care less what you believe."

Something flashed in those ice-blue eyes, and for the first time she thought that Terence might be a dangerous man. "Does the phrase 'the spirit of London' mean anything to you?"

She took a long drink of her iced coffee, almost draining it, and when she set it down the ice clinked in the glass. Then she reached for the bag, grabbed the strap, and pulled it onto her lap.

"Thank you for the coffee," she said. "But the conversation's gone a bit dull, don't you think? I'd best get going."

Yet she could not rise. Those blue eyes fixed her in place, so intense was his stare.

"Do you ever see ghosts down there?" Terence asked.

Her heart skipped a beat and she caught her breath, knowing that her face had betrayed her. Understanding dawned in his eyes. What the hell did he know? Jazz had been willing to chalk it all up to coincidence and let it go at that, but now she realized it could not be. Whatever this thing in her bag was, and whoever Terence might be, it was all connected. How this related to her mother's death and the Uncles she didn't know, but Terence had just asked a question that destroyed any assumptions she had made.

"You should come home with me," the thief said.

The words hung there between them. Jazz tried to make

sense of them, but her confusion had become a maelstrom. What was true? Who could she trust? Surely not this man she had just met, this gentleman bandit?

Jazz leaned across the table and lowered her voice.

"You might think yourself something more, Terry, but you're no better than me. You wear sophistication the way you wear that suit and tie, carry around your looks the way you carry that shoulder bag. Maybe you live high, but you might as well be down in the tunnels with me. You're a thief, not a bloody baron."

His brow furrowed and he stared at her a moment, then sipped at his cappuccino again. He sat in contemplation, searching her face for something—Jazz had no idea what. Slowly, Terence sat forward so that they leaned toward each other across the table. Prior to that moment, observers might have thought them uncle and niece, even father and daughter. But now passersby would think them quarreling lovers, no matter her age.

"I am a master."

"You're not *my* bloody master."

He tapped one finger on the table, then sat back. "I could be. You have aspirations? I could teach you. Help you fulfill them. I could show you a life that would otherwise always be out of your reach. You have natural talent, but with proper training you could achieve a lot more. You could have almost anything, really, but given your present circumstances, you might begin with a warm bed, clean clothes, the finest foods. And the security and confidence not to be so frightened all the time."

Jazz nearly shouted at him, denied being frightened. But

he'd already pointed out the way she looked around, always on guard. There would be no point in lying now.

"I have friends. I couldn't just—"

Terence stood, sliding his chair back. "You could. We've already established you haven't been down there long. How close could you have gotten in that time? How well do you even know these friends?"

"Better than I know you," she said.

But the question was not lost on her. The fact that Harry had chosen Mort's house to rob lingered in the back of her mind. But as for how close she had gotten to the others in the United Kingdom, Terence had no idea. A single thought of Cadge was all she needed to know that she had friends in the Underground. And maybe, where Stevie was concerned, more than friends.

"They'll be worried about me," Jazz said, holding the bag on her lap.

Terence glanced at it, then reluctantly pulled his gaze away. He plucked a wallet from his pocket and tossed a twenty-pound note on the table. It was far too much for their coffees, but he showed no inclination to wait for change. The money meant nothing to him.

And if the money meant nothing, then why had he broken into Mortimer Keating's house today? Why did he want that strange serrated blade?

"Tell me something," she said. "What's this apparatus you asked me about? What does it do?"

Terence hesitated a moment, then gave a small shake of his head. He pointed at the bag on her lap. "I need that. You have no idea how I need it. But I'm not going to try to take it from you. I'm hoping that at some point you'll be willing to give it to me. But I also meant what I said about teaching you. You're a remarkable girl, Jasmine. Only the dead belong so far underground. It's time for you to come back to life.

"I'm going now. But think about what I've said. If you want to try a different path from the one you're on now, meet me tomorrow afternoon at half-two in front of the Victoria and Albert Museum. I'll wait, but not for long."

Jazz stared at him.

Terence smiled, slung his jacket over his shoulder, and gave a small bow of his head. "A pleasure to meet you."

"And you, strangely enough," she replied.

He turned and strolled across the patio, weaving around other tables, and out into the park. In moments he was out of sight.

Jazz picked up her glass and drained the last of her coffee.

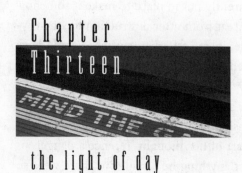

Chapter Thirteen

the light of day

For weeks, Jazz had felt as though the gloom and shadow below the city were her natural habitat, and every time she went upside, into the daylight world, her eyes had to adjust. But she'd been aboveground most of the day, and by the time she descended once more into the Underground, she had to learn to adjust to the darkness all over again.

With the bag over her shoulder—the weight of the blade Terence so desired seeming to want to pull her deeper—she followed the tracks of an abandoned tunnel and descended farther. The geography of the underworld had become second nature to her now. Jazz moved as though on autopilot, her mind absorbed by her conversation with the gentleman thief, his blue eyes locked in her memory. She stepped through the hole Harry had found in a hastily bricked-up wall and then started down the corridor to the Palace.

On the other side of that broken wall, she found the bucket that Bill had set there with several torches inside. Jazz took one and clicked it on. The light seemed to be swallowed by the darkness. As she started down the arched corridor—its marble columns apparently put in place to make it somehow more acceptable a retreat from utter destruction for the royals, ministers, and members of Parliament who would have used it—she wondered if any of the others would have been positioned out here by Harry to wait for her.

Jazz faltered. She gripped the strap of the bag and swore under her breath. Flashing the light around, she tried to decide her next step. Part of her thought Terence a dangerous man and did not trust anything he'd said. But there were so many other things to consider. Her life had been nothing but a terrifying puzzle since her mother's murder—a puzzle with a lot of missing pieces. Terence clearly had some of those pieces. Then there was the fundamental question of her future. Her mother had wanted her to hide forever, but there was more than one way to hide.

Her pulse raced with indecision. She didn't want to deceive anyone, and she refused to betray the kindness of those who had given her a place to belong. But she had to think of herself. *No one is to be trusted,* her mother had told her so often. *And sometimes you can't even trust yourself.* Jazz knew what she meant. Emotions could get in the way of the smart decisions.

She needed more time to think.

Slipping the bag from her shoulder, she glanced around. The torch picked out a square metal door, about three feet wide and waist high. The metal was rusted. Jazz went to investigate. She paused to listen for any sound that might indicate she was not alone in the corridor, but the only sounds were the rumble of a train above her head and the steady drip of water from somewhere nearby. Then the muffled sound of laughter reached her. It came from the Palace, but there were two doors and thirty feet of winding stairs separating her from the United Kingdom. For the moment, she was alone.

Shifting the torch to her left hand, she grabbed the handle on the rusted hatch and pulled. The door jerked. Rust sifted down. She tugged it again and it slid to one side. Jazz shone the torch into the hole and frowned. Searching with the light, it took her half a minute to realize what it was she was looking at. Though the pulleys must be just as rusted and any ropes rotted away by now, once upon a time this little three-foot-square box had been a lift of some kind, like a dumbwaiter in an old hotel. Whoever had built this retreat to keep bombs from raining down on the monarchy must have used the lift to bring down supplies and equipment. On the surface, it would have long since been covered over by something else. The mechanism was useless, but for the moment it would serve her well.

Unzipping her bag, she slid out the two framed photographs and put them inside the rusty metal box. The blade followed. She looked at it for several seconds, trying to make sense of the hole in the metal—big enough for her to slip her hand through—and the jagged teeth at the end of the thing. It might do someone a wicked bit of damage, but now that she studied it, the thing didn't really seem like a dagger or sword at all, rather a part of something else, some other . . . *apparatus.*

A screech of metal came from down the arched corridor.

Jazz thrust the blade into the old lift and slid the door closed as quietly as she could, pulse racing madly. She zipped the bag and put it over her shoulder, then pointed the torch down along the corridor in the direction of the sound—which had to have been the door that led to the spiral stairs down to the Palace.

"Nothing up my sleeve," a voice whispered behind her.

She spun around just in time to see something tumble to the stone floor. Her torch caught it as it struck the ground—a top hat with a thick brim. It rolled in an arc along the stones. When it came to rest, something moved inside. Jazz held her breath. A tiny rabbit poked its face out from inside the hat, sniffing querulously at the rust-flaked air. The little creature emerged, paused a moment, then darted toward the wall, where it vanished.

Jazz's throat felt dry. It had looked so real, not like a phantom at all. She crouched and reached for the brim of the top hat, but it faded out as her fingers passed through it.

She raised her torch and pointed it back into the darkness the way she'd come. The magician again. She had seen him more and more frequently, and he seemed to be growing more tangible somehow. Yet like the rest of the spirits of old London that lingered in the Underground, he had always been just an echo, never showing anything resembling awareness. So if he was a ghost, either a manifestation of the resonance that past events had left on the city or actually the spirit of a person who had once lived, why did he show up more than the other ghosts? The other specters haunted the Underground, but it had begun to feel as though the magician haunted *her*.

A cough sounded from the direction of the Palace. Jazz swung her torch round.

"Who is it?" came a voice from along the corridor. The

orange glow of a cigarette burned in the shadows. "Who's there?"

She sounded afraid. Jazz couldn't blame her after those men had discovered their previous shelter—after Cadge's murder.

"It's just me," she said, hurrying toward the other girl, bag over her shoulder.

"Jazz?"

"Yeah."

Then they were close enough to make out each other's face in the illumination of the torchlight. Leela stood gaping at her, cigarette dangling from one hand. The girl's exotic beauty transformed into a fool's grin and she rushed to embrace Jazz.

"Fuck's sake, girl. We've been worried sick. Harry's out of his mind." With a laugh Leela stood back and looked Jazz over. "None the worse for wear, are you? Let's get you home, then."

The girl tossed her cigarette down and ground it underfoot. She took Jazz by the hand and hurried her back to the metal door, and they descended the spiral staircase to the United Kingdom's lair. When Leela opened the door at the bottom and they stepped out into the monarchy shelter, most of the others didn't even look up. Hattie and Gob were playing cards on the floor. Switch, Bill, and Marco were eating big bowls of pasta with red sauce at a round table. Off to the right, near the shelves of books that were their mentor's own personal library, Harry and Stevie were talking quietly, drinking from tumblers of whiskey.

"Harry," Leela said.

"Back so soon?" Harry asked as he turned. Then he saw Jazz and his eyes lit up. "Well, now, my pets, didn't I tell you she'd be back? Come in, Jazz girl! Come in!"

The others started calling her name. Bill remained silent, as always, but gave her a smile and a thumbs-up sign. Gob and Hattie jumped up and rushed toward her, but Harry beat them to her. The old man wrapped her in his arms. Jazz couldn't help smiling, and she loved the musty scent of his clothes and the dash of cologne he sometimes used. His stubbly cheek scraped hers. Then Harry stepped back, holding her at arm's length.

"Let me look at you! Still in one piece. Good. Good."

"Glad to see you, Harry."

"Glad to see me, she says!" he crowed, looking around at the others. "We were worried sick about her, weren't we? I sent 'em all out looking for you, Jazz girl, but no sign of you at all. Even kept an eye on the police station myself, just in case they'd brought you in."

Stevie drifted up behind Harry during this speech. He had his arms crossed, betraying no interest in hugging her, much to her dismay.

"I told him not to panic," Stevie said. "You were off and running."

Hattie came up beside Jazz and bumped shoulders with her. The girl wore a purple French beret, hair tucked underneath it, and smiled saucily at her. "Don't listen to a word, Jazz. Our Mr. Sharpe was even more worried about you than Harry. Thought you'd been hurt or lost or fell down a hole or something. Jazz through the looking glass."

"Well," Stevie said, glancing awkwardly away before

meeting her gaze again. "Had to come up with some reason for you to have been gone so long. What I said was, I knew you hadn't been nicked. And the bloke with the bag who was chasing you, we slowed him down enough so he just gave up. Wanted to get out of there even quicker than us—hopped in a cab and was gone."

Harry linked arms with Jazz and escorted her to the table. The others all gathered round as she sat down. The old man had seemed spry enough, but as he leaned on the back of a chair, she saw how much the injuries from his beating still pained him. His smile faltered but he did not let it vanish.

"What about that gent, love? I'm afraid when Stevie told me about the fellow, I couldn't make any sense of it. You all saw the mark leave the house and set the alarm. Far as we know, nobody else lives there, so where did this mysterious man come from?"

Jazz fought to keep her smile on her face. Harry talked about the mark—about Uncle Mort—like the house was chosen at random. But from what Terence had said, and what Jazz herself had seen in that house, that was simply too much coincidence for her to swallow. One of the thugs the mayor had sent into the tunnels had been a BMW man who worked for the Uncles, and now one of the wealthy men they'd stolen from had been an Uncle, a man present at the murder of her mother.

The temptation to confront him with her questions that very moment was strong. But Jazz felt sure that Harry wouldn't make it so simple. She had no doubt his concern for her was genuine, but there were many things she suspected he wasn't telling her, and that troubled her.

"No idea who he was," she said, putting on a mystified expression as she gazed around the gathered faces of the United Kingdom. "But he's a thief too."

She proceeded to tell the story of her break-in to Mortimer Keating's house, including the moment the motion sensors clicked off and her flight from the premises upon being discovered by the house's other intruder. But Jazz didn't mention that Terence had caught up to her, and she told Harry she hadn't even gotten a good look at the man's face.

"He knew what he was doing," she said. "Had these little hi-tech gadgets that he attached to the keypad for the alarm to keep it from going off."

"What did he steal?" Gob asked.

Jazz shrugged. "No idea."

"Who cares? The question is, what did Jazz take?" Leela said, blowing plumes of smoke from her nostrils. Harry didn't like them smoking down here, but in the excitement, he didn't seem to have noticed.

"Excellent question," Harry said, eyeing the bag she'd set on the ground by her chair.

Jazz grinned and pulled the bag up onto her lap. Her pulse sped up again and she chided herself for being nervous. It wasn't as if anyone could tell that she'd had anything else in the bag.

"First and most importantly, there's this," she said, pulling Hattie's pink bonnet from the bag. Hattie squealed, grabbed the hat, and held it against her as though she were five years old and Jazz had just returned her favorite stuffed bear.

"Otherwise, not much, I'm afraid. Our mystery man was there almost immediately." She reached into the bag and pulled out several silk ties, a quartet of antique books, a couple of rings, and the wedge of cash she'd found in Mortimer Keating's sock drawer.

Marco reached for the money and Harry slapped his hand away. Picking it up, he counted silently, fanning the bills with the speed of a bank teller. Harry's smile grew wide.

"Over two thousand here. Considering the circumstances, well done, Jazz."

"Who keeps two thousand pounds in their sock drawer?" she asked.

Switch laughed. "Rich fucking bastards, that's who."

"Language," Hattie snapped, and Switch looked properly chastened.

"There's also this," Jazz went on. From the bag she took a gold watch with diamonds set into the face. It sparkled in the dim light of the bunker.

"Now, that *is* lovely," Harry said, nodding. "You keep that for yourself if you like, Jazz girl. No less than you deserve for your quick mind and fleet feet today."

"I couldn't," she replied. "Besides, it wouldn't fit me. You take it."

Harry seemed overcome by the gesture, but she couldn't tell if his reaction was genuine or merely theatrics. He clutched the watch to his chest, nodding, and then looked up at her.

"What I'd really like to know, lass, is where you've been all this time. We truly did fear for you."

Jazz felt her face grow warm and wondered if the light was bright enough down there for Harry to see her cheeks flush pink. Did he suspect she had lied to him?

"I'm sorry to have worried you all. I'd just had such a fright that I needed to clear my head. I took the Tube to

Covent Garden and wandered for a while, had a coffee, watched the mothers strolling with their babies. When I realized how much time had passed, I came back as quickly as I could."

Harry nodded as though he understood perfectly. "You had a close call today, and no arguing that. But I hope it hasn't put you off our little endeavors."

Jazz smiled. "Not in the least. We still came out on top. And a coincidence like this—it couldn't happen twice, could it? Two people trying to rip off the same house at the same time. What are the odds?"

"Precisely," Harry said, but in his smile she saw a flicker of some doubt.

In the dark, late at night, Jazz felt as though she could hear the voice of the city coming up from deep beneath the ground. They were already so far down it was difficult to imagine anything deeper, but Harry had told those stories about tribes of people who had lived in natural-cavern formations far below the Underground for generations without ever seeing the light of day. Perhaps what she heard was the chanting of some subhuman clan. But Jazz could not make herself believe that. What she heard didn't really come to her through her ears but in her mind and in her gut. It resonated in her like the low hum of electrical wires, but with the rise and fall of music. It pulled at her. Often, of late, she had felt as though something called to her from deeper underground, and the lure of it was even more powerful when everyone else had gone to sleep and she could do nothing but lie there and listen.

From time to time, she heard the distant shriek and rumble of trains passing by. The air vents brought the occasional sound all the way from the surface. But for the most part, the Palace was silent.

But Jazz couldn't sleep. Thoughts and doubts churned in her head, playing on her hopes and fears and loyalties, her love for her mother and her need for justice, and the exhaustion that had begun to weigh on her. Even now, when she should be resting, she could not. Living down here, hiding, drained her of strength and spirit.

Often she dreamed of her mother, and of Cadge, but sometimes her dreams were nothing more than visits to her old house, to her school, mundane nights out for a curry with some friends. But now all of those school friends were no longer a part of her life; she had left them behind without so much as a thought. True, she had never been as close to them as she might have been. The way her mother had raised her made it difficult for her to grow close to anyone, to trust anyone. Jazz didn't think she'd had a best friend since the age of six or seven, until she'd met Cadge.

Harry and the United Kingdom were her friends now. At least, she thought they were. They cared about her, and Harry was always so proud of her. Her mother was dead and she had no one else—no one to run to, no one who could hide her. Terence had hinted that he could be that safe harbor, but she had only just met him.

You didn't know Harry when he took you in, she thought.

The truth did not comfort her. Jazz plumped up the folded blanket she was using for a pillow and turned onto her other side, eyes open in the dark. Only the tiniest bit of illumination came from a small light that Harry left burning in the corridor to guide them to the toilets during the night.

What time is it? she wondered. The Palace was large enough that most of them could have had their own rooms, but, with the exception of Stevie, all of the kids had instinctively grouped into twos and threes. Safety in numbers, Jazz figured. She had paired off with Hattie, who snored quietly nearby. Her breathing was low and steady. Jazz listened carefully but could not hear anyone rustling in the dark. It must be late for them all to be so deeply lost in slumber.

In the dark, she imagined she could see Terence's ice-blue eyes.

Jazz did not want to die down here. If there was any possibility that she could have a better life yet still stay safe, wouldn't her mother have wanted that for her? Wouldn't Cadge have told her she was a fool not to at least try?

And beyond safety and the future, there were other concerns. Jazz wanted answers. The connections were there. The Uncles, the BMW men, the mayor. Harry had sent her to rob Mort's house, and now she wondered about the other two houses they'd robbed. Who owned those? What did Harry know, really, about the Uncles? What did Terence know about the ghosts of old London? What the hell was the Blackwood Club?

"Bloody hell," she whispered.

With a sigh, Jazz gave up on sleep entirely. She rose quietly, slipped on her trainers, and left her room. In the corridor, she paused to listen for any sign that others were about, but all she heard was Harry snoring loudly at the end of the hall. Grabbing her torch, she padded quietly to the door and went up the spiral stairs. If Hattie woke, she'd think Jazz had gone to the bathroom.

The door at the top of the stairs scraped the floor, so she had to open it very slowly. She left the door ajar and went along that arched corridor to the old rusted dumbwaiter, slid aside the door panel, and shone the torchlight inside. The light glinted off the blade.

But when she reached in, she grabbed one of the framed photographs instead. The blade had some terrible significance to Terence, and she could feel when she carried it that there was something unusual about it. The photographs, however, had lingered in her mind even more.

Jazz held the frame in her hand and shone the torch on the picture of that grim assemblage. Mortimer Keating stood on the left. She recognized other Uncles and wondered whether theirs were the voices she'd heard in her house while her mother's corpse cooled.

And there was her father.

The Blackwood Club? Logic at least suggested it. Josephine Blackwood controlled the Uncles, who were in turn served by thugs and lackeys Jazz thought of as the BMW men. Since her father's death, she had been aware that he was involved with the Uncles, but she had never known how, and any time her inquiries to her mother had strayed into that territory, the subject was changed. Once or twice, her mother had warned her away. They were being looked after; that was all that mattered. But even when her mother assured her of this, Jazz had known the woman did not believe it.

Come on, then, Dad. Help me out. What the hell is the Blackwood Club?

She stared at the image so long that she lost track of the time. Her father had been involved in something ugly, that much was evident. But a photograph wasn't going to give her the answers she wanted.

Beyond tired, eyelids drooping, she went to put the photo back into its hiding place and caught the frame on the edge of the metal door. It fell from her hand. Jazz tried to snatch it up again but only succeeded in striking it with her torch. The photograph hit the ground, shattering the glass and cracking the frame.

Dropping to a crouch, she shone the torch on the broken glass. The picture looked undamaged, but the frame was ruined. Glancing around to make sure no one had heard, she carefully picked the largest pieces of glass off the floor and put them inside the rusted dumbwaiter, over to one side so that she wouldn't accidentally cut herself later when retrieving the blade or the photos. The broken frame followed in pieces. Soon, only the picture itself and a bunch of glass shards remained on the stone floor. Some of the glass had gone down into the grooves of the mortar, and she would never be able to get them up without a broom. Careful not to cut her fingers, she brushed as much of the glass as she could onto the photo and dumped it with the rest of the broken shards inside the old service lift.

Before hiding the photograph again, she studied it one last time. The glass had nicked it in many places, but she was glad to see it hadn't ruined the picture. With her torch's light to guide her, she went to put the photo back, and only then did she notice the writing on the reverse side.

It was the imprint of a photographer's stamp. Curious, she held it up and read the words.

15 July, 1981
Harold Fowler, Photographer

The grand entrance to the Victoria and Albert Museum was a bit of loveliness dropped in amid an otherwise austere facade. The receding arch around the doorway made it look as though the museum were the home of giants, and the people passing to and fro in the intersection of Cromwell Gardens and Exhibition Road seemed Lilliputian in comparison.

Terence stood leaning against a lamppost with his hands thrust into his pockets, as casual as you please. A shopping bag from Harrods rested on the pavement by his feet. Like the museum, he had a certain austerity about him, but he also had the dashing looks of a 1940s film star. Today he wore khaki trousers, brown shoes, and a green short-sleeved linen shirt. He might not have been wearing the suit, but Jazz thought his clothes still looked quite expensive. The man seemed to breathe money and confidence. She had known girls who went weak in the knees in the presence of arrogant men, but she'd never been one of them.

Now she understood that there was a difference between arrogance and confidence. Terence had swagger, and in spite of herself, she liked it.

Jazz had tied her hair back in a ponytail and donned big dark sunglasses she had nicked from a street-corner vendor just after coming off the Tube. She wore a crushed lilac-hued gypsy skirt and a white spaghetti-strap top and carried a big knit shoulder bag. Had she tried to leave the Palace dressed that way, there would have been many questions, so she had worn a loose cotton top over the tank and a pair of jeans, then changed clothes in the ladies' at Waterstone's a few streets from the museum.

She considered trying to sneak up on him but instead purposely let him see her coming. After so many weeks attempting to be as inconspicuous as possible, it felt strange and liberating to switch gears. Jazz strode across the street as though it was some fashion runway in Milan. Several car horns blatted the approval of male motorists and she waved to one driver. She was just a girl out shopping today. If the Uncles were looking for her, they would be searching for a frightened creature scurrying in the alleys of London, not this young woman. In her time with Harry Fowler, Jazz had learned more about perspective and appearance than in any of her meager efforts at onstage drama.

Terence stood up straight, smiling as she approached.

"You clean up nicely," he told her as she stepped onto the sidewalk.

Jazz gave him a flirtatious toss of her head. Without the glasses, her eyes would have betrayed her turmoil. She kept them on.

"I'll choose to take that as a compliment."

"It is," Terence replied. "No one would mistake you for a tunnel rat today."

"Not even you."

He cocked an eyebrow. "I wasn't sure you'd come."

"I wouldn't have," she admitted, still hiding behind her glasses. "But I had a bit of an epiphany last night. I'm not going to find the answers I'm looking for down below."

His expression turned grim and he replied with a knowing nod. Then he gave her a more thorough inspection and bent to pick up the Harrods shopping bag.

"This may be easier than I thought," he said.

"What's that?"

"I picked up some things for you. Camouflage, if you will. But I think you'll do as is. At your age, the Bohemian look is a fashionable choice. Though I'm impressed you're able to keep clothes so clean down there. Wherever there is."

Jazz put a hand on his arm and leaned in to speak to him in an exaggerated whisper. "I only stole them this morning."

Terence gazed at her again. "Well done, you. We're better off, I think. I had to guess at sizes. I do hope I succeeded with the shoes, however. Those simply won't do."

He pointed to her feet and Jazz looked down. The sandals she wore were not particularly ragged, and she'd worn trainers until she changed at the bookstore.

"What's wrong with them? You said the Bohemian look was fashionable."

He smiled, blue eyes sparkling with mischief. "True enough. But there's the genuine Bohemian and then there's the young and rich who adopt BoHo to dress down. The shoes and the jewelry always give them away."

Terence reached into the Harrods bag and took out a shoe box. Jazz stared at him a moment, trying to figure out what the man had in mind that required her to wear different shoes. Out of curiosity, she surrendered. Taking the box from him, she opened it to find a pair of very expensive-looking shoes, all straps and high heels.

"You have some kind of fetish?"

"We all have fetishes. Mine don't involve shoes, if that sets you at ease."

"Not much, no," Jazz said. But she slipped off her sandals, put them into the box, and put the heels on instead. "Perfect fit."

Terence admired her feet and legs. "Excellent. They change your whole appearance."

"They're only shoes."

"You're taller in them. They alter your center of balance so that you stand differently. They accentuate your legs, draw attention, and succeed in making your age ambiguous. And they suggest a certain affluence, which is the most important element."

"Of what?" Jazz smiled at him. "You're a very strange man, Terence."

"I'll never deny it, love. But bear with me. I predict you're going to have a very entertaining day. Exciting, even."

He took the box—now with the discarded sandals in it—and returned it to the Harrods bag. Then he drew out another, smaller box, and offered it to her. Jazz knew of only one thing that routinely came in such small boxes, but was still taken aback when she opened it and discovered a quartet of thin gold bangle bracelets.

"What the hell are you doing, you mad thing?" she asked, staring at the gold.

"We have work to do, Jasmine, and you need to be dressed for the job. I told you if you came to meet me today, I would show you a different way to hide and to live. This is step one. Class is in session. Put them on. All on one wrist, please."

Jazz put aside any hesitation and slid the four gold bands onto her left wrist. They were simple, but she liked them a great deal. Whatever the hell Terence was up to, she had to admit that she couldn't wait to see where it led next.

He put that box back into the Harrods bag as well and

then offered her his arm. With a nervous laugh, she took it, and they strolled together away from the Victoria and Albert Museum. It had not escaped her notice that the thief had not yet mentioned the blade. She carried it in her shoulder bag, wrapped in her blue jeans.

"You're really not going to tell me where we're going?"

Terence gave her that look again, mischief dancing in his eyes. "We have several stops to make, actually. Promises to keep, and miles to go before we sleep."

They walked for a while, and for the first time since her world had changed, Jazz found herself not at all concerned with her destination. Terence presented her with a game of discovery, and she went along with it quite willingly. Even for late summer it was quite warm, but a breeze blew her skirt around her legs and the heat of the sun was welcome on her skin.

When Terence led her across the street toward a boutique salon, Jazz slowed, teetering a little on her new heels. He urged her on, but when they reached the sidewalk, she stopped and forced him to face her.

"What are we doing here?"

He raised his eyebrows. "Don't you have a mirror down there? Tying back that hair doesn't make it any less a rat's nest. You've got to have it cut and washed. A change in color would suit you as well, if you're trying to hide in plain sight. And your nails are worse than a hag's. Manicure and pedicure are both in order."

Jazz blanched. She drew her arm away from him, staring first at Terence and then at the salon. He had to know what he was suggesting. If she had her hair done professionally, cut and dyed—never mind a bloody manicure—she would never be able to explain it to Harry and the others. She'd have to tell the truth, an idea that troubled her deeply given the secrets she suspected Harry was hiding from her.

Only if you go back.

Her throat went dry. She licked her lips and took a step away from him. Terence stared at her, but Jazz studied the ground instead. In the back of her mind she had known all along that by coming to meet him she was expressing her interest in changing course, in discovering if he could change her life the way he'd promised the day before. But she'd only come because of what she'd seen on the back of that photograph of her father and the Uncles—*Harold Fowler, Photographer.* She'd wanted to see Terence again, there was no denying that. But she'd told herself she had come only for whatever information he might provide about the mysteries surrounding her. She had not planned to leave the Underground for good. Not now. Not at this very moment.

Jazz slipped the gold bangles from her wrist and started to offer them back to him. Terence closed her hands in his, bracelets inside, and through sheer force of will made her meet his gaze. His eyes were full of a grim determination and kindness that belied his profession.

"Put yourself in my hands, Jasmine. You won't regret it."

She stared at him. "I can't."

"I understand why you wouldn't trust me—"

"I don't trust *anyone.*"

Terence released her hands. His face lit up, and she could not turn away from those mesmerizing blue eyes.

"Then you've got nothing to lose."

Chapter Fourteen

invincible

The shop smelled like an explosion in a perfume factory. The scent was cloying and sickening, hanging heavy on her throat and in her nose. Her eyes smarted. *How can people work in here?* she thought. At every counter there was another made-up lady, women whose job description seemed to include using as many of the products they were trying to sell as possible. Heavy lipstick, thick eyeliner, foundation, blusher, much of it apparently pasted on with tools more suited to a building site. Jazz actually found herself slightly perturbed by some of the women, their visages so solid that it seemed they would crack if they dropped their constant smiles. She imagined them knocking off after a day at work, grimacing and frowning in front of the mirror while their makeup mask fell off in chunks. Underneath, there would be the real person.

She caught sight of herself in another mirror and paused yet again. It would take her a long time to get used to the new look. While the stylist had been working, Jazz felt a thrilling sense of expectation, the past shouting at her to take control, the future offering that control to her. Her hair was several shades darker, six inches shorter, and cut in a trendy tousled look that she knew caught people's attention. She'd attracted more than one appreciative glance since leaving the salon. Inevitably, the lookers' eyes switched from her to Terence, their smiles replaced by distracted frowns.

Maybe she shocked them. She liked that.

"There's no way I'm going to sit here and let one of those monsters turn me into someone else," Jazz said. Terence stood beside her, the sleeve of his shirt just touching her shoulder, and he uttered a quiet laugh.

"I don't blame you," he said. "But you need a touch of something."

Jazz beamed up at him. "Meet me out front in ten minutes." Terence raised an eyebrow and Jazz walked away, not looking back.

She felt more like herself than ever, yet her look had changed so much. Maybe it was freedom born of making a positive choice. As she weaved between the counters she thought of Harry, and the United Kingdom, and her smile slowly slipped.

"Can I help you with something, madam?" a made-up lady asked.

"No thanks," Jazz said. "Just browsing."

And she browsed. Moving from counter to counter, one display to the next, passing her hand across a hundred different shades of the same color, consulting charts and sniffing at testers, and a couple of minutes later she saw Terence pass by in a mirror, a knowing smile on his face as he headed for the front of the shop. *I hope he thinks I'm making a run for it*, Jazz thought, but at the same time she knew that was unlikely. He could see that he excited her.

Five minutes later she went into the ladies' restroom and spread her haul on the shelf above the sink. Good stuff, most of it, but she'd never been keen on makeup. She chose lip gloss instead of lipstick and a touch of something around her eyes. When she reached for the blusher, she realized she did not need it; she was already flushed.

Smiling, she left the stolen makeup in the bathroom and went to meet Terence. Out on the sidewalk, he smiled appreciatively and offered quiet applause. They fell into step together quite naturally.

A black BMW drifted by as they turned the corner into Brompton Road.

Jazz turned away and looked into a shop window, browsing children's fashions at ridiculous prices. She stared past her own reflection at that of the BMW, saw that the windows were down, and tried to make out who could be inside. *They won't know me*, she thought. Not now. Not like this. But there was little comfort in that thought, because if they saw her, they *would* know her. She hadn't changed that much. Different clothes and a new haircut could not make her a new person, and if she caught their eye, they would see the fear and uncertainty that still rode her shoulders.

"What is it?" Terence asked.

Jazz shook her head. The BMW picked up speed and moved on, overtaking a cyclist who lifted a hand and shouted something unintelligible.

"Really, dear, I don't think we should settle down just yet."

Jazz turned away from the kids' clothes display and glanced after the BMW, then looked at Terence. She tried to smile but it would not come.

"Oh," he said. He looked after the receding car as well, then nodded as another passed them by. "Plenty of those here. Posh area. Some would say exclusive. Park your rusting Ford Sierra here and it's liable to be towed away."

Jazz nodded. "I'm okay." *Just bloody terrified.*

"Do you want to—"

"No, no. No more talk. You were taking me somewhere?"

Terence smiled uncertainly, then held her hand and linked her arm through his once again. "Plenty of time," he said. "Secrets are good, but remember: a secret that hurts is best shared."

"Where'd you get that from, a fortune cookie?"

"Winnie the Pooh."

Jazz laughed out loud, a few faces turned their way, and she wondered how she could possibly feel so safe with just one man.

They walked along Brompton Road until Harrods stood before them, one of its main corner entrances marked by two men in top hats and tails welcoming customers in and bidding farewell when they left.

"I thought you'd been here already today," she said.

"Yesterday," Terence said. "I wanted to buy you something, and it was a good opportunity to pinpoint a few of the more obvious dangers."

"Dangers?"

Terence leaned in close until their heads were almost touching. "There are cameras everywhere in there," he said quietly. The noise of the traffic would drown his voice from everyone but her. "Store guards walking the floors all day. Security contacts on every display case with coded entries for certain people holding certain keys. If something big is lifted, the whole place goes into lockdown. Lifts stop, electronic doors close and lock, and every alarm is linked to the local police station."

"You are seriously telling me we're going to rob Harrods?" Jazz asked, and even saying the words sent a thrill down her spine.

Terence stood up straight again and laughed out loud. London passed them by and ignored them, because that's what London was, an impersonal place crammed with people. Millions of stories to be told, and every one private. "Not *all* of it," he said. "Just one small bit."

"I just want a carrier bag," Jazz said, smiling.

Terence held her hand, ready to cross the busy street. "Now listen," he said. And he told her what they were about to do.

Jazz knew that she was being tested. Terence had seen what she could do at Mort's house, but once could so easily be luck. Sure, she'd nicked her clothes this morning, lifted a few tubes of lipstick and eyeliner from Boots, but any street kid could do that. Practice made perfect. Some scores, though, could never be practiced. They would count on sleight of hand, confidence, calmness, and a total awareness of one's surroundings while never becoming the center of someone else's attention. Almost anyone could *learn* to be a good thief, but few were born with all the skills required to make it come naturally.

Yet she welcomed this test. Not only because it would be exciting but because it would be proving herself in Terence's eyes, and that was becoming more important to her than ever. She was a girl full of questions, and for a long time she had feared the answers. Now, when the questions were multiplying more rapidly than ever, something in Terence made her less afraid.

She also believed he had answers. The weight of the blade in her shoulder bag, the apparatus he had mentioned but not explained, why something as important as this blade seemed to be was kept in Mort's house—here was a man with secrets. Jazz was sure that once he viewed her as more of an equal, he would take Pooh's advice and share them.

As they reached the pavement near the corner entrance, Terence slipped the bag from Jazz's shoulder. "Can't take this in there," he said.

She turned to him, ready to confront him over the bag. *He could just take off with it*, she thought. *I'll bet he's faster than me, when he needs to be. And I'll bet he knows this area too, which alleys to slip into, which doors will be unlocked, which shops have a back entrance* . . . She fisted her hands, not quite sure whether she was ready to fight, and felt her shoulders tighten with tension.

But Terence smiled casually at her and threw her a surreptitious wink. "They look more closely at people carrying bags," he said. He strode on toward the main entrance as if he did not have a care in the world.

If only she could feel like that. A world without cares. She had never known that, ever, and neither had her mother.

As she followed Terence, Jazz felt a sudden rush of emotion about her mother, stronger and more unexpected than anything she had felt for weeks. It struck her like a punch, clouding her eyes and building a rapid pressure behind her face. *She never had a day without fear,* she thought. *Never got up in the morning and looked out the window, saw birds in the garden and clouds in the sky, thought about what a beautiful day it was. She always looked further. Past the birds and the garden, searching for people who wanted to do her harm.*

Jazz knew that if she cried now, she would blow the whole day. She would fail the test, and Terence would likely never trust her again.

She never had her own life to lead. She always led mine for me, worried about me, building fears about me.

She watched his back, staring at a point between his shoulders and concentrating on the way his shirt moved as he walked. Damn him, not only was he smooth and intelligent, he was also fit. Damn him!

And I know what she was thinking . . . when they held her down, came at her with the knife . . . She was thinking . . . about . . . me!

"Wait for me, for Christ's sake!" Jazz said, blowing her anger and venting the pressure behind her eyes. Terence looked back, hiding his surprise well. The doorman glanced at Jazz, a small smirk touching his face, and she rolled her eyes and shook her head.

"Sorry, babe," Terence said, recovering sharply.

Jazz shook her head and blew air up at her new ragged fringe. "S'okay. Hot, that's all."

They reached the security point at the entrance and Terence strode straight to the desk. "Afternoon," he said. "I don't suppose I could leave this with you for safekeeping?

I'm an antiques dealer and I've just bought this, but it's bulky and heavy."

"No problem, sir," the tall doorman said. He tore a ticket from a small book and handed it to Terence, tying its corresponding number around the bag's handles. "I'll just pop it in our bag room."

"Many thanks." Terence waited for Jazz this time, offering her a smile, but she could also see the hint of something else behind his eyes. Anger? Maybe. She hoped so. She liked the idea that something she did would shake him up.

The doorman opened the door and they stepped in, Jazz giving him her most dazzling smile.

"What was that?" Terence asked quietly as they walked inside the great shop.

"Attracting attention to ourselves. We're good, honest people, leaving our bag at the entrance."

"Really?"

"Yep. Really. Oh, look at this!"

They walked the floors of Harrods, the cheerful couple, the wealthy shoppers. Jazz pointed out some suits and Terence looked, felt the fabric, and nodded appreciatively. They passed the waxwork of Mohamed Al Fayed and swapped a whispered comment, Terence smiling and Jazz giggling as they passed into the cosmetics sections. Jazz had had enough of cosmetics for one day but she browsed nonetheless, squirting a couple of testers onto her wrists and pressing them up to Terence's nose. He sniffed dutifully, screwed up his nose, and shook his head. The second time she touched his lips with her wrist, accidentally, she thought, but as she turned and walked into the cheese section of the store she wasn't so sure.

Terence seemed more at home here. The smells were tremendous, and Jazz followed him as he cruised back and forth along the counters. He asked for samples of several cheeses and offered her a bite, but they all smelled too strong for her taste. They moved through into the tea and coffee section, then the chocolate and cakes, and while Jazz perused the grand displays, Terence acquired small bags of produce. He did not seem especially excited about any purchase, and Jazz wondered whether he shopped here regularly.

For her part, she did her best to hold back her sense of awe. She smiled as she contemplated the wondrous chocolates and the mountainous cakes, never quite able to exude boredom but happy with a middle ground. She took a few chocolate samples when they were offered, nodding in sumptuous appreciation. She checked out the prices on a couple of the cakes and tried not to let her shock show.

Terence stood beside her and put his arm gently around her, cupping her elbow in his hand. "Left here is the meat section," he said. "I want to pick something up for dinner. You like lamb?"

Jazz was amazed at his presumption. "Dinner?"

"Unless you were planning on going home this evening?"

She looked away, confused, silently cursing him for doing this to her here and now. *Testing me*, she thought. *He knows I nearly blew it on the way in, so now he's trying to distract me. One wrong word or movement from me, and the whole nick is off.* She knew that if that happened, the distance between them would expand rapidly, and by the time they left Harrods, Terence would likely take the blade from her—by force if necessary—and that would be the last she ever saw of him.

"Lamb's good," she said. "I assume you know how to cook it properly?" Jazz herself had no idea, but she wanted to appeal to his vanity. Steer him away from trying to trip her up.

His only response was a smile.

The smell in the meat section was similarly heady, the tang of fresh blood blending with fresh fish to provide an aroma that reminded Jazz strangely of the makeup shop. It consumed the atmosphere of the place, and any amount of extract ducts and air-conditioning could not change that.

Jazz berated herself for glancing up at the ceiling. Air-conditioning, yes, and extravagant plasterwork, decorative light fittings, and hams hanging from heavy hooks. But, as Terence had said, there were cameras everywhere in here.

After Terence selected a cut of meat and added even more to his collection of bags, he touched her arm and gently guided her back through the fruit section—more heady smells, more glorious displays—and into the jewelry rooms.

Nothing too extravagant, he had said. *Nothing too expensive. All the really pricey stuff is well protected, and much of it isn't even on display. But we'll not go through this for something cheap.* He told her that he'd leave it up to her what she decided to take. Another test.

They were the perfect happy couple as they passed into the fine-jewelry section. Jazz's heart sped up at what was to come, and she could feel her senses heightened. It might well be that Terence was testing her. But this, she promised herself, was going to be fun.

"That one's gorgeous."

Jazz tapped her fingernail on the glass display cabinet above a tray of necklaces. It held five pieces of jewelry and she was indicating the most garish one, a heavy metal chain with bulky mountings for the five diamonds.

"Which one, madam?" the jewelry manager asked.

"That . . . Oh, that one's nice too."

"Can we see them all?" Terence asked.

Jazz rolled her eyes at the assistant. "Steve!"

Terence held out his hands in a what-can-I-do gesture. "Show her this one, she'll like that one. Show her that one, she'll like this one. By the time she chooses, her birthday will be over." He frowned and leaned forward. "Oh my, that *is* a beautiful piece!" He was examining the assistant's necklace, a subtle, thin chain with a single sapphire in a tasteful mount. The woman actually blushed, smiling at him just a little too long for comfort.

Jazz smiled inwardly. *Oh yes, she likes him.*

"Don't you think, Lucy?"

Jazz glanced at the woman's neck and saw a nervous flush starting across her chest. "Quite," she said.

Terence smiled at the assistant and nodded down at the display case. "Well, we'll have a look at those," he said.

Jazz wasn't sure she liked this I'm-in-charge act from Terence, but it seemed to be working. The assistant barely saw her anymore, and even when she withdrew the tray, unclipped the necklace, and placed it around Jazz's neck, it was Terence she looked at.

"Not bad," Terence said.

The woman nodded. "It's gorgeous. Catches her eyes."

Her, not *your.* Jazz batted her eyelids at Terence, knowing that the assistant would not see.

"How much is it?" Jazz asked.

The woman moved back slightly, taking the necklace from Jazz's throat and laying it out across both of her hands. It caught the artificial lights and dazzled, throwing light a thousand different ways. "This piece is seven thousand pounds," she said. "It's quite unique, handmade, and there are matching earrings and a bracelet if you're interested."

"Seven thousand," Jazz said, trying to sound disappointed. *Seven fucking thousand!* she was actually thinking, but she was delighted at her act. Her face did not actually drop, but she feigned sudden disinterest.

"This one looks glorious," Terence said. "More similar to your own, madam."

The woman blushed deeper, fussing around as if trying to hide it. "Sorry to say, mine isn't quite the same quality."

"Jewelry is given worth by its wearer, not its maker. That's what I always say." He was looking right at her and continued to do so until the woman met his gaze. She looked away again, and Jazz saw a brief, wry smile curl his lip.

He knows all about himself, she thought. But there was a big difference between arrogance and confidence. And, anyway, it was all part of the job.

The woman swapped necklaces and held the second one to Jazz's throat.

Terence hummed in appreciation.

Jazz asked how much this one was.

"This is nine thousand four hundred," the woman said. "It really does catch your character, madam. So stylish and modern."

"Nine thousand," Jazz said. She reached up and held the necklace. She did not actually force the woman to let go, but still the assistant took one step back, keeping her eyes on the piece.

"Perhaps we should look more in the five-figure range," Terence said.

Jazz threw him a smile, making sure the woman saw.

"There." Terence leaned across the glass display case and tapped its top, indicating a piece a couple of trays along from the first.

Jazz placed the second necklace back on the tray with her right hand.

For a second the woman looked away, eyes flitting across Terence's athletic form, then down to the tray he was pointing to.

Jazz lifted her right hand to her face, scratching an imaginary itch on the side of her nose. The movement caught the woman's attention, Jazz smiled at her and rolled her eyes again, and with the index and middle fingers of her left hand she lifted another necklace from the first tray.

"Now *this* is the one, Lucy. This is definitely the one."

Jazz moved to Terence's side, pocketing the necklace and then clasping her hands in front of her chest, all in the same movement.

"That one?" she said. "Yeah ... s'pose ..."

The assistant hurriedly locked the first tray away and moved along to them, standing primly while "Steve" and "Lucy" played out their act.

They looked at several more necklaces, and when Terence saw another couple waiting to be served he shrugged, held

Jazz's arms, and looked at her as though she were an unruly child. "What am I going to do with you?" he asked.

What indeed? Jazz thought, and for a beat he actually scared her again.

"I'm sorry," Terence said. "If I could have persuaded her to follow your taste..." He pointed at the assistant's neck again, bringing out more of her flush. "But perhaps next time."

"I certainly hope so," the woman said.

Jazz was already walking away, completing the act by leaving first, unfulfilled and petulant. When she glanced back, the woman had moved on to the next couple, standing by while they perused a display of outlandishly priced bracelets.

As Terence approached Jazz, the woman took a long, frank look at his ass. She glanced up and caught Jazz's eyes, looking away quickly. But there'd been no shame in her expression. *She thinks I'm a spoiled little tramp*, Jazz thought. *Well, fuck her.*

They left through the candy shop and bakery, Terence pausing only to buy some floured bread rolls.

Sleight of hand, Jazz thought. *I magicked it away.* She remembered that vision she had seen several times in the Underground, the Victorian magician who seemed to be looking more intently at her every time she saw him. Sleight of hand, that's how the greatest tricks were done. Misdirection, skill, confidence. None of the other ghosts paid her any attention at all. None of the others saw her.

Maybe next time, Jazz could show *him* a thing or two.

At the security desk, Terence picked up Jazz's shoulder bag with a brief but polite thanks. He turned and handed it to Jazz, waiting while she shrugged it back on. Then he invited her to link arms as they exited into the busy streets of London.

A black BMW stopped at the curb. Jazz barely flinched. A tall young woman climbed out, followed by a scruffy man dressed in jeans and T-shirt. He seemed drunk.

Right then, Jazz felt invincible.

"Dinner?" Terence said.

"Of course." She walked with him, this mysterious stranger who seemed so keen to help change her life. And she realized with a jolt that a sense of invincibility was the surest way to fail his test.

But she could not shed the buzz, nor temper her excitement.

"Are you dangerous?" she asked, relishing the risk inherent in such a question.

He looked at her sidelong. "Deadly."

"Yeah," Jazz said. "Pussycat."

Terence said nothing else all the way home.

Chapter Fifteen

lessons in art

Terence's home was not what Jazz had expected. She'd been thinking of an apartment in the Docklands, a posh flat in Chelsea, or a maisonette in Kensington. Or if not that, then perhaps a big pad somewhere in the country, an easy commute into London but remote enough to be set within a dozen acres, with its own private woodland and lake and a keeper's house rented out to one of the locals. The country-squire look wouldn't suit him, but Jazz knew there would be much more to his choice of home than style and location. He had his profession to think about. Wherever he lived would be a big part of his cover.

When they got off the Tube in Tooting and began weaving through a maze of streets, Jazz thought perhaps he was teasing her. Maybe he'd just left his car here (a Porsche? No, too tacky. Mercedes, perhaps). They passed the police station, turned left, and Terence approached a paint-peeled front door.

"Welcome to my humble abode," he said, slipping in his key and opening the door. An alarm buzzed inside, and he fumbled in his pocket, switching it off with some remote device.

Jazz looked either way along the street. At one end, a white transit van sat on two wheels, the missing two with concrete blocks in their place. At the other end, children played football in the street, shouting and laughing, screeching in startled delight whenever a car came along.

"This isn't you," Jazz said, instantly regretting her words.

"Oh?" he asked. "And what exactly *is* me?"

Jazz shrugged.

Terence sighed and looked around. "So are you going to come in? We don't want my neighbors to think I'm forcing you inside, do we?"

Keep your cool, Jazz, she thought. She glanced up at the second floor of the house and saw a woman looking down at her, hands resting on the window jambs, net curtains hanging on either side of her face like a funeral veil. The woman did not seem to blink.

"It's a maisonette," Terence said. "Mine's the ground floor."

Jazz nodded and walked through the door. "Who lives upstairs?" she asked. *No one,* she expected to hear. *Young woman lived there a year ago, but she disappeared and no one's ever seen her since.*

"That's Janine," he said. "Did you see her?"

Jazz nodded.

Terence smiled. "She does that. Scares people. Spends hours at that window."

"She didn't scare me," Jazz said, a little too hastily.

"Right." Terence closed the front door behind him and put his array of carrier bags down in the hallway. "Look, Jasmine, this is my home, and I want you to feel welcome here. You're on edge. I'm going to cook you a nice meal, and while I do that maybe you'd like to use the bath? I have spare shirts and jeans you can borrow."

"You want me to have a bath in your place?"

"No..." he said, drawing out the word. "I'm offering you a bath if *you* want one."

Jazz relaxed then, a loosening of her tensed shoulders that brought a sigh and then a yawn.

Terence breezed by her, passing two doors on his left before entering a small dining room along the corridor. "Bathroom's back here," he said. "Shall I start a bath running?"

"Can do," Jazz said, noncommittal.

She stood in Terence's hallway, looking at the simple decor—tasteful rugs on the quarry-tiled floor and the pictures on the walls. There was a landscape of somewhere that looked like Cornwall, then a series of prints that reminded her of Leonardo da Vinci's sketches of mechanical devices, all cogs and wheels, struts and engines. There was something almost animal-like about them, as if each image was an X-ray vision through something living.

Jazz slipped the bag from her shoulder and set it down at her feet.

"I have some wine," Terence called.

"No thanks."

He appeared at the end of the corridor and offered her a gentle smile. "Look...let's eat. Be at home, really. I promise you, I'm a good guy. No date-rape drugs here, no ulterior motives. And after you've rested, and you *believe* that, it'll be time for us to talk."

"Talk about what?"

Terence glanced down at Jazz's bag, then back at her face. "Lots of things."

The bath was sumptuous—hot, bubbling with foam that gave off the scent of pine and lavender—and the bathroom filled with steam, clouding the mirrors and condensing on tiles and window.

Jazz stood at its center for a moment, looking around at the small, sparse space and wondering whether she really knew anything about Terence at all. He was involved, that much was certain, and he had spoken of some "apparatus" as though Jazz should know about it. Her mother had taught her never to believe in coincidences; there was something about that blade, Mort's house, and Harry's involvement with the Blackwood woman that Terence must know.

She looked at the door. There was no lock on it, and that made her anxious, but she also felt a thrill, because she knew what this was. "Another test," she whispered, and the steam swirled before her like dancing ghosts. So she stripped off the new clothes she'd nicked that morning, dropped them in a pile beside the bath, and stepped in.

Jazz sank down into the hot water and bubbles, sighing as she was enveloped in pure luxury. How long since she'd had a bath? She'd almost lost track. She lay there for a while with her eyes closed and mouth slightly open, leaning her head back against the bath and hearing the whisper of bubbles bursting all around her. She imagined each bubble having a story, all trying to tell her their tales.

From along the corridor she heard the steady sound of Terence chopping ingredients for their meal. He started whistling, then broke into a song, immediately cutting off after two lines. Maybe he'd forgotten she was here.

"You can carry on!" she called.

She heard him laugh. "I'm no Pavarotti."

"Sing me a song."

He was silent for a while but for the chop and scrape of his meal preparation. A saucepan lid rattled, she heard the click-roar of a gas flame being lit, and then water ran into a metal container.

"I really can't sing," he said at last.

Jazz felt strangely disappointed. But as she drifted into a light doze, buoyed by the beautifully warm water, there was something comfortable about the continuing silence.

"Men," her mother said. She stared at her daughter, sitting across from her in the restaurant. Jazz was fourteen at the time. She picked at her food. She'd never been a fan of pasta, but her mother loved Italian, so Jazz never complained.

"What about them?" Jazz asked after a while. Her mother had muttered the word and left it hanging there, as though it would expound on itself.

Her mum sighed. "I suppose I need to talk to you about them."

Jazz laughed. She couldn't help it.

"Mum," she said, "I know all about *that*!"

Her mother ate another mouthful of lasagne. As she

chewed she looked at Jazz, examining her face, her hair, her mouth and neck. "You're such a beauty," she said.

Jazz posed prettily and fluttered her eyelashes. "Follow my mum."

"Of course you do." Her mum put her fork down and glanced around, her expression neutral. It was like a nervous tic her mother had developed. Jazz hoped she never ended up that paranoid, that afraid.

"You may know about *that*, but not what leads to it. There's sex and there's seduction. One is an act and one an art, and you need to be able to identify and deal with the artist."

"Okay," Jazz said. "Let me have a guess. A Dali would woo me with his intellect, a Picasso would make me see things in a different way, and a Warhol would just show me his dick."

"Jasmine!" her mum said, but she was smiling.

"I have an appreciation of art, Mother."

"You've done it at school, you mean. There's lots more to it, sweetie. You can learn about geography sitting in the classroom, but there's nothing like actually going places to get a true understanding."

"Fine. So . . . men?"

Her mother sighed, and for an instant her eyes were taken with that wretched look of sadness that filled them from time to time. She truly scared Jazz then, because she thought her mother was seeing the future, visualizing where this strange life of theirs would someday lead. "Trust is hard to come by," she said.

"You tell me that all the—"

"I mean it! Trust *no* one, Jazz!"

"What, *ever?*"

"Never! You can't, sweetie. They'll tell you you're beautiful and buy you such things, sing to you and take you places. But you can't put your fate in anyone else's hands. That's especially true of men. And more so when the men are trying to seduce you."

Terence knocked on the bathroom door. "You awake in there?"

"Am now." Jazz sat up, startled, and her eyes flicked to the unlocked door.

"Dinner's bubbling away nicely. You've got about fifteen minutes."

"Right." She wiped her hands across her face. *Damn, that was stupid of me!*

As she climbed from the bath, dried, and dressed in the clothes Terence had laid out for her, Jazz smelled the mouthwatering scents of dinner drifting under the door. Cooking meat, spices, and baking bread. She closed her eyes and breathed in deeply. With the United Kingdom she usually ate food that could be cooked in a microwave. On rare occasions, Harry fried sausages or steaks under a vent. They never went hungry, but when Harry was in one of his more paranoid moments, he made them eat cold, afraid that the smells of cooking would give them away to someone higher up. Meal times had been quiet, the food eaten quickly and from necessity rather than any real desire.

She guessed that now things would be different.

Dried and dressed, she exited the bathroom and walked through into the kitchen. Terence was at the cooker, stirring something in a large frying pan and whistling softly again.

"Nice bath?"

"Very, thank you."

"No problem." He glanced up at her and smiled, looking her fleetingly up and down, taking in the rolled-up jeans and shirtsleeves. "They look better on you."

"More my sort of clothes anyway. I don't usually dress up. What's the apparatus?"

"Oh," he said. He continued stirring, bobbing pieces of meat beneath the surface of the thick, aromatic sauce. "I had rather thought we could chat over dinner."

"Okay," Jazz said. "I'll help you serve it up. I've done everything you wanted today, and I think I've passed the tests pretty well."

"Tests?" he asked, raising an eyebrow.

"Don't piss me around, Terence."

He blinked. "I hoped you would emerge from the bath calmed and laid back."

"I am calm. But ever since meeting you, I've felt like I'm in the middle of something huge, and it's all rotating around me. Does that make sense?"

Terence nodded and sighed, a sad sound that reminded Jazz of her mother. "It does. Pass me that spoon, would you?"

Jazz removed two plates that had been warming in the oven and watched Terence serve their meal. He did it without any arty flourishes, yet he had created a dish that would not have looked out of place in any restaurant Jazz had ever been to. Bowls of saffron rice, ladles of curried lamb, its sauce containing red peppers and roughly chopped shallots, and on the side, dishes of onion bhajis splashed with mint sauce. Jazz helped him carry the plates to the table, then he returned to the kitchen and emerged with several jars of chutneys.

"You don't make your own?" Jazz asked, making a big point of examining the label on one of the jars.

Terence shook his head. "I know my limitations. Making chutney is an art, and no artist is good at every discipline."

"What's your art?"

"I would have thought that was obvious." He forked in the first mouthful and sighed in genuine appreciation of his own cooking.

"Stealing is an art?"

Terence paused with the next mouthful raised halfway. "You seriously ask me that?"

Jazz shook her head. "Doesn't matter."

He pointed at her plate with his fork. "You're not going to try?"

She collected up some lamb and rice, made sure it was liberally coated in the sauce, and popped it in her mouth. It tasted heavenly. She half-closed her eyes as she chewed, making approving noises, using the side of her fork to slice off a portion of the bhaji and ready it for her next mouthful. That was equally superb.

"Is there anything you're not good at?" She hated herself for asking, but damn him, he'd prepared a feast in the time it took her to have a bath.

"Chutney."

Jazz smiled. "So," she said, resisting talking through another mouthful. "The apparatus."

"Hmm." Terence chewed and looked up into the corner

of the dining room, thoughtful and contemplative. "Well . . . that blade you stole is part of it."

"Right. So it's a weapon."

"Oh no, not a weapon! And that's not really a blade. It's a gear."

"So what does it do?"

Terence ate some more, chewing slowly and taking a sip of wine. He had not asked her again whether she wanted any, and Jazz was beginning to regret saying no. He examined her frankly, staring as though trying to see past her outer self to the real Jazz beneath. *This* is *the real me*, she thought. She wondered whether he heard.

"I'm going to trust you. Partly because I like you and I think you're trustworthy, but mostly because you have secrets too, Jazz. Lots of secrets. And something tells me that once we start talking, we'll be helping each other a great deal. We both hold pieces of a puzzle, I suspect. Perhaps this evening we can make it whole."

"Perhaps," she said. "But you know nothing of my secrets."

"Of course not," he said, eyes glittering. "Which is why they're secrets. But Pooh was right: some secrets are heavy, and a burden shared is easier to carry. And some are dark. And a friend can shed much light."

"So now we're friends?" Jazz asked.

Terence shrugged and ate some more of his meal. He left the word hanging, and it seemed to echo around the small dining room.

Jazz laughed a little, looking around again. "This really doesn't seem like you," she said.

Terence held his hands up, mock-offended. "It's home!"

Home, Jazz thought. *Maybe that's my first dark secret he can brighten for me. I never really had a home.*

"My father always wanted to be a magician," Terence said. He put down his knife and fork, took another sip of wine, and rested his elbows on the table. "But when he found out the price of magic, everything changed. He couldn't gain the knowledge he wanted if it meant visiting pain on others. So instead of a magician, he tried to become a savior. But the Blackwood Club killed him."

"They killed your father," Jazz said in a monotone.

Terence nodded.

"Why?"

"Because the cause of the Blackwood Club—their reason for being, from the day of their inception right up until today—has been the acquisition of magic." He took another sip of wine, then without asking poured some into Jazz's glass as well as refilling his own.

"Go on," Jazz said.

"You know some of this," he said. "Don't you?"

She took a drink. It was cool and refreshing, but she heard her mother's warning voice at the back of her mind. *Drink too much, and you'll lose your way so badly you might never get back. You need your wits about you all the time, Jazz.* Jazz sighed, half-lowered the glass, then took another mouthful.

"Tell me your story," she said. "Then I'll tell you what I know. And if we meet somewhere in the middle—"

"We will. We *do*!"

Jazz stared at her host.

"The spirit of London," Terence said. He waited for a reaction, but when Jazz gave him none he continued.

"There are ghosts down there in the Underground—the Tube lines, the shelters, the sewers and storage places, and places far deeper too. The souls of London past, played out again and again; the spirit of the ancient city itself. All big cities have a hidden soul, do you know that? London has always been a turbulent place, a place of learning and mystery. There were plenty of people who lived here long ago who had a much better grasp of arcane knowledge than most people do now. Now, a child's mind is polluted from an early age with the wrong kind of input, made so that it can't be taught the things that many were taught two hundred, six hundred, a thousand years ago."

"Polluted by what?" Jazz asked.

"TV. The cult of celebrity. Society nowadays places importance on the wrong things and often the wrong people. Three hundred years ago, it was the learned types of London who held most respect, and many of those men and women had their fingers on the pulse of the city. Now... someone sells a movie of their ex-girlfriend fellating them, and they're both instant superstars. Where's the magic in that?"

"I have no heroes," Jazz said.

Terence became animated, pointing at Jazz with his fork. "Yes, but you're unique!"

Jazz ate her final mouthful of food and followed it with more wine. Terence looked off into the corner of the room again, tapping his wineglass with the signet ring on his right hand, almost lost in his own world.

"Your father?" Jazz said.

"My father. Alan Whitcomb. A magician who tried to become a savior. He knew what the spirit of London was, you see. He knew there was true *magic* there, down beneath the streets, just waiting to be picked up and learned by whoever had the desire. But sometimes that spirit screams, and when he first heard that he recognized its true state: tortured."

Jazz paled and Terence stared at her, but she said nothing. *Let him finish his story*, she thought. *Then I'll decide whether I should talk to him ... or run.*

"My father was a very clever man. A genius, from a long line of geniuses. All my life, I've aspired to his greatness. The more he knew about the tortured spirit of the old city, the more he wanted to help it. He researched old London, looking through books and records. There are places in London designed to keep secrets, which keep them still, but my father found his way in. He spent fifteen years gathering knowledge, and at the end of that time he started building."

"The apparatus," Jazz said.

"Yes, the apparatus. The Blackwood Club knew of him already, of course. You can't investigate the hidden secrets of London without them eventually knowing your name. But where his genius came in was making them think he was no threat. He started building an apparatus made from arcane segments and parts, which, when finished, would put the spirit of old London to rest."

"And the magic?"

"The magic would go down with it. The time of magic and magicians is dead, Jazz. Humanity has moved on. The past weighs on society like Marley's chains. A people, a culture, a city like London must molt from age to age, like a snake shedding its skin."

Jazz frowned. "Sorry. I don't understand."

Terence gave it a moment's thought, then forged on. "The direction of my life has been totally defined by the murder of my father. But it's common for people to be forged by their past, even shackled by it. Until we put the past to rest, we can't move on. We might as well be carrying our dead ancestors on our backs."

Jazz shivered, thinking of her mother's murder and the death of her father so long ago.

"Think of a deposed king who cannot accept a world in which no one bows to him anymore," Terence continued. "Even ordinary people are often affected by the memory of their glory days. Now extend that idea to an entire city. Once, London was the heart of an empire. Magic thrived here. The collective consciousness of London had an image of itself not unlike that king. But the king is dead, Jazz. It's a world of technology and celebrity now. The future is here, and London can't let go of its past. That collective consciousness? It's dead, and it haunts the modern city, weighs London down, just as my need to finish my father's work weighs *me* down.

"Rid London of its connections to the magic of another age, put its ghosts to rest, and the city can finally shed the skin of its past and become something new. Not an empire maybe, but a thriving, vibrant piece of the future."

Jazz arched an eyebrow. "That's a beautiful sentiment, but it's all a bit metaphysical for me. How do you know this isn't all a load of shit?"

Terence leaned back and studied her. "You can feel it, Jazz, down there in the tunnels. Don't tell me you can't. You must. As for the restless spirits of old London, they're all too real. There's little enough magic left, but it isn't entirely gone. What's left could be collected and harnessed. My father knew that if the Blackwood Club eventually gained such magic, everything would change."

"Are you sure that would be such a terrible thing?" Jazz asked.

"The city would remain a relic, antiquated, forever a part of the past. London would go the way of Babylon. If the Blackwood Club even allowed it to survive that long. Don't you see? The magic is of another age. These men are not real sorcerers. They're old, bitter, corrupt, and they could never use it for good. Worse still, they're amateurs. Allowing them to pull together the lingering occult energies of the past could only lead to catastrophe. The entire city might go mad, or sleeping evils be wakened. Even if they managed to control the magic for a time, they'd be corrupted by power. Anarchy would tear London apart, hastening its fall into ruin. The only way to assure the safety and the future of London is to gather the magic, destroy it, and set free the city's old ghosts."

He drank more wine, and for the first time Jazz saw a break in his composure and confidence. His eyes were watery and his cheeks flushed, but she thought it was more than simply the alcohol causing it.

"All right. I understand," she said. "Go on with your story."

Terence nodded. "What happened next showed how right my father was."

"*What* happened?"

"Somehow they found out what he was doing. Until then, the club had apparently been a peaceful group. Gathering knowledge, translating more magical information every time the spirit of London screamed. Sometimes years passed between the screams; other times they happened every few weeks."

"Hour of Screams," Jazz said. "That's what it's called."

Terence nodded, focusing intently on Jazz in the hope that she would say more. But she looked back at him, blinking slowly, waiting for him to continue.

"When they murdered my father, everything changed. Their thirst for knowledge had become a greed for power. They dismantled the incomplete apparatus and spread its component parts about London. And ever since, I've been stealing them back."

"Why not destroy it? If they wanted the opposite of what your father wanted, why did they just break down the apparatus and hide it?"

Terence smiled grimly. "If only it were that simple. But he made something that accessed the magic in order to put it down. And they saw that as the fast route to what they'd been gathering, piece by piece, for decades. My father built that thing to help London move on, but the apparatus has to gather the city's magic before it can be destroyed. The Blackwood Club didn't *want* the machine destroyed. They wanted to use it to achieve their own ends, to gather the magic for themselves."

"And that blade I took from you is part of the apparatus."

Terence nodded. "They've been moving the parts around, of course, trying to keep them from me. But I always find them. That gear you have is almost the last part."

"So what's left?"

Terence poured more wine, stood, and took another

bottle from the fridge. He still moved gracefully, but there was a tiredness about him now, which Jazz was certain had to do with his murdered father. "Your turn," he said.

They killed my mother too, she wanted to say. *And my father, I think, a long time ago.* But to tell him that would be too revealing, and beneath his cultured exterior there was a definite streak of danger. Sometimes he seemed to be her friend, and occasionally something more, but she knew that he was a man intent on his own needs and desires. She could be far more involved in this than he could ever guess—and she was not sure that now was the time for such a revelation.

"So you chose your course in life," Jazz said.

"Strong people do."

"Not always. Sometimes it's forced upon you. Strong or weak, sometimes it can't be helped."

"Okay," Terence said cautiously. "So...?"

"My mother died. I had to go belowground. And when I was down there..." She trailed off, confused now, not sure how much to say and how much to hold back.

"You met Harry Fowler."

She stared at him, the impact of what he was saying sinking in. Her mind was hazed with confusion. She drank wine to give herself more time, closing her eyes, swilling it around her mouth and swallowing. *He knows Harry!*

"He took me in," she said.

"He does that."

Her mind was spinning. Terence knew Harry, Harry was the photographer for the Blackwood Club, and they had both been trying to rob Mortimer Keating's house. Had Harry known about the gear for the apparatus contained in that place? He had not seemed interested in anything in particular, choosing the house ostensibly because it would hit back at the mayor and his cronies, a weak form of vengeance over what had happened to Cadge. If he'd been after the gear, surely he'd have told Jazz what to look for?

"Were you in the Blackwood Club?" she asked.

Terence frowned and sat up straight. "No," he said. "I've told you about them and what they did. I haven't lied."

"How do you know Harry?"

"We used to work together."

"He was a photographer." Jazz watched closely, looking for any trace of a lie in Terence's response.

"Did he tell you that?" he asked.

"No. I found out."

Terence nodded, frowned, tapped his ring against the wineglass again. "In Keating's house?"

"Yes. There were photos on the wall upstairs. I knocked one off when I was hiding from you, it smashed, and I saw his name on the back. I thought the reasons why Harry wanted us to rob Mort's house were clear, but—"

"Mort?"

"Mortimer Keating."

"Knew him well, did you?"

Jazz thought of Mort leaning from her bedroom window, watching for her return to the house where her mother already lay murdered. *Call me Mort*, he'd said to her when she was a little girl, and she'd never spoken a word to him. Just another Uncle.

"It's what Harry called him," Jazz said.

Terence shook his head. Stared at her. Poured more wine. "I've been open and honest with you," he said.

"You've told me nothing," Jazz responded. "I still don't

know anything about you. You're trying to build a machine that'll lay old ghosts to rest, keep magic out of the wrong hands—or any hands, really—but that doesn't tell me who you are, where you come from, or what you're all about." She waved around at the small dining room. "This isn't you. You come across as someone who likes the good things in life, and when you say you'll take me home, I find myself... somewhere else."

"Do you have a home, Jazz?"

"I used to."

"Until your mother died and for some reason you had to go underground? And you talk about *me* not saying anything." He stood from the table, smoothed his shirt, and picked up the plates. Jazz sat in silence for a while, watching him wash the plates in the sink before piling them beside it, clearing the cooker, each movement deliberate and balanced. If the several glasses of wine he had already consumed had gone to his head, he was not showing it. The only chink in his armor she had seen was when he mentioned his father, and she was sure now that behind that chink was more strength and determination than he would ever betray.

"You're driven," Jazz said.

"Yes," he said, without turning. He leaned on the worktop and looked down at his hands. "Absolutely, resolutely driven. And that's why I never let anyone come close."

"What about me?"

"What *about* you?" He turned around and looked at her, as though she had all the answers.

"Am I close?"

"Are you?"

"Stop *fucking* with me, Terence!" She stood from the table, knocking it with one leg and setting her wineglass swaying. A splash of rosé hit the tablecloth, spreading like thin blood.

"Help me steal the battery," he said. He looked suddenly exposed, his expression betraying the risk he must believe he was taking.

"Last part of the apparatus?"

"Yes. And I'm thinking, my dear Jasmine, that you have issues with the Blackwood Club that are as intense and personal as my own. Help me steal this last piece, and between us we can destroy everything they've been striving for."

"Issues," Jazz said. She nodded slowly, not looking at Terence, because she was sure he'd read in her eyes what she was thinking. *Mum*, she thought. *Dad. Cadge.* "Yes, I have issues."

"So help me."

"Why?"

"Because you're very good. And because I can give you back your life. Harry Fowler is a gentleman who has turned into a rat. And now he lives with them."

Jazz bristled and stood up straighter, pressing her lips together.

Terence crossed his arms and leaned back against the worktop.

"Where's the apparatus?" Jazz asked.

He smiled. That assured man had returned, suave and confident and forever posing questions. "That," he said, "is a secret."

Jazz finished her wine in one gulp. "I'll sleep on it," she said. "If you'll show me to my room, Terence, I'd be most grateful."

He smiled, bowed, and waved his hand at the door. "After you."

She walked by him and started along the corridor, aware that he was following a few steps behind. "By the way," she said, "fantastic meal."

Jazz had never believed that she could kill someone.

During those dark weeks following her mother's death, she had mentally put herself in the position where murder was possible: holding the Blackwood woman down with a knife at her throat, perhaps the very same knife used to kill her mother. Kneeling on the woman's chest. Pressing down on the handle. Seeing the first dark dribble of blood when the skin was pierced, the woman's eyes opening wider as dreaded realization hit home, then slashing hard right to left, pushing forward at the same time to open her throat to the spine.

She had imagined the scenario, but each time she became more and more certain that she could never do it.

Yet revenge was not exclusively about murder. There were other ways to destroy people than killing them. As Jazz closed the bedroom door behind her and surveyed the room, she wondered whether Terence had offered the best chance for revenge she would ever have.

At first glance, the room looked as sparse and unassuming as the downstairs, but after a quick look around, Jazz saw that this was far from the case. The rug on the polished oak floor was of a very fine weave, and when she lifted one corner she found a cloth tag imprinted in a language she did not know. The double bed sat on carved hardwood legs, columns of wood with snakes and other creatures curled around them. The bed's headboard was inlaid with a complex leather design—a series of symbols that perhaps meant something in another unknown language. *Maybe it's the language of magic*, she thought. The idea appealed to her.

The room was small but beautifully decorated, with several delicately framed photographs hanging on two of the four walls. Any one of them could have been a prizewinner. There was a morning scene with sun burning through mist, a street scene from New Orleans, a bee buzzing a flower, and an old, rusted car in a field, home to a spread of flowers and shrubs.

Beside the bed was a bedside table, with a glass half full of water and a book open and facedown. The book was Dickens's *Great Expectations*. Jazz realized that Terence had given her his bedroom.

Behind the book and glass sat a tabletop picture frame. In that frame, a ghost.

Jazz clasped her hands to her mouth, holding herself steady as the world seemed to spin around her. *The eyes are the same*, she thought. The man in the picture did not wear a top hat or white gloves, but the eyes were the same.

"The magician," she whispered, watching the photograph for any sign of movement. She had seen him three times belowground, and each time he appeared, he seemed more and more real. She'd thought he was a random manifestation among the many wraiths she had witnessed, but seeing him here made her feel even more a part of something over which she had no real control. *The magician, and I'm so bloody stupid because I didn't recognize those eyes.*

The photograph was black and white—of course, because it was maybe a hundred years old—but the similarity between the man in the frame and the man who had just guided her along the corridor to his own bedroom was startling.

She sat on the edge of the bed for some time, attempting to piece together the extra pieces to the puzzle. Maybe it was shock, or maybe the quantity of food and wine she had consumed, but the disparate pieces refused to fit. She could concentrate on one point at a time—Terence's murdered father, or the apparatus, or the Blackwood Club and the corrupt organization they had turned into—but any attempt to see her place in all of this led only to confusion. Her eyelids were drooping. She was not sure whether she wanted to laugh, cry, or sleep.

"Shouldn't have had so much to drink, eh, Mum?" she said, laughing quietly. She looked at the door, crossed the room, and pushed it gently until the latch closed. There was no lock. Those piercing eyes stared at her from the picture on the bedside cabinet. No, not quite the same as Terence's. Very similar, but this man had something missing from his gaze that Terence, in those dark moments when his guard came down, could not help displaying: hatred.

He hated the Blackwood Club.

"That makes him my ally, Mum," she said. She laughed again nervously, because talking to herself was the first sign of madness. But she was not mad. Lost maybe, and confused, and floundering in a stormy sea of secrets that seemed to get deeper and stormier the more she found out.

She lay on the bed and picked up the book. It was strange reading from where Terence had ended, as though she had for a moment taken over his life. She read four sentences before sleep took her.

That was a memorable day to me, for it made great changes in me. But, it is the same with any life. Imagine one selected day struck out of it, and think how different its course would have been. Pause you who read this, and think for a moment of the long chain of iron or gold, of thorns or flowers, that would never have bound you, but for the formation of the first link on one memorable day.

She dreamed of invisible stains of blood binding her mother to Josephine Blackwood, and daisy chains in the park.

She woke several times and stared at the door, and every time it remained closed. She had left the curtains half open so street light bathed the room yellow, a false dawn whenever she opened her eyes. When the true dawn came, accompanied by the sounds of early-morning bustle from the street outside and Terence moving around in the kitchen, Jazz pulled the duvet up to her chin and sighed. She felt warm and cosseted, but she knew she had a decision to make.

Terence did not only want her help because he thought she was talented. That was part of it, she was sure, and she felt an unavoidable pride in thinking that. But he was also aware that she had secrets. What better way to reveal them than to keep her close and work with her?

But there were Harry and the others: Stevie, Hattie, Gob...She owed them a lot. They had taken her in when she most needed help, given her their food, let her stay with them in their secret underground lair, taught her their ways, and they had lived through the grief of losing Cadge together. They trusted her, and now she had betrayed them by trying to change. Because that's what she had been doing, hadn't she? Accepting those shoes from Terence, letting him pay for her haircut, accompanying him to Harrods? He offered her protection and a new life, but in truth she sought far more than that from him. She had been lured with things she had never seen while living with the United Kingdom. *All the good things in life are in your mind*, her mother had once told her, sitting in their small backyard and staring at the fence that badly needed painting. She had stared for a long time.

The United Kingdom seemed a million miles away from her right now. But there was someone much closer who could help her avenge her mother's death, and Cadge's death too.

"Maybe we can work together," she whispered. Her voice was startlingly loud, and she glanced at the old framed photo beside the bed, afraid that the dead magician would be staring at her. He was, but with the same expression he had worn the night before. Daylight changed nothing.

She sat up in bed, stretching. Then she shook her head. The idea of Terence and Harry working together seemed foolish—a waking thought that lost all clarity when the dregs of sleep melted away. *We worked together*, Terence had said, but she could not imagine that now. The men were just too different, and it had little to do with the places they chose to live.

There was a knock at the door. "Breakfast?" Terence asked.

"I'll be out in a minute." Jazz sat on the edge of the bed and listened, and for a moment she was certain that he was still standing outside the door, listening, hand on the handle. She stared at it, waiting for it to dip, as if she were a doomed twenty-something in some trashy horror movie. Then she heard a kettle boiling and Terence whistling in the kitchen. She sighed.

After dressing quickly, she walked along to the kitchen and watched him preparing breakfast. He must have known she was there, but he gave no sign, setting the table carefully, placing the full *cafetière* in the center along with croissants and honey, grapefruit juice, and a selection of cold meats and cheeses.

He looked up at last and smiled. "So, did you sleep on it?"

Jazz frowned, images of thorns and flowers flashing across her mind. She nodded. "I just need a bit of fresh air," she said. "Do you mind if . . . ?" She nodded at the breakfast table.

"Not at all. But fresh air in London?"

She shrugged. "Just a walk. Stretch my limbs."

"I'll just lock up—"

"I'll be fine, Terence. Fifteen minutes, and when I return we'll have breakfast. Just want to clear my head."

He nodded, his stance tense as though he had so much more to say. But he must have seen something in Jazz's expression that silenced him, because he walked past her to open the front door. "Coffee's getting cold," was all he said as she breezed by.

Jazz turned, stretched up, and gave him a kiss on the cheek. Even early in the morning, he smelled fresh and clean. "Thank you."

"Left here," he said. "Around the block. Some nice antique shops, but watch out for pavement pizzas."

She laughed at his use of such an unrefined term and decided not to look back. That would be too keen, too eager.

The main street was bustling. People of all shapes, sizes, and colors weaved around one another on their way to work, many of them jabbering into mobile phones, others lost in their own private iPod worlds. A shop owner swept broken glass from the pavement, while two young men hammered boards across his smashed shop window. A policeman stood with his arms crossed, face set in stone as he was subjected to the shopkeeper's wife's fury. The policeman caught her eye and watched her pass by, and Jazz looked down at her feet. *If that doesn't look guilty, I don't know what does.*

She turned left, following Terence's directions, walking slowly so that she could think. She was not sure exactly what he was offering. He was twice her age, but sometimes there was a tension between them that she was certain was not only in her imagination. But he was a clever man, aware of his looks and confident of his abilities to play with perceptions and emotions. He had proved that only too well in Harrods, and the more she thought about that nick yesterday afternoon, the more she realized how complex a test it had been.

Someone shouted on her right, a woman calling a good-natured greeting. Jazz looked up. Across the street, a tall black woman was waving with both hands, and Jazz turned to see who she was waving to. Farther along the street, outside a butcher's shop, a man waved back. He was smiling.

As Jazz went to turn back and start walking again, someone stepped out in front of her. A policeman.

I don't look the same, she thought. *New haircut, darker hair, new clothes I nicked only yesterday... It's all about appearance, confidence, style.* She gave her dazzling smile up at him—he was very tall—and stepped sideways to move around.

"Excuse me," she said.

His arm closed around her wrist. "Hang on, miss."

"What is it, Shane?" his partner asked, emerging from a shop.

Jazz glanced sidelong at the second policeman, and there was nothing like recognition in his eyes.

"Bit of business," Shane said. Then he leaned down so that he could whisper into her ear. "Come with me." He punctuated the words with a quick, harsh squeeze that made her wince.

They walked along the street until an alley opened up between shops.

This could be something else, Jazz thought, but already she knew it was not. Maybe the copper recognized her from some CCTV footage from a shop the United Kingdom had done—careful though they always were, chance dictated that some of them would be filmed at some point.

"My mum's expecting me home," Jazz said, wide-eyed, innocent, and scared. The scared part didn't take much acting.

"Yeah, right," Shane said. He dug a mobile from his trousers, eschewing the radio clipped to his pocket, and flipped it open. "Mayor's offering a nice little reward for you, my love."

Nice little reward . . .

She had no choice.

Jazz mustered every bit of her strength and kicked Shane the policeman in the balls. She twisted her upper torso to follow through, adding weight and power, and the copper went down like a sack of shit, barely even able to gasp. His eyes were wide and glazed.

Jazz took a second to stamp on his dropped phone, then she ran.

"Hey!" Shane's partner called.

Don't look back! Jazz thought. *Concentrate, run, focus!*

The end of the street was ten seconds away. If she turned left she'd be heading back toward Terence's house, where she'd left the gear. But she'd give him away. She might not even reach his house before they caught her. Right, and three hundred yards along the road was Tooting Tube station, and a world she already knew so well.

She heard the sounds of pursuit—pounding footsteps, people shouting in surprise as they were shoved roughly aside.

Someone pushed a huge fruit-laden trolley from a shop doorway in front of her. She skipped right, stepped from the pavement, and ran across the street without looking back.

Decision made for her, she sprinted for the Tube station. The morning sun broke through the light cloud cover, and the heat on the side of her face seemed like a final good-bye.

Chapter Sixteen

china plates

Jazz descended the stairs that led down into the lair of the United Kingdom as carefully and quietly as she could. Opening the hatch door at the top of the steps ought to have brought a creak of metal hinges, but she moved slowly and opened it only wide enough to slip through. It wasn't that she planned to sneak up on Harry and the others. It was more that, after so many weeks learning to be a thief, stealth came naturally now. Her mother had raised her to be invisible when she wished—unseen—and unwittingly gave her daughter the skills and philosophy to become an excellent thief.

As she neared the door at the bottom of the stairs, she caught the smell of frying sausages, and her stomach growled. Terence had made her breakfast. He'd been nothing but a gentleman to her, and now he'd be thinking she had lied to him and run off, even though she had left the gear behind. He seemed so sincere that she had been tempted to trust him, had wanted to take a walk and consider how much of her own life and her own theories she would reveal to him over breakfast. Now the question had become moot.

Harry liked his sausages burned, the same as Jazz. The aroma made her mouth water. God, she was ravenous. But she had a feeling Harry wouldn't be in the mood to cook her breakfast.

Not that she cared about Harry's mood.

As she closed her fingers around the door handle, she paused to listen. She heard muffled voices; Harry wasn't alone. It had taken her nearly an hour to get to the Palace from Terence's, taking the Tube and then navigating the labyrinth of the Underground on foot. It had to be half past nine at least, which meant the United Kingdom would be out for their first shift of the day, some of them searching for pockets to pick, others for goods to nick from shops and street vendors. The rest would be doing errands, including picking up Harry's newspaper.

Jazz had no difficulty hazarding a guess as to who might have stayed behind.

She turned the handle and pushed open the door, stepping into the Palace. Harry stood at the stove with a frying pan. Stevie sat at the table, cutting a sausage on his plate. A strongbox lay open on the table, stacks of pound notes bound in rubber bands inside. Towers of one- and two-pound coins stood beside the metal box. Doing their accounting over breakfast.

Their conversation halted and they stared at Jazz. For a

moment she only stared back, but then she closed the door behind her, crossed her arms, and raised her chin to fix her gaze on Harry.

"You and I need to talk."

Harry did not smile. His eyes were hard. "I suppose we do." He turned his back and stuck a long toasting fork into each sausage, flipping them over. "Stevie, we'll finish tomorrow. Eat up, then put the box away. I've been thinking about teaching Hattie to play the guitar. Go and see if you can't manage one, would you?"

Jazz raised an eyebrow at the incongruity, then glanced at Stevie. He forked another piece of sausage into his mouth and chewed slowly, staring at her as he might have a strange insect. The frisson of attraction that had existed between them before had evaporated. Suddenly, they were strangers again.

"I'll see what I can do," Stevie said, standing up from the table.

He scooped the coins into one hand and dumped them into the strongbox, then locked it. Without glancing at Jazz again, he went through the room to a door at the back and disappeared. She guessed they had a safe down here somewhere. Stevie would lock the money away and, if he followed Harry's bidding, go topside in search of a guitar, of all things. Harry, playing father to the kids in his United Kingdom, giving Hattie guitar lessons. Stevie was the big brother, half the time searching for Father's approval and the other half desperate to start a life of his own.

So what does that make me? Jazz thought.

"Sit down," Harry said, turning off the stove and taking the pan to the table. "Will you have some sausage?"

Pleasant as anything, as though nothing at all had happened. Jazz had the answer to her question then. If Harry was the father and Stevie the eldest brother, she was the prodigal.

"I'm famished, actually," she confessed, despising herself for it.

He put a couple of sausages onto the plate that had been Stevie's, taking it for himself, and put the other two on the clean plate he'd intended to use. "There you are."

The pan went back onto the stove. Harry sat down at the table while Jazz only stood and watched him. At length he glanced up. "Well? Don't let 'em go to waste, Jazz girl. I actually paid money for those, and they came dear."

Something seemed off. Yes, she'd been gone all night, and all the previous day, and that accounted for the cold shoulder Stevie had given her. But the edge in Harry's voice and demeanor spoke of more than that.

Jazz slid into a chair, picked up the knife and fork Harry had originally set out for himself, and cut herself a piece of sausage. She'd come to confront him, but his behavior made her curious, and hunger persuaded her to eat a little. Halfway through the first of the sausages, she caught him staring at her, but instead of the suspicion or even malice she might have expected, his gaze contained only sadness.

"Your hair looks lovely," he said, wiping his mouth with a napkin. "Bit of makeup, that expensive cut, you could be a television presenter or something, up in the world. Is that it, then? You think you can still return to the illusion they paint as normality? Steady pay, a husband, and a couple of kids? Probably want a dog too."

She lost her appetite, let the fork fall to the plate, and

pushed back from the table, glaring at him. "All I want are answers."

Harry sighed. "And you think Terence can give you those? Poor girl. Bloke takes you to a posh salon, and in spite of everything you've learned about the way the world really works, you still think you can be a princess, live happily ever after."

Jazz stared at him. The words cut her, and a part of her wanted to scream at him, tell him just how full of shit he was. But the tempest of her rage had been undone.

"How could you know that? Were you following us?"

"I didn't have to follow you, pet. When you described the thief you met at Keating's house, there was only one man it could be. Then you didn't come back last night, which created two possibilities. The cops had you, or you'd seen Terence again. From the new hairstyle, the smell of perfumed soap, and the clothes you're wearing, I surmise you haven't spent the night behind bars."

He waited for a response. As she stared at him, the idea of Harry Fowler as parent and herself as errant, prodigal child began to fester.

"You know what? That'll be enough of that," she said, pushing her plate away. She jabbed an accusing finger toward him. "I don't owe you an explanation for anything. You're the one with all the lies and secrets, Harry, and it's time I had answers. You act like you're this benevolent creature, some fucking shepherd, gathering your flock of lost lambs. But you're not so innocent, are you? And it may've taken me a while, but I'll tell you now: I'm no fucking sheep."

Slowly, leaning back in his chair, Harry began to applaud.

"Bravo," he said, rising to his feet and striding toward a cabinet set against the far wall. "Truly. A little ferocity will take you far, Jazz girl. Could keep you alive as well. Might be you'll need it soon."

Harry opened a drawer and began to slide something out.

"What are you talking about?" she demanded.

He returned to the table and she saw what he held in his hands, and for a moment words failed her. Harry set down the two photographs. The one of the Blackwood Club, whose frame she had accidentally shattered while retrieving the stolen piece of the apparatus, he placed on top. Her father's face stared up at her from the group photo, and for the first time, she noticed that the photograph had been arranged so that her father was the focal point. The Uncles were all there—Mort and the rest of them—but James Towne was the center.

"Where did you get those?" she asked.

Harry studied them, not looking up. "I saw broken glass on the floor in the corridor upstairs, just below the door to the old service lift. I've walked that way dozens of times; would've seen it if it had been there before. So I had a look. Careless of you, really. But when I found these inside, I knew we'd be talking soon. There are things I wished you would never have to know. But it's too late for that."

Jazz uttered a small noise that sounded almost like a laugh. It was anything but.

"Who are you, exactly, to decide what I should and shouldn't know?"

Harry began to reply, but she waved him to silence.

"No. It's a rhetorical question. I've had a think, and I figure you can't be working for the Blackwood Club or the mayor, 'cause they'd never have beat you like that, and you'd have served me up to them by now. Maybe you think that makes you some kind of hero. Well, I hate to shatter your illusions, but you're not. You're an old man who's run away from something. I know plenty about hiding, Harry. And you can keep it up, for all I care. But this concerns me. My family's all wrapped up in it, tangled in fucking barbed wire, and I want to know what *you* know. How you and Terence know each other, how you ended up photographing the Blackwood Club, what you know about the damn apparatus and London's ghosts—all of it."

She leaned over the table. "But the first question is this: was it all a setup, me finding you? We're connected, Harry. You, me, Terence, and the damn Blackwood Club. But you didn't find me. I came upon the old shelter by chance. Fucking stumbled into it. Seemed that way, at least, but I can't believe in a coincidence like that, Harry. So tell me, how did you do it?"

For the first time since she'd entered the Palace this morning, Harry's face lit up with a smile of real humor and mischief—the smile of the Harry Fowler she'd known.

"I didn't do a thing, pet. Not a blessed thing. It's magic, isn't it? The entire history of England is constructed on the fates and destinies of people. Some of them were extraordinary, and some ordinary. Once upon a time, magic influenced everything. And with magic, there's no such thing as coincidence."

Harry had been fascinated by magic his entire life, but not the sleight of hand that Terence Whitcomb's father had enjoyed. He claimed to have had numerous encounters with magic during his childhood, and it had scarred him, both physically and emotionally.

"How did you meet Terence?" Jazz asked.

"Magic again. And thievery. The twin stories of my life," Harry said. He wouldn't look at her now. His gaze was fixed at some distant point, as though simply by speaking of these events he could see into the past.

"In another age, the Fowlers were fairly well-to-do. My father taught university, though his family had left him enough money that he could've retired at thirty. Instead, he taught until the day he died, at the age of sixty-four. I was just shy of forty when I returned home for his funeral. My sister, Anna, awaited me there. Hadn't seen her in five years or more. Afterward, we went back to my father's house to find that someone had broken in during the service. Oh, there was no damage. But there were things missing, including my mother's wedding ring. She'd been dead five years by then, and the ring had been on my father's nightstand ever since.

"It gutted Anna, losing that ring. Some of Mum's other jewelry had been taken as well. My father had nothing of value for himself, save a library of antique books. While he lived, nothing had mattered to him but my mother's things. A queer desperation struck me then. I felt he wouldn't rest until I got them back. Anna was distraught. For her, and for my father, I did something I'd sworn to myself I never would do." His eyes grew dark as he spoke, and his nostrils flared with self-loathing.

Jazz studied him a moment, and she knew. "You used magic to find the thief."

Harry put his hands over his mouth and nose. His gaze seemed lost. "Yes."

"But...magic. It's all storybook stuff to me. You and Terence talk about it like it's...like you could just reach out and touch it."

"Not so simple as that, love. Oh, it's here now, all around us. And some people—you and I included—can sense it at times. Those who dare, those who know the right words or gestures or symbols, can tap into it. But magic has faded, the same way the stories about it have."

Jazz rolled that around in her brain for a few seconds. Once it would have seemed completely absurd to her, but she had witnessed the ghosts of old London and heard the Hour of Screams, and she knew there was more to the world than what the worker bees rushing around the city could see.

"And the thief? It was Terence?"

Harry clapped his hands together. "Precisely. One of my father's students, in fact. Twenty years my junior. Yes, I'm afraid I'm not quite as old as I appear. Time has not been kind to me.

"As you surmise, I located the thief, but his reaction was not what I would have expected at such a discovery. Terence was so pleased that I'd been able to track him down that he gave me back everything he'd taken from the house without my even asking. He wanted to know how I'd done it, of course. Such things fascinated him. Thought there must be some trick to it and wanted to learn. I ought to have turned him in to the police, but I did not. I told Anna that I'd found a bag tossed aside in the garden and there would be no way to catch the thief. I said we ought to be content just to have gotten our things back.

"Terence and I crossed paths again a few days later. Anna and I had been packing up my father's things to vacate the house—university property, you understand—when he appeared at the door and insisted I tell him how I'd found him. The mystery had been driving him mad, he said. We made a bargain. Simple enough. He'd show me some of the tricks of his trade if I'd tell him the truth. I was sure he wouldn't believe me, you see. But, then, I didn't know about his father or the apparatus he was building. You see what I mean about fate, Jazz girl? It seemed like more than serendipity that the two of us had come together."

Harry paused then, and at last his gaze seemed to focus on their present circumstances. He looked at Jazz.

"How much did Terence tell you?"

Jazz considered a moment, then said, "Not everything, I'm sure. I know they killed his father. They wanted the apparatus for themselves, to gather up all the city's old magic. But they didn't have the battery, so the apparatus was useless to them. Terence said they took it apart, scattered the parts about, so nobody else could use it."

Harry nodded. "And they've been looking for the battery ever since. So has Terence. I looked with him for the longest time. We spent years stealing back pieces of the apparatus. These—" He gestured to the photos on the table. "I created an elaborate ruse, even set up a photographer's shop with family money and used all of the connections my late father's status would allow to manipulate myself into the good graces of the Blackwood Club. I needed to know the identity of each member, so we would know where to look."

Jazz held up a hand to halt him. "All right, I get it. Now, suppose for a moment that I believe all this. How did you get from there to here? You had money, status, and a purpose. Terence is still topside, still on his crusade. But you're down here in the dark."

Harry let his gaze drop, a rueful smile on his face. "Terence tried to teach me as best he could, but the shameful truth, my dear, is that old Harry never became half the thief Mr. Whitcomb was. Nor half the actor. They found me out, tried to make me tell them who else I worked with. Didn't speak a word about Terence. Not a word. I thought they'd kill me. But they weren't always as hard as they are now. They knew me, yeah? Knew my family. They told me to disappear, to vanish myself forever. That if any of them ever saw me again, they'd kill Anna. Couldn't have any contact with her. Not ever."

Shamed, he hung his head, but after a moment he glanced up, eyes damp with tears. "The worst of it is that Anna died last year. Cancer took her. I went to the hospital, tried to say good-bye, but she didn't know me by then. Barely conscious. She's dead and they've got nothing over me now, but I'm still down here." His laugh was bitter.

"Wouldn't know what to do with myself topside anymore. I don't know how to live in that world. And I've got the young ones to look after, don't I? Who knows what would happen to them without me?"

Jazz studied him. Despite her natural suspicion, everything Harry had said had the ring of truth. His grief was painful to see. But looking at him, she was certain he had not told her everything.

"You knew my father."

Harry frowned. "Only to photograph him."

A niggling thought worked at the back of her mind,

puzzle pieces attempting to fit together. "The Blackwood Club killed Terence's father and threatened to kill your sister. You see where I'm going?"

"You want to know if your father fell victim to his friends. The Senate burying their knives in Caesar."

"Caesar?" she said, and a ripple of revulsion went through her as she realized what he meant. "My father was...what? Club president?"

Harry got up and walked to a cabinet, poured himself a snifter of scotch, and leaned against the wall. "I don't think they have such titles," he said, taking a sip. "Not so far as I know, anyway. And, yes. James Towne ran the Blackwood Club, at least back in those days. The club goes back a long way, you see. More than two hundred years. But Josephine—the ice queen in that photo—thought that, as the only living Blackwood, she ought to lead them."

"She murdered him?" Jazz heard how small her own voice had become.

"Nothing of the sort. Your old man tried a bit of magic that was too big for him. Something dark and ugly, from what the whispers said at the time. Cost him his life. Right after that was when they found me out, drove me off."

"And my mother?"

"Never met the woman."

Images of her mother's corpse sprawled halfway off her bed and the words smeared in blood on the wall filled her mind. Jazz blinked hard, holding back tears, but she knew that when she spoke, the quaver in her voice would reveal her anguish.

"All those years, why did the Uncles—the Blackwood Club, I mean—why did they look after us like that?"

Harry threw back the scotch in his glass and squeezed his eyes closed. When he opened them, his gaze was intense. "They were obsessed and ambitious. Nasty, greedy bastards. But they had a loyalty to the club. I can't know for sure, you understand. Just a theory, but from what little I knew of them, I expect it was just them taking care of their own. You were James Towne's family, so they looked out for you. And maybe they wanted to make sure you didn't know anything that could hurt them."

Jazz's throat felt dry. She wouldn't have minded a scotch herself. "Then why did they kill her?"

"That, I haven't the faintest idea."

His expression was blank, not a trace of a smile or frown, and Jazz knew he was lying. Her pulse fluttered and she searched his eyes.

"Harry, don't—" she started to say.

A gunshot interrupted her, echoing down to the Palace from the stairwell and muffled by the doors. Jazz stood, knocking over her chair, and took two steps away from the door.

"Christ!" Harry said.

She turned and reached out a beckoning hand. "Come on," she whispered. "We've got to go out the back. It's got to be them."

Harry stared at the door. "I'm not sure about that."

He set his glass down on the table and went to the door. Jazz wanted to shout at him, ask him what the hell he was doing, but making noise didn't seem like the smartest idea. She took a step toward the rear exit. Even if they came through, she could still make it out as long as she reached that back door and locked it from the other side.

She held her breath.

A knock came on the door, slow and methodical. Jazz flinched. She hadn't heard footsteps or voices, just that one shot and now the knocking. Harry stared at the door a second, but then he turned the handle and swung it wide open.

A figure stood framed in the doorway. For a moment all she could make out were the eyes, and they were familiar enough to make her shiver. *The magician*, she thought. But then she saw that he had no hat, and the clothes were different. This was no Victorian ghost but a flesh-and-blood man, and when he took a step into the light she blinked in surprise. How could she have mistaken Terence for a ghost?

Stevie Sharpe followed behind him, pressing a gun against Terence's back. Stevie's lower lip had been split and blood trickled down his chin. He wiped it away with his free hand, keeping the gun on Terence.

"Fuck's sake, Stevie!"

But he didn't even glance at her, his face grim and sullen.

"Hello, Jazz," Terence said, smiling at her. "I'm sorry to say it, but I suspect your breakfast has gotten cold."

"But you've *got* the gear!" she blurted.

He raised an eyebrow, shrugged. "Hmm."

Harry crossed his arms and stared at Terence for a moment before glancing past him.

"Well done, Stevie. Smart lad."

Stevie spit blood onto the floor. "Hattie's guitar'll have to wait. Thought I'd keep an eye on the tunnel, see if any rats came down after the cheese."

Jazz stared at the small pistol in his hand. "Where the hell did you get a gun?"

His smile was bitter. "You don't know everything, you know? We were doing just fine before you came along. Would've been better off if you'd stayed gone."

His tone belied the words. Her staying out all night had stung him. Stevie was angry, which stunned her. All the time she had fancied him, she'd never been sure how he felt. But none of that mattered now. If they'd ever been on a path that could have led to some shared future, Jazz had left that path, and there could be no going back.

"Hello, Harry," Terence said.

"Terry. Nice of you to pay us a visit. We were just ruminating on the little web that seems to have entangled us all. Apparently you didn't think enough of her to tell her the whole story."

Despite his struggle with Stevie and the gun pressed against his back, Terence still managed a roguish smile. But Jazz had seen the look before and knew it was a mask.

"I meant to continue the conversation over breakfast, but I found myself eating alone."

His gaze penetrated deeply. She did not want to trust him, did not even want to think well of him. But at the same time, the idea that she had hurt him troubled her in ways that Stevie's feelings of betrayal never would.

"It wasn't by choice," Jazz said. "I really did just go for a walk to clear my head. But a copper spotted me. He got hold of me but didn't try to arrest me. He got on his mobile, said something about the mayor giving him a reward if he brought me in. If I hadn't gotten away . . ."

She let the words trail off, hating that she was making excuses.

Terence and Harry exchanged a dark look.

"Stevie, the time for bullets has passed," Harry said.

Reluctantly, Stevie made the pistol disappear inside his jacket. Terence gave him a nod, as though the boy had just done him a courtesy.

"Jazz," Terence said, "did your mother ever say anything at all about the apparatus or about the battery? Anything at all? It's vital that you try to remember."

Harry snorted. "Honestly, do you think they'd have left the woman alive all those years if they thought she knew anything?"

"I don't know what to think," Terence said, his eyes never leaving Jazz. "They must have decided she did know, after all, or else they wouldn't have killed her. And if they want to get their hands on Jasmine this badly, there's only one reason I can think of—they think she knows where the battery is."

Harry tilted his head to one side as though in thought. "Perhaps."

"You bastard," Jazz whispered, staring at Terence.

He flinched, narrowing his eyes. "Excuse me?"

"You knew who I was all along. I must have 'issues' with the Blackwood Club, that's what you said. But you knew what my bloody issues were."

Terence opened his hands in surrender. "I just wanted it to come out in its own time. I was afraid you'd think I was involved with them somehow."

"Aren't you?"

Harry and Terence both started arguing with her at once. Jazz waved them silent.

"Oh, shut up. You *are* involved. I know you didn't have anything to do with killing her, but you're connected to all of this down to the roots, the both of you." She glared at Harry. "You still want to tell me this is all coincidence? All fucking destiny?"

Harry shrugged. "I'm afraid it is. Unless there's something *you're* not telling us."

Jazz quieted at that. There *were* things she hadn't told them. Harry knew she saw and heard the ghosts of old London—hell, *he* saw them as well—and Terence had hinted that he suspected as much. But she hadn't shared with them the vividness of her visions of the ghosts or mentioned the way the magician's wraith had seemed to notice her in a way the other specters were incapable of doing. She hadn't told them about the impulse she felt from time to time to descend even deeper underground, to go through certain doors.

They had kept their secrets from her well, these two old disenchanted friends. Through one part spite, one part caution, and one part sheer stubbornness, she determined to keep what secrets she had left from them.

Terence looked at her strangely, but Jazz ignored him.

"Now what?" she asked.

"I've asked Jazz to help me steal the battery," Terence told Harry.

Stevie moved around to the table, eyeing him with great suspicion. He took Harry's glass and poured himself a shot of scotch, knocked it back, and grimaced as it went down. Then he crossed his arms.

Harry raised his eyebrows. "You know where it is?" he asked, but it was clear he didn't believe it.

"Not precisely. I've got all of the other pieces, save the battery. I've been inside the homes of every member of the

Blackwood Club. To say they're displeased would be understating it quite a bit. I'd planned to come and see you once I had all the pieces of the apparatus. Jasmine moved my plans up by a day or so."

He smiled softly at her. Jazz smiled back, unable to help herself.

Stevie gave a derisive sniff.

"I need your help, Harry," Terence said.

Harry glanced at Jazz. Something about the way he looked at her made her skin crawl, as though he was evaluating her somehow.

"That's all in the past for me. You know that."

"Why?" Jazz asked.

All three of them looked at her in surprise.

She shrugged. "Your sister's dead, Harry. There's nothing to stop you helping Terence now."

Harry shook his head in obvious disappointment. "Your memory is short, Jazz girl. Have you forgotten our Cadge so quickly? These people murdered him. I won't risk the lives of the others."

"Shouldn't that be up to them?" Jazz said.

Throwing up his hands, Harry crossed over to the table and sat down. "It doesn't matter, anyway," he said, poking a cold bit of sausage with a fork. "I looked before, remember? Nowhere left to search. And the Blackwood pricks never had the battery to begin with."

"Maybe not back then," Terence said, all humor leaving him. "Last couple of years, they've been after me harder than ever. I've had to give up on two houses in the past twelve months because they almost found me, they were moving the few bits of the apparatus I hadn't already lifted more and more often . . . and the only reason I can think of is that they were close to finding the battery and afraid I was too."

Jazz frowned. "You don't know that. You don't know a damn thing. They could have been watching you all along or just been content that if they couldn't find it, neither could you. Jumping to conclusions would be stupid."

Terence gave her a sharp look. Jazz did not flinch.

"Let's say they *did* find it," Harry said. "It could've been moved a hundred times. A thousand."

Terence dismissed them both with a gesture. "I haven't found it, so they *must* have."

"All right, spit it out!" Jazz said. "Where is it?"

"You said you'd been in all of their houses," Stevie Sharpe said, suddenly taking an interest.

"I haven't been in the mayor's house."

They all stared at Terence.

"The bloody mayor's house!" Stevie snapped.

"He's not even a member of the club," Harry said.

"True enough," Terence replied. "But he's their man, isn't he? Does their bidding, yeah?"

"That's what you want my help with?" Harry asked.

Terence glanced at Jazz. "I couldn't do it by myself. Once I saw young Jasmine's talents, I knew it could be done with her assistance. But it'll take more than that. I'll need people outside, a distraction. And it wouldn't hurt any if you could take a walk past the house and tell me if you can sense anything."

Jazz frowned. "What do you mean, sense anything?"

Terence arched an eyebrow. "Harry didn't tell you about his little sixth sense? It's why he was so helpful to me, back before he became a tunnel rat. He may not touch magic anymore, but he's got a sense for it. He can practically smell it."

"Bullshit," Stevie said, snickering at the absurdity of it all.

But Jazz was watching Harry, and he didn't laugh at all. Didn't even smile. After a moment, Stevie's smile went away as well.

"And if it isn't there?" Harry asked.

Terence shrugged. "Then I'm no worse off than I am today."

Long seconds passed until, finally, Harry lifted his gaze. He studied Jazz, glanced at Stevie, and turned at last to Terence.

"All right. We'll give you a hand. The mayor sent a crew down here to drive us out, make some nice headlines about fighting crime, cleaning up London. They killed one of my boys. I owe the fucker. So there's a bargain here. You'll go in. You'll take Jazz, but you're taking young Stevie as well. He's the best I've got, and I suspect you'll need him. And while he's there, he's going to do a bit of damage and nick as many baubles as he can lay hands on. Mayor Bromwell's got to pay for Cadge."

Terence narrowed his eyes. "This isn't about revenge, Harry."

Harry smiled. "Isn't it? You can talk all you want about the way the world ought to be, how we've got to put magic behind us to find the glory of the new age, or whatever bollocks you're spouting now. And maybe there's something to all of that. But once upon a time, back at the start, it was about the bastards murdering your dad. We all have debts to collect, Terry."

Terence glanced at Jazz. "You in?"

She nodded. "Doesn't mean I'm not still angry with you."

"Fair enough," he said.

He walked to the table and put out his hand. Harry stood and took it, and the two thieves shook, sealing the bargain.

Chapter Seventeen

served cold

Jazz hated feeling excluded. She knew it was for the best—the copper would have contacted the mayor's men, and a new description of her would be circulating across London even now—but with one of the most audacious thefts in London's history in the offing, the last place she wanted to be was in the dusty, grubby confines of the Palace.

Terence had gone back up to collect some equipment from one of his houses. He didn't tell them which one and neglected to mention how many houses he owned, but Jazz guessed it must be several all across the capital. A man of mystery such as Terence could not exist in one place alone.

Harry and Stevie had gone up with him. Stevie was going to a long-term parking place he knew to purloin a car for the nick, while Harry would take a stroll past the mayor's manor to see whether his weird sixth sense tingled. He'd given Jazz a strange look as he left—part suspicion, part complicity—and she wondered how much of what she had seen in the Underground played across his internal vision as well.

Tell that magician I said hello, she wanted to say. *Whatever he is to Terence, tell him I see him, I know him.* But she said nothing of the sort. Such talk would feel so intimate and secretive, and Harry held icy anger for her in his manner. She honestly thought things would never be the same again between them. And the more she thought about that, the more she honestly did not care.

There was more to life than the Underground. Terence had shown her that. Though he was a man out for revenge—and however he tried to prettify his motives, that was the basis of his aims—he was at least pursuing it in style.

"Just promise not to leave me out of this," she had said as the three men left the Palace.

"Lovey," Harry had replied, "you're a bigger part of this than any of us."

She'd smiled and wished them safe journeys when they left; then she had the Palace to herself for an hour or more. She wandered around the place, searching the rooms with a new eye, but there was little down here she had not seen before. One room held a small door at floor level, a fresh scrape across the concrete floor showing where it had been levered open recently. She guessed this was where Harry and Stevie were hiding the box of money. Lot of good it would do them stuck down here.

You're a bigger part of this than any of us, he had said. That troubled her and she didn't know why.

Be anonymous, her mother had told her. *Don't be seen. Part of the crowd is as faceless as the crowd itself.*

"I don't want to spend my life being faceless," Jazz said. And there it was: the stark truth. Harry might be able to find himself most at peace down here, and maybe some of the others had grown, or would grow, into such a way of life. But yesterday, topside with Terence, walking the streets and feeling the sun on her wanted face, Jazz had realized that she was destined for greater things. It was ironic that her mother's attempts to keep her hidden away had perhaps contributed to Jazz's burgeoning desire to do so much more.

Hattie was first back to the Palace. She brought a handbag with her, expertly chosen to match the hat she had worn out that morning.

"You're back!" Hattie said, her pleasure at seeing Jazz untainted by suspicion. "I *love* your hair!"

"Hi, Hattie," Jazz said, genuinely pleased to see the girl. "Like your new handbag."

The girl smiled wickedly. "Wait'll you see." She upended the bag, spilling purse, mobile phone, and electronic organizer, as well as a slew of expensive makeup and a beautiful silk head scarf. "Silly cow left it on the back of her chair while she sat in Covent Garden drinking a ten-quid coffee with her snobby mate."

"It's nice," Jazz said. "Hattie?"

The girl raised her eyebrows, hearing something strange in Jazz's tone. "Jazz?"

"I need your help. Just for today—hopefully for the last time—I need to not be me."

Hattie grinned, delighted. "You've come to the right place," she said. "I'm an expert at being someone else. Come on." She led Jazz out of the main chamber and into the bedroom the two girls shared. "I missed you last night. Kind of scary sleeping in here by myself. Sit yourself down and let me fetch my box of delights."

Hattie went to a built-in metal cabinet in the corner of the room, and beneath the clothes hanging there was a big basket that everyone knew was Hattie's private property. There was a strong moral code among the United Kingdom, and no one would have ever considered invading another member's privacy. Jazz felt honored.

"Now, then," Hattie said. "Young or old?"

"What?"

The girl laughed. "Come on, Jazz. You're a beauty, and I'm sure you know you can play on that if you want. Or you can be an innocent teen. Up to you. Depends on the score."

"Big score," Jazz said. "The mayor's house."

Hattie's face went slack. "Fucking hell." It was the first time Jazz ever heard her swear.

"So, I think old," Jazz said. "But nothing too constricting. I may need to move fast."

Hattie recovered from her shock quickly, put on her usual cheerful smile, and started pulling things from her stash.

By early afternoon, everyone was back. They sat around the main room of the Palace, the United Kingdom familiar and relaxed with one another, Terence the outsider, and Jazz feeling apart from everyone. Harry did most of the talking. From what he said and the way things were going, Jazz didn't feel the need to ask what he had sensed while walking past the mayor's home.

As ever when planning a big score, Harry invited questions at the end of his pitch. There were none. A seriousness had descended over the group, one tinged with the still-raw death of Cadge and this prospect of getting back directly at the mayor, in however small a way. No one asked who Terence was or what he was doing there, though many of them eyed him suspiciously. Jazz was pleased to see a hint of discomfort in his forced smile.

After his address, when the kids were scurrying around the Palace in preparation, Harry and Stevie disappeared into a side room. Jazz glanced at Terence, who merely raised an eyebrow, then she followed. She found them huddled together in Harry's bedroom. They both looked at her, not surprised to see her but not very welcoming either.

"Jazz girl," Harry said. "Like your hat."

"You taking that gun?" she asked Stevie. He looked at her and blinked slowly but did not reply.

"That's his business and his alone," Harry said.

"No," she said. "It's *my* business if we're breaking into the same house together. We all know the mayor's thugs might be armed."

"It's my gun," Stevie said. "Not Harry's. My choice."

"And it's my choice whether I'm a part of this or not," Jazz said.

She stared at Harry and Stevie, who both stared back. She left the implied threat hanging in the air. Neither of them bit. *I should walk away*, she thought. *There's very little holding me here now other than revenge. And though they say it's sweet, more often than not it'll come out sour.*

"Shit," she whispered. Neither Harry nor Stevie changed their expression. She turned and walked away, suddenly feeling part of something over which she no longer had any control.

As she entered the main room once again, catching Terence's eye and deciding whether to say anything to him about Stevie's gun, she sensed something closing in. A scream in the distance at first, heard more in her mind than through her ears, and a sudden heartbreaking sadness swept over her. She uttered a wretched sigh and fell to her knees. Leela and Gob both turned to look at her, both about to ask what was wrong.

Jazz and Terence stared at each other, a moment of startling understanding passing between them. *This is about so much more than revenge*, Jazz thought then. *It's about saving worlds other than this*. And then Terence offered her a tired smile before closing his eyes.

"Everyone sing a song," Jazz said, and as a few groans of dismay rose up, the Hour of Screams rushed in.

It sounded like a train coming from the distance, but the noise of its wheels on the track were screams of pain, and the sound of its metal parts clanking together made desolate words out of nothing.

Jazz's song came to her without thinking, and it was her mother who sang it.

Wish me luck, as you wave me good-bye.
Cheerio, here I go, on my way.

Her mum had always joked that she'd like it sung at her funeral. Jazz cried, an outpouring of grief that racked her body and caught in her throat every breath she took, because here and now was when she laid her mother to rest. There would be no funeral. However the Blackwood Club had disposed of her body, it was long gone to rot and dust. Here, during this Hour of Screams, was when Jazz sang her mother's soul down into peace.

So she sang.

The air felt heavy, and every breath hurt. It was strange to bear witness to such violence upon the senses, and yet the solid walls and ceiling around them gave no sign, the floor did not shake, and the only dust in the air was kicked up by the United Kingdom falling to their knees in the old shelter.

At last it faded away, and Jazz felt something flit by beside her and stroke her cheek as it passed.

Sweet dreams, her mother would say, touching her daughter's cheek when she thought Jazz was asleep. But Jazz would always lie there awaiting this loving touch.

"Sweet dreams, Mum," Jazz said.

The Palace fell silent, and Jazz closed her eyes.

By the time they were in position, it was almost five in the afternoon. Terence and Harry had agreed that this would be the best time to strike. The stream of visitors to the mayor's home would peter off around then, and those on guard would start to relax. The streets in this exclusive neighborhood were quite busy as well, mumbling with Bentleys and Mercedes, Porsches and BMWs, as those who lived here started arriving home from work. Less-flashy cars flitted here and there too—other people leaving the area now that their job as hired help was over for another day. Nannies and gardeners, cooks and cleaners, common cars dodged the elite as class began to find its own level once again.

Stevie had nicked a Vauxhall Astra. It was quite new, so not shabby enough to be noticeable, but a basic model, so nowhere near flashy enough for anyone to pay them any undue attention. It was as nondescript as the three people inside could wish for, and for the last ten minutes they had sat at the side of the road without attracting one single glance.

Jazz sat in the front next to Stevie, while Terence lounged comfortably in the back. There didn't seem to be an ounce of anxiety about him. He even closed his eyes for a time, breathing smoothly and evenly, though Jazz knew that he was not asleep.

This is the culmination of years of hunting, she thought. She turned and glanced over her shoulder at Terence, and in his calm face she could see the evidence of strain; muscles twitched, and his eyes were not quite closed.

"Almost time," Stevie said. He had not looked at her since they'd pulled up a street away from the mayor's house. He had not even commented on her new look—a beret from Hattie, hair a mass of curls, frameless sunglasses. He tapped one finger on the steering wheel and whistled something under his breath, and it felt like they had never even met.

"I wasn't born down there," she said.

"Doesn't matter," Stevie said casually, and she was not quite sure what he meant.

"Stevie, I don't think I—"

"Doesn't matter," he said again, looking at her for the first time. His expression was like ice. "Time to go." Before Jazz or Terence could say anything, Stevie had opened his door and climbed out.

Jazz did the same and heard Terence following suit. It would look strange if the three of them did not get out together.

All thought of discussions flitted away. They were on the job now, it had begun, and Jazz knew she had to concentrate fully to make sure she didn't screw this up. So much hinged on this.

She linked arms with Terence. She felt his brief resistance, but then he looked at her and smiled. Jazz smiled back. "Shall we walk?" she asked.

Terence nodded. "Let's."

Stevie led the way along the street to the small road that connected with the adjacent road. The houses here were all grand and expensive, some of them almost hidden from sight behind high hedges or past wooded driveways. Brass nameplates beside gateways were often accompanied by speaker grilles and buttons, the gates electronically locked, cameras hidden away in trees or atop thin poles so that the owners could see who had come to pay a visit.

"My mum would have loved this place," Jazz said, speaking without thinking.

"I have somewhere not too far away," Terence said.

Jazz looked at him, surprised.

"Oh, nowhere near as grand as any of this. A modest five-bed. But it has its own grounds, and a wall, and there's a secret tunnel to the house next door."

"You have a house with a secret tunnel," Stevie said, barely trying to mask his sarcasm.

"Well . . . no longer *that* secret, of course," Terence said. He smiled smugly, and Stevie turned away and carried on walking.

Jazz laughed softly. But she was not foolish enough to believe that the antagonism between these two had anything to do with her.

"Here," Stevie said a few minutes later. "Follow me."

They approached the mayor's residence. It was a huge house, quite modern in London brick but built in an attempt to give it the gravitas of age. The architect had mostly succeeded, but even from the street they could see the shiny reflections and sharp edges of technology. There were cameras fixed on the house itself and also to several poles placed strategically around its grounds. Its six-foot-high boundary wall was topped with a wicked-looking metallic structure, too short to be a fence but spiked and sharp enough to deter any but the most determined invaders. It also had an entry system at its gate, though Jazz tried not to stare too hard. As they passed by the wrought-iron gates, she saw movement from the corner of her eye, and she risked one glance.

There were two black cars parked in front of the house. Several people milled about the stepped entrance, though they were too far away to make out properly. They all wore dark suits.

"Might be them, might not," Terence said cheerily. He was smiling, and Jazz copied the act.

"Whoever it is, let's hope they leave soon," Stevie said. He was already past the gate and striding along beside the wall.

"They will," Terence said. "Your friend Harry will see to that."

Harry's idea of a distraction was as simple as it was audacious. Underground, the mayor's men were shielded from the world, their action witnessed only by rats and the human rats they believed the United Kingdom to be. But up here . . .

"When does he start?" Jazz asked. She and Terence passed before the gates, and she risked one final glance as they did so. People were already climbing into the cars to leave. *Election time*, she thought. *They could be anyone sucking up to the mayor's ass.*

Stevie stopped so sharply that Jazz and Terence almost walked into him. The long-haired boy turned around and grinned, and Jazz saw just how dangerous he could be. His eyes were dark but glinting with the excitement to come. *Keep your cool*, she wanted to say. But she was afraid how he would react.

Stevie looked past them and the grin grew wider. "Right about now."

Jazz turned around just in time to see Harry and the rest of the United Kingdom emerging from a side street a couple of hundred yards away. Harry led the way, and behind him the kids carried furled banners and flags, along with bags of eggs, flour, and rotten fruit.

"Let's go," Terence said. "We've got three minutes at best."

Jazz, Terence, and Stevie hurried away from the main entrance, and if anyone saw them they were simply three people trying to get away from potential trouble.

"Bromwell *out*!" Harry's voice called, and Jazz smiled at the venom there. "Bromwell *out*!" The kids took up the call as well. They reached the front gates, unfurling the banners and waving them, lobbing eggs over and through the iron railings, throwing torn bags of flour and overripe fruit to explode across the drive.

"Here," Stevie said. He'd reached the corner of the mayor's property and turned without sparing a single glance back the way they'd come. Jazz paused, forcing Terence to wait as well, and watched Harry and her friends.

The police would have been called already. They'd be here in minutes, though not as quickly as for a midday disturbance. Rush hour would slow them down. Harry and the others shouted their slogans, threw their soft missiles, and not one of them glanced along the street at Jazz and Terence. True professionals.

"Come *on*!" Stevie hissed.

There was a British Telecom junction box against the wall here, giving them a vital three-foot start. Stevie took one quick glance around, then hoisted himself up. He took off his heavy leather jacket and, holding one sleeve, threw it up and over the vicious metal blades atop the wall. He gave one experimental tug, then used the snagged jacket to haul himself up.

Jazz held her breath as Stevie carefully stepped on, then over, the low, dangerous metal fence. He looked down at her and smiled quickly, then jumped out of sight.

They heard him land, and Terence looked at her for a loaded moment. This was when they would find out whether the nick was on or not. If they heard the noise of barking dogs, running men, or Stevie involved in a struggle, they would know to run. If there was no sound at all, they would climb.

"Bromwell out!" they heard from around the corner, the chants intermingled with some colorfully obscene language. From over the wall, nothing.

"Go," Terence said.

Jazz leaped nimbly onto the BT box, grabbed the trailing sleeve of Stevie's jacket, and hauled herself up. She stepped over the low fence atop the wall and jumped, landing with knees bent, rolling to the right and coming up in a crouch. She scanned the area quickly. They'd landed among some trees, just as planned, and she saw Stevie's shadow beneath the canopy a dozen feet away. He was staring through the undergrowth and across a wide well-maintained lawn at the house.

Terence landed lightly beside her. He'd held on to the jacket sleeve as he jumped, bringing it over to this side of the wall. This was just one of their potential escape routes.

There was a plastic box fitted to the wall here, a thick black cable duct protruding from its base and sinking into the ground. Terence gave it one good kick and the cover broke and fell away. There was a spaghetti of colored wires inside, junction points and circuit boards, and a knot of wires almost as thick as Jazz's wrist snaked through a hole in the wall to the Telecom unit outside.

Terence took a pair of heavy pliers from the small bag over his shoulder.

"How do you know which ones to cut?" Jazz asked.

"Only one." He snipped a white wire, then took out a small device from his pocket. He checked its batteries, turned it on, and nodded in satisfaction when it emitted a short beep. There was a forest of wires protruding from the device, each ending in a small crocodile clip. Terence stripped the cut wire, connected both ends into the unit, and began stripping plastic and attaching clips to other wires in the bundle. He worked quickly, almost randomly, but Jazz knew there was nothing random about this. She could see the concentration on his face as he worked.

"There," he said after a minute. "Should give us a bit of time."

He and Jazz knelt beside Stevie. From beneath the trees

they had a good view of the side of the large house. To the left were the two black cars, but the people who'd been milling around were now down closer to the front gate, still out of range of the eggs and fruit but forming a protective semicircle in case one of the protesters climbed in. To their right, at the rear of the house, stood a large conservatory with timber decking built all around. The double glass doors were open and there was no movement inside.

Between them and the house, the garden was spotted with several large flower beds, mostly planted with mature roses growing on frames. Plenty of cover.

"No dogs," Terence said.

"Not that we can see," Stevie replied.

"They'd have let them out by now," Jazz said.

"Conservatory?" Stevie looked from Jazz to Terence, then back at the house.

"There'll be other entrances around the back," Terence said. "Let's see when we get there."

"Harry should be knocking off now," Jazz said, looking at her watch. It had been over three minutes since he and the United Kingdom started their distraction, and if they were not careful they'd still be there when the police arrived. Last thing anyone wanted was for them to be caught. But this was a dangerous job—the most dangerous they'd ever pulled—and that called for extreme risks.

"I can just see them from here," Stevie said. "Harry's right at the gate. Think he's smiling. Maybe he sees the punks that beat him up."

"And killed Cadge," Jazz said.

"Yeah, Cadge." Stevie did not turn around, but Jazz heard the break in his voice.

"So let's get our own back," Terence said. He was the first to move, breaking cover and running crouched over to the first planting bed. He glanced back quickly, looked around the shrubs, and ran on. Stevie followed, and Jazz brought up the rear.

They had considered breaking in at night, but then all the security measures this house employed would be in place. Floodlights in the garden, maybe patrolling security guards and dogs, contact alarms on all the windows and doors, motion and heat detectors inside, panic alarms, trip-wire alarms perhaps, and every one of them would be linked directly to the local police station. And, perhaps, to the homes of the BMW men. Weighing those risks against breaking in when the mayor was up and about, there had been little choice.

Terence reached the timber decking, vaulted the low fence, and lay along the conservatory's dwarf wall. He stretched to look in through the open doors, signaling back that the coast was clear.

Harry and the kids let out a final roar, then their voices died out quickly as they left. *Be safe*, Jazz thought. There were sirens wailing in the distance, but she knew that the United Kingdom was expert at avoiding capture.

She broke cover first, dashing across the lawn and step-ping lightly through the open doors. No alarm sounded, no shouts erupted, and no dogs barked.

Stevie was beside her then, crouched down low, and through the glass walls of the large conservatory they saw Terence skirt around toward another door farther along the rear of the house.

"Take care," Stevie said. He gave her a quick smile that

reminded her of how it used to be, and for a second she wanted to reach out and touch him. But then he was gone, so light on his feet that she heard nothing, just saw him disappear quickly into the house.

This was the most dangerous part of the operation. They hoped that the people around the cars would be leaving now, instead of coming back inside. They suspected that the mayor's staff would be relaxed, many of them preparing to go home for the day. Maybe the mayor himself was even having a snooze after a hard day's campaign planning. But they could rely on nothing other than their own stealth and talent to get them through the next half hour.

Jazz took a quick look around the conservatory and thought, *We don't even know what the hell we're looking for!*

The battery, Terence had said. *Something strange and out of place. Something unusual that doesn't belong. You'll know it when you see it.*

There were several huge pots in the conservatory, home to various exotic cacti, thorns long and cruel. A bit of furniture, a table with a few empty cups and a spread of paperwork, nothing unusual.

Room by room, Jazz thought. *So here we go.*

She slipped into the huge kitchen. There were three doors in here, and she knew that Stevie must have taken the one on the right. Jazz headed left, crouched low and listening all the time for approaching footsteps. The air smelled of old food. As she passed one work surface, she saw the detritus of a meal: bread crumbs, meat scraps, shreds of browning salad. There were a few plates piled up beside the double sink, and on an island unit in the center of the kitchen sat several full shopping bags.

She opened the first door she reached, still crouched down low. She winced as the hinges creaked, stared through the narrow gap, squinted against the bad light. It was a walk-in larder, at least eight feet per side. The walls were lined with shelves stacked with all manner of canned and bagged goods. The entire rear wall was taken up by a wine rack, at least two-thirds of it filled with bottles. There were built-in cupboards at floor level, all of them shut with padlocks.

Weird, Jazz thought. *So what's in there? Posh food?* She closed the door gently behind her and switched on the light.

The cupboards were solid, and when she tapped the first door it sounded heavy. Metal lined with wood laminate, perhaps? She jiggled the padlock, but the hasp and eye were bolted firmly into the door. If she had a crowbar, perhaps she could pull it off, given time. But she had neither.

Last place to look, she thought. *If we don't find it anywhere else . . .*

She turned off the light, opened the door slowly, peeked out, and exited back into the kitchen.

The final door from the kitchen led along a short corridor to a large dining room. This was a grand place, with a table that seated at least twenty being the only item of furniture. The walls were paneled with dark wood from floor to ceiling, and a portrait held pride of place in each separate bay. At first Jazz thought they would be pictures of the Blackwood Club and that the accusing eyes of her father would soon bear down upon her. But then she recognized one of the paintings as the previous mayor of London, and from the end wall Mayor Bromwell stared at her. She smiled and gave him the finger.

Jazz hurried through the dining room. It didn't seem to

be a place that was used very much; there was a film of dust on the table, and the air was musty and old. *They should air this place*, she thought. *Get rid of the stink*. There was a pair of doors at the far end, and she opened them just a crack.

Then froze.

The doors opened inward, and beyond was the mansion's main hallway. To her left she could see the spill of light where the main entrance doors still stood open. Directly across from her, another set of doors stood closed, and just to her right was the stairway, eight feet wide and climbing to a balcony that overlooked the hallway on three sides. On the first stair stood two men. One of them wore an eye patch.

Philip, Jazz thought. The BMW man she'd seen batter Cadge to death.

"Fuckin' tunnel rats!" Philip hissed.

"He's got guts, coming up here," the second man said.

"Yeah, well, I'll happily open his guts to the air." Philip's face seemed twisted into a permanent grimace, and a twitch pulled at the corner of his lip as though someone had a hook in him.

"Don't like being reminded—" the second man said, but Philip cut him off.

"Pussy! Those bastards did something to us down there." He twitched again, his head flipping to the side. Jazz saw his good eye, and it was almost completely black. "Gassed us or poisoned us. Bastards! Get my hands on 'em ... Get my knife in 'em ..."

"Calm it, mate," the second man said, and from his tone he was obviously scared of Philip.

"Yeah," Philip said. "Calm." But he seemed anything but calm.

"Where's the mayor now?"

"Upstairs in that room of his. Fiddlin'."

"Weird," the second man whispered.

"He likes to be left alone," Philip said. "Needs to concentrate."

"He really thinks it'll help him win?"

Philip shrugged, then grinned. "He'll win." The two men walked upstairs and passed from Jazz's line of sight.

She closed the doors. *Fiddlin'*, Philip had said. In any other place, Jazz might have suspected that meant something else. But not here, and not now, and not knowing what she knew.

"Upstairs," she whispered. Stevie was supposed to go directly to the second floor, and Terence would likely still be working his way through the first floor beyond the hallway. There were probably the library and living rooms over there, much more likely places to hide the battery than in the kitchen and dining room, and probably a second minor staircase buried in the bowels of the mansion. But the mayor was upstairs—in "that room of his"—and suddenly Jazz realized she had an advantage.

I need to find that battery, she thought. *Me. Not Terence, not Stevie. They've both got too much going on, and my need for revenge is fresher.*

Revenge might be a dish best served cold, but as Jazz opened the dining-room doors and crept to the foot of the stairs, she was burning inside.

She glanced carefully up the stairs. The two men had disappeared, either around onto the balcony above her or into one of the rooms up there. She listened for their voices but heard nothing. Behind her the main doors still stood open, and she knew she had to get away from there as soon as possible. Visible through the doors was the rear end of one of the black cars, which meant that there were likely more people still outside. Maybe they'd come in, maybe they'd eventually get into the cars and go. She did not want to wait to find out.

As she started climbing the stairs, keeping as far to the right as she could in case the two men were standing silently above her, she heard the screech of tires. A police siren sang briefly before falling silent again. Jazz paused and held her breath; if Philip and the other BMW man were on the balcony above her, they'd probably pass some comment now. But all was silent.

She ran up a dozen more stairs and squatted at the top, looking around. Before her, a corridor led toward the back of the house, a door halfway down on either side. To her left and right, the landing swung around above the hallway, and there were more doors and corridors leading off. Several of the doors were half open, others closed, and though she concentrated she could not hear voices from any of them.

Stevie could be anywhere.

There were several small tables set along the landing, most of them bearing vases with sprays of dried flowers. A couple were empty. Some had small drawers, others larger cupboards beneath. *Bloody thing could be anywhere!* she thought, realizing for the first time the immensity of their task. Terence did not know how large the battery was or what it looked like; all he knew, based on Harry's walk-by, was that it was here.

Jazz went left. The first door she came to was ajar, and she knelt low and pushed it open slightly until she could see inside. A bathroom: toilet, bidet, shower stall, bath, basin, a couple of chairs. The shower was steamed up and still dripping water, and the air carried the warm, heavy smell of recent use.

The next door was closed, and Jazz pressed her ear to the wood. She couldn't hear anything inside. She touched the handle, paused, and withdrew her hand. *Doesn't feel right*, she thought. Trusting her instincts, she moved on.

The silence of the house was intimidating. Such a big place, so little activity... She was glad, but it also felt strange. It felt as if, even though she *thought* she was being careful and quiet, the whole house was watching her. The tall ceilings pressed down, the walls closed in, and she was sure she could smell the must of ages drifting up from the carpets beneath her feet. She looked around for cameras but saw none. She listened for footsteps.

The front doors slammed shut. Jazz fell to her stomach and crawled quickly to the balcony, looking down into the hallway. If someone had shut the doors and was heading for the stairs, she'd have maybe a dozen seconds to find somewhere to hide.

There was a tall bald man in the hall. He engaged the locks on the front door and turned, heading right into one of the rooms Jazz had not seen.

She turned the corner of the balcony and headed toward the front of the house. There was one long wall here with a single door, and she paused outside, listening. There was someone inside—she heard murmuring, muttering, whispers interspersed with what could only be sobs.

Was this "that room" where the mayor always wanted to be alone?

There was the tang of something in the air, like the stench of hot electrics, only more animal, more natural.

Jazz knelt and tried to see through the keyhole, but it was blocked with a key on the other side.

She grabbed the handle, placed her ear against the wood again, and turned. If the whispering stopped, she'd have to run. If its tone or volume changed, the person talking could have turned their head to look at the door, and she would have to flee.

Concentrating, listening for footsteps from behind as well as a change in the voice beyond the door, she turned the old ivory handle some more. Felt the latch release. Pushed.

She blessed whoever maintained the house for keeping its hinges well oiled.

The wedge of room revealed did not seem to fit the dimensions or shape made apparent by its outside. The inside walls were curved, forming a perfectly circular space. There were no windows, and the only other opening was a closed door directly opposite Jazz. The walls were painted a dull purple. The ceiling was cream, the floor was covered with a pale, hard covering, and at the center of the room, the mayor sat cross-legged, naked, and shivering.

Sweat dripped from his straggly hair and landed on his flabby stomach. He stared down at the floor just before him, his right hand six inches above, index finger forming small, irregular circles in the air. He mumbled a few words in a language Jazz did not know.

Fiddlin', Philip had said. *In that room of his.*

The mayor's strange words seemed to travel around the curved walls, repeating themselves again and again until they were even more jumbled and unknowable than before.

A small weak light appeared on the floor before him, squirming like a slug sprayed with salt. It quickly faded away to nothing, and the mayor cursed and shook his head.

Magic, Jazz thought. *I'm seeing magic. But . . . is that it?*

And then the door across the room from her opened, just a crack, and Stevie peered in. He didn't see her, of that she was sure. His attention was too fixed on the mayor and what he was doing, eyes wide, fearful and excited at the same time.

Jazz opened her door another inch, willing Stevie to see her. He did not. Instead, he pointed at the mayor, and at first Jazz thought he was going to laugh. But she realized too late that the laugh was actually a grimace, and Stevie was not pointing with his hand.

The gun was black and ugly in the boy's pale hand.

"No!" Jazz screamed.

The mayor turned to look at her. And then his right eye and cheek erupted as Stevie shot him in the back of the head.

Chapter Eighteen

deeper

Mayor Bromwell tipped sideways and struck the floor, his shattered face making a wet *thunk* as it hit. Blood, fluids, and shreds of bone had spattered the floor, and more pulsed from the wounds. He moved slowly, like a creature uncurling from a long sleep, and made a terrible keening sound deep in his throat. Then he was still.

Jazz looked up at Stevie, and he looked at her. There was a moment of doubt in her mind, an urge to flee for her own safety, because Stevie still had the gun half raised. There was a blankness to his expression, as though he was looking through her to what might happen beyond, and Jazz thought, *He's going to shoot me because I saw.* But then his face fell slack, his mouth hung open, and life came into his eyes once again.

They looked at each other for what felt like forever. And

then the shouting began, and the footsteps, and Stevie's mouth closed tight.

"Jazz, we have to—"

"What the hell—"

"Later. Let's go."

Jazz turned around. A door burst open on the other side of the landing, across the hallway from her. Philip and the other man came out, staring at her, and even though she thought she was disguised, the recognition in the BMW man's eyes was instant and obvious. "You!"

Jazz entered the dead mayor's room and slammed the door behind her, turning the key. She skirted around behind the corpse, keeping to the curved wall so that she did not tread in any blood, and Stevie threw the door wide for her.

"Terence," Jazz said.

"He'll be okay."

"He didn't know?"

"Later." Stevie grabbed her arm hard and steered her along a small narrow corridor toward the rear of the house. He was still carrying the gun in his other hand. "Go!"

Jazz ran, heart thumping, sweat chilling her back, and the implication of what she had just seen was still very far away. There was no detail, though she felt it hovering around her, waiting to strike home. Her mind was a haze, the only clear thing in that haze the image of her dead mother. So much blood. Such murder.

"Turn right," Stevie said. He pushed her that way just in case she hadn't heard.

The house was coming to life. People shouted, footsteps pounded, doors burst open. She had thought the building all but deserted as she sneaked around, looking for something she knew nothing about, but it seemed that first impression had been wrong.

Voices came close, then moved away again. A door was smashed open to bang against a wall. Someone shouted in shock, and another voice wailed in grief—a sound that chilled Jazz. She stopped, the corridor before her ending in a sash window that was half open, and Stevie shoved her hard in the back.

"Through there and up!" he whispered.

"But—"

"*Just fucking go!*"

Jazz lifted the sash higher and peered out. She looked out upon landscaped gardens, and below and to her right was the roof of the large conservatory through which they had entered. That seemed like days ago but probably wasn't more than fifteen minutes. *Everything's changed*, she thought, and someone appeared in the conservatory. A tall thin man, standing beside the low table in there, partly visible to Jazz through the glazed roof.

Stevie placed his hand on her ass and pushed, but she slapped back at him and held her hand upright: *wait!*

The man looked around, scanning the garden, then he seemed to speak into his sleeve. He shook his head and went back into the kitchen.

Stevie pushed again. Someone must be getting close. He still had that gun, and Jazz didn't want anyone else dead. Not even Philip, that mad monster who'd battered and kicked Cadge to death. Not even him.

Below the window a steel platform was bolted into the wall, and to the left a hoop ladder rose eight feet to the roof. Jazz went for it, moving quickly when she felt Stevie press up close behind her, jumping up the first few rungs and then climbing quickly. *Surely we should be going down?* she thought, but perhaps that was the point. They'd be looking for people trying to escape, not those holing up on the roof.

But they'd be trapped up there.

Jazz reached the roof. There was a small platform and then the roof pitch, shallow enough to climb but still dangerous if she happened to slip. Beyond the ridge, she did not know.

"Up," Stevie said. "We've got to get out of sight."

"They'll shut the building down," she said. "We'll be trapped up here."

"We've got a couple of minutes to get away, that's all."

"You planned this?"

"Over the ridge in the middle of the roof, there's a flat area for air-conditioning and heating equipment. We turn right there, back up and down another pitched area, then there's a tree growing really close—"

"A tree?" Jazz said, aghast. "And what, we jump?"

"Yeah." Stevie pushed past her and started climbing the sloping roof, crawling on hands and knees, gun still clasped in his right hand.

"Stevie—"

"*Later*, Jazz! We don't get away, we're both dead."

She followed him up. They passed between two dormer windows. Jazz expected them to open at any moment. Men would climb out and come for them, grab her ankles, tug just hard enough to set her sliding and falling... *She fell. How tragic.* The police would believe them. They *owned* the police.

Stevie was right. They crested the ridge, dropped down

the opposite slope, and stood on a large flat section of roof hidden away from outside view by pitched areas all around. There were no dormer windows on this side, but there were two doors, both of them closed. Various pieces of machinery sat on paving-slab plinths, humming and buzzing away as they heated or cooled. Pipes lay everywhere.

"Over here," Stevie said. And then one of the doors opened.

Jazz froze. Her view was partially blocked by a big condenser, but she saw the shape step quickly through the door and close it. *Terence!* she thought. *Let it be Terence!*

The man stepped lightly across the roof between some equipment. He disappeared for a moment. Stevie was crouched down several feet away, looking at her, eyebrows raised. Jazz shrugged.

The man emerged a few steps from her and smiled. "Little girl," he said.

Stevie stood up and aimed the gun, holding it with both hands as if he knew what he was doing. "Don't fucking move."

"Or what?" the man said. "You'll shoot me?" He was smart, short but strong-looking, and his expression betrayed only confidence. He didn't seem to be carrying any weapons.

"I shot that bastard mayor."

"No you didn't," he said, frowning, and Jazz thought, *Maybe some of them don't even know yet*. But then the frown turned into a sad smile. "He committed suicide. Tragic. But at least that means the police won't be looking for anyone else in connection with his death."

Stevie shifted from one foot to the other, but the gun never wavered. "Kneel down," he said.

"No." The man shook his head.

"Turn around, kneel down, and put your hands—"

"Fuck you, shit for brains." The man's voice was soft and calm. He shifted his gaze from Stevie to Jazz. "This turn you on?" he asked, nodding at Stevie. "This hard-man act?"

Stevie fired.

The man's eyes went wide in surprise, then his left leg folded and he went down.

To begin with, Jazz couldn't see where he'd been hit, and she looked frantically for the wound. Then the man's trouser leg turned dark as blood pulsed from his thigh.

"Shit for brains," Stevie said.

The man smiled, a pained grimace.

"People will have heard that," Jazz said. "We need to go now!"

Stevie glared at the downed man, gun still pointing at him, and Jazz gave him a hard nudge. *"Now!"*

Jazz pushed past him, skirted around a piece of humming machinery, and started climbing the slope. Her foot slipped on a loose slate and she fell, the slate sliding down to the flat roof. She climbed again, more careful this time, and she heard Stevie scrambling up the slope behind her.

"Here!" the wounded man started shouting. "On the roof!"

When she reached the ridge, she paused and took a careful peek over. The other side of the house was mostly lawn, and there was the huge old oak tree that Stevie had mentioned. It grew very close to the house, a thick branch pointing at the building like an old finger. It was a six-foot jump at least.

"You're kidding," Jazz said.

"Got a better idea?"

"On the roof!" the man screamed again, and they both heard a door burst open behind them.

"Go!" Stevie said.

Jazz swung one leg over the ridge and started sliding. She clawed at the slates, a fingernail snapping back as it caught, but her weight pulled her down. She tried to gain her knees but she rolled instead, and with each roll she saw the edge of the roof coming frighteningly closer.

A hand closed around her ankle. She gasped as Stevie clasped tight, and her left foot and hand dipped into the gutter at the roof's edge. It was filled with dead leaves and slime, and it flexed and dipped alarmingly beneath her weight.

Looking back, she saw Stevie stretched headfirst down the roof. He still held his gun, and his lips were pressed together, veins standing out on his forehead as he struggled to keep hold of her.

Jazz carefully knelt, then sat on the roof, leaning back so that her center of gravity was lower. Stevie let go of her leg and gasped in relief.

"Thanks," Jazz said.

"Jump," Stevie said. "We have seconds."

She glanced at Stevie and the gun in his hand and wanted to say, *Don't make things any worse*, but she realized they were as bad as they could get. If these men caught them, they'd be dead.

Jazz eyed the limb of the oak tree, balanced on her feet with her arms outstretched for balance, then leaped. The branch punched her in the chest and she held on, legs swinging, hands scrabbling for purchase.

"Swing left!" Stevie called, and behind his voice were others, quieter and less panicked, more in control.

Jazz swung her legs to the left and kicked a branch. One trainer caught and she heaved her other leg up, swung both arms over the branch before her, and then lay across it, looking back to Stevie.

"Come on!" she said, but he had already turned to look up the slope of the roof. A shape appeared above the ridge and he shot at it, aiming again even as Jazz saw that it was a diversion.

"Look out!" she shouted. Farther along the ridge a man rose up—Philip, a loose slate in each hand. He flung them. The first bounced from the roof and shattered, shards flying over Stevie's head. The second caught him square in the face.

He dropped the gun. It slid from the roof, caught in the gutter for a second, then spun down to the ground below. Jazz watched. There was solid paving down there, a patio, and it was at least twenty-five feet down.

"Stevie!" she shrieked.

He turned to her slowly, but he could not see. The slate had caught him across the bridge of the nose and just beneath his eyes, and the wound it had made was horrendous.

"Jump!" Jazz said, but it came out more like a sob.

Philip and another man were sliding down the roof toward him, taking their time because they knew they had him. Philip grinned madly. They could see the blood, and the shiver that went through Stevie was all too apparent.

Perhaps it was a final act of defiance. Maybe Stevie was already unconscious. Jazz would never know. But she would never forget the sight of him falling forward from the edge of the roof and striking the ground headfirst. Nor would she forget the sound his body made as it hit concrete, or the disappointed expressions on the men's faces as they realized Stevie had denied them their revenge.

Jazz had no fear now; she was numb. There was little thought about where the best handholds were. She reached the trunk of the tree and climbed down, finding another heavy limb that led out toward the street. She walked along this one, ducking below other branches, holding on to whatever she found above her, until she could see the tall boundary wall below her. She lowered herself down, jumped from the wall, and landed on the pavement, rolling to the left.

Hands grasped her shoulders.

"Come with me!" Terence said softly. He helped her stand and guided her across the road, and she followed in mute acceptance. She knew that if there was any chance of escape, it would be with him. He cursed as they ran, muttering to himself and hauling Jazz as though she were a bit of baggage.

Terence ripped off her hat and glasses and buried them in a bin, ruffled her hair, tried to wipe her tears away. Unable to stop herself, she cast one last glance at the mayor's house.

Mortimer Keating stood on the street corner, beside the open rear door of a black BMW. He seemed calm, as though the events that had just unfolded—the sound of gunshots and the appearance of Jazz from the branches of that tree—had been no surprise at all. Uncle Mort held something to his ear, a radio or a phone. From that distance she and Terence could easily have outrun him, but he didn't make any move to pursue them. Instead, he simply waved at Jazz and smiled, as though he had a secret.

"What the hell is that about?" she said.

Terence looked back as Uncle Mort slipped into the backseat of the BMW. The car pulled away.

"What's what about?" Terence said.

Jazz didn't reply. Her mind whirled. As she hurried along the street, she stole glances down alleys and into parked cars, even looked up at the windows of houses. The back of her neck burned with the feeling of being observed. Her mother had raised her to be paranoid, but she couldn't shake the idea that this was more than her upbringing.

Why hadn't Mort chased her? Only two possibilities presented themselves to her: either he did not want to, or he did not need to. Either way she felt confused and uneasy, even in the midst of her horror and grief about what Stevie had done and how he had paid for it.

Jazz and Terence were walking along a tree-lined street now, the houses not as opulent as in the mayor's district but still large and imposing. At the wail of a siren, they slipped into an alley to await the passage of a speeding police car.

"Did you see it?" he asked, as they set out walking again.

"Yes," Jazz said. Her voice sounded empty and flat. "Shot him in the head."

"The battery!" Terence said. "Did you see the *battery*?"

Jazz frowned, thinking for a moment that perhaps Terence had lost it. But she could see the knowledge of what had happened in his face. He knew. He was not stupid.

"The battery?"

"When you saw the mayor, before Stevie killed him, did you see the battery?" They'd stopped on the street and Terence held both of her shoulders, ready to shake. If they'd wanted to attract more attention to themselves, she supposed they could have stripped and started screwing on the pavement.

"Stevie's dead," Jazz whispered. "He fell. I watched him fall, and—"

"Fuck it!" Terence shouted. He looked around then, shook his head, and ran a hand over his ruffled hair, as if flattening it down would smooth over the fuckup this had become. "Come on."

As they started walking again, Jazz said, "Did you hear me? Stevie's dead."

"His fault," he said.

"What?"

"And Harry's. Harry's more than his, I suppose. That old bastard steered him."

They turned right into a narrow lane that led to the rear of the houses, passed several parked cars—Audis, BMWs, sporty soft-tops—then Terence vaulted a fence and held out his hands for Jazz to follow.

She hesitated, looking around. The presence of the BMWs troubled her. In her mind she could still see Mort's smile and that casual wave.

"Where are we going?" she asked.

"Tube," he said. "I have a flat in Colliers Wood; we can hole up there for a while." He seemed distracted, never quite meeting her eyes. He was fuming, and she sensed him ready to boil over.

"I don't know you," she said. Terence looked at her, then away again, straining over the fence.

"Come on!" he said. "I won't wait all day."

Tube, Jazz thought. *Safest place for me right now.* She was momentarily surprised at how she had come to view the

Underground as safe, but there were things down there she was starting to understand more and more, and things up here she knew less and less. Her world seemed to be changing with every breath. She could fight those changes or follow.

"I believe you," she said. "I just don't know you anymore." She grasped his hands and he pulled her over the fence.

As they walked, her legs hurt more and more. She had cut herself on the top of the security wall and gashed her shin on a broken roof tile but barely been aware of the injuries until now. In spots, her trousers had turned dark with blood, but her injuries were not serious; nothing a few bandages and some antibiotic cream wouldn't cure. They hurt when she walked, but she welcomed the pain, because Stevie could not feel pain anymore, nor could Cadge or her mother. She was hurting because she was still alive, and even though she had just seen two people die, she felt a moment of utter joy, a shocking euphoria. A bee buzzed them, weeds bent beneath their feet and sprang up again, and when they reached a busy main street she looked up at clouds, colorful window boxes, and the way life filled this place.

A police car cruised by, and Terence turned her to face a bookshop window. She saw his reflection, and even there his eyes seemed dark.

"There was no battery," Jazz said.

"We didn't search the whole house."

"There was nothing in the mayor's room but the mayor."

"That means nothing. Damn it. So close!" She knew he wanted to shout, but he whispered instead.

She looked along the street and saw the familiar Tube symbol above the pavement. *Almost there*, she thought. They walked on. Jazz thought about linking arms to give them the look of a couple, but Terence was frowning at the ground as he walked now, arms swinging by his side and lips pursed in concentration. When they reached the Tube station, he turned right and paused at the ticket machine, buying two Travelcards for them. He handed one to Jazz, passed through the turnstile, and started down the stairs. Jazz followed. He seemed to be moving without giving thought to where he was going, and right now that suited her well. She'd happily get lost down here forever.

She wondered whether Harry knew what had happened. Probably not, but he had his ways and means.

They waited on a crowded platform, Terence still staring down at his feet but no longer frowning. His face now seemed blank.

When the train arrived, he got on without looking to see whether Jazz followed. She almost did not. But as the doors started to slide shut she jumped on, eager to stay close to Terence simply because she still felt vulnerable. They'd be searching for her, now more than ever before. The way Mort had smiled at her—he'd seemed so confident he had her—worried her deeply. Had he really known they would break into the mayor's? Had he known they were searching for the battery there? And what else did he know?

Terence might be ignoring her, but the last thing she wanted was to be alone.

He had sat down, and he swayed in time with the train's motion. Jazz hung on to a strap, and when they stopped at the next station and there was a spare seat, she sat down beside him. He glanced at her, then stared, and he smiled. It did not look good on his face. It was the smile of someone with nothing to live for.

She leaned in close. "There *was* no battery," she said. "Just him in that room and—"

"There was no battery *ever*," Terence said. "Not in that house. Taken a while to figure that out. That's not like me."

Jazz sat back and looked at the man across from her. He was about Harry's age, smart, and he stared at her feet as the train shook and shimmied its way through the tunnels. *No battery ever*, she thought, and she remembered Stevie aiming through the door at the mayor as the man tried magic. She'd thought he was laughing for a moment, but Stevie had rarely had any laughter in him. So dour for a boy his age. So serious.

"Harry," she said. "He set it all up."

Terence laughed, a little too loud for her liking. He drew a few stares. "Harry!" he said. "Yeah, Harry." He leaned in close. "I hate being used," he said, quieter and in his real voice. She'd always thought that beneath the outward veneer he could be dangerous, and those words were as threatening as any Jazz had ever heard.

"He never meant for Stevie to die, though," she said.

Terence shrugged. "Bad luck, that's all."

"You don't care?" She turned to face him, smelling his breath and looking straight into his eyes.

Terence raised an eyebrow. "Really? No. In the scheme of things—"

"You're a machine. That's it for you, isn't it? The scheme of things."

"Yes," he said. "What I'm doing is *serious*, Jazz. I'm not

playing games here. Not messing around like your Harry and his precious United fucking Kingdom." He kept his voice low, but he was more solemn than she had ever seen him. No flirty smiles now, no calm assurance. This was Terence at his most basic. She didn't like it one bit.

"People are dead," she said.

He shrugged again. "Everyone dies."

The train began to slow. Jazz didn't even know which station it was, but she knew she would be getting off. And if Terence tried to stop her, she'd scream for help, and everyone on the carriage would be on him.

"If that's the case, why still seek revenge for your dead father?" She stood and held on to a strap, swaying left and right as the train ground to a halt. For a second she thought he was going to call her back. But he was too proud for that, too angry.

As the train pulled away, Terence smiled at her, and Jazz knew that she would see him again.

She caught the next train, got off three stops along, and caught another, staggering her journey in an effort to lose any potential pursuers. Mort's smile still lingered in her mind. And the sight of Stevie falling. She felt alone and lost, shielded somewhat by the weight of the ground around her but assaulted by the stares of a thousand strangers. Her cut legs were hurting like a bastard now that the shock was wearing off, and more than once she thought about her journey through that oak tree to the wall. How she had made it, she had no clue. Something must have guided her feet, steered her hands, breathed luck into every step she took down through the tree and over the wall.

Every time she closed her eyes for more than a blink, she heard Stevie's head hitting the stone patio.

She had trouble acknowledging what had happened, though in reality it was startlingly, brutally simple: Harry had used them all to get his revenge upon the mayor for Cadge's death. Terence's suggestion that the battery could have been at the mayor's residence had seeded a plan in Harry's mind, and his offer to help Terence steal it was the perfect cover. He'd done his walk-by, and whether or not he truly had the power to sense magic, he'd likely felt nothing. Getting in had all been about Stevie and his gun. They couldn't have done it without Terence's gadgets to disable the alarms, and Harry had known that Terence would not have gone in without Jazz.

She'd almost died. If Stevie hadn't grabbed her as she rolled down that roof, it would have been her head making that awful splitting sound as it struck the mayor's patio. It would have been her body resting in some shallow grave, or being eaten by pigs, or however else the BMW men would get rid of Stevie's remains. She would have been dead if it weren't for Stevie, and Harry was obviously prepared to have that on his conscience.

She had nowhere else to go. She had to stay down here, away from the glare of the sun and the searching men dressed in suits and ties. Away from Mort's knowing smile.

And besides, something was drawing her down. It was more than the sense of safety afforded her when she was down in the Tube stations, more than the feeling of coming home, which she had tried to deny for a long time but which resounded through her every cell. This was something as inexplicable as magnetism.

When she came to a part of the Underground she recognized, she waited until the platform was all but deserted, then entered the tunnel. She walked quickly along to where she knew there would be an opening, silently counting down to when the next train would come through. Blown tiles crumbled beneath her feet like dried shed skin. Water dripped from a broken main in the ground above. It was warm as blood. Rats squealed, and she wondered if they could smell *her* blood.

She shook her head and cursed, trying to drive down such morbid thoughts. She heard a sound in the distance like a hundred people moaning in unison, and at first she froze, expecting an Hour of Screams. She did not *fear* it. Old death was nothing to be afraid of. But it was a train, and she quickened her step until she found the opening.

Through doors, along dank corridors, across unused lines, and through excavations long forgotten by anyone else, Jazz made her way down. At one point she paused at a ruined door, suddenly feeling the need to turn left where there was no opening. She stared at the curved wall there, closing her eyes and feeling the draw even stronger than before, and when she looked again she could make out the different shades of cement. Picking up a fallen brick from back along the corridor, she bashed at the wall a few times. Cement came away, wet and rotten. She exposed two areas of contrasting brickwork, one old, the other even older, and the oldest area seemed to describe the shape of a doorway.

"What's beyond?" she whispered. Her voice was very loud, and she realized that question must have been asked down here a million times before. The Underground was an escape, never a home, and anyone living down here was simply borrowing the space from something else.

She went on, and at one point she heard a sound behind her, metal against stone. She stopped and held her breath, hunkered down in the darkness and listening for a repeat of the sound. But there was nothing. There were always strange noises down here, some of which could be explained, many that could not. She supposed such mysteries always came with ghosts.

She found one of the United Kingdom's torch stores and welcomed the light to guide her down. Upon reaching the grand arched entrance to the Palace, she started crying, and try as she might she could not hold back the tears. When amorphous shapes appeared before her, she dropped the torch and held out her hands, welcoming them in, not knowing whether they were alive or dead and not really caring.

"Stevie's dead," she said. Her voice was cool and blank, despite the tears.

Harry stepped back as though she'd slapped him in the face. She heard gasps of shock from the others—Hattie, Leela, Gob—and she tried not to look their way, because she knew she'd see her own grief mirrored there.

"He did what you sent him to do, like a good little servant, and then they chased us and killed him. He saved me first...He stopped me from..." She held her face in her hands and cried some more, and when Harry touched the back of her neck, she shrugged him off and walked across the subterranean room.

"I never meant for this," Harry said. "He went with a

task, but I never meant for this." He was being careful what he said, and Jazz realized he didn't want everyone else to know how he and Stevie had conspired. It would taint the kids' opinion of him, knowing he was a murderer by intention. At first she closed her eyes and tried to judge how heavy that knowledge would be, unshared. Did she have the right to shatter their illusions of their savior?

She looked at Harry, his wide watery eyes, the long coat, and she tried to imagine him walking past the mayor's house and sensing nothing. Standing at the gates and chanting abuse. Knowing that Stevie, Terence, and she were breaking into the wolves' den, and however much he told her now, he would have known there was a good chance one of them would get hurt or killed. A very good chance.

And Jazz realized that, yes, she absolutely did have that right. Because the United Kingdom needed to know who Harry really was.

"You sent him to kill the mayor. You sent him to murder."

Harry stepped back, looking for a moment like a startled dog. He looked around the big room at the other kids and shook his head.

"Yes, Harry," she said sadly. "Yes."

"For Cadge," he said. "Poor little Cadge—now, don't you think he deserved something, Jazz girl?"

Jazz could not answer. Tears were threatening again, burning behind her face and filling her throat. Hattie came to her and stood by her side.

"It was for him," Harry said.

"And what of Terence?"

Harry scoffed. "Him and his precious battery? Fool! He

thinks he can do what his father before him couldn't, and I've no time for such daftness, Jazz girl. Now listen—Leela will fetch the first-aid kit and have a look at your legs," he said, gesturing toward her bloodied trousers, though Jazz could have told him the bleeding had stopped. "And then we'll talk, you and I. Have a real good adult chat about—"

"Adult," Jazz said, laughing softly. "Stevie was barely that, Harry. I saw his head burst open when he hit the ground." She stared at the tall figure of Harry Fowler and tried to see something in his eyes when she said that, something that would give her a shred of hope for his soul. Perhaps it was the poor light in that place, or a blurring from her tears, but she saw nothing.

"Hour of Screams!" Faith said, dashing in from one of the other rooms. Her blue eyes were wide with fear, and she knelt down, covered her ears, and started singing a song.

Harry glanced at Jazz. "Second time today," he said. "Something's happening." He stared at her for a moment, so intensely that she thought he was going to run at her, strike her. Then he sighed and sat down, singing his own sad song.

Jazz stood and ran. She could not bear to share the experience of London's pain with this man or be in the same place as him when she felt the ethereal tendrils of the old town's ghosts passing by. She went back into the tunnels, passing the place where she had hidden those photos. That seemed like so long ago now, and she almost saw the form of her younger, more innocent self squatting there, picking away broken glass and closing the dumbwaiter on the images of her father. She sat against the wall opposite and felt the screams beginning deep within her bones. It always came that way first, a feeling, before the true sounds came in. It was almost as if the ghosts came from within instead of without, and Jazz wondered whether it was like this for everyone.

She hugged herself, eyes open, and sang softly as the Hour of Screams washed over, around, and through her. The air in the corridor became opaque at first, and then the walls seemed to fade away to welcome in a long column of marching people. At first she thought they were soldiers, but then she saw the weary faces and sad eyes—none of them turned her way—and she recognized kindred spirits. These were lost souls, wandering the Underground because daylight would not welcome them.

Jazz followed, gasping as a line of people walked right through her.

Out in the main tunnel, the figures had faded away, but there were others now, blurs of motion, movement, and sensation that threatened to overwhelm her senses. Several of them turned to her as though pleading that she continue watching. She kept singing softly as she followed them away from the Palace. The tunnel turned a corner and merged with a connection route between two larger tunnels, and here the images started fading.

Wait, she thought, because she had the pressing idea that they had something to tell her. Jazz stopped singing, ready to shout at them to wait for her. But as she exhaled, her breath seemed to forge a clear space through the fleeting shapes, as though they were made of little more than mist. They wavered in the air before her. The screaming diminished and started to echo, retreating even as the ghosts dissipated. And as the real screaming began behind her, a more solid shape swam through the fog of London's agonized past to stand before her.

Mortimer Keating raised a pistol and pointed it at Jazz's face. Her breath caught in her throat. And now she understood the smile on his face outside the mayor's house. They'd found Harry and the United Kingdom once before, and now they'd found them again. He'd been in no rush to give chase, because he'd already known where to find Jazz.

"You've led us a merry chase, Jasmine. Your old man would've been proud," Uncle Mort said.

Hatred gave her courage. "I'm sure he'd be pleased you murdered his wife. Now you'll kill his daughter too? What a friend."

The man's grim facade faltered a moment. "Tragic, that. But it couldn't be avoided. Your mum knew all along that you were the very thing we were hunting for. We tried to do right by the two of you, for the sake of your father's memory. But your mum hid the truth. When we figured out you were the battery, we came for you. If she hadn't fought us, she'd still be alive."

Jazz stared at him, eyes wide and mouth agape.

Mort frowned. "Christ, you didn't know?"

Shouts reverberated through the tunnel. Beyond Mort, she saw other Uncles and their thugs fighting with the kids of the United Kingdom. Gob kicked one of the BMW men in the balls and caught a blow to the face for his troubles. A dark-suited man struck Leela with a hard backhand, but then Marco leaped on his back, giving her a chance to run.

Jazz felt sick and hollow inside.

"The battery's inside me?" she asked, turning her gaze upon Mort.

"Not inside you, Jazz. You *are* the bloody battery. Took us forever to figure it out, but—"

She strode toward him. Mort frowned and started to back up.

"Then you won't kill me," she said.

He shot out a hand and grabbed a fistful of her hair. "Doesn't mean I won't hurt you. Oh, and thanks for sorting out the mayor, by the way. He'd become a liability lately. You've done us quite a favor."

Jazz punched him in the throat as hard as she could. The gun fired, bullet ricocheting off down the tunnel, the shot incredibly loud. Mort dropped to his knees, choking, and reached for his throat.

"Fuck off," Jazz said.

A roar erupted down the tunnel and she looked over the kneeling Uncle Mort to see Philip—one-eyed and half mad from exposure to the Hour of Screams—running at her. Mort might not kill her, but Philip certainly would.

She'd started to flee when a shadow rushed past her. She blinked, startled when she saw Harry Fowler brandishing a cricket bat. He swung. Philip raised his forearm to block the attack, and both bat and arm snapped.

As Philip cried out in pain, Harry spun on Jazz, and she saw the *knowing* in his eyes.

"Jesus," she said. "You knew!"

Of course he'd known. He could sense magic, couldn't he? He'd helped Terence locate the other pieces of the apparatus. It all came tumbling over her now. If she truly was the battery, Harry must have known from the moment he met her and never said a word. When it came time to break into the mayor's house, he had known that they wouldn't find anything. He'd manipulated them all just to get his revenge, and that had cost Stevie his life.

Philip shouted in fury and used his good hand to knock the shattered bat from Harry's grasp. They faced off against each other, an old thief and a madman.

"Just go, Jazz girl," Harry said. "Find a place where nobody knows who or what you are. Not Terry and not Josephine Blackwood. The world'll be better off if they all just leave it alone, let things happen in their own time."

Clutching his injured throat, Mortimer Keating began to rise to his feet, shaking. "Philip," he rasped, "kill him."

Philip grinned.

"Harry—" Jazz began.

"Run!" the thief screamed.

Two other BMW men rushed up then, joining Philip, and they fell upon Harry, beating him with their fists and kicking him once he'd dropped to the ground.

Uncle Mort looked around for his pistol. Jazz saw someone else move from the corner of her eye. At first glance she saw the spectral shimmer of a ghost, a familiar jacket and top hat, a flower in the phantom magician's lapel. But the ghost vanished and in his place was Terence Whitcomb.

He held Mort's pistol in his hand.

"Mr. Keating," he said.

Uncle Mort sneered. "Whitcomb."

Terence shot him through the left eye, the back of Mort's head bursting like rotten fruit. The chaos in the tunnel continued. It wasn't the first gunshot to echo around them all, and the Uncles and BMW men who'd come with Mort kept at their task—all save the two who were helping Philip. They looked up and fixed their attention on Jazz, realizing they'd found their target.

Jazz hesitated, wanting to save Gob and Leela and the

others. But if she was the cause of all this, the only way to make her friends safe was to get these bastards away from here. She had to surrender herself.

As if plucking the thought from her mind, Terence reached out and grabbed her wrist. "No. We can lead them away."

"But—"

"You can't do anything for them, Jazz! And the Blackwood Club *can't* have you." He held her arms and spoke into her face, their noses touching, and she could smell the fear on him. His lips touched hers as he spoke, but there was nothing more than words. "We have to leave. Now!"

"But where? Nowhere's safe anymore."

"Down," Terence said. "Deeper." And he pulled, holding her arm as if he might never let go.

Chapter Nineteen

daddy's girl

Jazz ran ahead of him, fleeing into the darker shadows of the Underground. They left the Palace behind, but not without being seen. Shouts followed, and then footfalls, and as Jazz emerged into a wider tunnel where the distant sound of modern Tube trains could be heard, she knew there would be no escape. There were too many Uncles, too many BMW men. Her mother had told her to hide forever, but there was nowhere left to hide.

Deeper, Terence had said.

Fuck that. Deeper only meant a dead end.

Jazz raced along the tunnel. The only light was the barest illumination coming from a couple of vents that were still open to the surface, not nearly enough by which to watch her footing. Yet she threw aside caution and simply ran.

"Damn it, Jasmine!" Terence shouted after her.

It felt fine. Wonderful, in fact. For too long she had allowed herself to be guided by the assertiveness of others. No longer. A hundred yards ahead, she knew of a passageway that separated this tunnel from another, abandoned but more recently in use. It still had rails, and there was a platform there whose many exits had long since been boarded over. But Stevie had shown her a way up, an emergency exit. It was the nearest path up from the Underground.

Her eyes were wide, trying to pick up any source of light, peering at the wall on the right in search of that passageway. More shouts came along the tunnel. Light from torches bobbed dimly behind her, helping to show the way. Then she saw it—a patch of shadow even darker than the rest of the tunnel—and Jazz ran for it. At the wall she paused, taking ragged gasps of air, and reached out with her hands to make sure she wasn't going to run into anything.

A hand clamped her shoulder, spun her around, and in the darkness she could just make out the shape of Terence's face. His scent was warm and comforting, sweat and cinnamon and rich earth. But she didn't want his brand of comfort anymore.

"Let me go!" she hissed.

More voices shouting. She glanced back the way she'd come and saw a dozen points of searching, bobbing light from the torches of the Blackwood Club and their minions.

"Go where? You don't think they'll find you up there?" Terence snapped. "There's only two ways this can end. One of them is with you dead, and I won't see that."

"I'm supposed to *trust* you?"

"You're supposed to want to put an end to them. Take

power from the people who murdered your mother. Prevent them gaining the magic that'll change them, corrupt them. Jazz, it could turn them into *monsters*!"

Jazz glanced into the passageway, swore, and shot him a hard look, hoping the darkness did not prevent him from seeing it.

"Deeper it is, then."

Terence sighed and took her hand, and they ran on together. Their pursuers had drawn closer during the pause. Bright torchlight swept around them.

"I see them!" a voice cried.

"Shoot fucking Whitcomb!" a man ordered.

"Don't hurt the girl!" a woman said.

A woman, Jazz thought. And she knew of only one woman who could give instructions to these men. Josephine Blackwood herself had descended into the Underground.

A gunshot echoed along the tunnel, and Jazz flinched. Terence just kept running. They darted to the left and the torch beams danced around them, trying to pinpoint them again. A short way ahead the tunnel forked, though the narrow left fork had been closed off and bricked over a couple of generations past. Jazz's breath hitched and she stared at the dark brick, feeling a tug on her gut and her heart. She'd felt something similar before, but never this strongly.

She started for the wall, but Terence pulled her along the open fork.

"No. We're supposed to go that way," she said.

"I'm glad you know that. Glad you feel it."

He drew her to a stop just a few yards beyond the split, and she realized there was a heavy wooden door set into the wall, separating one of the fork's tunnels from the other.

Terence turned the handle and it opened easily. He stepped through and crouched down, searching for something in the dark. Jazz heard a click, and light blossomed from a torch in Terence's hand. Just like Harry and the United Kingdom, he must have had them stored in various locations underground. What Jazz wanted to know was why.

"Where are you taking me?"

Terence narrowed his eyes. "Hurry."

It was good advice. The Blackwood Club was closing in. Someone called her name, as if they knew her, and it turned her stomach to realize that they probably did. Some of those men—the Uncles—had known her since she was an infant.

She started to follow Terence through the door and froze, seized by the lure of whatever lay beyond it. Jazz threw back her head, inhaling sharply as a wave of bliss passed through her. Then Terence took her by the hand, and for a moment it was as though the temptation that lay beyond the door was Terence himself.

Jazz broke the contact with him.

"Come on!" he snapped.

She glanced toward their pursuers. They were close enough that she could make out the silhouettes of the Uncles and the BMW men by the gloomy light of their torches. One figure was that of a woman. Josephine Blackwood seemed to float along the floor of the tunnel, long hair framing her face, catching the glint of the lights as though she was more a specter than the ghosts of old London.

Someone laughed, a booming thunder that rolled across the tunnel, and her skin crawled with revulsion. Philip, the half-mad. By now perhaps entirely mad.

"Jazz!" Terence shouted.

But she was no longer paying any attention to him, or to the Blackwood Club. The wind had started blowing along the tunnel, tousling Jazz's hair, and she could hear the banshee cry of the city's ghosts rising.

"Again?" she whispered.

The Hour of Screams had returned once more. The intervals between them were growing shorter and shorter. Harry had been unnerved by them coming so close together, but Jazz breathed deeply and let the breeze wash over her, let the screams come. The ghosts of old London were crying out to be heard. Harry might have seen the phantom images of the city's past, but he had never listened to their cries...their pleas. The time had come for someone to listen.

"Oh, Christ," Terence muttered. "Cover your ears, Jasmine. Find a song!"

Jazz shook her head. "Not this time."

The Uncles and their hired thugs began to shout in alarm. Philip howled like a wolf. Josephine Blackwood snapped off orders to those who had gathered in her name.

The Hour of Screams roared in, and all around Jazz the ghosts of old London began to rise again.

At first, the parade of echoes seemed familiar. There were visions from the days when bombs rained down over London, images of chaos and heartbreak, but the stream of ghosts soon produced more-mundane memories, which vividly revealed the life and laughter of the city, along with its tragedies. There were music halls and couples dancing, actors on a stage, streets filled with early-model cars giving way to brougham carriages. The ghosts of London swept around her like a rushing river, and Jazz stood in the midst of the current and let it wash over her.

She looked up, and the magician was there in his top hat and tails. From one sleeve he produced a bouquet of flowers, and from within his jacket a white dove. The dove took wing.

And it changed.

The Hour of Screams roared around her, and in the midst of that mournful wailing, the dove transformed into another sort of ghost. The entire spectral flow shuddered and rippled and changed.

"What is this?" Jazz whispered. Or perhaps she only thought the words, for the wind would have torn them from her lips.

They overwhelmed her, rushing around her and into her, all of the secrets of old London. She knew not only the pain and the grief but the magic that the city had once contained.

Terence was down on his knees just inside the door into the other tunnel, hands clamped over his ears. Somewhere farther along the ghostly torrent, the members of the Blackwood Club and their bone-breakers would be doing the same, or be tearing at their ears and eyes the way that Philip had.

But Jazz only stared in wonder.

The spectral flow coalesced, shaping itself into a vast chamber whose every wall was covered with bookshelves, a massive library of arcana. There were tables strewn with tools and metalwork, pipes and bolts, along with talismans and still more volumes of lore and magic.

But the heart of the room comprised an enormous confusion of pipes and gauges, gears and levers. It clanked and hissed with steam that emerged in clouds from small valves. The pipes and gauges were ordinary enough, but many other parts were oddly shaped and roughly crafted, obviously made specifically for this machine. They were like nothing she'd ever seen before. Except that wasn't true. One of the gears looked precisely like the blade she had stolen from Mortimer Keating's house.

The steaming structure could only be Alan Whitcomb's apparatus.

And the bespectacled man who stood before it, inspecting a gauge, could only be Whitcomb himself. The resemblance to Terence was not exact—perhaps because of his father's mustache—but it was there.

The Hour of Screams cried in the hiss of the steam from the apparatus. The ghosts of old London shrieked.

Alan Whitcomb stepped into the heart of his machine. He locked a metal arm across his chest and slid his arms into iron cuffs. He positioned his feet so that the sole of each shoe sat atop a different lever. Jazz saw the fear on his face—fear of the unknown—and she understood then that Terence's father had made the apparatus to function with himself as the battery.

In that fog of ghosts, she watched as the man withdrew from the machine. At first she thought he had lost his nerve, but when he sat down at a table with a sheet of calculations and a heavy, dusty *grimoire*, she realized that some essential element had not yet been completed.

The spectral image flowed and changed, and now she saw him seated in a meditative pose amid a circle of candles, letting his own blood flow with a sharp blade, spattering crimson droplets onto long metal gears inscribed with strange runes and a quartet of crystal spheres that seemed to absorb the blood.

This is for me, Jazz thought. Aside from the visits of that Victorian magician, all of her previous experiences with the ghosts of old London had seemed random, but there was nothing random about this. The Hour of Screams was the cries of those ancient echoes, the restless, anguished spirits of the city, and they had chosen to replay these events for her.

"Show me," Jazz said.

A figure manifested and she knew him immediately, though only from photographs.

"Dad," she whispered.

The ghost made no sign that he had heard her or even recognized her presence. With the exception of the magician, that was always the way. The shades of the past acted out some bit of ghostly theater, but that did not mean they were the wandering spirits of the actual people whose faces were revealed to her. The fading magic of London itself might have manifested those images or the collective yearning of those whose ghosts did still linger in the city.

This specter was not her father.

Yet Jazz's heart ached terribly as she watched him. The shouts and singing of the members of the Blackwood Club—themselves trying to survive the Hour of Screams—retreated beyond her awareness. Though Terence knelt quite nearby, he seemed a world away. In those moments, Jazz felt as though she had been swept into the substance of the spectral, becoming a ghost herself.

The gray shadow of Alan Whitcomb's occult laboratory still existed around her, the bulky apparatus with all of its odd juttings still in the center of the room, yet the image of her father existed in the same space, a ghost of her own past layered on top of one from Terence's. The phantom of the elder Whitcomb stood by the apparatus, fixing a bloodied—perhaps bewitched—gear into place.

Her father's ghost stood among the burning candles and the spatters of Whitcomb's blood, and he drew a curved dagger from his coat, moving within the shifting shadows toward the other man.

Jazz stared, eyes wide.

The specters weren't layered. The vision unfolding before her was not some odd combination of events but a single moment from London's past.

Her father spoke, though she couldn't hear his voice. Whitcomb spun, hands up instantly, ready to defend his infernal machine. James Towne gestured with the blade, which Jazz now saw had been marked with strange symbols not unlike those on the apparatus itself. He tried to force Alan Whitcomb away from his invention, but the man's face contorted with hatred and fury. Her father brandished the blade, a warning, a threat, and the two men began to shout at each other.

All Jazz heard was the wailing of the Hour of Screams, but she didn't need to hear the words spoken. She saw the story playing out on their faces. Her father wanted Whitcomb to back away from the apparatus, intending to either destroy it or use it somehow. Whitcomb had a zealot's eyes.

When her father made a move toward the apparatus, Whitcomb lunged at him, yet it seemed to Jazz very little like an attack. The inventor leaped upon her father, who tried to back away, tried to pull back his blade. The curved tip of that wicked dagger punctured Whitcomb's abdomen. Her father tried to push the man away, and then Whitcomb did something entirely mad. He wrapped his hands around her father's throat and began to throttle him, pushing him backward and down even as he dropped himself down onto that blade.

Blood flowed from his belly, soaking her father's shirt.

Her father pushed Whitcomb off. He clamped his hands on the sides of his head, staring at the inventor in anguish. He shook his head and began to shout. Jazz could read the cursing on his lips. The gruesome pantomime became even more bizarre as her father, panicking, raced to the apparatus and studied it for a moment before rushing to the table Jazz had seen Whitcomb seated at before.

He was frantic. Though that ritual dagger still jutted from Whitcomb's belly, it seemed obvious he hadn't meant to kill the man. In a frenzy, her father began to gather items from the laboratory, lining them up just outside the circle of candles Whitcomb had left on the floor. Then he grabbed hold of the bleeding, barely conscious inventor and dragged him in a swath of blood across the floor into the midst of those candles, leaving a crimson streak behind.

Alan Whitcomb's mouth opened, half a sneer and half a smile. He laughed and blood bubbled on his lips. When he spoke, even with the Hour of Screams around her, she understood every word. In that moment it seemed almost as though all the ghosts of old London were speaking with him, whispering the words into her ears.

Without a battery, it's just rubbish. Damn fool. Without me, it's useless.

The inventor laughed again, choking on his own blood. Jazz's father ignored him, relighting extinguished candles and unrolling a scroll that seemed ancient at first glance, until the designs and writing were revealed. These were plans for the apparatus. Her father tossed the scroll aside and grabbed another, and another still, until finally he had before him a pattern of symbols.

He had piled small dishes of dye or paint nearby, and now he plunged his fingers into one filled with ochre and daubed it at his temples, then inscribed circles upon his cheeks. Tearing off his shirt, he painted his chest with the symbols on Whitcomb's scroll, flecks of ochre flying like spittle. Even as he did this, his mouth was moving and his body rocked to some repetition of words, some spell or chant.

Then he knocked the ink pots aside and slid over beside the dying Whitcomb. He tore open the man's shirt and there, laid bare, were the same symbols he had just painted upon himself. His eyes were filled with regret and he hesitated, shaking his head in frustration.

Jazz watched her father place both hands onto the handle of the dagger.

"No," she said, the word both a plea and a denial.

Chanting, he withdrew the curved dagger from Whitcomb's abdomen, raised it, and drove the blade into the man's chest, stabbing him in the heart. Jagged lances of bright silver light crackled around the blade and raced up James Towne's arms. His hair stood on end, and the sigils he'd daubed on his flesh with ochre ink flashed with a brilliant light. As though electrified, her father shook, hands still locked on the dagger, a circuit of power traveling from his fingers down through the blade and into Alan Whitcomb's heart.

Jazz screamed, her voice mixing with the anguished moans and wails of old London. The wind of the Hour of Screams buffeted her, increasing in force and urgency. The fog of ghostly images wavered as though it might blow away, but instead it rippled and altered yet again.

Whitcomb's apparatus evaporated, the laboratory around it shifting. Lights cut the darkness, and at first she thought that somehow the Blackwood Club had overcome the Hour of Screams and was attacking, the lights their torches. Then she saw the silhouette of the car rolling through the fog and staggered back. The headlamps shone through the spectral mist, and in it she could make out dozens of tiny, dour faces.

The car jerked to a halt at a strange angle, half on the curb. The door swung open and her father staggered out, not bothering to close the door. Jazz stared at him and she knew something had gone horribly wrong. He'd gone to try to take control of Whitcomb's apparatus, but the inventor had sacrificed himself to deprive the Blackwood Club of the battery, because he'd made *himself* the battery. Her father had tried to use the same magic Whitcomb had manipulated to transfer the power into himself, to become the battery so that it would not die with Whitcomb. But he'd been rushed. Frenzied.

It had not gone well.

Whatever magic Whitcomb had used, in his desperation her father hadn't done it correctly. Looking at him, Jazz could see it all. His eyes bled scarlet tears. Silver light flickered behind them, and the sigils on his flesh glowed. His body had begun to wither. This must have been the very same night, but he looked twenty years older, as though some cancer had eaten away at him.

He staggered toward the house. Jazz nearly crumbled when she saw it, sketched there in the fog of ghosts. Her childhood home. Only when she tasted the salt of her own tears on her lips did she realize she had begun to cry. She shook her head, wishing she could call back to her father across the years.

Jazz watched him go up to the door, fishing in his pocket for the key. "I don't want to see," she whispered, the words a kind of keening cry, a prayer, a wish.

But she could not look away from the sight of him staggering up the stairs and into her bedroom, where he stood over her crib. He swayed as he gazed down at baby Jasmine.

He reached down into the crib and picked her up, then made his way—stumbling once and nearly dropping her—to the rocking chair in the corner. Withering even as she watched him, crumbling in upon himself like wilting flowers, he collapsed into the chair, holding baby Jazz in his arms.

Crying, he kissed her forehead.

In the now, Jazz dropped to her knees and wept along with him, the ghosts swirling around her head with a final gust of wind.

Silver light spilled from her father's lips and his tears, and it crackled like lightning in a burst of illumination from the sigils on his papery skin. In his arms, the infant gurgled happily as her entire body flared with brilliant light, eyes gleaming silver. The glow slowly vanished.

James Towne's last breath rattled in his throat.

Baby Jasmine settled down, slipping back to sleep.

A slap cleared her mind. Blinking, Jazz stared up at Terence, her cheek stinging from the blow. From the depths of her sadness, anger flared, even as she became aware again of the ground under her knees and the cool air of the tunnel. Her tears began to dry on her face.

"What the hell—" she began.

He grabbed her wrist, pulling her to her feet. "Pay attention, Jasmine. While you were off with the fairies there, the Hour passed. Or didn't you notice the screams were gone?"

Jazz glanced around. In the midst of the vision that had played out before her, she hadn't noticed at all. But he was right. The Hour of Screams had ended. A ragged voice came to her from down the length of the black tunnel, exhorting others to rise and give pursuit. Torches clicked on, one by one.

Some of the Uncles and the BMW men might have been affected by the Hour, but not all. Josephine Blackwood would have seen to that. They were still after her.

"Come on!" Terence whispered, tugging her through the door and into the parallel tunnel. His torch lit the way, picking out dripping sludge and a scurrying rat.

It was her nature to resist, but not this time. Jazz let him lead her along the tunnel, careful with her footing and trying to pick up the pace. She had to make sense of what she'd seen, had to decide what it would mean for her.

"Faster!" Terence said.

His grip tightened on her hand. Jazz shook her head to clear it and matched him step for step.

"What happened to you back there? What did you see?"

She took a deep breath and cast a sidelong glance at him. All along she'd held her secrets close. Her mother had taught her never to share too much of herself. A dreadfully sad lesson, now that she considered it, but Terence had done the same, and Harry as well. All of them with their secrets. If only they'd been truthful with one another, things might have turned out much differently.

"You know about the ghosts," she said, and it wasn't a question. Of course he did.

"Harry sees them," Terence said. "I had an idea early on that you see them too. Now I know."

A loud crash behind them signaled the arrival of the Blackwood Club. The Uncles and the BMW men would be pouring through the door between tunnels now. A glance back showed her the wavering glow of a trio of bright torches, but there would be more.

"Where are we going?" she asked.

"I told you. Deeper."

Jazz gave a soft, sickened laugh. Still more secrets.

"I know the story now. How this all began," she said. And then she told him, as succinctly as she could, the tale of their two fathers and their shared tragedy.

"I've never been much of a believer in destiny," she whispered, breathing heavily now with the exertion of their flight. "But this is all so tied together, it can't just be coincidence."

Terence could only nod.

They were still holding hands and Jazz felt the contact acutely.

"So what am I supposed to do? It's magic, isn't it?"

Terence darted abruptly to the left, hauling her with him and nearly colliding with the stone wall. She put out a hand and leaned against it, feeling the rough surface under her fingers. He held his torch pointed at the ground, and the yellow gloom it cast made them both look like ghosts.

"That's not why we're here," Terence said, his gaze grim. "We're here to move on from magic, not to grow stronger from it. If you have a destiny, it's to finish the job my father started—the job your father interrupted."

She felt his grief and relented. Whether he was right or wrong, Jazz wasn't sure it mattered. All of the tales she had heard about magic—Terence's and Harry's and her own—they were all tragedies. Had her mother known the truth of what her baby had become all along or only learned it in the end?

It no longer mattered. She'd tried to run away from the part she had been meant to play. Her mother had tried so hard to prepare her for that. But she could never have run far enough or hidden deep enough.

Terence shone his torch on a rectangular metal hatch about four feet high and two wide. He pushed it open, and once more Jazz felt that tugging, a fishhook set deeply into her chest, pulling her through and downward. A narrow curving stone staircase lay before them, and they quickly descended.

"Quiet," Jazz said, concerned about the sounds of their footsteps.

"It doesn't matter. Josie Blackwood's got a little magic of her own. The whole club dabbles, fancying themselves as true sorcerers. They want to take the old magic of the city into themselves, have the kind of power no one's seen for centuries. But for now she's got enough to follow our trail. How do you think they found you? It took a while, but they found you every time. And she's come too close to lose us now."

The stairs continued winding downward. Jazz had not thought to count them, but just when she began to think they must have descended two hundred or more—and the shouts of their pursuers started to follow them down—they reached another iron door. Terence swung it open on thick, squealing hinges and flashed the torchlight into the chamber ahead.

Shadows retreated, strange silhouettes scattering into the deeper darkness. Jazz might have asked what they were, but Terence pulled her through into the chamber and then they were running again. What she saw of the floor and walls in the torchlight unnerved her. The stones that had been built into the foundations and arches of these subterranean caverns were ancient things, dating back at least to Roman control of London, perhaps further. These were the halls of old kings or the churches of archaic gods.

They raced through corridors and courtyards and chambers, down short flights of stone steps. At last Terence drew them to a halt. Jazz shook her hand loose from his, simultaneously relieved and disappointed at the loss of contact. Without the feel of his hand in hers, she felt alone. The weight of the entire city hung over her.

Terence fished in his pocket and withdrew an object. Jazz narrowed her eyes, trying to make out what it was. He snapped it open and gave it a flick, and a tiny flame blossomed to life. A lighter. What did he need with that when he had a torch?

He dropped it into a narrow gutter to the left of the door they had just stepped through, and a small rivulet of oil ignited. A line of fire raced along the perimeter of the circular room, a ring of flame that illuminated the vast chamber and threw dancing shadows on the high, domed ceiling.

Alan Whitcomb's apparatus filled the center of the chamber.

Jazz caught her breath. "You've been building it down here all along?"

"I couldn't do it aboveground. They would have found me eventually. And this was my father's intention from the start, to use it down here in what was once the heart of the city."

In the flickering firelight, she stared at the massive contraption. It sat awaiting its final component, the battery that would bring it to life.

"They're not far behind us," Terence warned.

"I know that!"

The visions she had seen in the tunnels above were fresh in her mind. Whitcomb had prepared all of the parts of the apparatus. She had seen him testing the gears and levers in his occult laboratory.

Taking a deep breath, she approached the apparatus. She could see the levers where she was supposed to put her feet, the metal braces that would hold her arms, the bracket that would close upon her chest. The ghosts had not only given up the secrets of Jazz's past. They had shown her what they required of her.

"I don't understand," she said, wrapping her hand around a cold metal pipe that made up part of the apparatus. It thrummed in her hand like the rails in one of the Tube tunnels, alive with distant power. "You rebuilt this thing, but you didn't know the battery was a person?"

He shook his head. "I knew someone had to operate it from the inside. I've strapped myself in a hundred times, trying different power sources. There are connections for outside power; I suppose he left them intact only to test the apparatus, but I always presumed the battery would attach there. How could I have known the battery would be a human? Who could have imagined it?"

Jazz took a deep breath. Trembling, she gazed up at the gauges and bars and steam valves of the apparatus. When Terence put a hand on her shoulder, she did not turn to meet his gaze.

"What will happen to me?" she asked.

Down there in the cold heart of the city, the only sound was the crackling of the flames that lit the chamber. Then Jazz heard approaching voices and footfalls and knew that they were out of time.

Terence did not reply. That was good. If he'd said anything other than *I don't know*, it would have been a lie, and the time for lying was over.

Jazz grabbed hold of two thick pipes and stepped up into the apparatus. It began to hum.

Chapter
Twenty

off the rails

The ghosts had been waiting for her. As Jazz locked herself into the apparatus—even before she began to put her weight on the levers beneath her feet—apparitions began to manifest in the fire ring and in the shadows of the domed ceiling above her. Phantoms of all eras faded in, as though they'd been there all along but were only now revealing themselves. Victorian ladies and newsboys drifted alongside the starving specters of Shadwell thieves and the madmen of Bedlam. Yet there were so many others, clad in the garb of wartime and peacetime alike, from centuries of London's life. None of the spirits seemed to notice one another, nor did they pay any attention at all to Jazz. They simply waited.

The beams of half a dozen torches approached from beyond the chamber. Figures stepped through the firelight, more substantial than the ghosts. Josephine Blackwood raised a hand and pointed at Jazz, shouting something—perhaps a command. Jazz could not hear her. She felt as though she were drifting far away, and when she looked down she saw that the levers had been slowly released by her weight.

Gauges spun. Gears began to clank, and steam hissed from release valves. Terence had prepared the apparatus to receive its battery and now it roared to life. The pipes thumped and the gears churned, and Jazz blinked and stared in amazement as the apparatus began to fade, becoming almost transparent. She glanced down at herself and realized that her own body also had faded. Still among the living, she was becoming a ghost.

"Mum!" she shouted, panic overcoming her. For just a moment she'd forgotten her mother was dead, and there was no one left among the living to whom she would call for help.

The men she'd called Uncles and the thugs in their employ began to spread out among the ghosts in that chamber, careful of the flames at its edges but unmindful of the wraiths. They couldn't see the spirits of the city. Several of them had guns drawn, aimed at a shadow in the midst of the room.

Jazz blinked, realizing that the shadow was Terence in his dark clothes, somehow both more solid than the rest of them and less substantial even than the phantoms of London's past. He also held a gun. Ignoring those whose weapons were pointed at him, Terence aimed at Josephine Blackwood. Jazz could see his mouth moving—shouting a warning, perhaps—but she couldn't hear a word. It was as if she had slipped out of the world.

The gunshot dragged her back in. That, she heard.

An Uncle had pulled the trigger. Terence darted aside but not quickly enough. The bullet caught him in the shoulder, spun him halfway round. He swung his gun hand, sighted along the barrel, and shot the man in the chest. The other two with guns began to fire, but Terence was already moving. Philip—mad, one-eyed Philip—charged toward him. Terence shot him twice, once in the abdomen and once in the leg.

But he had nowhere to hide.

Josephine Blackwood raised her hands and the shadows began to coalesce around her fingers. She chanted something and the air shimmered. They might all dabble in magic, but whatever of it remained in the world, she had tapped it.

Jazz opened her mouth and screamed.

London answered with anguished cries from its past. The fire crackling around the circumference of the room flickered as a wind roared through the chamber. The Hour of Screams had arrived once more, but differently this time. Steam cried from the valves of the apparatus. Jazz howled her frustration and fury. The ghosts of old London joined her in a chorus, and then the chamber seemed to contract for a moment before exploding in a rush of apparitions.

A phantom train roared through the room, right through the apparatus, and Jazz was its screaming whistle. Piccadilly Circus flooded with people throwing their hats into the air, women kissing men who were total strangers, hundreds and then thousands embracing, celebrating the fall of Berlin. Parades marched by. Killers stalked victims in dark alleys. Lovers walked hand in hand. Rough-hewn men unloaded crates from ships along the filthy Thames. Bobbies walked their beats. Children played in parks and gardens. Tires screeched and horses whinnied as accidents took the lives of innocents. The wealthy walked past street beggars with nary a glance. Little girls sold flowers. Dancers performed upon a stage. An old woman pulled her shawl around her and wept for a love lost, a life unfulfilled. And more.

The ghosts of old London filled the chamber, the apparatus summoning them into a hurricane of memory and emotion. Jazz saw them all, and she felt their yearning for rest. For solace.

She arched her back, pressing down on the levers of the apparatus with all of her strength. Her eyes went wide as the first of the ghosts rushed into her. They began to push into her throat, sliding in through her nose and eyes and ears and, with a chilling rush, sifting through the pores of her skin. They filled her entirely, and as they did, the stories and secrets played no longer before her eyes but across the stage of her mind. All of the tales, funny and tragic, sweet and wistful and heartbreaking and horrifying, became hers.

All of the magic passed into her.

With a thunderclap, it ended. The apparatus gave a hiss like a final gasp and the gears began to slow. The screams were gone, along with the regret in the heart of the city. Jazz inhaled deeply, and the air down in that vast subterranean world smelled clean. The world had moved on. She understood now. The world had moved on, but London had clung to the past, dragging the weight of its ghosts like iron chains.

But she had felt its sigh of relief. And now the city was free to seek its future.

Jazz freed herself from the apparatus. Its gauges were cracked and broken, the gears bent and rusted. How the thing had ever worked, she could not imagine. She slid out between the pipes and jumped to the floor of the chamber.

In the flickering of firelight, Terence Whitcomb and the members of the Blackwood Club lay sprawled across the stony ground. Slowly, groaning, most of them began to rise. Two men lay still, either unconscious or dead. Terence staggered toward her, a weary smile on his face, yet there also seemed to be an air of sadness around him. He had dedicated his life to this moment, and now that it had arrived, what would he do?

Josephine Blackwood and the Uncles seemed shriveled and diminished. The woman raised her hands, malice etched upon her face, but she looked foolish sketching the air as she tried to cast some kind of spell. The realization shattered her. Jazz saw it fill her eyes, watched as her body went slack. She was just a sad old woman now. All of the power she'd lusted after, like youth, was a lost dream, forever beyond her grasp.

As Jazz looked on, they all seemed to be growing older. One by one, heads hung in despair, they turned away and began to shamble back the way they had come.

All save for Josephine.

She crouched and picked up a fallen pistol.

"Josie, no!" Terence shouted, scanning the ground for his own gun.

The crone pointed the gun at Jazz and fired. As Josephine pulled the trigger, Jazz felt her gorge rise as though she might vomit. Instead, what burst from her was a human figure—a gray shimmering form in a top hat and tails with a simple prestidigitator's wand. He waved it even as the bullet passed through him, but what struck Jazz was a wilted daisy.

The gun in Josephine Blackwood's hand had become a bouquet of flowers.

The old woman crumbled to the ground and began to weep quietly.

Terence stared at Jazz and then at the ghost of the magician. "It can't be."

The magician reached toward him, spectral fingers passing through Terence's cheek and reaching behind his ear to produce a silver coin. Then he bowed deeply, stepped backward into Jazz, and vanished within her.

The stories and secrets of old London had not disappeared or been destroyed; they had found a new home.

Jazz reached for Terence and pulled him close. He winced at the pain from the wound in his shoulder. She drew his face down to hers and brushed her lips against his in a gentle kiss, then kissed him more deeply, a maelstrom of emotions rushing through her.

"Jasmine," he said.

She shook her head, gave him a final glance, and then turned from him. When she walked past Josephine Blackwood, the old woman didn't even look up. Terence called after her once, but Jazz did not falter. She had descended so far into the underneath that the journey upward would take time, and she was keen to get started.

London awaited.

On a Tuesday in the last week of October, Jazz sat on a low wall in Regent's Park, away from the zoo and the rose garden and the major pedestrian traffic. A man with a guitar strummed and sang on a nearby footpath, instrument case open but for the moment filled only with the hope of future generosity.

A small group had begun to gather around her, an odd coterie that included a tidy young professional, a couple of aging homeless, and a dark-eyed junkie thief unused to being as exposed as the park required. The thief's eyes were skittish, but Jazz often found that she loved them best of all.

Tuesday. Jazz had discovered that she liked knowing what day it was. That had taken some getting used to once she had returned topside and become part of the city again. But she liked the feeling. It made the day hers, in a way.

London was enjoying an Indian summer, and the sun felt warm on her arms, now turned a rich bronze from many such days. Her hair was tied back in a ponytail and she wore a spaghetti-strap tank top, cutoff shorts, and a cute pair of sandals she'd retrieved from the closet in her old bedroom. After all she had been through, robbing her own house before the bank finally sold it off hadn't been difficult.

A few others approached cautiously, seeing her there on the wall. Among them she saw Aaron, a nouveau punk, maybe twenty, sauntering toward her with his usual arrogance. When he reached the small, strange group sitting on the grass in front of the wall, his entire demeanor changed. He stood up straight and even smiled. The green hair must have seemed out of place elsewhere in the park, but not here. No one was out of place here.

"Mornin', Jasmine," Aaron said. He had a pack slung across his back and now he brought it down, unzipped it, and produced a bottle of water. "Here's for you," he said, handing it over, "and I've got a bunch more. Give 'em to whoever."

Jazz touched his hand. "Thanks, Aaron. You're a good one."

He shrugged and glanced away, almost sheepish.

Jazz took a long sip from the water and looked at the gathering again. A homeless woman, perhaps forty-five but looking sixty, met her gaze with damp blue eyes. The woman reached up and tucked a long strand of greasy hair behind one ear, a gesture that reminded Jazz that once the woman had been an ordinary girl with the usual concerns—school and boys and clothes.

"What's your name?"

"Peg."

"Hello, Peg."

The woman smiled so gratefully it nearly broke Jazz's heart.

"What's on your mind?" she asked.

Peg lowered her gaze a moment, then looked up. "It's my sister, love. She and her husband lived in a flat in Battersea. When things took a turn for the worse for me, I was too embarrassed to ask for help. Hadn't talked to her in years. Had a falling out, you see. Two, three years ago, I finally realized how stupid I'd been, what I let happen to myself, you see. Went to try to find her, but they'd moved. Don't know if she's still in the city or even still alive, but—"

Jazz smiled and reached out for her hand. Peg rose and clutched at her fingers, trying to stifle her hope.

"You know the address where she used to live?"

"Twenty-seven Watford Close."

A shiver went through Jazz, as though a chill wind had passed through Regent's Park, but the sun still shone warmly down and the Indian summer heat would not have been abated by a simple breeze. She closed her eyes, and in her mind's eye she raced across the city, through alleys and over rooftops, into the Underground and all the way out to Bromley.

A twinge of sadness touched her heart.

"Your sister's husband has been dead five years, Peg. Cancer. But Polly herself is still alive and living in a flat in Bromley." She took up a notebook that lay on the wall beside her and scribbled the address down, ripped off the page, and handed it to the woman.

Peg took the page and stared at her writing, lips moving as she read the address to herself. She shook her head as though she could hardly believe it, and then a tentative smile touched her lips.

"Oh, love, you've no idea what this means."

But Jazz knew *exactly* what it meant. "Good luck," she said.

Peg took her hand and kissed her knuckles. "Thank you, dear. Thank you so very much."

She hurried away. Jazz watched her go, but as she did, something colorful caught her eye. Coming to join the small gathering was a young girl wearing a pretty wide-brimmed hat with fake flowers tied to a ribbon around the crown. It looked like something the queen would have worn in the 1980s.

Jazz and the girl saw each other's faces at the same moment. The girl's expression changed from that familiar, tentatively curious look to one of recognition and surprise.

"Hattie," Jazz whispered.

The girl took a step back, as though deciding whether or not to run away. Jazz slid off the wall and started toward her, leaving the others behind.

"Hattie!" she called.

Then Hattie was moving toward her as well. Laughing, they ran up to each other and embraced, spinning around.

"Jazz," Hattie said. "Oh, Jazz, I missed you."

They held each other at arm's length then, and Jazz saw that Hattie's nose had been broken and not healed properly and her smile was absent two teeth, all the remnants of the beating she had sustained that night in the tunnels.

"I love your hat," Jazz said.

Hattie kissed her nose, then pulled her in for a tighter hug. "I heard whispers about this oracle in Regent's Park. Got me thinking if the story was true, about this girl who could find anything in the city, maybe she could help me find you. I missed you so much."

Playfully, Hattie pushed Jazz away. "But I never imagined she'd *be* you!"

Jazz faltered then, her smile fading. "I'm sorry, Hattie. I should've come to see you. But after what happened, I couldn't go back down there. I don't belong in the Underground anymore. No more hiding in the dark."

Hattie nodded. "I know. That's what Harry said. He told us you weren't coming back. But I missed you."

Jazz took the girl's hands in hers. "I've missed you too."

Harry had survived, though he was still recovering, broken bones healing. Jazz had sensed that, just as she had sensed that Leela and Marco were dead and that Bill had left the Palace, returning topside as Jazz had done.

"I'm sorry about the others, about Marco and Leela," she said.

Hattie's eyes glistened with tears, but she took a deep breath and nodded. "Me too. We gave 'em to the river, just like we did with Cadge. The coppers kept Stevie's body, though. Never could find out what happened to it."

Jazz knew. Stevie still had family, and they'd claimed his remains. Where he'd been buried, she couldn't have said, for they lived beyond the outskirts of London and she did not feel anything out that far. Terence had gotten what he'd wished for; the city's ghosts had been laid to rest. London could put the past behind it now and move into the future. Instead of crumbling into diminishing echoes of an ancient empire, it could embrace the new millennium and seek glories yet to come. But there had been a side effect that Terence had not foreseen. Perhaps even his father, who'd designed the apparatus, hadn't fully understood his invention.

All the lingering bits of London's magic were inside Jazz now; all its secrets had been fused with her. She knew the city in ways that nobody else ever could, every person, event, street, and shady corner. Every brick and garden. Jazz and London were irrevocably linked. With all of the wisdom of the city inside her, she would never be alone again, as long as she lived. And though it had occurred to her to wonder what would happen when she died, she'd decided that was beyond her control. Perhaps the city's secrets would pass to someone else, and perhaps not. Somehow, she felt sure the wisdom and magic that the city had shed in order to survive—and which she had taken into herself—would endure long after she was gone.

"It's all past now, Hattie," Jazz said, smiling at her.

"I miss it, a little," Hattie said.

The half dozen or so people who had gathered by the wall to see Jazz kept a respectful distance, though they watched her and Hattie with fascination. The girl fidgeted a bit, not liking the attention.

"You ever comin' back down to see us?" Hattie asked.

Jazz tightened her grip on the girl's hands. "I don't think so. I'm glad Harry's alive, but I don't really want to see him, Hattie. Neither him nor Terence. I've changed—"

"I'll say you have," Hattie said, nodding toward the gathering.

Jazz laughed softly, a bit self-conscious.

"But I can still come to see *you*?" Hattie asked. "We can still be friends?"

Jazz smiled. "You can always come to see me. I can show you all my favorite parts of London. If you'd like that."

"I'd like it very much," Hattie said.

Together they walked back toward the wall, past the people who had come to the oracle to find the things they had lost or simply to find answers in a city full of questions.

In that, Jazz thought, they were really no different from anyone else.

about the authors

CHRISTOPHER GOLDEN'S novels include *The Lost Ones*, *The Myth Hunters*, *Wildwood Road*, *The Boys Are Back in Town*, *The Ferryman*, *Strangewood*, *Of Saints and Shadows*, and *The Borderkind*. Golden co-wrote the lavishly illustrated novel *Baltimore, or, The Steadfast Tin Soldier and the Vampire* with Mike Mignola, and they are currently scripting it as a feature film for New Regency. He has also written books for teens and young adults, including the thriller series *Body of Evidence*, honored by the New York Public Library and chosen as one of YALSA's Best Books for Young Readers. Upcoming teen novels include *Poison Ink* for Delacorte, *Soulless* for MTV Books, and *The Secret Journeys of Jack London*, a collaboration with Tim Lebbon.

With Thomas E. Sniegoski, he is the co-author of the dark fantasy series *The Menagerie* as well as the young readers fantasy series *OutCast* and the comic book miniseries *Talent*, both of which were recently acquired by Universal Pictures. Golden and Sniegoski also wrote the upcoming comic book miniseries *The Sisterhood*, currently in development as a feature film. Golden was born and raised in Massachusetts, where he still lives with his family. At present he is collaborating with Tim Lebbon on *The Map of Moments*, the second novel of *The Hidden Cities*. Please visit him at www.christophergolden.com.

TIM LEBBON lives in South Wales with his wife and two children. His books include the British Fantasy Award–winning *Dusk* and its sequel *Dawn*, *Fallen*, *Berserk*, *The Everlasting*, *Hellboy: Unnatural Selection*, and the *New York Times* bestseller *30 Days of Night*. Forthcoming books include the new fantasy novel *The Island*, *The Map of Moments* (with Christopher Golden), two YA novels making up *The Secret Journeys of Jack London* (in collaboration with Christopher Golden), the collection *Last Exit for the Lost* from Cemetery Dance Publications, and further books with Night Shade Books, Necessary Evil Press, and Humdrumming, among others. He has won three British Fantasy Awards, a Bram Stoker Award, a Shocker, and a Tombstone Award, and has been a finalist for International Horror Guild and World Fantasy awards. His novella *White* is soon to be a major Hollywood movie, and several other novels and novellas are currently in development in the USA and the UK. Find out more about Tim at his websites: www.timlebbon.net and www.noreela.com.

If you loved *Mind the Gap*, then you are in for a treat!

Because now Christopher Golden and Tim Lebbon
take us across an ocean, and to another hidden city:
the storm-torn wreckage of New Orleans. There,
in the months following Katrina, one man finds
himself on a most unusual quest to save the
life of the woman he loves.

So be sure not to miss:

THE MAP
OF
MOMENTS

A Novel of The Hidden Cities

by

Christopher Golden &
Tim Lebbon

On sale spring 2009
from Bantam Books

Here is a special preview:

The Map of Moments
on sale spring 2009

In Max's dream, Gabrielle still loves him. And she is still alive.

They're in the attic of the wood-frame house on Landry Street, making love. Golden light streams in and makes her cinnamon Creole skin glisten, and Max's heart catches in his throat as he moves inside her. She's the kind of beautiful that clouds the minds of men, that makes even the most envious woman marvel. Yet she has a wild need in her eyes, as though a fire burns inside her and she believes he might be able to give her peace.

"Don't ever stop," she says, gazing up at him with copper eyes.

Stop what? Making love to her? Loving her? He's known her only a handful of weeks, been intimate with her only this once, and already he realizes that he will never be able to stop. The spell she has cast over him is irrevocable.

Gabrielle shudders with pleasure, her breath hitching. She wears a tight tank top with lace straps, her socks, and nothing else. But the light shouldn't be like this. It should be night, with the sounds of car engines and pounding music from the street below. Instead, there is no sound at all, save for her breathing. It's like listening to a dead phone line—not just an absence of sound, but a vacuum.

Her fingers twine in his hair and she pulls him down. He loses himself in the hunger of her kiss, but the wrongness still troubles him. The attic is too clean, and somehow he notices this.

Floorboards creak and the attic is different now, impossibly huge. Posters hang on the walls—things he'd had in his office at Tulane University—and in the shadows of the eaves, figures loom. He knows these faces, the silent observers who watch him and Gabrielle. He recognizes some of his colleagues and students, Gabrielle's grandmother and her cousin Michelle. And also two men from Roland's Garage, the bar on Proyas Street where she'd taken him once; he'd been the only white face in the place. They watch him, now, but he feels no menace. Only sadness, as if they've come for a wake.

One figure remains in shadow. Max cannot see his face, which is all right, because he doesn't want to. The shadow scares him.

He focuses on Gabrielle. Only on Gabrielle, shutting them all out. He wants to bring her joy, and he touches her face.

Only then does he feel the water beneath him.

Frantic, he glances around, and sees water flowing up through the spaces between the floorboards. He tries to ask where it's all coming from, but when he opens his mouth, water spills in. Panic surges through him. He cannot breathe. The water fills the attic. The roof tumbles away, and Gabrielle slips into black waters and is gone.

And he wakes . . .

Max had a moment of dislocation, and then the hum of the passenger jet's engines filled his ears, and he remembered.

"Jesus," he whispered, forcing his eyes closed for another moment before opening them, surrendering to consciousness.

The obese woman in the seat beside him shifted, absorbing even more of the space he'd paid to occupy. It seemed she'd gotten larger since the plane departed Boston, but of course that had to be impossible.

Don't be a prick, he chided himself. Such thoughts were out of character for him on most days, but most days he wasn't traveling to the funeral of the person responsible for both the greatest joy and the greatest pain he'd ever known.

"Ladies and gentlemen, we'll be landing shortly. At this time, please turn off all electronic devices and return your tray tables and seatbacks to their upright position."

Somehow Max managed to get his seat upright. He rested his head against the window frame and stared down at civilization below.

Did I ever really know you? he thought. And though the question was meant for Gabrielle, it could easily have applied to the city of New Orleans as well. He'd barely scratched the surface during the semester he'd taught at Tulane, figuring he'd have years to explore the mystery of what had once been called the Big Easy. It had been a city of music and exoticism, a place of both excess and torpor. But Gabrielle had hurt him so badly that he'd fled home to Boston, taking a new position at Tufts University.

Still, she wasn't entirely to blame. Yes, she'd told him that she loved him, and pulled him into her life and her bed with a fervent passion he had never before encountered. But Max was thirty-one years old when he met Gabrielle, and she only nineteen. He'd been her professor. He'd known the rules, and broken them with abandon.

No one had blamed him. Not after they'd met her. Even Anne Rutherford, his sixty-year-old department head, had understood—and that spoke of the power Gabrielle had. She left the world breathless.

Yet despite the way everyone who discovered the relationship seemed willing to give him a pass, Max blamed himself. He'd looked into those bright copper eyes and *seen* the love she felt for him, believed it wholeheartedly. When Gabrielle had told him that she'd dreamed of finding a man who would leave *her* breathless, and that she'd found him in Max, he'd believed her. When they'd made love that first time, in the attic on Landry Street, she'd wept and clung to him afterward, and wished them away to some place where no one else could ever reach them. And he had felt like the man all men wanted to be—the hero, the knight, the lover and champion.

Yet the one thing that he'd learned in his time in Louisiana was that New Orleans was a city of masks. Everyone wore one, and not just for Mardi Gras. Only the desperately poor were what they seemed to be. Otherwise, how else to explain the way the populace had so long ignored warnings of their beloved city's vulnerability, or the libertine air of sexual and epicurean excess and jazz improvisation that fueled the tourist trade, while sixty percent of the city remained illiterate, and thousands lived in shotgun houses slapped together like papier-mâché? New Orleans had two faces—one of them a stew of cultures and languages, of poverty and success, of corruption and hope, all conspiring to forge a future; and the other, the mask it showed the world.

How could he have been fool enough not to see that Gabrielle also wore a mask?

Max had asked himself that question far too many times during his move back to Boston. He ought to have been settling in, enjoying the preparations for his new job and trying to get on with things. But he'd been too lost in that question to pay attention, wondering how he had fallen in love so fast, and so hard. Wondering how long it would be before it stopped hurting.

And then August had come, and with it, hurricane season.

Watching the television reports as Katrina moved into the Gulf of Mexico, he'd wondered why no one seemed terrified. Couldn't they see the monster about to make landfall? But even as those questions rose in his mind, he understood. Some of the people in New Orleans would put their faith in God, others in luck, and others would simply chalk it up to fate. If the storm was meant to take them, it would. And some would just be stubborn; until someone called for a mandatory evacuation, they weren't going anywhere, and maybe not even then. Someone would have to go and round them up, get them out of there.

For too many, no one ever came.

Far, far away, Max had sat in his little faculty apartment on the Tufts campus and watched the suffering and the dying begin, and the anguish of the aftermath.

He had little faith in the spiritual, but Max had felt a soul-deep certainty, in those initial few days, that Gabrielle had not survived Hurricane Katrina. Days turned to weeks, numbness turned to shock, and shock to mourning. Chaos had still not released its hold on the Gulf Coast, and it seemed order might never be restored.

On the 18th of October, just over seven weeks after the storm, Max's phone rang. Without even realizing it, he had gotten into the habit of holding his breath when he glanced at the caller ID window. That night, the readout had said *unknown caller*, but what struck him was the area code. 504. Louisiana.

Max had picked up the phone. He'd hated himself for the hope in his voice when he said "Hello?"

"It's Michelle Doucette."

And he'd known. "She's dead, isn't she?"

For a moment, the line went silent. Then, just as he'd begun to think they'd been disconnected, Michelle spoke again.

"I told her to get out of there, but she wouldn't go. Said she couldn't leave, that it was the only place she'd be safe. They were saying all the neighborhoods in the bowl would be flooded, but she just went up into that damn attic and wouldn't come down. I told her she was crazy, Max, but you know Gaby. No talking to that girl."

Michelle's voice had broken then.

Max had listened to Michelle as she went on about evacuating to Houston, and how she'd called and tried to get the police or someone, *anyone*, to go by and check the house on Landry Street. Most of her family had left New Orleans, and of those who planned to return, none of them wanted anything to do with Gabrielle, dead or alive. Except for Michelle, Gabrielle's family had written her off years before.

In late September, Michelle had reluctantly returned to New Orleans. She'd gone straight to that deserted house in Lakeview and found it uninhabitable—crumbling and contaminated. And in the attic, she'd found Gabrielle.

At last, when Max had heard enough, he'd finally spoken up. "Why did you call me?"

It had brought her up short. "What?"

"After what happened. Why would you call me?"

Her nerves had to be frayed. She'd laughed, and the sound was full of hurt and anger. "Jesus, Max. I called you because I thought you'd want to know. Maybe she fucked with your head, but I figured you were the only one . . ."

Her words trailed off.

"The only one what?" Max had to ask.

"The only person in the world besides me who would cry for her."

Max had wanted to tell Michelle that he'd done his share of crying for Gabrielle when the girl was alive. That it hadn't helped then, and it wouldn't help now. But he couldn't get the words out.

Nearly three more weeks had passed, and now he found himself on this airplane, about to touch down. During the layover in Memphis, he'd nearly turned around, gotten on the next plane back north. Or he'd pretended to himself that he could. What a joke. He could no more turn around than he could snap his fingers and make the grief go away. Leaving the way he had, this chapter of his life had never reached completion.

Perhaps Gabrielle's funeral might finally put an end to it.

He'd grieve, but he would not cry. Perhaps it was a good sign that he couldn't shed any more tears for her. Or maybe it meant that he was dead inside.

The next morning, Michelle picked him up and they drove out of the Quarter, following Esplanade up through New Marigny. Their route took them mainly through areas that had remained above the floodwaters, and thus far he'd not encountered the level of devastation he'd seen in photographs and on television. He wondered if Michelle had been purposely sparing him that, or if she'd rather just avoid it herself.

When they reached Holt Cemetery, however, there was no way to avoid the reality of what had transpired in the city. Max had driven past it before, had seen the rows of tilted crosses and slate-thin headstones, but he'd never been inside the gates. In most of the Catholic world, All Saints' Day just meant another trip to church. But in New Orleans, every first of November brought massive gatherings to the city's cemeteries. People went there to leave flowers and notes and photographs, or just to remember.

As Michelle drove slowly along the narrow cemetery road, Max shuddered to think what All Saints' Day had been like this year. Markers were scattered like broken teeth, many undoubtedly far away from the graves they were intended for, lying on brown, lifeless grass.

At the gravesite, Max fixed his tie and adjusted the cuffs of his jacket. Even in November, he felt too warm in the charcoal suit he only ever wore at weddings and funerals. Perhaps the New Orleans weather was to blame—humid and warm today—or perhaps he just felt out of place here. The jilted ex, much too old for the dead girl to begin with.

No longer able to fight its pull, he at last focused on the coffin that sat on the ground beside the open grave. It was a shabby metal box, but he suspected it was better than a lot of those interred at Holt would have. He stared at it, trying to imagine that Gabrielle lay inside, and could not.

His throat closed up, emotion flooding him. How could anyone not have loved her? How could he ever stop?

"Are you all right?" Michelle asked, appearing beside him.

Max flinched, then slowly nodded. "I will be."

"You don't look it."

He smiled, keeping his voice to a whisper. His words weren't meant for other ears. "I thought I was a fool, coming down here. What kind of guy travels this far for a girl who slept with someone else, you know? But I'm glad I came."

Michelle touched his arm gently. "She was hard to understand."

That was the understatement of the year. Max glanced at the other mourners. "I thought you said it'd be just us."

"It is. Father Legohn's congregation is mostly gone. The one with the nice shoes is the undertaker. The others are what's left of the church, just here to help carry her, say a prayer, and put her in the ground."

The truth of this hit Max hard. Despite the warning Michelle had given him, the idea that there was nobody left in New Orleans who cared enough to say good-bye to Gabrielle was bitter and ugly.

Except there was one other person, Max noticed now. A little white two-door coupe that looked forty years old had pulled up on the cemetery road. The man who stood by the car must have been thirty years older, with hair as white as his car and skin darker than his funeral suit.

When the funeral ended, the white-haired old man approached the graveside.

"You're Max Corbett," he said. His skin was so dark his hair looked like snow on top of tar. Of all the things Max might have expected to come out of his mouth, this wasn't it.

"That's me. Who are you?"

"You have questions for her," the old guy said, and it wasn't a question. "Things you wanted to ask her."

Uncomfortable, Max glanced at him. "Why? Did she talk about me? Give you a message or something?"

"Some, but nothing like what you mean." The old man

reached out and touched the thin metal of the coffin, stared at it a moment, then looked back up at Max. "I'm just saying if you have questions you want to ask, it might not be too late."

"Look, no offense, but—"

"Your lady's gone," the old man whispered.

Max glanced at the coffin, thinking he meant Gabrielle. But then he heard the sound of a car starting and looked across the cemetery to see Michelle driving slowly away. She didn't turn around, didn't look at him, but neither did she seem in a rush to leave. Almost as if she'd forgotten he was even here.

"Time to talk, Max," the old man said. Max was not sure whether it was posed as a question or a statement.

"How'd you know my name?"

The old man shrugged, in a smug way that Max knew would become bothersome very quickly.

"And what do you mean when you say—"

"I know a nice little bar," the old man said. He stretched, and Max was sure he actually heard bones creaking. "Not far from here. Least, used to be nice. Since the Rage, the whole place has gone sour."

"Rage?"

The man rolled his eyes at the clear blue sky. "The storm. Katrina. Such a sweet name."

"Why would I go anywhere with you?"

"'Cause you're intrigued," the man said, shrugging again. Then he smiled. "And 'cause your lady's gone."

As he climbed into the passenger seat of the white coupe, Max realized that he had made no plans beyond the funeral. He'd arranged the trip, booked the flight and hotel, spoken with Michelle about her picking him up from the airport, but his focus had always been on the moment that had just passed. He had watched Gabrielle's coffin as words that meant little to him were spoken, and now that it was over, he was lost.

Three days left in New Orleans, and nothing to do.

Max closed his eyes for a moment and saw Gabrielle's face,

and the thought that he would never see her again seemed to cut him in two. Since leaving, he had lived with the certainty that she was out of his life forever, but at least she had still existed in the same world, still shared the same atmosphere. He was still *aware* of her. Now she was gone, completely and finally, and he sucked in a breath that contained nothing of her.

The old man drove slowly from the cemetery, steering around grave markers that had been washed onto the road. He turned left, eventually edging them past the muddy ruin of City Park and driving so slowly that Max thought they could probably walk faster. He glanced across, and the expression on the guy's face was one of quiet contemplation.

"Bar's called Cooper's. I've been drinkin' there some thirty years, and it was there long before that. Cooper's long dead an' gone, but his boys, they still run the place. It wasn't the nicest place you'll find in the city, even before, but . . . it's one of the best. You can smell the honesty when you walk in. Know what I mean?"

Max didn't, but he saw where the old man's non-answer was leading. "All right. We can talk when we get there. Do I get to learn your name?"

"You can call me Ray."

"Ray," Max repeated. The framing of the answer wasn't lost on him. The guy seemed to sidestep every question, and this was no exception.

When they reached the bar, the place looked dead. The sign had been blown away, leaving a bent metal hanger above the entrance door, and most of the windows were boarded up. Three others were exposed, glass grubby, and surrounded by what Max first took to be bullet holes. Then he realized that they were nail holes, punched into the frames and walls when the windows were covered before the storm. Behind one window was an old neon beer sign, swathed with brightly-colored paint to give it some semblance of life.

Someone had spray-painted "We shoot looters" across the facade, the double "oo" of "shoot" missing now that the entrance door was visible again. Just below that stark warning, two feet above pavement level, was the grubby tide mark that Max had already noticed around the city. It showed how high the waters had come. The limits of life and death.

"Place got off lightly," Ray said. He slammed the car door and stood beside Max. He was a good eight inches shorter, but a palpable energy radiated off him like heat. For someone so old who drove so slow, he certainly seemed very much alive.

"Doesn't look that way."

Ray pointed along the street. "Ground level falls the further you drive. Half a mile down there, water was ten feet deep."

"I don't want a tour," Max said, immediately regretting the comment. How could he not expect Ray to want to talk about the storm? The Rage, as he'd called it.

"Good," Ray said, and Max knew that he meant it. "'Cause life and death move on." He opened the door to Cooper's and beckoned Max inside.

You can smell the honesty when you walk in, Ray had said, and Max had not really understood. Yet upon entering, he knew exactly what the weird old man had meant. It no longer looked like a normal bar, if it ever had been. Floorboards had been replaced with thick plywood flooring, joints rough, nail holes already filled with dirt and cigarette ash. The furniture was a mishmash of plastic garden chairs and tables, wooden benches, a couple of church pews, metal chairs with timber seats tied on with wire, and a large round table made from piled car tires and a circle of the same plywood used for flooring. Flickering candles sat on each table and on rough shelves across the walls, providing a pale illumination.

Along the back wall was the bar itself, with beer crates stacked five high, and an open shelving unit screwed to the wall and containing dozens of liquor bottles. A tall, thin black man sat on a stool beside the pile of booze, a cigarette hanging from his mouth and his eyes half closed. Another tall man walked the room, collecting empties, chatting with the dozen people there, fetching more drinks. These, Max assumed, were the Coopers. They had refused to let their place go to stink and rot, and had instead reopened it as best they could. No illusions, no pretense; this was a place to drink and talk. It stank of sweat and spilled beer, because there was no power for air-conditioning. It stank of defiance.

"Bother you, bein' the only white face?"

"I thought you'd been drinking here for thirty years?" Max asked. *So where was the welcome? Where were the raised hands from the Cooper brothers, or the other patrons?*

That shrug again. "Keep to myself."

"Okay," Max said, unconvinced. "And no, it doesn't bother me."

"Good," Ray said. "'Cause if you looked bothered, it'd bother them. Drink?"

"Yeah," Max said. He wondered whether Michelle was drinking now, and what she was thinking about, and why she'd left him with Ray.

"Water?" Ray said, a twinkle in his eye.

"Whiskey."

"I'm partial to Scottish single malt myself. But hereabouts it's mostly bourbon. Folks are suspicious about anything that goes down too smooth."

"Whatever." Max looked around and spotted a plastic table in the corner of the room, two old school chairs upside down on its yellowed surface. He took the chairs down from the table and sat, and Ray came across with a bottle of Jack Daniel's and two glasses. Max wasn't a big drinker, but right now it was just what he wanted.

Max had a hundred questions about Cooper's, but a thousand about Gabrielle, and Ray saw that. The old man sighed and sat, pouring them both a double shot, and lifted his glass. Before he could say anything, Max cut in.

"What? A toast? To Gabrielle?"

"If you like," Ray said.

"For now I'll just drink. And I'll listen."

Ray nodded, his face suddenly serious for the first time since they'd met. Max wondered whether this was his natural look.

"Gabrielle's truly one of New Orleans' lost souls," Ray said. He drank his whiskey.

"You mean a hurricane victim?"

Ray shook his head. "I'm not talkin' about that, not now. This goes deeper, and further back. Right to the heart of this place." He smiled, and gave a more casual version of that annoying shrug. "But you ain't from New Orleans."

"No buts, Ray," Max said, trying to keep his voice level and low. "And no more of this mystery-man crap."

"Oh, I'm not sayin' I'm not goin' to tell you. Already decided that, in this old head of mine. All I'm sayin' is, you won't understand."

Max wanted to stand, leave Cooper's Bar and walk as far and as fast as he could, following the terrible tide marks to higher ground and finding his way out of this city once and for all.

"She could have been so special," Ray said.

"She *was* special."

"You can save her, boy. If you choose to do as I say, if you're willin' to follow the path, you can save her from herself."

"She's dead," Max said. "By now, she's in the ground."

"Dead now, yeah. But she *was* alive, *so* alive. More'n any woman I ever met." Ray stared into his glass for a moment, seeing unknown pasts in the swish of amber liquid. Then he drank the remnants of his whiskey and poured some more. He filled Max's glass as well, which Max was surprised to find empty.

"I don't know what I'm listening to here," Max said, drinking the whiskey in one swallow. It tasted good, felt better.

"There's a man who can help you, name of Matrisse. He's a conjure-man."

"Magic," Max said. "Right."

"Not magic like you know it. Not that tourist shit. Matrisse, he don't have a shop front on Bourbon Street selling charms and magic dust. He's known in the city, but only to some." Ray leaned forward across the table and lowered his voice. "True magic, boy. None of this meddlesome fakery peddled to wannabes. His heart is tied with the heart of this city."

"And he's still here after the storm?"

"Yeah, still here. His heart aches, but he can never leave this place. It's a New Orleans thing." Ray sat up again and smiled, pouring more whiskey into his glass. They'd got through a third of a bottle already, and Max was feeling the effects stroking his senses. The candlelight looked brighter, the outlines of the other patrons sharper, but the door looked much farther away than before.

"True magic's an oxymoron, Ray. No such thing. Even if there was, what do you think this guy can do for Gabrielle? Make her a zombie?"

"Forget Hollywood," Ray said, his smile no longer holding any trace of humor. "Forget all the stories you think you know. Matrisse, he has ways an' means to do more than you can imagine, boy. An' one of those things . . . well, he can open a door to the past. Maybe get a message through."

His chin tilted down, so his eyes were lost in shadow. "Maybe get a man through. It ain't easy, and he don't do it too much . . . but he'll do it for you. For Gabrielle."

"Why?"

"I told you why. 'Cause she could have been special." Ray drank more whiskey and filled his glass again, no longer topping up Max's.

It was a hell of a fantasy. Send a message back to Gabrielle, warn her about what was coming. But a fantasy couldn't raise the dead.

Max stared at Ray. "Even if I believed any of this, how would I find this Matrisse?"

"He'll find you. First, though, there's a map you have to follow. You got no magic about you. No aura. You're from outta town, but in cases like this that can be good. An advantage. A clean slate."

So sincere, and already talking like Max had agreed to go along with this bullshit. He almost scoffed, but stopped himself. He was asking the questions, wasn't he? Maybe it was the whiskey talking, but he couldn't stop his mind from following where Ray's words led, and wondering.

"Clean slate for what?" Perhaps it was their surroundings, lending that honest power to everything the old man said. Or maybe it was just the deadly combination of grief and Jack Daniel's.

"For gatherin' magic to you. I can give you the map, if you

commit to followin' it. Follow it, magic yourself up, like runnin' your feet along a carpet to build up static, and at the end of the map, you'll find Matrisse. And if he finds you as well, then maybe he'll help you through."

"And maybe I can get a message to Gabrielle, back before any of this happened?"

"Maybe. Or maybe you bring it yourself. Right place, right time . . ."

Max wanted to laugh. He wanted to mock this old fool, tip the table over, and storm from the bar. But he could not. And he knew it wasn't just the whiskey keeping him in his plastic school chair. It was something about the old man and his words, and the fact that he obviously believed every one of them.

"Why are you telling all this to me?" Max said. "You knew Gabrielle. You obviously cared about her. Why don't you do it?"

"'Cause it's dangerous, and I'm old, and I doubt this body could take it," Ray said. "You want to see the map?"

"Yeah. But . . . won't it all be changed?"

Ray grinned. "This ain't a map of just places, boy. It's a map of moments." He took an envelope from inside his jacket, extracted a folded sheet of paper, and spread it across the table. He glanced around just once, and for an instant Max saw something like danger in his eyes. And Max knew that this harmless old man could be deadly as well, if the time and need called for it.

He leaned over the table and looked down at the map. "That's just a tourist map of the city."

"It was, 'til it was changed. Look closer."

Max did so. Wavering candlelight seemed to make the Mississippi flex like a sleeping snake, and Lake Pontchartrain loomed across the top of the map, dark blue and menacing.

"It's your choice now, boy. I've told you enough, and I can't hold you down an' make you do this. I ask one thing, though." Ray smiled at the empty bottle of whiskey. "You owe me half a bottle, so do this one thing for me. Go to the first place, an' the first moment. You'll know where an' when that is when you study the map. Drink this beforehand, an' it'll help you." He laid a small clay bottle on the table.

Now Max did scoff—too loudly, fueled by whiskey. "Magic potions? You're shitting me." Every head turned to look at them.

"Just humor an old man," Ray said. "Ain't nothin' in this bottle gonna hurt you. And you know I ain't lyin', just like you know the rest of it's true."

Max stood, and the whiskey hit him hard. His legs shook and his head seemed to sway atop his neck, and he wasn't sure whether everyone was looking at him, or everyone was looking away. He grabbed the map from the table and folded it, then snatched up the small clay bottle. It seemed the right thing to do.

"This . . ." he said, waving the bottle before Ray's face. But the old man was still chuckling, and he watched as Max edged his way across the bar.

Standing by the front door, conscious of the poor light inside and the harsh sun without, Max glanced back at the old man. There was a fresh bottle of whiskey on his table, his glass was full, and he was talking at the chair Max had just vacated. He gestured with his hands, nodded, and gave that annoying, dismissive shrug once again. *Talking to himself*, Max thought. *Now I just* know *he's nuts.*

Then Ray did a curious thing. He reached inside his jacket pocket and pulled out a small glass vial with a glass stopper. Carefully, he poured a few drops into the second glass—the one Max had just left behind—and followed it with a dash of whiskey. He slid the glass across the table, toward the empty seat, and smiled, talking, as though to some companion Max couldn't see.

Nutjob.

Max tugged at the door and stumbled outside. The stark autumn sun blinded him for a moment, and he slid down the wall and sat on a sidewalk strewn with litter and grit, just another midday drunk washed up on the shores of New Orleans.